Predator's Heart

MARIAN YATES

First Published by Marian Yates 2016

ISBN: 064944487
ISBN-13: 978-0-646-94448-7

DEDICATION

To Stephen without your encouragement I never would have written this book. To Liza Holmes and Rachael Bermingham, you ladies rock! Thank you for your time and honest feedback.

EXCERPT

"So the bastard was right, this is a trap," his lip curled in disgust. "You won't get any information from me," he ground out.
Chris walked over to the prone figure. "Sure we will dickwad," he smiled down at him. Regan thought it was one of the most evil smiles she had ever seen, it seemed as if Chris had let some of the bear out of its cage and it sent a shiver down Regan's spine to see it.
"You get nothin' from me."
Regan frowned as she noticed his face was changing from flushed to a sickly pasty white. Sure Chris was a big bastard and right now with the grisly close to the surface, he was menacing – but he hadn't even "made any threats let alone caused any pain. So why had this moron gone so pale, and was that foam at the corner of his mouth? Regan leaned forward, drawing in her breath, trying to assimilate the changes she could see happening."

CONTENTS

Dedication
Excerpt

Chapter 1

Chapter 2

Chapter 3

Chapter 4

Chapter 5

Chapter 6

Chapter 7

Chapter 8

Chapter 9

Chapter 10

Chapter 11

Chapter 12

Chapter 13

Chapter 14

Chapter 15

Chapter 16

Chapter 17

Chapter 18

Chapter 19

Chapter 20

Chapter 21

Chapter 22

Chapter 23

Chapter 24

CHAPTER 1

Apprehension wound through her as sweat trickled slowly down Regan's spine, forcing her to vanish silently back into the shadows. She was tall and thin with a sleekly muscled frame that moved with cat-like grace – perfect for slipping through the night shadows undetected.

She sensed the danger that hung in the night air – an insidious malevolence that crept up in the dark. "Shit, shit, shit!" she muttered under her breath. "This is my home and there's no way in hell anyone will hurt me here!"

Her face took on an intense look of fierce concentration that accentuated her feline features as she opened her senses to the night. Drawing the fresh evening air into her lungs, Regan tried to capture the scent of whomever, or whatever was causing her nerves to quiver with anxiety, but the breeze at her back let it escape from her. She could see better in the dark than anyone else she knew, but from this distance, she couldn't see anything out of place around her small cottage. Yet she was *certain* someone was inside her home; her instinct for danger was never wrong, and it told her that one or more people were inside, laying in wait.

"Well if they're expecting a victim to show up, they're in for a nasty little surprise. Those days are long gone." The corners of her mouth curled up into a wicked smile, baring a set of white teeth with unusually sharp incisors.

In silence, she moved further back into the trees and circled around the house to the back entrance rather than the front, where they would expect her to appear. Two yards from the back door was a path leading into the dense forest that bordered the cottage. The reason Regan purchased it was because of the easy escape it provided if she ever needed to hide.

As she cautiously approached the back door, she picked up the scent of the intruders from within her home. *Obviously they're not waiting with friendly intent*, she thought, *or they would wait on the front porch for an invitation.* She paused just outside the entrance and surveyed the darkness with keen perception, making sure there was no one waiting to blindside her.

Breathing deeply she calmed herself and allowed the night to bring her more information. Once again, anxiety shot through her like a bolt – *something* else was wrong. She sensed two men awaited her inside the darkened house, but her intuition told her there was another threat, something more ominous that was yet to reveal itself. Two men, even armed with guns as these two were, was not something to overly concern her now that she had the advantage of surprise.

Shrugging off the uneasy feeling, Regan tightened her muscles and roped her long black hair back into a ponytail, then silently slipped into her house. She eased her way through the kitchen, coming from the opposite direction to what the intruders expected.

When she entered, she spotted two men leaning against either side of the front door watching the entrance, laying in wait for her arrival, oblivious to her presence behind them. *I mean how fucking dumb can you be,* she thought, shaking her head. She took a moment to assess the threat of her adversaries. Both men had dark brown hair although the one on the right was taller with a military style buzz-cut, while the other had his hair pulled back in a ponytail. The taller man looked like he knew his way around a gym, looking at the muscles on his arms, yet his bulk would slow him down. Whereas the shorter man was younger and had youth on his side. They both emitted a distinct air of violence, as if over the years it had seeped into their very pores.

With inhuman speed, Regan charged the smaller man first, startling him enough to cause him to drop his gun. Using every ounce of her strength, she aimed a punch straight at his face with such force it dislocated his jaw, and caused his head to slam into the door. He stumbled away from her holding his face while groping the ground with one hand; searching for his weapon in the deep shadows of the room.

The second man swung his weapon round and held it out in front of him, defensively. With another quick swing of her hand, Regan knocked the gun from his grasp with her palm. She then turned back to the first man who was still fumbling in the dark for his gun, and stomped her foot down hard on his hand, shattering his bones with the heel of her boot. Her lips curled into a satisfied smile at the sound of his bones crushing – unlike him, Regan was able to see perfectly with the small amount of moonlight seeping through the window.

She motioned for the second man to follow her into the center of the room, allowing them more space to fight. He took up the offer, sheathing his weapon he lunged at her, his attack attempting to knock her to the ground, but she easily slid back out of reach.

"So what are you two bastards doing here? Why are you in my home?"

She dodged a kick aimed at her knee.

"Watch your mouth bitch! You might have been able to sneak

up on us, but now that it's just you and me, you should try to stay on my good side."

"Which side is that? You're big, slow, and ugly, I don't think you have a good side." She laughed as he launched a series of punches that missed as she twisted out of reach, too fast for him to land a blow.

With speed faster than her opponent could follow, she stepped in and slapped his face hard enough to split his lip, then danced back out of his range. For the first time, she could see apprehension on his face, as he considered that she might be better than he was.

"Now I've asked politely what you're doing in my home, if I have to ask again; you'll have more to worry about than a split lip."

"Bitch, you don't know who you're dealing with. If you come with us quietly, you will suffer a lot less than if you make them send more of our associates for you. Trust me, we are the civil ones compared to some of the others in our corporation."

With a sigh, Regan lunged in close and backhanded him across the face this time splattering a dark arc of crimson blood.

"You didn't answer my question," she persisted. "Tell me! Who wants me and why?"

"I do daughter."

Thomas wasn't as tall as his daughter, but what he lacked in height; he made up for in brute strength. He was a heavily muscled man of 5' 10', with a mouth like a knife's slash under his broad nose, and deep sunken eyes that viewed the world with cold hostility. His violent history was written in the scars that littered his face, which was flushed with the gratifying thought of causing Regan pain. He loved the sense of power he got from hurting her – she was his, and he'd missed their *training sessions*.

Air hissed from Regan's lungs, dread clawing sharply at her insides, she'd hoped to never again hear the wretched sound of her father's voice. The past began bulging against the walls she'd built to contain it. If they crumbled, the memory of that dreadful night when she last saw her father would rush in and drown her in pain. It had been many years, yet the horror that was her childhood still threatened to swamp her as if it had just been yesterday. Breathing harshly, she pushed the memories back down. If Regan was to survive the next few minutes, she needed her wits about her. She needed to control herself as she had done for so many years.

She inhaled harshly forcing the memories away. Regan would not go back to that night; if she did, she knew she wouldn't be able to break free of the nightmare. She had spent years gaining control over her fear and would not surrender control again. Regan would not let herself be swallowed up again into that dark place...

~~~

She heard the woman pleading for her life as Regan's father pummelled blows upon her face and ribs. When she was no longer able to stand, he held her up by her blood-drenched hair as streams of blood flowed freely from her broken nose and lacerated mouth. Repeatedly he punched her, never saying a word, or showing any emotion – just bent on killing her in the most painful way he could.

Flashes of the past started flickering through her mind like crime scene photos. Regan lifted her hands to her ears as if to shut out the tortured moans from so long ago of that barbarous death. A death she had been helpless to prevent.

Pleasure crossed Thomas' bullish features as he watched his daughter's reaction to his presence.

"Regan will you come with me willingly or do I need to *persuade* you to accompany me and my associates?" his deep voice grated along Regan's nerves like course sandpaper. His narrow lips twisted into a cold smile as he wondered how much pain his daughter could sustain these days. *Had she become harder as an adult or softer?* He would soon find out.

Regan didn't hear the question, as she was still fighting her
~~~

memories. The gruesome parade of thoughts flicking through her mind as she remembered the wretched sounds from the woman she loved, her mother, straining for air as she was strangled. But the sharp explosion of pain from the jab to her unguarded stomach brought her back to the present. As she gasped from the excruciating pain, Regan straightened up and shifted her weight to prepare for the fight of her life.

Not bothering to answer him, Regan struck out trying to smash her father's knee, but he slid effortlessly out of her way. "So that's how it's going to be? You'll soon be reminded – it is a lot easier to do as I say, than to fight me, girl."

Her stomach twisted with the anxiety of the memories of pain, as she prepared to dodge her father's attack.

Thomas rushed at Regan with vicious violence, forcing her to hasten around the room in a defensive pattern. Sweat broke out on her brow as she used every fragment of skill and agility she had left to avoid his savage attacks.

The fear she had been keeping at bay grew insidiously, draining her confidence. As the painful minutes dragged by, the constant pressure of her father's assault caused her thinking to freeze. Her small mistakes allowed him to breach her defenses and punish her with cruel precision. Escape was hopeless – trying to land a punch on him was impossible enough, let alone attempting to hurt him enough to run. Regan needed to do something, or Thomas' relentless pursuit would tire her out and destroy her.

Her distressed muscles screamed for oxygen as she panted for breath, with sweat dripping into her eyes and blurring her vision. Regan misjudged yet another of Thomas' punches, and it hit her cheek with brutal force, stunning her momentarily. She leaped back, trying to give herself time to recover but not quickly enough to avoid a vicious kick to her stomach, followed by a savage kneeing to her face.

Regan struggled to maintain her balance as she felt the cartilage in her nose crush and the warm blood gush freely. Each ragged breath she inhaled was a labor, threatening to choke her, and pain ripped through her will to continue. Self-preservation told her she desperately needed to escape, as she staggered backward towards the door, seeking a way out.

Her father's vicious assault persisted – punching her in the face even as she raised her arms to protect herself; the rest of her body open to his attack. The room was filled with the sounds of her ragged gasps of pain, and the harsh unrelenting sound of flesh hitting battered flesh. She knew the ferocity would stop only when she lay bloody and broken on the cold floor.

Regan closed her one still open eye against the sight of her father standing over her, gazing down with those soulless blue eyes. Tears glistened along her lashes, as she lay on the floor in a drowsy haze. *Get up!* She told herself, but her muscles no longer responded to her will.

Her father grabbed her by the upper arm and dragged her across the floor towards the front door. Her head rolled to the side as she concentrated on pushing the pain to the background. Regan tried to think, but the unrelenting waves of pain over her body stole her focus, and darkness crept in at the edges of her blurred vision. Groaning in endless agony, she tried to gain control of her feet. Her father fixed his reptilian eyes on her swollen bloody face before coldly backhanding her, causing pain to explode once again in her skull.

"Stay down and I won't have to hurt you anymore. It's your choice, Regan." His tone appeared to be composed, but Regan knew her father relished in doling out pain and her compliance would not stop him from continuing to hurt her. She gritted her teeth, forcing herself to stay conscious – to let him take her away was a death sentence.

As he dragged her across the floor, her hand brushed across something cold and heavy. She turned her head and saw the gun dropped by the man whose hand she'd broken. With shaking fingers, Regan tried reaching for the gun; her fingers clumsily missing it as her father continued hauling her away from what looked to be her only hope of salvation. Nevertheless, she refused to give up. She hooked her foot through the gun's strap, and carefully slid it back within reach of her hand. Fresh pain tore at her, but her fingers closed around the handle. Catching her breath, she raised the gun towards her father.

"Gun!" her first attacker called out in warning, while at the same time shards from the living room window exploded inward in all directions as a large male lunged through it, gun held out in front, scattering glass across the battle scene that had once been her living room.

The new intruder's gaze swept the dark room instantly taking in all exits, potential cover, and players in the room. The man with the buzz cut turned his gun towards the intruder, who fired a single shot into his head, killing him instantly without remorse. As happened in combat, everyone moved in different directions simultaneously. He swung his gun towards the figure lunging for the front door, but before he could pull the trigger, the wounded woman fired from her prone position, hitting the fleeing man, but he couldn't tell where.

Through blurred vision, Regan had watched as her father hit the floor and rolled towards the door. Aiming, she squeezed the trigger, hitting him in the stomach before he lunged through the entryway and out into the night.

The third man had fled through the door furthest from the interloper when he crashed through the window. He began to give chase but pulled up as the man disappeared into the thick woods behind the house; his gut reaction was to go back to the woman and protect her rather than give chase. This didn't make sense to him, he needed information, information the fleeing man might have, and the woman meant nothing to him, but the wolf side of his nature demanded that he return to the woman and protect her.

Re-entering the demolished living room, the man noted the woman had dragged herself to the entry way and now sat with her legs splayed out and her back resting against the hall wall. He caught the wounded woman's eye and signaled for her to wait while he checked the rest of the property, noting she never lowered her gun from him as he moved about. He admired her spunk, she'd been badly beaten but she wasn't giving up.

After seeing that the area was safe and there were no more intruders, the man went back to the battered woman. Tucking his gun into the back of his jeans, he spread his hands wide in the universal sign of peace as he slowly walked towards her, "It's alright little one. My name is Rafe. I am here to help. We need to get you out of here before the authorities turn up and start asking questions. Will you come with me so I can help you?" He pitched his voice low and soft as he crouched in front of her; he was a big man and knew his size was intimidating. He needed her to come without a fight, he didn't want to hurt her any more than she already was, but he also couldn't risk the police finding them at the scene of a murder and he refused to leave her here.

It was essential for shifters to stay below the radar; they couldn't afford to come to the attention of human authorities. Hopefully, his team would have this cleaned up before the authorities arrived, but if not he and Regan needed to be long gone.

As he remained crouched in front of her, she continued to hold her gun aimed at his chest although at this point, she was having trouble holding it steady. There was no trust in the blood shot eye focused on him; the other eye was now completely swollen shut. Bile rose in his throat to see the beating she had taken, from the way she was holding her other arm across her chest and her shallow breathing he had to assume she'd had broken ribs and her face... *Dear God why would they do this to her?* Her tangled black hair was soaked with blood from her facial wounds and blood dripped slowly from her chin. The swelling from her injured swollen shut eye continued over her cheek, already darkening with bruising. Her short shallow breaths were panting through her mouth, as her mashed nose was useless. .

He ached for her even as he respected her courage. This woman had the soul of a warrior. The thought of handing her care over to one of his men had his wolf growling a low warning. This protectiveness he felt toward her made no sense; she hadn't even spoken to him, and still held her gun on him at point blank range.

"Give me your hand little one and I'll take you somewhere we can protect you and see to your wounds." Her eye didn't waver from him as she considered his words, "You're safe with me," he added and then waited, willing her to believe him.

Regan looked at the big man squatting before her so calmly, holding his hand out to her, unfazed by the gun she aimed at him. He was a virile, athletic looking bastard, with thick coffee colored hair that reached his shoulders, strong features that were harshly aesthetic, he was the kind of man women's eyes turned to follow as they walked by. Dressed in a navy blue T-shirt that clung to his muscled chest and tight abdomen before tucking into black jeans, above well-worn steel capped boots, he looked self-assured, experienced, someone who could shoulder any load necessary and keep going. He held an air of accomplished authority and the pressures of life had left its mark on his chiseled features. He had the air of leadership about him, that he'd be making the decisions, not following them.

His liquid brown eyes held sympathy for her pain, and the promise of help. Nevertheless, could she trust him? He had killed without hesitation and now wanted to go before the police arrived and he hadn't mentioned taking her to a hospital. She needed to make a decision whether to go with him or try to make a stand and call 911 herself. She didn't kid herself that she would be able to stop him if he forced her to go; even now, her vision was fading at the edges as darkness closed in. She desperately wanted to curl up and escape the pain but she shook her head trying to focus. Why wasn't she afraid of him? Where were her senses that always told her if she was safe or there was danger? Why was he even here? She struggled to hold on, to get her senses to respond, but even as she tried to form a question, she felt the world tilting on its side as she slipped into the oblivion of darkness.

Rafe watched as Regan lost her valiant fight for consciousness and gently lowered her to the ground as she sagged to the side. He quickly ran his hands over her ribs feeling the obviously broken rib; he cupped her cheek and jaw in his large hand to see if either was broken, when the iridescent blue spark leapt between them from the skin-to-skin contact. He flinched his hand away nearly falling over backward, he shook his head. How could this be?

She wasn't a shifter, how could she be his mate? Only two shifters could form a mating bond. The sparks flew between two mates when they either first touched skin-to-skin or at a later date when both were in a highly emotional state. Never both, it was either one or the other. No one understood why some couples knew instantly while others could know each other for years before the mating spark flared to life. One thing was undeniable; once the sparks flared, the couple was drawn to each other by an irresistible sexual chemistry. This was nature's way of forcing them to deal with each other.

No one ever resisted the pull for long; the vast majority of shifters anticipated their mating with relish. That's not to say all shifters were guaranteed a mating. Only just over half the population received the blessing of a mating. Shifters weren't like humans whose numbers continued to increase; shifters only produced one or two, and on rare occasions three offspring, keeping their numbers at a status quo. Tentatively he reached for her hand and watched in fascination and growing horror as the luminous blue spark arced between them one more time before flaring out.

Dread filled his heart and realization filled his mind as he stared down at her. He'd only just started working for the Sentinels straight out of high school all those years ago. The team he'd been assigned to was tracking a shifter who'd murdered an unknown number of human women. Rafe remembered the resentment he'd felt at being pulled off the hunt to go check up on some kid. He had been asked to verify if she was a shifter. If she was one of them, he was to offer her and her mother sanctuary within their community of shifters, even though her father had chosen to live outside the safety of the shifter society. It was in everyone's best interest if children were brought up within shifter communities to help maintain their secrecy and help the young ones adjust as their animal natures started to influence them. Kids couldn't be expected to hide their secret so they were sheltered within shifter communities until they could understand the necessity of hiding their abilities from humans. They were also taught how to control their natures, which were often aggressive.

He remembered driving by her house and seeing her with her mother in the front yard playing happily together. Neither of them showed the luminous aura that surrounded shifters, an aura that only other shifters could see. He remembered watching the black haired tike running away from her mother as fast as her little legs would carry her, squealing with delightful laughter as her mother chased after her. He'd assumed that all was well with the family and checked them off as of no interest to the clan. The atrocities later dealt to Regan could be laid directly at his feet for the decision he made that day.

God, she would hate him when she came to realize what his decision had cost her. He had done one drive by and forgotten her existence until her father had come onto his radar recently when his name had come up in his current investigation. She would hate him when she realized the full ramification of his decision all those years ago.

Trailing the back of his fingers gently across her forehead he sighed, “Little one I hope your heart is strong and generous as you will have to learn to love the one who left you behind to suffer. You will need to love the one who betrayed your right to a cherished childhood. For you will have no choice but to share your heart with me as I will not let you go, and I will accept nothing less than your whole heart as you shall have mine.” So saying he gathered her gently and left her house for his car that he had hidden further down the street, his head bent over her protectively. Once he had her settled on the back seat, he called Jordan, his second in command, to organize the cleanup of Regan’s house. Hopefully, her cottage was isolated enough that none of her distant neighbors had called the police, but life was never that easy.

CHAPTER 2

Rafe sat in the chair next to Regan's bed and watched her resting in her coma-induced sleep. His lovely mate was a tall woman, sleekly muscled, but lying there she looked like a broken porcelain doll, lost amongst the thick feathered comforter, vulnerable, and defenseless. His heart ached as she made a low keening sound deep in her throat, her hand moving restlessly searching for something. He could no more stop himself from taking her hand in his, than he could stop himself from breathing.

"It's OK sweetheart you're safe here. We've got you now." His heart eased as she settled. His wolf stopped its incessant pacing and settled into watching her, its worry for their mate pervasive. His wolf was part of him and yet separate, like having a consciousness living with you every minute of every day. Rafe couldn't talk to his wolf but he could feel its influence. When he changed into his wolf form he was still

Rafe, but with a wolf's instincts.

Regan settled back into a quiet sleep at the sound of his voice, her face relaxing as she surrendered to the drugs. Reluctantly he released her hand, conscious of keeping their skin contact to a minimum. Over the last twenty-four hours, her sleep had become more and more disturbed. Their doctor Kylie Warner had assured him it was normal and a sign that the worst of the injuries had been repaired, as shifters heal at a much faster rate than humans, and Regan's body was ready to awaken. Kylie had reduced the dosage saying that Regan would wake up when she was ready.

Rafe studied her face resisting the urge to run the pad of his finger over her finely arched brows. Instead, he wrapped a lock of her jet black hair around his forefinger smoothing his thumb over the silken texture again and again. Over the last couple of days, her aura had begun to develop, a halo of exquisite ochre indicating she would shift into one of the larger hunting cats, probably a panther like her father.

Her features were influenced by her inner cat, now the swelling had receded he could see her nose was slightly flattened at the bridge and flared slightly at the bottom, but with her high cheek bones and square jaw her face became striking rather that odd. Any skin that wasn't bruised held a healthy golden sheen. All in all, she wasn't classically beautiful, but instead she was arresting, alluring, and with her bone structure she would stay that way as she aged, he hoped he would be with her to witness the changes the passing seasons would bring.

He'd looked at their problem with apprehension from every possible angle over the last five days as Regan's body recovered from her beating. He had decided that he needed time for her to bond with him before telling her of his life-altering decision and abandonment of her as a child. If there were no feelings to bind her to him, she would have no reason to forgive him.

He'd asked Jordan to find everything he could about her history. Jordan's genius with computers allowed him access to any database, be it government or private. What Jordan had discovered had left him devastated. Dropping his head, he rubbed at his eyes with his free hand as he imagined Regan's suffering. Whatever Regan had witnessed, the night of her mother's murder had broken Regan in some fundamental way. At first, she'd retreated into a type of mental breakdown and rather than having the clan surround her to cherish, comfort, and help her through, she'd been left alone in an overstretched public hospital with strangers that would never understand her. Never had he been so close to crying as when he'd read those heartbreaking reports. The things they had done to her, her resilience was amazing. She had endured so much hardship in her twenty-four years.

After her mother's savage murder Regan had been unable or unwilling to talk to anyone. Rather than wrapping her in love and giving her comfort, they'd stuck her in a public ward. She'd lain in the cold sterile environment surrounded by a constant rotation of cold, uncaring staff. Regan had retreated further and further inside herself. When she'd stopped eating, they'd used a tube to force feed her and a drip to hydrate her. Either Regan's own will to survive or maybe her cat had started to assert her influence when it felt Regan's will to live fading, and had forced her out of her catatonic state. She'd started eating and responding when people spoke directly to her.

The police had searched for her father for questioning in her mother's murder but they'd never found a single lead to his whereabouts. They eventually turned it over to cold cases. She received no counseling or love from the overworked hospital staff, and it appeared like there was a complete lack of compassion amongst the social workers. Soon Regan was moved into the foster system to free up the hospital bed.

They had prevented her from starving herself to death but had done nothing to help her spirit and mind heal. There had been no one to care for her, to talk with her, to hold her and let her cry, to encourage her back to the surface.

Rafe was filled with shame. He had done this to her. Her time in hell was because he had been too busy proving his manhood to his fellow sentinels, to take the time to check on her properly. Now she would be tied to him for the rest of their lives as a mate. Knowing what her father had done, it seemed an insurmountable obstacle they faced. He could not let her go yet surely she would want nothing to do with him once she knew. He ached for the pain they were both to suffer until she could find a way to forgive him.

Consciousness drifted ever so slowly towards Regan and with it, the pain returned. Time had no meaning as pain swallowed her, drowning her in shards of jagged agony. Moaning, Regan fought the blackness towing her back under to the bleak darkness, trapped and alone, the unending silence a crushing weight on her chest. Struggling for her breath, she fought to move through the black stench struggling to find something, someone; she didn't know what, her thoughts were fractured. Desperately she moved through the dark searching for someone. She couldn't stay here trapped, forsaken, forgotten. She struggled doggedly upward into that unrelenting pain that meant she still lived. Whimpering she kicked free to the surface. Gasping Regan let the pain roll over her, it was a validation that she still lived.

Swallowing to bring moisture to her dry mouth, she tried to figure out where she was. Slowly she remembered the horrendous fight with her father and his men, and the stranger who came to her assistance, but she couldn't remember anything after her father ran out the door. Had the stranger left her, had her father come back for her while she was unconscious? Her heart raced. Slitting her eyes open, the room slowly came into focus, she was in what looked like a motel room. A bedside lamp cast the room in a soft glow; her bed was queen size, there was a small lounge and matching chairs made of some light toned wood, and innocuous beige carpet. A small television sat on an entertainment unit against the far wall. There were two doors, the open one led to a bathroom, the other was closed and must lead outside. This definitely wasn't a hospital.

The compulsion to leave set in, raising the hair on her arms, she didn't think she was safe here. Regan's stomach rolled at the thought of facing her father in this condition. Additionally, if the stranger had brought her here that was all wrong too. A helpful citizen would have called an ambulance and she'd be in a hospital. This wasn't right, anxiety scored along her nerves, she had to move, the need to hide herself away in order to heal was an overriding command in her mind.

Pushing the covers back her breath was torn from her as pain crushed her skull. It also radiated from her stomach and ribs. Breathing through the coursing agony, she let the waves wash over her until she was able to control her breathing and the nausea subsided. Breathing shallowly but steadily, she clenched her teeth refusing to groan at the pain splintering her ribs as she sat up. Persevering, she swung her legs over the edge, then sat still once again allowing the jagged fragments of pain to rip through her, not fighting it, letting herself endure the pain, to raise to this level and maintain. Face contorting she stood, reaching out as the room spun, and her vision faded, biting her lip she rejected the agony of sitting again.

Hatred for her father swelled in her, she refused to black out, raw anger had sustained her before, and it would again. She used the anger, forcing herself to move, she would *not* permit herself to be used as a punching bag again. She was not the helpless child he was accustomed to dealing with. She was strong, her hatred made her strong. Pain and endurance made her strong. She would not allow herself to be caught here in this weakened condition, she would not be trapped. Clenching her teeth she shuffled over to the wardrobe, she needed clothes. Of course, it was empty. "Damn it what am I supposed to do now?"

"Getting back in bed would be a good idea," a male voice replied.

Spinning to face the ruggedly handsome stranger from her house resulted in shards of pain stabbing at Regan's ribs and head. Regan cursed her stupidity while the room darkened and her limbs became heavy as she clumsily struggled to hold herself up using the wardrobe door for support.

Rafe reached Regan as she folded in on herself. Gathering her close to his chest, he turned toward her bed intending to settle her gingerly back under the covers. His wolf pushed against his control wanting to keep Regan with them. It had found its mate and wanted to cosset her until she awoke. The urge to keep her in his arms tucked safely against his chest was strong and he couldn't entirely blame his wolf for the need. Unable to help himself he dipped his head and heavily breathed in her rich scent, barely resisting the instinct to rub his own scent over her, temporarily marking her as his. It felt so right holding her close to his heart, yet his human side understood the necessity of placing her carefully back on the bed. He needed to keep the skin to skin contact to a minimum until he'd had a chance to woo her; otherwise, the hormones both their bodies were producing would drive them both into an irresistible sexual frenzy. He didn't want the mating craze taking Regan's choices away from her.

He'd forced himself to take a step towards her bed when Regan turned her body into his and drew his scent into her lungs, subconsciously seeking comfort from her mate. Rafe closed his eyes and tipped his head back, his mind swimming as she made a soft purring sound before settling herself against his chest with her head resting in the crook of his neck. Arousal punched him in the gut. His mate was lying trustingly in his arms. His wolf urged him to keep her there and ignite the animal arousal between them into a blazing inferno when she awoke. He knew he could do it too. She was responsive to his magnetism in her unconscious state.

He could lay her down, remove her tank top and panties before easing her legs open enough to see her hidden femininity. Using the softest of touches, he could arouse her body. A feather light touch of his fingernail scraping her nipple until it beaded under his watchful gaze. The rough calluses of his hand would rasp the silken smooth skin of the inside of her legs moving ever closer to her liquid core, a breath of air against her moist opening, so when she awoke, need had her wrapped in its tight fist. Before coming fully awake, he could use his questing tongue to sharpen her arousal, to build her sensory pleasure until her body craved his. It would be so easy; Kylie had assured him Regan had recovered from the worst of her injuries. His wolf growled in anticipation. Once she was fully awake and burning with animalistic need, he imagined the pleasure of arousing her need until she begged for release. Sensual passion pounded through his powerful frame as he stared down at her face.

Rafe shook his head, trying to control his lust and his wolf's focused need. He forced himself to move to the bed and reluctantly settled her under the covers. His fingers trembled as he drew the blanket over her, trying to control his pounding heart and the throbbing need surging through his manhood. Turning he paced away from her to look out the window until he gained control of himself and his wolf. Worry wove through his jumbled thoughts; already the sexual thrall of the mating was challenging his control. Had he overestimated his ability to resist the pull and court his mate as he intended?

He ached to hold her close to his body's warmth. But he didn't want her thinking he was some sick prick getting his jollies while she was struggling to even stay conscious. He noted her cheeks were flushed when he walked back to her, drawn to be closer. Concerned he reached out to touch her, at the last instant remembering not to. The more skin-to-skin contact they had the more hormone would be released into her system increasing the sexual intensity between them which would bring on her first shift. He needed time with her, for her to come to know and understand him, before her body and his forced a mating between them. The sexual need between them would grow to a pounding, unrelenting pressure until satisfied; arousal would plague them until fulfilled. His only chance of holding it off was to keep physical contact to a minimum. Soon he'd have to go for a run and let his wolf race until exhaustion burned her out of their system, at least for a while.

While he paced beside her bed waiting for her to awaken again he pondered how much she knew about the lives of shifters, their mating habits and what instigated the first shift for females. Did she know the males shifted when they hit puberty while females didn't shift until they met their mate? Her mother was human and would have only had the information Thomas gave her about shifters. With Thomas choosing to live outside the shifter communities, more than likely Regan would be in total ignorance of the communities shifters lived in and that she could change forms.

It was unlikely her family had ever lived amongst shifters. From the information Jordan had dug up, her father had never fit in and would have found it hard to hide his violent nature surrounded by shifters. Additionally, shifters did not look the other way when a man hit his wife or child, as humans were apt to do. So had the bastard told her about shifters and all it involved or had he left her ignorant? Rafe was betting on ignorant. Her old man would not want to help his daughter understand why she felt so different from humans. His controlling nature would want her feeling isolated and alone.

Rafe sighed, the obstacles between he and his mate were problematic but could be insurmountable if she had an inflexible, uncaring personality. How would she react to shifters and their need for constant touch and sharing every facet of their lives with each other? Would she be able to accept this new way of life, so different from what she had ever known? From the research Jordan had done on her, she had never bonded with the foster family she had been placed with. She hadn't stayed in contact with any of them when she left at seventeen after finishing high school and getting a job. Not even a Christmas card, nada, nothing. She had just walked away as if the six years she had spent living with them had never happened.

She didn't even keep in contact with the other kids fostered by the family. Surely, she should have bonded with at least one of the other kids. But no, she had been a loner. That she hadn't bonded with anyone, worried him, she was all-alone in the world and it just wasn't in a shifters nature to be so. They all instinctively sought touch and company. They were gregarious by nature. Had Regan been so scarred by her childhood that she couldn't function normally – couldn't form bonds with others? Had her father actually knocked that desire out of her? He couldn't imagine how lonely she would have felt as a child. Cut off from all others that could have understood her, who would have just held her until she could cope with her mother's murder. However, she had been left with humans who didn't know of a shifters inherent need to be held. She was now cut off from her emotions and inner cat. Would she let him help her get to know this other side of herself, or keep him at a distance?

Could he bring her into such a tight knit community like this or would it be too overwhelming for her? So many questions, and the answers escaped him. He didn't want to contemplate leaving, it would be like severing his arm to move away from everyone – but his mate's happiness would come before his own and if she could not cope with the shifters, for her sake, he would leave Eden's Retreat.

Rubbing his hands over his face, he watched as she dozed on the bed. If she could walk away from a family that had looked after her for six years, how was he going to get her to stay with him when she discovered he had turned his back on her and left her with that monster of a father? When she found out that it was his decision, which had ultimately led to her mother being beaten to death in front of her, how would she react? He needed to find a way into her heart before she discovered that he was the one who had sealed her fate. If he had brought her mother and Regan here to live, Regan's mother would still be alive and Regan would have grown up loved and protected. Instead, he had consigned her to hell.

He needed time with her but he didn't want it to be all about their sexual need for each other, he wanted her to *choose* to stay, not be forced by a chemical reaction that would make them crave each other. That would be a living hell for them both. Such mating's were horrendous to watch. It didn't happen often but Rafe had witnessed one mated pair who hated each other but were forced to share sex because the arousal from the bond was so intense between them they couldn't stay away. Over the years, both had become bitter and resentful. The community in general pitied them but at the same time avoided them because of the sourness. No one wanted a mating like that. Rafe had always envisioned a mating like his parents, where a deep abiding love for each other held them together as much as the mating bond. To be faced with the potential disaster of his own mating made him sick at heart.

Rafe stepped out into the hallway and called Kylie, she would be able to see to it that Regan was kept comfortable. Kylie had kept Regan in an induced coma for five days to allow her shifter metabolism to repair the worst of her concussion, broken nose, and ribs. The swelling and bruising around her eye and cheek had gone down, the bruises were now black edged with yellow showing that they were already healing, as were her ribs, although it probably didn't feel like it to Regan.

Rafe looked up a short time later as Kylie turned the corner into the hallway where Rafe waited outside Regan's door. She moved with the sureness of a wolf, all economy of movement, always in balance. Caught in the light streaming in from the hallway window as she passed, her tawny hair was the color of fire. The creamy complexion of her skin was smooth as porcelain, with her lush figure it always amazed Rafe that Kylie didn't have more men panting at her door. Although they had been friends since childhood, he could count the number of men she had taken as lovers over the years on one hand and still have fingers to spare. Maybe she was waiting for her mate, it was unusual for wolves to stay single for the long periods that Kylie did, but not unheard of.

Although he and Kylie had been friends forever and could talk about anything – her love life was one topic he found uncomfortable discussing with her. She felt too close to being a sister for him to be comfortable discussing intimate relationships, it was just wrong – put a shiver down his spine thinking of it. He hoped she found her other half soon, as she deserved the best. She was now in her thirties like him and no doubt was ready to settle down and start her own family.

Kylie squeezed Rafe's arm reassuringly.

"She'll be fine. I checked on her earlier, her fever's gone, her ribs are mending, and the bruising and swelling are well within normal range for the attack she sustained."

"She was out of bed when I went in, but passed out before she could sit down," he did nothing to hide the concern in his voice.

Kylie opened the door, moving over to look down at the sleeping woman.

"Honestly don't worry, by this afternoon she'll still be sore, but she will be up and about." She gave him a sidelong look from beneath her long, dark lashes, "Have you decided what approach to take with her? Full disclosure up front or dribble the information out in bits and pieces?"

"I'll tell her about shifters if she doesn't already know – but not about our bond."

Kylie shook her head, the cinnamon and gold hair was highlighted under the fluorescent lighting she'd turned on to examine Regan's wounds, "She should be ecstatic to have such a mate as you. I don't understand why you would try to hide such information from her."

Rafe frowned at the undertone of resentment he heard in Kylie's voice, wondering where it had come from.

"She wasn't brought up with the knowledge of there being one perfect mate out there for her. I don't think she is going to believe me if I say to her *"Oh by the way you're my mate so get your stuff together and move into my unit and we can get straight to fucking ourselves senseless and live happily ever after."*

Kylie's lips kicked up into a slight smile, "I can think of nicer ways of saying it, but yeah I think you should come straight to the point with her. You're forgetting she is going to be unreasonably attracted to you anyway, why beat around the bush – like I said she should be ecstatic she's got you."

His head tilted as he again caught the slight bitterness. This was so unlike Kylie, normally she was serene, gentle with her patients, giving and loving towards her friends. It was like a burr in his fur to see this animosity coming from her, he'd have to remember to take her aside when he had time and find out what was going on with her.

Rubbing his hand over her narrow shoulders and down her back in a sign of affection he rested some of his weight against her, "Thanks for the vote of confidence – but you aren't taking into account her childhood."

"And you aren't taking into account the physical pull you have going for you. I'm just saying don't waste it." Looking back to Regan, she asked, "Do you want me to stay with her until she wakes up?"

"If you don't mind – I'm desperate for a run and I need to contact the sentinels out in the field to see if anyone has anything we can use to catch these bastards hunting us. Call me as soon as Regan wakes." With one last look at the woman on the bed, he left the room as silent as the predator he was.

Kylie moved over to the lounge placed near the window, sat down, and pulled her tablet out of the backpack she always carried with her. Sitting here, she could look out the window and watch the antics of the people in the compound while going through and updating her medical files. She needed to read a journal article, on new treatments for immune disorders. Although shifters had stronger immune systems than humans did, they still had some chronic illnesses that the human medicines could help with and she needed to keep up with the latest research. As she waited for her computer to hook up to the network, her gaze drifted to the girl on the bed.

"You better appreciate how lucky you are, scoring Rafe for a mate. If you start any of this standoffish bullshit as you've done with your foster family, you and I are going to have words. That man deserves the best and you had better get your shit together and be your best."

Kylie found it hard not to resent Regan, actually, if she was being honest with herself, which she tried to be – she was resentful as all hell. She was just trying to get a handle on it. She and Rafe had been friends as far back as her memory went. They fit together so well. God how she had prayed as a teenager, that they would prove to be a mated pair. However, the sparks that would prove they were a fated match never appeared throughout her adolescence and by the time she was twenty, she'd had to come to terms that they weren't going to appear. Rafe had never shown a sexual interest in her. As far as he was concerned, she was a friend and that's all. Nevertheless, Kylie's feelings of friendship had turned to infatuation as a teenager and into love as an adult. Over the years she had reconciled herself to just being friends. She was glad now that she had come to that decision, realizing how awful it would have been to be in a relationship with Rafe when he found his destined mate.

Not only would she be dumped but also she would have to

watch Rafe with his real love, the hurt and jealousy would have driven her from her home. She knew she wouldn't have been able to endure their joy while her world shattered around her. It was far better never to have had him in the first place. So, she had reconciled herself to keep their friendship platonic and she had really believed she would be happy for him when he found his mate. Boy had she been kidding herself, she felt nothing but resentment. It was one thing to contemplate losing Rafe in theory, but it was another to witness the reality.

From everything Rafe had told her about Regan, she wasn't going to be a good partner for him. His life was hard enough being head of the sentinels, an enforcer of their laws, he was the one who made the tough decisions when it came to protecting their community. He needed someone whose warmth and love could balance out the bitterness of having to hunt down and kill his own kind because they had harmed humans, or risked exposing them to humanity by their behavior. He did not need this girl who was so cold and dead emotionally that she had cut all contact with her foster family; the girl had no friends. It was as if she was the antithesis of a shifter. While shifters craved physical contact with their kind and shared each other's lives, this girl lived in total isolation.

Kylie understood that a large part of her antagonism for Regan came from seeing her dream die, and the disappointment of the final confirmation that she and Rafe would never be lovers. Unknowingly she must have still held some hope that she and Rafe could be together. Now her friendship with Rafe would change, he wouldn't have the time for her that he used to and it would leave a big hole for her to fill in, somehow. Her time with Rafe was the highlight of her week – what was she going to look forward to now, more work? God she did enough hours already for two people. The hollow loneliness of the coming weeks was already sucking her down into depression.

Dropping her head back against the lounge's headrest, she let that aching loneliness wash over her, her chest ached with unshed tears. Each breath racked shards of glass over torn flesh and at last the tears fell as the first rasping breath tore from her chest. Her face contorted as she tried to hold back the sobs. She wanted to scream at the unfairness. *Why not her? Why this girl? What did she have that Kylie didn't? Why was fate doing this?* Breathing through the barbed agony of her loss, she fought back the sobs. God it hurt. She sat in the misery of her loss, as tears tracked down her face. The only sound in the room was her harsh breaths.

Time was meaningless as she grieved. Time moved indifferent to her pain, tiredness replaced the anguish slowly, unnoticed at first but weighing down on her when she roused. She was exhausted, her head and chest ached, but the pain had receded, for now she would prevail. Maybe she would look into moving to a new shifter settlement, maybe a new start would help her more, better that than staying to witness Rafe and Regan's courtship. Kylie wasn't a bitter person and she did not want to become one, which she feared she would if she had to have her face constantly rubbed in their happiness.

Taking a deep breath to release some of the ache in her chest, she wiped her face on a tissue from her bag. Looking up she found Regan watching her from the bed.

Kylie cleared her throat but her voice was still scratchy, "Good to see you awake. How are you feeling?" she asked as she rose to her feet and crossed to the bed.

"Like someone took to me with a baseball bat. Where am I?" Regan's voice came out a harsh whisper; she swallowed trying unsuccessfully to bring moisture to her parched mouth.

"I'm Dr Warner – I've been looking after you for the last five days. How's the head feeling?" Kylie filled a glass of water from the jug left on the bedside table and handed it to Regan after helping her to sit up.

Shrugging as she took a sip of water Regan admitted, "It hurts but not as much as the first time I woke up." Keeping her eyes on the doctor, she swallowed more water easing her parched throat. "So you didn't answer my question, where am I?"

Kylie's eyes narrowed at the flat tone of Regan's voice. "You're welcome, nothing like a patient being appreciative of all the hours I sat with them to make sure they didn't suffer any complications from the beating they took."

Regan nodded her head in acknowledgement of the reprimand, "Thank you for looking after me. Could you please explain why I'm here rather than in a hospital and where here is?" Kylie noted that the tone had only been dialed down marginally. What a piece of work, absolutely no gratitude!

Standing Kylie headed to the door; "I'll let someone else fill you in on that. My advice to you is to listen with an open mind and an open heart. *Not that I'm sure you have one.*" she muttered to herself as she left the room.

Regan watched the doctor leave; she had never been comfortable around medical staff after her mother's murder. One thing the doctors' short visit had accomplished was to lessen Regan's fear. Her father wouldn't have provided this level of comfort, so he hadn't captured her after she'd passed out. Therefore, her rescuer had brought her here and had ensured she received medical treatment, now she just needed to find out why he did that and where *here* was.

The abrasive doctor reminded Regan of the overworked doctors she'd been forced to endure after her mother's murder. They had poked and prodded her but hadn't given her the one thing she'd needed – empathy. Regan understood as an adult why they kept her in there, but as a traumatized girl, she just wanted to escape from all those strangers, go home, curl up in her bed, and cry. Cry until the pain overwhelmed; cry until there were no more tears to cry; until she had reached the bottom of despair, as was her mother's due. Her mother should not have gone quietly from the world. Regan had needed to scream, to tear at her hair, to shatter glass, to shriek her rage until her throat was raw. She had needed to destroy. It had been her pain and she had needed to wallow in it – to let her mother's spirit know she was shattered.

Instead, she had internalized all that barbed agony. By the time they had released her into foster care, she had been unable to shed even one tear. All that anger and pain was locked so deep inside her it felt like a cold jagged lump of rock filled her chest. She lived with that every day until she became deadened to the pain. She felt little; it was as if something had died inside her. It wasn't just the loss of her mother; it was as if all her trust and interest in humanity had been stolen. How could she trust anyone when her own father had killed her beautiful mother? She truly didn't care what people thought of her, when you were totally cut off from everyone there was no pain to feel except your own, which for her had cooled into a hard dead knot in her torso. Life was about survival and that is what she did.

From her earliest memories of her father, she'd been terrified of him, his unpredictability leaving her always on edge. She never knew if he would be civil with her, beat her, or do something in between. She lived in constant fear of the moods of her father. She vividly remembered one instant when he was laughing and tossing her up in the air, she was squealing with laughter as he caught her and tossed her up again. The next throw he caught her and shouted at her because she hadn't laughed enough, he'd taken her by the upper arm and had shaken her like a rag doll. Regan grimaced as she caught herself rubbing her shoulder with remembered pain. Even that young she'd known not to make a sound as he'd continued to shake her, if she had cried he would hit her instead and that was much worse than being shaken about. He'd stopped shaking her as quickly as he'd started, giving her a hard hug.

"That's my brave girl you did well. It's ice cream time for you."

He'd taken her into the kitchen fixed her a bowl of ice cream as if they'd had a grand time together and left her to eat it. Once he'd left the kitchen tears had silently slid down her face, she'd been too sick to eat the ice cream and had quickly taken it to the sink to flush away all evidence that she had not eaten it, in case he came back.

If he had just been a drunk she would have known when to

avoid him – but that wasn't the case. Regan had never been able to discover what triggered his rage and neither had her mother.

"Do as he asks as quickly as you can poppet" had been her advice to Regan. "If we keep him happy he might not hit."

Wow what a motto to live by.

Growing up the only support Regan had was her mother. Her mother had mentioned she was an only child but had refused to talk about Regan's grandparents. To this day, she didn't know who they were or if they were even alive.

When she was in her first year of school, her shirt had gotten paint on it and her teacher had taken it off to get the worst of the paint off. When she had seen the purple and black bruises on Regan's body, she had asked how Regan had gotten them. Regan had shrugged and thinking it was no big deal, told her that her father had hit her. A parody of a smile twisted Regan's lips as she remembered how at the time she'd thought that's what all fathers did to their little girls. If they didn't move fast enough they got backhanded out of the way, and if they fell down, they'd then get kicked for losing their balance.

Regan had earnestly explained to her teacher that she had to learn how to take pain. *"I still lay on the ground too long, I've got to get up quicker."* She'd further explained. Her teacher had asked her a few more questions about her father then she'd handed Regan her shirt back and had gone back to teaching the class, reaffirming in Regan's mind that her home life was just like anyone else's.

Regan didn't connect the incident with her teacher to the social worker arriving at their house a week later to conduct an interview with her mother. It might have just ended there, with her mother being able to fob off the social worker but her father had walked in. Regan to this day didn't know what happened in that interview but the social worker had eventually left with a smile and warm handshake for her father.

After the social worker had backed out the drive, her father had called her into the living room. On entering the room, Regan had sensed his rage, her stomach churned and she'd struggled to breathe through the panic. Before the first fist struck, she'd been crying promising not to do it again, even thought she'd had no idea what she'd done.

He had told her that the punishment her mother was about to receive was because Regan had told someone that he hit her. "This is our family and what happens in this house stays here. You will never tell anyone that I hit you or your mother." His voice had been eerily emotionless. "If you ever tell anyone again, the punishment your mother is about to receive is nothing, compared to what will be dealt out to you. Do you understand?"

Tears had streaked her ashen cheeks, "Please father, it was my error please don't punish mummy. Please!" she'd begged. His first blow had been to her mother's face splitting her lip and crushing into her cheek. Regan had moaned at the sound of flesh hitting flesh. She'd cringed, wrapping her arms across her stomach but her mother had stood stoically through the following barrage of punches to her face and stomach until she could stand no more and sagged to the floor. Blood trickling from her mouth, nose, and a split near her eyebrow. No sound escaped her mother though. His beating of her mother had been methodical and systematic. No bones had been broken, no internal damage done but the punches had been placed for the pain they would cause, and the visual reminder they would give Regan as the cuts and bruising slowly healed over the following weeks. It was a lesson Regan never forgot.

She'd often wondered as a child why her mother never left her husband, why she had never taken Regan away, but Regan had never doubted for a moment that her mother loved her. After that assault, her mother had never showed any disappointment or resentment over Regan's behavior. No her mother had cuddled Regan on her lap and rubbed her back as Regan had sobbed into her neck. Her soothing voice telling Regan over and over that it was all right, that everything was OK until Regan's tears had petered out.

Her mother had never referred to the incident but Regan had

never forgotten her mother's willing acceptance of Regan's punishment. And Regan had never again placed her mother in harm's way by allowing anyone to see her own bruising or speaking out. She came to realize that what her father was doing to them was not normal behavior nor acceptable. But, Regan would never take the risk of her father hurting her mother, because what if the authorities failed to remove Regan and her mother immediately from her father's reach?

Movement in the doorway brought Regan out of her memories, anticipation zinged through her and she latched onto the anticipation gratefully, she hated thinking about her past and this male standing in the doorway was a worthy distraction. He smiled down at her showing off his perfect white teeth and a set of dimples that was just criminal for such a hulking male to possess. As he leaned negligently against the wooden doorframe she guessed, he was just over 6 foot, tall without being a giant. He was gorgeous and he knew it but she could see no conceit in his manner. He had laugh lines at the corners of his eyes showing that he knew how to enjoy life, but that did not detract from the strong jaw or firm lips indicating that this man would be no push over. His muscled body reinforced her first impression of him at her house as being a man of action who could hold his own in a fight. His thighs clad in jeans were all hard muscle and drew her eye to the zipper in his jeans that was obviously concealing something substantial by the bulge being held back, said bulge now being at her eye level.

"See something you like?" he asked with a cheeky grin once again flashing those damned dimples.

Warmth heated her cheeks as Regan realized where she had been caught staring.

Letting her off the hook he turned from her allowing Regan to recover her composure as he moved across the room to grab a chair. Regan couldn't resist copping a look at his ass before he turned back. She always enjoyed looking at a good set of gluts and his jeans framed his nicely. Yummy!

Bringing the chair over he placed it next to where Regan sat, resting her back against the headboard.

"My name's Rafe McIntyre and I head up a private security agency, I'm guessing you have a lot of questions, so fire away," he said as he settled himself into the chair.

Rafe was pleased to see Regan sitting up with color in her face rather than the deathly pallor of the last few days. The fact that she seemed interested in his body gave him some hope they might have a chance as a mated pair.

Regan started with the question concerning her most, "Why am I here rather than a hospital?"

"We can guarantee you safety from your father here – whereas the logistics of keeping you protected in a hospital is a nightmare."

A frown pulled at her brows "How do you know my father? Come to think of that, how do you know he's *my* father?"

"Ahh now we are getting into the trickier information." He paused as he calculated again how much to reveal.

Regan arched one of her black brows at him and crossing her arms over her chest waited him out.

He flashed another charming grin although she noted the dimples didn't come into play this time. He settled back fully into his chair, "Depending on how much you know of your heritage, what I'm about to tell you may make perfect sense or you will think that I'm crazy and am missing a few requisite brain cells."

"Your father used to belong to a small neighboring clan until he was banished, which is how I know of him. He has an aura I can see and you have the same aura although faint, which indicates you are his biological daughter. The reason I can see this aura around you and your father is that you are both shape shifters. To be more specific you are both cat shifters. Your father is a black panther or if you want to be technically correct black leopard and I assume when you make your first shift you will also be a panther as your auras are nearly identical."

Rafe had watched her aura developing over the last few days as she lay in bed, though it was still faint compared to other shifters. He had no idea why she'd had no aura previously as every shifter he knew had their auras from birth. Maybe it was because her mother was human. He could only speculate that coming into contact with her mate had initiated the development of hers. Other shifter abilities would no doubt be developing further now; her cat would be waking up and influencing Regan.

Rafe watched her reaction as he spoke. Yeah it would've been too much to hope that she knew about shifters but from the way she was looking at him, he could tell she thought he was certifiable. What was the best way to convince her – keep talking or just show her? Talking to her might be less traumatic but showing would save a lot of time and cut through a lot of bullshit – soooo show and tell it would be.

Before Regan could begin to formulate a reply to the load of bull he'd just fed her, he held up his hand signaling for her to wait. He then stood and pulled his shirt off over his head. OK, while the view was exceptional, he was sleekly muscled, and his smooth skin tanned to a deep teak from the sun, she could not just sit there while the crazy man stripped naked.

One part of her brain was screaming, *Get up and move your skinny ass out of here*! *This man is dangerous, you've already seen him kill, and you're just lying here. You're not at full capacity to defend yourself.* The other half of her brain, that she didn't recognize was encouraging her to stay and watch, and was intensely curious about what he was going to do next. It felt playful and expectant instead of threatening. Regan felt as if another entity had taken up residence in her mind. These were not her thoughts; never would she choose to leave herself in this vulnerable position. Where was her fight or flight instinct that was so finely tuned? Normally she'd be up and out of this room while he was still talking. Not sitting here waiting to be assaulted by the deranged half naked guy. *Hello????? How stupid can I be?*

Oh goody – there go his jeans – time to get out of here – wait ...... what.... Is that for real? He had a lot of meat jammed into those jockeys – *surely, he couldn't get much bigger when he was aroused – because ouch that thing would hurt!* Before Regan could pull her eyes away from his groin, he turned and in one motion yanked his jockeys off. Before she could really appreciate those fantastic glutes, he turned into a wolf. Regan rubbed her eyes as she sank back onto the mattress – yeah there was a wolf standing there, looking at her with Rafe's intelligent brown eyes.

CHAPTER 3

"Holy crap," she whispered as her confused brain shut down. How else could she explain that instead of running from the room screaming as any normal rational person would, she felt drawn to the wild animal? She felt no fear, only a strange calm settling over her. It was as if something had been missing from her was now whole; the relief flooding through her was euphoric. Compulsively drawn to him, she slid from the bed and approached him with her hand held out.

The wolf sniffed her hand then nuzzled his massive head against her stomach rubbing gently back and forth. Her hands reached along his neck and smoothed over the thick rough fur of his back. It was incredibly dense; she could bury her hands and grab fists full of fur. Burrowing her fingers into his gray coat she ran her hand down his flank pausing to rub her fingers along a raised ridge of scar tissue, it was a substantial wound, and she wondered absently how he'd received it. As she ran her hands over him, awe wove through her.

She had always felt different from everyone and she knew to her soul that it was more than her trust issues that had kept her from engaging with others. She knew to her core that she was different, she'd never felt as if she belonged. Now she knew she had no interest in those around her because they weren't even the same species as her. Oh, this explained so much, her excellent night vision, her quicker than normal reflexes and speed, her ability to sense danger for no explicable reason.

Excitement thrummed through her; maybe at last she could find someone to connect with, to not always be so alone, and to not always be wary of everyone around her. She hugged Rafe to her as the opportunity of belonging somewhere engulfed her. A feeling of veneration, of possibility, of hope rolled over her. Moisture gathered along her lashes. For the first time since her mother's death, there was hope that something wonderful could happen. There was possibility out there, that there was more to life than endurance.

Eventually Regan reluctantly released her hold on Rafe and stood up. As she did so her sense of caution returned. Experience taught her she didn't fit in and she would be setting herself up for rejection again if she didn't keep that in mind. Anticipation drained leaving her slightly nauseated as she swung from vibrant hope to reality. She did not belong here anymore than she had belonged to that foster family.

Using her arm, she wiped her face as she waited for Rafe to materialize before her once again in his human form. The change was spontaneous, one instant he was an overly large wolf the next a ruggedly handsome man. A *naked* ruggedly handsome man, she swallowed dryly trying to drag her eyes away to give him some privacy while he casually dressed.

As he bent down to slide his feet into his boots Rafe assessed Regan's reaction.

"Tough girl aren't you?" his lips quirked upward as he continued, "Most people who don't know about shifters usually run off screaming for help right about now."

"Oookaay, I have to say that was unexpected." She paused "Does it hurt?"

Rafe laughed, "No, it sort of feels like a spike of adrenalin, you feel hot, tingly and full of energy."

"What happens to you when you shift does the wolf take over?" Regan didn't like the idea of another creature living inside her and taking her over.

"You're still there and in control, it's just your cat's instincts will be stronger in your shifted form, but you are aware and with practice can control her influence."

"So how do you do it, how do you change?"

Rafe shrugged, "You will it to happen, and it does. The first couple of times your cat will instigate the change – but you'll need to learn how to push her back and instigate the change when you are ready, not her."

Regan pondered that for a moment; obviously, she had a lot to learn. "OK so give me a brief overview on shifters."

Nodding he sat back down indicating that she should do the same. Once she was settled back on the bed resting her back against the headboard he began.

"OK a short history of shifters. We have been around for as long as humanity. We can trace our history along with humans; at some stages we were treated as gods – at some stages as high priests, and at other stages, we have hidden ourselves from persecution as we have in modern times. Our life spans are similar to humans. We can breed with humans, although if we do only a certain percentage of the offspring are able to shift, as seems likely in your case. I saw you with your mother once in passing – but she didn't have the aura of a shifter." His gaze left hers briefly, before returning his gaze to her, Regan sensed that he was nervous – although why he would feel uneasy eluded her, something to think about later.

"Back then you didn't have an aura either, which I've never heard of in a shifter, we all have auras from birth." Shrugging he added, "Maybe you have some rare recessive gene, I honestly don't know."

"We can tell a shifter by their aura. Different shifters have different auras. Male shifters have their first change at puberty, for some reason females don't change until they meet their mates." Again, his eyes shifted briefly from hers. She sensed he was withholding something – but since he was being so forthcoming with the information he was giving her, she didn't want to question him and chance him clamming up altogether.

"You'll find now days that most shifters will live in clans usually varying in size from fifty to two hundred. The clan will often own several neighboring farms or all the houses in a small gated estate so we can control who comes in. There are the odd clans that own a high-rise and a certain number of floors will be dedicated to shifters. We have to be careful about how we go about it and it's not unusual for a clan to move regularly so as not to arouse questions about why neighbors can't buy a house or unit that the clan controls. But by keeping the humans out it allows us to be ourselves and have somewhere we can shift safely. Most clans will own tracks of native forest nearby where members can go to shift and run their animal.

When you're ready, we can go for a walk outside and you can meet some of our people. The enclave here is called Eden's Retreat. You'll notice we are a lot closer to each other than humans, so don't be put off if people keep hugging you. It's just our way to have a lot of physical contact. You'll notice your inner animal craves the contact. It brings a sense of peace to us and reaffirms our connection to each other."

Regan grimaced at the thought – she hated being touched. She didn't trust people to get that close to her, a left over from her father's *training*.

"*Never let anyone close to you girl, because you never know who your enemy is. Anyone can turn on you, anyone can hurt you,"* as he had proven to her again and again. If she ever dropped her guard around him, he'd lash out pain, his favored training method.

Rafe paused allowing Regan to assimilate the information he had provided so far.

"How did you end up at my house just in the nick of time, saving me from *daddy dearest*?"

Rafe grimaced, she would have to ask that wouldn't she; nothing like telling your mate that you're going to kill her father after torturing information from him. Even though the man had beaten her and killed her mother – she was sure to find it difficult to forgive him the cold blooded murder of her only living relative.

He would also have to reveal that her father was betraying shifters, capturing and handing them over to *Titan* an exclusive club open to a select few. The requirement for membership was obscene wealth or a sponsorship from a member and a love for hunting exotic animals. Moreover, what could be more exotic than the newly discovered shifters? Oh yeah another requirement: no morals precluding you from stalking and killing innocent people who's only sin is their ability to shift. If you had a code of ethics that prevented you from hunting and shooting unarmed people, you couldn't be a member of this select little group.

Justin, a member of the Sentinel group, who'd managed to escape before being transferred to the park to be hunted, had overheard the guards discussing various aspects of the operation. They'd often taunted Justin with what his future held, confident that he would soon be dead. Justin had learned he was to be released into an enclosed park around 100 acres in size. Although he didn't know where the park was it had to be in an isolated area with few people to hear the report from the rifles. He'd inferred from the guards comments that the area was remote, rugged, with steep terrain and fully forested, making the hunting more challenging.

The fence was fully electrified and too high to jump. They'd laughed at the memory of the shifters who had tried to escape that way and had been hung up in the barb wire, electrocuted until they could be tranquilized, and the fence turned off. They would be stitched up then sent back out into the park to be hunted again the next day.

Justin was to be released into the park and five hunters would track him in order to kill him. It didn't matter to the hunters, whether the shifters were in their human or animal form, they were still killed.

For months, there had been rumors of such a hunting club but no one had ever found evidence until Justin's escape. Regan's father had captured him, taking delight in taunting him with how the hunters would wear him down, forcing him to shift in an attempt to survive. The hunters preferred to kill the animal that way they could gut him, skin him, and tan his hide for a souvenir. Then the hide would be displayed in the clubhouse as they smoked their cigars, drank their scotch, and compared previous hunts.

Now thanks to Justin, Rafe and his team of Sentinels had three leads to follow: the name of the club, the fact that there was a park out there somewhere, and the most promising lead, Thomas Reynolds was involved.

As yet, they hadn't been able to trace the club *Titan.* It wasn't as if you could Google a group like that. There were a lot of multi-millionaires in the United States to investigate, and who was to say the members were only from the United States? They were also using satellite imaging to try to identify the park but once again, there was a lot of data to sift through. He also had investigators out quietly questioning locals about hearing high-powered rifles, but as they were searching in remote areas, it wasn't that unusual. There were legitimate hunters, farmers, and poachers using high-powered weapons everyday in the potential sites.

That left them with Regan's father as their most promising lead. Unfortunately, the bastard was as cunning as he was mean. He knew how to stay off their radar. It was Jordan who had reminded Rafe that Thomas had a daughter. The man never ceased to amaze Rafe with the information he could retain. His brain was incredible at putting small pieces of information together and forming patterns, finding information there that no one else could see. Rafe never regretted promoting Jordan to the head of their intelligence section. Although Jordan had fought the promotion, because he wanted to stay in the field, he had proven himself invaluable again and again at obtaining information they desperately needed.

As soon as Jordan had informed him that Regan lived in the same city, he'd driven there intending to interview her about her father and see if she knew his whereabouts or could contact him. He had also organized surveillance to start on her in the hopes she'd lead them to her father if she turned out to be uncooperative.

As he pulled up to her house he'd been trying to remember

what she had looked like as a kid, he'd had a vague memory of elfin features and dark hair, he'd only seen her the once and only from his car as he'd slowly driven past.

All thoughts of that long ago day had fled his mind when he'd walked up the path and smelled the scent of fresh blood, he'd taken a quick peek through the window to assess the situation. He'd seen Thomas dragging a badly beaten woman across the floor. His every instinct had pushed him to protect her. Now that he knew she was his mate, that response made perfect sense to him. Shifter males were genetically predispositioned to protect their mates and cubs, to die for them if necessary.

Regan nudged her foot against his – she could tell he was sifting through information trying to decide what he would reveal and what he would withhold.

"Spit it all out, if you want me to keep my mouth shut about shifters you have to give me a reason to trust you and want to protect you. Withholding information, especially when it's related to me doesn't inspire trust."

He narrowed his eyes on her before nodding his agreement.

"You do tackle things head on don't you? OK," he rubbed his hands over his jean clad thighs, "to summarize; your father has been capturing and selling shifters to some humans who then release us into a remote area and hunt us with high powered rifles. I was at your house to see if you had any information that would help us track your father."

Regan assimilated this, she didn't doubt Rafe, and nothing her father did would ever shock her. "But why was he trying to capture me? I can't shift so I'd be of no use for hunting." She ran a hank of her hair through her fingers as she thought over what she'd been told. She met his astute brown eyes, "I must have some other value to them. I can't shift until I find my mate, right?" At his nod she continued, "Could they have my mate? Would they know who he is?"

Rafe shook his head "No one knows who will be their mate until they actually meet and touch setting off the sparks, or the sparks can fly at a later date, usually when both are emotionally charged. My guess is your father is having trouble finding shifters to capture. We are very good at moving our communities and hiding ourselves. Your father hasn't lived with shifters for over thirty years and has lost our trail. Therefore, unless he trips over one of us randomly he can't easily supply *Titan*. Even though you can't shift yet, you have more speed, strength and endurance than a human." His voice turned derogatory, "Maybe they thought you'd provide enough sport for them just in human form."

Rafe had to say he was surprised at Regan's reaction, or lack thereof, she wasn't noticeably upset – as if it was an everyday occurrence that a father would sell his daughter so she could be killed for entertainment. His resolve to do whatever it took to make this mating work firmed. His mate would learn what it was like to be cherished; to have her happiness valued above all others, to have a family, to have security, to feel safe and loved, to have a community who would never sell her out – that would fight *for* her.

He would somehow break through the defensive wall she surrounded herself with. He understood that she had needed it to protect herself emotionally from the crushing blows her father leveled at her, but now Rafe would be her wall, her protection, allowing her the freedom to love.

He accepted in that moment that it would take longer than he had anticipated to win her heart. He would have to plan a campaign to break through her protective shell. She had built that protection over many years and she would not let down her guard easily. He would need a multifaceted approach.

He would proceed slowly: get her accustomed to his touch, he would never lie to her – to break her trust at the early stage would be to lose her, he would tread carefully around his abandonment of her as a child and his mateship with her, he wouldn't lie, but he was going to be doing some fancy side stepping. He also needed to involve her with the community somehow. She would need a job at Eden's Retreat; he needed to tie her to their community with as many strings as possible. Because if he knew his mate at all he would bet she was already planning on where she was going to move to next, in order to stay ahead of her father.

He smiled to himself as right on queue Regan asked.

"Is there any pertinent information I need about being a shifter before I hit the road?"

Funny how much Regan didn't want to leave this man, it *felt* like the wrong decision when she knew it was the right one. She was more comfortable in her own company and the thought of staying with a community of people who were highly tactile caused a shiver of distaste to race down her spine. Besides she had had more than enough of being the odd person out during her foster years it wasn't an experience she was in any rush to revisit.

Her stomach tightened as she remembered the sideways glances and snickers of her classmates. She refused to expose herself to ridicule or being ostracized again, because she didn't fit in. Then there was the way she studied people assessing their weaknesses, people on some level knew, it understandably made them wary of her. Soon enough they avoided her, but she couldn't stop herself. As more than one foster sibling had pointed out to her – Regan's cold eyes were freaky enough without the feel of them constantly tracking their movements. She knew she didn't respond to people appropriately, but she no longer knew how, and had long ago lost the inclination to try or even to care.

For the first few years after her mother's murder, she was so shattered she hadn't noticed that the other kids avoided her, by the time she did notice, she hadn't known how to change their attitudes to her and soon found she didn't want to. It was easier to rely on herself for company. She didn't need to worry about what people thought of her, or if they would include her in their groups. Her few attempts at friendship had been treated with such hostility by the other children that she had quickly retreated back into herself and stayed there; isolated but safe.

She did not feel any inclination to go through that rejection process again. Even if it meant she could spend more time with this intriguing, sexy man.

Rafe leaned forward in his chair resting his forearms on his thighs. "Why don't you stay with us for a day or two?" before she could deny him he held up his hand. "You have been seriously injured; it would be pertinent to be in better physical condition before you go on the run from your father. If he catches onto your trail, you are in no condition to outrun him. It will also give us a chance to get some belongings, money, ID, etc. from your house for you so you don't have to go back and risk he has someone waiting for you." He continued before she could say no.

"It will also give you a chance to learn more about what it means to be a shifter. We have an extensive selection of books in our library about shifters and you can observe shifters – even if you only want to look from your window." He flashed Regan another dimpled smile "Although I hope you won't waste the opportunity to spend time with us and learn more about what it means to be a shifter." He could see she was considering his words.

"You realize when you meet your mate you're going to shift soon after and that could be traumatic if you don't know what to expect. Come on Regan," he coaxed, "give yourself a chance to heal and learn about your heritage."

"I can leave when I want? I'm not trapped here – I'm free to come and go?" she scrutinized him intently as he answered.

"You're free to come and go. I'll be honest- if you leave Eden's Retreat, someone will tail you to see if they can spot your father and try to capture him. We need to know who these hunters are and we need to stop them."

"How can my father find me if I don't go back home?"

"That's another thing about shifters; parents are connected to their cubs and can feel where they are. The closer they are the stronger the feeling. If he were on the other side of the country to you, he'd just know you were to the north, for example. The closer he gets the more specific the directional pull. Here at Eden's Retreat a parent would be able to tell if their cub or kit left school and went home."

Regan hunched in on herself as the ramifications struck her, "So I'll never be free of him?" she asked in a wooden voice.

Rafe tried to resist the temptation to hold Regan in his arms, she looked defeated as she sat on the edge of the bed, her long straight hair hiding her bruised face as she plucked absently at a lose cotton thread from the pillow she'd pulled onto her lap. The need to comfort her was irresistible. He scooped her off the bed and cradled her resisting body against him as he sat back down in his chair.

"Relax Regan – I offer only comfort. Take strength from me. We are tactile creatures, share my warmth, breath my scent. You will feel stronger and more able to meet this challenge. I seek nothing in return."

When she continued to strain against him, he quickly placed her back on the bed before she could feel trapped. He then shifted to his wolf form and with a practiced shake, he removed the clothes hanging off him. He settled his large frame onto the bed resting up against Regan's side holding his breath until she slowly began to relax. Within minutes, Regan began rubbing her hand through his thick ruff. He groaned with sheer joy, his mate was touching him voluntarily, thanking the God's she could find comfort in his wolf, while at the same time cursing the fates that she couldn't trust the man.

At first Regan just marveled at the gigantic wolf leaning

against her side. He was much larger than a normal wolf and stretched out would nearly reach the bottom of the bed. She could see the intelligence in his eyes as he watched her patiently but she felt no fear, no sense of suspicion, no need to protect herself as she had when he'd tried to hold her in his human form. Again, she felt peace weave through her, easing her tension as she continued to pet his massive form.

For so long she had felt ice cold inside, and now this man was easing her pain, in a way she didn't understand. It had been years since someone had touched her to offer comfort. With a sigh, she closed her eyes and lay down on her side facing his back she breathed in his scent. A shudder rolled through her body as more heat eased into her. Just for this short time, she would accept this man's comfort – but she couldn't allow herself to become accustomed to this feeling of warmth and contentment, of acceptance and belonging. To do so would make the ice-cold isolation of her world intolerable when she moved on.

The warmth of his body heat eased the residual pain from her wounds at the same time it brought comfort to her soul. She felt a contentment she had never experienced before. She had never realized she could be so at ease. Until this moment, she had never realized what she lacked. She allowed herself to sink into a sense of wellbeing. Like the cat she supposedly was, she sat up enough to rub her cheek against his shoulder.

Rafe scarcely dared breathe as Regan rubbed her cheek across his back and shoulder, unknowingly rubbing her scent into his fur. Her cat was starting to rise already. His wolf's sense of smell allowed him to scent the enticing spicy aroma she was rubbing into his fur. Her cat was marking him so other shifters would know she was staking a claim, warning others away. Regan might be unaware but her cat knew exactly what she was doing.

His heartbeat deepened and strengthened, anticipation arose as he realized her cat would accept him, actually wanted him. He would now have her own nature wanting to mate with him. For the first time, there was something in favor of their mating rather than only the obstacles. He felt anticipation for their courtship rather than just determination. He would let her assimilate the knowledge that she was a shifter, and then he would pursue the sexual bond between them as Kylie had suggested. He hadn't anticipated her cat rising so swiftly or showing signs of acceptance so quickly. He would use the sexual attraction between them as one of many fetters to tie them together.

Due to their mating bond, her cat's libido would be insatiable; she would literally be like a cat in heat. Since she was already rising, she would heighten Regan's sex drive. He almost felt sorry for Regan.

Mind you, he still expected her to put him through his paces.

Female panthers were notorious for making their mates suffer through the courtship. One minute enticing their male the next instant turning on him and lashing out with lethally sharp claws, before once again waving their tail in their mates face. A rumble of anticipation vibrated in his chest.

"I have always stood alone, always looked out for myself," she spoke into the silence.

Rafe changed back, pulling the covers over his hips in an effort to minimize Regan's discomfort, he was comfortable with his nudity, but he didn't want Regan flipping out on him. She still jumped off the bed with an alacrity that was downright offensive.

Controlling his piqué he assured her, "I know honey. But, right now in this moment you don't have to be alone. Learn what it is to be a shifter. We are a pack for a reason, not only does it feel good – but we gain strength from contact with each other."

When she didn't respond but paced over to the window and gazed out sightlessly he prompted, "So what do you think – will you stay and give yourself a chance to heal and learn about shifting?" He watched her eyes as she turned back to him he could see the battle within her; to leave as her isolated human half urged, or to stay as her cat required. He saw the instant her cat won out.

Her nod of agreement was hesitant, "I'll stay a few days,

thanks. Hopefully we can also come up with a plan to capture my father while I'm here."

Hiding his relief at her agreement to stay, he stood and bent to gather his clothes.

"Whoa there's a sight I could go a life time without seeing and live happily!"

CHAPTER 4

Regan turned to see a teenage girl standing in her doorway with one arm covering her eyes as she used the other to hold the door open.

“That’s what happens to brats who forget to knock before entering people’s bedrooms,” Rafe’s voice was light with affection as he slid his jeans over his lean hips.

“Yeah but she was in a coma this morning when I dropped in, I thought you’d have the decency to let her recover before starting any hanky-panky with her. Gees Rafe give the poor girl a chance!” she teased. “Can I look yet?”

Rafe shot his youngest sister a vexed look when Regan stiffened at her words. Honest to God, his sister had no filter between what went through her mind and what came out her mouth.

A low warning growl rumbled in his chest, “Yes you can look

now," he grouched as he finished dressing.

Laughter lit his sister's brown eyes as she sauntered into the room; she was slightly built for a wolf shifter. Her fine features almost elfin in design, brown shoulder length hair with caramel highlights attesting to the amount of time she spent outdoors. His sister's skin was a healthy golden brown and she currently revealed too much of it in her denim shorts and hot pink crop top as far as he was concerned. A mischievous smile lit her open face as she ignored his warning.

"It's only fair that Regan knows you're a hound dog as well as a wolf."

Moving over to Regan, she gave her a hug totally ignoring Regan's not so subtle attempt to avoid the contact.

"It's great to see you up and about Regan, I'm Stephanie, but call me Steph, everybody does. I'm Rafe's youngest sister and only family here at the moment. Mum and dad and the rest of the siblings have moved to a ranch outside Dallas where the rest of the extended family is residing now days."

Steph shrugged off her backpack and started pulling out clothes tossing them on the bed next to where Regan had retreated as she continued.

"Dad used to head up the Sentinels so we all used to live here, but he retired a couple of years ago and Rafe was elected as his replacement. So I come for regular visits cause ya know Texas is OK, but we're so isolated at the ranch I come back here for a bit of couture and shopping. These clothes are for you, get dressed and I'll show you around if you are up to it. Otherwise I can just hang with you here and keep you company."

"Jesus Steph, draw a breath will you?" Rafe chastised her lightly as he grabbed her from behind, locking his forearm across her throat in a mock choke hold as he wrapped his other arm around her middle and hugged her.

Regan watched the playfulness between the two siblings, it was apparent that Rafe adored his irrepressible sister as he gave a mock growl and leaped away when Stephanie reached back and tickled him along his rib cage. Dusting her hands together, Steph turned her sherry brown eyes back to Regan, her lips curled in a satisfied smile.

"I'll let you in on a family secret," she stage whispered to Regan, "Rafe is outrageously ticklish. If he's ever got you in a hold just go for his ribs. Works every time," she winked conspiratorially.

"Gees Steph, is nothing sacred with you?" Rafe wined pitifully. "How am I supposed to command respect from the pack when you go and spread rumors like that?"

"Right, rumors." Steph snorted. "Anyway, go away will ya, so Regan can get dressed without you drooling all over her.

Then I'll show her around," she flicked her hands at him in a go away gesture.

Rafe looked at Regan who was watching them intently from her position near the bed. He hadn't thought of it before but it would be fantastic if Steph took Regan under her wing. Steph was irresistible, he'd bet even Regan wouldn't' be able to hold Steph at arm's length for long. If Steph decided someone needed her as a friend, she'd just ride over any reluctance or avoidance until the other person inevitably gave in. It would mean Regan had a friend here, and Steph could ease her into the rest of the community. He'd have to talk to Steph later and give her a heads up about how hard it would be for Regan to assimilate into shifter culture with her past holding her back.

Looking at Regan, he offered a reassuring smile, "Steph will look after you. If you start getting a headache from the incessant chatter, retire to your room, because it won't matter how much you ask her to stop talking, she'll just keep going." He turned to Steph and wagged his finger at her, "Don't overdo it. She's not that strong yet, and for Christ's sake don't talk her to death." With one last look at Regan, he left the room after placing a kiss on his sister's head.

"So come on girl, I'll wait here while you shower and get dressed. Betcha can't wait to wash your hair huh?"

Before Regan could open her mouth, Steph continued.

"We'll stop and grab a sandwich to eat as we walk. If we stay in the hall to eat you'll be overrun with inquisitive shifters and never get out of there, so this morning we'll just keep moving and not give 'em a chance to assuage their curiosity about you. Do you think you'll be OK in the shower or do you want some help?"

At Regan's quick headshake Steph continued, "Alright I'll just wait here for you, take your time, I'll read one of the magazines I left here earlier for you. What do you prefer Vogue, Allure, or Cosmopolitan? Personally I'm not much of a fan of Vogue who needs to spend that much money on a watch or perfume, ya know what I mean? Wait until we get outside it's a spectacular day, the sun's out, the air is so crisp, and clear, you feel as if it's actually sparkling. If being outside today doesn't make you feel good nothing ever will."

Regan took a deep breath as she shut the bathroom door on Steph's chatter. Wow, could that girl talk, maybe Rafe was right, Steph would end up talking her to death. But she was ready to get out and explore, she was a little shaky but was sure after eating some solid food she'd feel much better. Being with Steph she wouldn't have to worry about talking with any strangers, either, no doubt the girl wouldn't let anyone else get a word in. Regan anticipated for the most part she could just watch and learn. She'd spend her time assessing these people and maybe learn a bit more about herself in the process.

Regan felt like the proverbial new woman after her shower. After leaving her room they'd gone straight to the food hall and snagged a couple of sandwiches each and were currently following a winding gravel footpath through the immaculately manicured parkland that separated the front entrance to Eden's Retreat from the buildings. Whoever had designed Eden's Retreat had left a stand of native forest surrounding the whole compound, which created an impenetrable privacy screen allowing the residents the freedom to shift whenever they pleased. Steph had also informed Regan a security fence surrounded the retreat and was monitored 24/7 in case some human became curious about what was behind the fence, as happened from time to time.

"We have over a hundred acres here, about ten of it is partially cleared for housing, offices, the school, hospital etc. the rest is fully forested so there's plenty of room for running in either human or animal form. We have true freedom here to be ourselves. It's fantastic, we have this magnificent native wilderness, and we're still only a thirty minute drive from the city center. There are about two hundred shifters living here, making this one of the larger packs. Byron Anderson is our alpha, and his word is law although he has a council to advise him. Because we are one of the larger packs and tend to move around the central states of America, we have the head office of the Sentinels stationed to this pack.

There are Sentinels stationed with every community and they act sort of like the human police force. Rafe is responsible for all Sentinels in the United States, you know just in case you were wondering what he does for a livin'," Steph threw Regan a sly grin and bumped shoulders with her playfully before continuing on with her usual hip swaying saunter.

"Hey there's Jordan he's a great guy you'll love him." Steph assured Regan calling out, "Jordan! Over here!" she waved her arms at the lean man heading from the car park towards the buildings housing various offices including the Sentinels, as Steph had been careful to point out to Regan earlier. *"In case, you know, you need to see Rafe, nudge nudge."*

Regan didn't know what to make of the girls continued innuendo that there was something between her and Rafe. She couldn't imagine trusting a man enough to want a friendship nevertheless a sexual relationship as Steph obviously thought was going to happen between her and Rafe. Maybe shifters were more promiscuous regarding sex than humans and swapped partners frequently with no recrimination aimed at the women? The thought of allowing a man to touch her in such a way sent a repugnant shudder through her.

Regan assessed Jordan as he walked towards them, he wasn't as tall as Rafe maybe 5' 11" and was leanly muscled like a long distant runner. He had the thickest ginger red hair she'd ever seen on a person, he wore it long enough to see it was dead straight; she imagined if he wore it any shorter, it would stick up everywhere. He moved with a fluid grace, his sharp eyes assessing her as he came closer. He was dressed in steel capped boots, jeans, and a dark T-shirt. He was one of the most aesthetically appealing men she'd ever seen, his high cheekbones stopped his face from being too narrow, his pointed nose, was proportioned to perfection. Sooty black lashes surrounded his copper colored eyes, highlighting the metallic color and distracting your attention away from the cunning intelligence. This was a man who would listen to what wasn't said, as much as, to what was said. Regan knew not to underestimate this shifter.

"Jordan, I'd like you to meet Regan, Regan this is Jordan Dodd one of Rafe's closest friends and our computer guru. If you ever need information this is the man to see, his intelligence is off the grid and he's a genius at writing computer code and analyzing data."

"Enough short stuff or you'll embarrass me," he laughed as he went to enclose Regan in an embrace, Regan quickly held her arm out with her hand up stopping him.

"I don't do the touching thing. No offence meant," she added at his surprised look.

Jordan recovered quickly and gave her a reassuring smile.

"None taken," he assured as he turned his attention to Steph gathering her into a tight hug. Smiling Steph returned his embrace; resting her cheek against his chest before turning her face to rub her cheek along his in an affectionate caress. Regan studied the pair; she didn't pick up any sexual awareness between them although they continued to hold each other Regan could only sense friendship between the two.

Steph and Jordan chatted for a couple of minutes both trying to draw Regan into the conversation, Regan tried to contribute, for although she was wary of Jordan he didn't cause her alarm, but he was a stranger and a potential enemy. It was impossible for her not to be reserved.

She'd never learned the art of idle chit chat and on occasions like this felt totally inept. This was why she avoided social situations she was useless at it and found it easier to avoid rather than feel this awkwardness. I mean why bother, she was a loaner, she'd learned long ago not to open herself up to rejection from others.

Jordan cut the conversation short; he could see Regan was feeling increasingly uncomfortable. His heart went out to her; he'd done the research for Rafe on Regan's past and knew how she'd been left out in the cold and the damage that had to have been done to her psyche. Rafe's mate was going to need the hand of friendship extended repeatedly to her before she'd trust anyone not to hurt her. Now after meeting her, he was determined to help her settle into Eden's Retreat. His pack mates wouldn't understand her reticence as they didn't know her history, but he could be patient and win her trust. After all he was a fox and foxes were renowned for their cunning, if he couldn't insinuate himself into her life no one could.

After Jordan left to go to his office, Steph explained that she wanted to go see another friend. Regan decided she had enough for one day and opted out of going along.

Two hours later, Regan wandered along a narrow bush track that followed a meandering creek through the forest within Eden's Retreat. The water was shallow and crystal clear. Up ahead dappled sunlight permeated the dense canopy. As she reached a sun drenched glade, she rested her hand on the rough bark of the giant tree next to her, spellbound by the sight before her. Nature had created a private beach within the ancient forest. The picturesque creek wove itself into a U turn and over the years, gravel had built up in the tight turn creating a beach. Verdant grass grew up to the beach with ferns scattered along the perimeter of the glade created by the trees. The sound of the burbling water and the occasional trill of a bird added to the peaceful tranquility of the clearing.

Regan breathed deeply, taking in the rich earthy scents of the forest mixed with the warm grass of the glade. The sun warmed Regan's face as she walked over to the beach and sank down on the gravel, running the fine particles through her fingers. The colors were bold after being under the dark canopy. The abundant plant life a hundred vibrant shades of green, the sun reflected off the moving water creating shimmering sparks too bright to gaze at for more than a moment, the sky a deep azure without a cloud breaking the breathtaking color.

Regan settled back and basked in the warmth of the sun. As peace settled over her she let herself drift, giving herself respite from all the information Stephanie had imparted to her about shifters and Eden's Retreat and the ramifications to herself. Later she would hit the library, gather more information, and try to verify what Stephanie had told her, but for now, she let her mind wander where it would. She rolled over on her side and watched the light breeze ruffle through the undergrowth.

Stephanie had given Regan a brief tour of the buildings at Eden's retreat. Thankfully after meeting Jordan, whenever they'd come across other shifters, Steph had just waved or acknowledged them with a smile but hadn't stopped to talk or introduce Regan. Regan had the impression she'd done that for Regan's benefit, saving her and the other shifters from the discomfort of Regan refusing their touch. She'd also like to take a bet with someone that by dinner tonight,

Steph would have ensured everyone living here knew not to assume Regan would welcome contact.

Thinking of that girl made her shake her head. Steph was so sunny and light hearted it was hard to keep her at a distance. It seemed like whatever thought went through Stephanie's head came straight out her mouth; there was no intent to manipulate. She gave freely of her time and seemed to want nothing in return but Regan's company. It had been interesting to see Stephanie and Rafe interact, the girl held no fear of her older brother, which was telling, and it was obvious from watching the easy camaraderie between the two, that Rafe enjoyed his sister's company. Deliberately Regan pulled her thoughts away from Rafe, thinking about him made her feel....restless was the best way she could describe it.

~~~

Regan left the dark interior of the forest with its rich earthy scent and walked across the sunlit parkland that separated the forest from the buildings of Eden's Retreat. Wandering pathways wound amongst strategically placed gazebos that were tucked under beech trees or old oaks, with their sprawling branches providing shade on hot summer days. An artificial creek flowed through the park with a pond in the center. Native water birds had taken up residence and as she walked over a quaint little bridge, she paused to watch some
~~~

ducks bobbing for food. A smile kicked up her lips as she saw what by the looks of its gangly legs had to be a juvenile wolf, launch itself into the pond with an exuberant belly flop and doggy paddle after the ducks, which just kept flying a few yards away whenever it got too close. Obviously, the birds didn't see the wolf as a serious threat.

She left the young wolf behind and headed towards the library Steph had pointed out earlier. The buildings of Eden's Retreat were all built of the same dark timber in an early settler's cabin style and all had the same slate grey tile roofs. They avoided monotony by using different size buildings, angling them away from each other, and creating different gardens around each. Whoever had designed the layout of the buildings and gardens had brilliant visualization as each building had its own individuality and privacy with tree placement and building placement yet as a whole it was cohesive. There were four three story-housing complexes all with verandahs on each level as wide as the buildings themselves. As she walked, the residential buildings were spread out around the edge of the park to her right, the communal eating area was straight ahead, and their business, hospital and school to the left.

Although she hadn't seen anyone in the forest here in the open parkland she watched as a small number of predators headed to and from the forest, obviously there were enough trails within that they weren't all tripping over each other. A group of wolves was playing a game where one wolf had an old T-shirt in its mouth and would race off with it while the others would try to tear it away. Once successful the others would then turn on the new claimant and try to rip it away. There were a lot of bodies tumbling over each other and generally getting pummeled. Regan noticed the big cats looked on disdainfully as they lazed in the sun.

It was hard to keep her nerves at bay at the number of lethal predators watching her as she walked by. Most only paid her passing interest, but some turned their heads and watched her fixedly until she disappeared from their line of vision. Steph had assured Regan she was safe here, and although her mind could accept that these were people who held no ill will towards her, it was hard to ignore her instinct, which told her that the big fucking tigers and lions were eyeing her up for a tasty afternoon snack. It took all her resolve to walk past them as if she didn't have a care in the world.

She marveled at the variety of predators living here, if an animal fit into the carnivore genus they seemed to be represented here. At a chorus of howls, Regan turned her head to see a hawk had swooped in and stolen their precious T-shirt and was now flying above the pack holding the T-shirt just out of the reach of the leaping wolves. It was slowly leading them towards the central pond and Regan paused to watch as two of the wolves so fixated on the T-shirt took a header into the water. The falcon's trill whistle sounded remarkably close to laughter before it dropped the shirt back into the pack and flew off. Obviously there were no hard feelings as the wolves immediately took up their game again. The rambunctious wolves eased some of Regan's disquiet. Seriously, how could she be afraid after watching that? She continued on to the library.

~~~

Regan set aside the book she'd been reading about shifters and leaned back in the club chair she sat in, tucked away in one corner of the library. It was interesting that the cats, although they still lived in communities, weren't as communal as the wolves that made up the majority of shifters. She'd confirmed her theory if an animal was a predator then there were shifters of that breed. "They probably ate all the cute fluffy ones," she muttered to herself.

Anyway, maybe she came by her standoffishness naturally. Maybe she was just an extreme example, besides if she was a panther, which were actually leopards just black in color she was even more inclined to enjoy her own company than the lions who gathered in prides. According to the book she'd read there were a couple of traits all shifters shared. They all mated for life, *if* they found their mate. They were extremely tactile and nearly always lived in communities. Apparently, her father was an exception; it was extremely rare for a shifter to live on their own or with only immediate family,
~~~

like she'd grown up.

Being ostracized from a community was so abhorrent to a shifter that they instinctively acted in the best interest of their community. Hence, the communities flourished wherever they were in the world. Everyone worked towards providing a safe environment for their young to grow. If your talents lay in the area of finance then you made money for the community as well as yourself. If your talents were in science then the community would fund your education but once the person started working, it seemed their research inevitably wound up being beneficial to the shifters as a whole.

There was travel and movement between the communities for those who needed to stretch their wings. If the books were correct, everyone participated in some way. Apparently the innate drive shifters had to provide and protect the cubs or kits didn't allow them to take without giving back to the community in some way. They were human enough for jealousy; greed and envy to still play their roll. Most conflicts were resolved in organized fights where the only rule was no weapons. They could shift to their animal form during the fight and often did. They pounded out their grievances' and generally accepted the win or loss. It was interesting to her that although most fights were amongst the young males, it wasn't unheard of for females to enter the ring to resolve personal conflicts. Each community had an alpha, whose word was law, but most alphas had an elected council who provided advice. They had their own police force, the Sentinels who ensured the alphas commands were carried out and who were also responsible for ensuring the safety of all shifters, from themselves and humans.

The sound of continued snickering intruded on her concentration; it annoyed her enough that she looked up from her reading. Regan watched a young teen lean into the face of a smaller boy. She could tell from the smaller boy's body language that he was intimidated but trying not to show any reaction. The larger boy grabbed the younger by the ear and yanked his head up to face him. The younger kept his eyes down in submission, indignation shot through her as the older boy spat in the youngster's face. Regan's eyes narrowed as the prick leaned in and whispered something to the boy before swaggering away. Surprise briefly flickered across his face when he realized Regan was watching him before he insolently ran his eyes over her and walked out of the room.

Regan knew what that boy was going through; she had lived it so many times herself with the abuse from her father. She gave the younger boy a few minutes to wipe his face before approaching him. Squatting down in front of him she waited until he raised his resignation filled eyes to hers.

"Would it be better or worse if I told someone in authority

what just happened?"

Misery darkened the kid's eyes, "Worse, please don't say anything."

"Is that sort of thing common?"

He dropped his gaze as he shrugged his thin shoulders. His ragged brown hair fell into his eyes, hiding him from her perusal.

Regan tilted her head to the side and studied him. He was malnourished and his demeanor was that of a puppy who'd been repeatedly beaten. He had no spark in him, no curiosity in what the day would bring. She'd volunteered frequently in various women's shelters over the years, she'd seen her fair share of abused children in that time, and she'd lay down money this little guy fell into that category. If it wasn't physical, it was emotional, and frankly, Regan felt emotional was just as devastating to a child.

Having dealt with bullies in the foster system and at school Regan understood the ways they would make the kid miserable. No place outside his home would be safe; food would be taken from him as a show of their power over him. By the look of his protruding bones, the poor little guy was missing more than was good for him.

Regan felt nothing but contempt for his parents. How adults could turn a blind eye to this kid and ones like him never ceased to amaze her. What were they thinking – that he was so happy he was starving himself for fun?

"So what's your name kid?"

"Ben," he muttered without looking up from his lap where he was picking at a loose thread in his cotton shorts. It was obvious he wanted her to go away.

Poor kid didn't realize he'd just picked up an advocate. She smiled to herself, he wasn't getting rid of her, and before she left Eden's Retreat, she would ensure his situation was much improved.

She had planned to grab a plate from the communal dining room and eat in her room, but to ensure the little guy ate at least one meal today she'd confront hell itself, not just a room full of strangers. They meant nothing to her – what were a few stares from curious shifters compared to making sure Ben ate a solid meal in peace?

"I'm Regan and I'm new here. Could you show me where the food hall is and keep me company while I eat?" She could see him try to decide if food was worth facing his antagonists. He obviously hadn't eaten in longer than she'd figured as he capitulated quickly enough and agreed to eat with her, giving her a nod of assent.

A ripple of awareness ran through the dining area as Regan and Ben entered the large atrium where communal meals were held. It was hard for Regan not to gape at the architecture of the room. Earlier Steph had run inside to get their sandwiches while Regan waited outside for her. Massive beams of dark hardwood with a high glistening sheen had been used to span the large room. Huge plates of glass were placed at the ends of the raked ceiling as well as along three of the walls allowing the outside in. The glass doors were massive bi-folds which when folded back as they were now allowed the scent of the freshly mown grass to waft through on the early evening breeze. The high ceiling added to the sense of openness and the polished wooden floor gleamed in the soft lighting. When entering the room you stood at the top of a small set of steps, which led down onto the floor of the main dining area, this allowed you to see everyone seated before stepping down. Once down on the main floor it was broken into sections by using potted shrubbery.

Scanning the area, she could see it would easily seat 200 people. Staff continually refreshed the smorgasbord of food laid out on one side of the room. The rest of the large room was divided into sections by various potted palms, ferns, and shrubs. All the greenery, the vaulted ceilings and massive windows lining the room gave one the feeling of being outdoors rather than inside a dining hall. This room was designed with shifters in mind, so they would feel like they were in their natural habitat.

People weren't blatantly stopping and staring as Regan and Ben made their way to the tables piled with mouth watering food, but she was aware of the sideway glances and subtle shifting of bodies so people could keep her in their line of vision. Regan's nerves tightened but she pretended to be unfazed for Ben who looked like he was seriously reevaluating his need to eat. Before he could slink away like a cowering puppy she broke her own rule of not touching and laid her hand lightly on his shoulder. She felt the ripple pass through his body, clearly the boy wasn't used to being touched any more than she was.

She puffed out a breath to relieve the tightness in her chest, the kid was worming his way into her heart, and he wasn't even trying. For some reason she felt a connection to him unlike anything she had felt for anyone, ever. She wanted to be there for him, someone he could turn to and know without doubt would help him. The need to tie them together with actions that matched the thread she felt binding them together was inexplicable. She didn't understand it but she already knew she wouldn't be leaving until Ben's situation was sorted out and already she held a deep conviction she would always keep in contact with him no matter where her life led her.

Besides she assured herself someone had to stand up for the boy and since everyone here, was doing a piss poor job of it she'd be stepping in. Anger burned for the neglect he was suffering. What was wrong with these people? Why have a child if you have no intention of looking after them properly? That was what the pill was there for, for Gods sake. It wasn't rocket science – just take one a day.

Breathing deep, she guided Ben over to the plates and handed him one. Her mouth twitched as she watched him industrially pile his plate. Obviously, she wouldn't have to coax him into eating now that they were here. After grabbing a glass of water each, they made their way to a secluded alcove which had a table for four hidden amongst some palms.

Both settled into eating, half way through the mound of food on his plate Regan noticed Ben glancing her way. Obviously starting to wonder about her, now the worst of his hunger was taken care of.

"Ask anything you want Ben, you won't offend me and I'm not going to snap your head off, I can assure you," she encouraged him with a quick smile.

Ben eyed her carefully before nodding, "Are you visiting or are you moving here? Do you have family here? Why are you eating with me instead of them," he tipped his chin indicating the room full of people.

"Visiting. No. I like you. Actually, I really like you. Plus I can help you deal with idiots like that one back in the library today."

His expression changed from confused to skeptical to disbelief. He snorted "Yeah right. What are you going to do? Tell on him to one of the elders, who in turn will hand out some punishment to him, so that Peter will turn on me worse than he already is? Yeah thanks but no thanks." His head went down cutting any interest in her off as he started stuffing his face again obviously trying to eat as much as he could while he had the chance.

"Umm no. I wasn't going to do that – I was intending to teach you to fight in such a way that you'll be able to beat the crap out of him. Moreover, I was hopping you'd do it in a public place to embarrass the shit out of him while you're at it. If you humiliate him badly enough he will think twice about coming at you again, especially if you cause him some real damage in the fight. Interested?"

CHAPTER 5

She had Ben's attention, yet again his metallic eyes were guarded in his thin face; she could see he didn't believe her.

"Skeptical. He's nearly full-grown and I'm still a cub – an undersized cub at that. That's a big advantage he's got over me."

Regan folded her arms on the table and leaned towards him, "Yeah, but you've got intelligence and your need is greater than his. You will be willing to endure more pain than he can even imagine in order to win. In addition, the training I'm offering you will negate the advantage of his size. I'm not going to sugar coat it for you; he will get some good hits in on you. Nevertheless, think on this, he already hurts you, this way instead of it going on for years into the future it will all be over in minutes. A real fight doesn't last long, ten minutes and it will be all over." Leaning back in her chair, she watched him consider her.

"It's up to you Ben. How much do you want him off your back? How much do you want to be able to come in here and eat in peace? How much do you want to go to school and be left alone? How much do you want to stop looking over your shoulder, worrying about when he'll come at you next? I can teach you how to beat him – but you have to want it, to hunger for pay back."

He gazed at her, his food forgotten. Regan could see him running through what the years ahead would be like for him if he didn't change things. Slowly he nodded, "What do I have to do?"

She could see he was still skeptical, but it was a chance he wasn't willing to let pass without investigating. His clear bronzed eyes told her he didn't hold much faith in her. Regan took a breath, was she really doing this? If she committed herself, she would be here for months preparing Ben. It wasn't as if her job meant anything to her; it was only a way of keeping food on the table. But, to move here so she could train him and live among shifters, did she really want to do that? Looking at Ben whose eyes were steady on her, the cautious hope she read there sealed the deal for her. She was not walking away from this kid.

She smiled at him.

"OK we are going to train three hours every day. It is going to have to be somewhere so that idiot doesn't find out about it. We have to surprise him when the time comes – that's going to be a huge advantage to you. His overconfidence in his size probably means he's not fast and not as skilled as he should be by his age. We don't want him thinking he should be training.

I'll have to speak with your parents and get permission to train you. Do you think they will object?"

"Nah. They'll be happy to have me out of the house. Mum and my stepfather have only just mated. Mum's never been interested in me, but now with Brian on the scene it's worse." He shrugged his thin shoulders at the anger in her eyes. "Don't get too upset until you've heard the full story." Looking away so he wouldn't have to see her revulsion, or worse her pity he continued, "Mum was raped and I'm the result. I remind her of what happened every time she looks at me. And Brian – he doesn't hate me but I'm a living reminder of what happened to mum and it sends his wolf insane to know he wasn't there to protect her. They only met recently and he's still coming to terms with it."

"Bullshit."

His startled gaze jerked to her face.

Christ it pissed her off when adults dumped their shit on their kids and the kids accepted the abuse because they truly believed they'd done something to deserve it. Regan saw that Ben accepted the reason for his mother's mistreatment of him. But the rejection of a mother for her child caused tormenting pain, the new exclusion by the stepfather would add to the excruciating rejection and Regan could literally sense his hurt. His pain burned her senses as if she could actually feel his despair at this new rejection. She could imagine the hope he would have felt when Brian entered their lives. At last someone to care for him to remind his mother that he wasn't evil, only to be totally rejected again. Any hope of his mother coming to love him squashed.

No wonder the other kids picked up on the vibe that something was wrong with him and harassed him. Ben probably believed he was unlovable and deserved the other kid's rejection and subjugation because after all, if his own mother couldn't love him how could he expect anyone else to want to befriend him? He would withhold himself, expecting their rejection, other kids would feel it, especially shifters, and in turn, they would reject him. He was a self-fulfilling prophecy.

"Pot calling the kettle black?" her conscience pointed out. "*Maybe I do keep people away so they can't hurt me emotionally* but *don't forget the training I endured from my father. I was trained not to trust anyone*," she argued back. *"Point."* Her conscience conceded. *"But you're not that scared little girl anymore."*

Regan grasped one of Ben's hands ensuring she had his full

attention. “Ben I’m sorry your mother was raped. I truly am, but that gives her no right to take her anger and pain out on you. You were an innocent baby in need of love and care; if she was incapable of that, she should have asked for help. What she has done and continues to do is wrong.” She squeezed his hand hoping she was getting through to him. “Something in your mother is broken. You are not of your father’s ilk, if you were like him, you would already be lashing out in anger and hatred, but you are not filled with those emotions. You don’t seek reprisal against your mother. I bet you accept her abuse because you think you’re helping her vent her anger.” She knew she’d judged him correctly, when his eyes dropped away briefly. “You have a soul of innocence; it shines in you for all to see. You aren’t belligerent and I bet you cause no trouble.” With a rueful smile she added, “If you had, someone might have stepped in and helped you.”

“Listen to me, I’ll admit I’m clueless as to why I feel this connection to you, and responsible for you but I promise you can rely on me. Once I give my word I keep it.” She waved her other hand at him, “I know you don’t believe me yet but time will prove the truth. We are going to fix this thing with that idiot from the library and we’ll also look at your home situation. I won’t promise to fix that but something will be done, changes will be made.”

Rafe entered the dining hall in search of food and Regan.

Steph had told him of Regan's intent to go to the library, he'd missed her there but had picked up the trail of her enticing scent and had followed her here. The whole day his wolf had urged him to drop what he was doing and go claim their mate, there was no reasoning with the animal. It didn't understand the problems facing their courtship, it recognized its mate and wanted her, now. It surprised him, the effort he was exerting to control his wolf. Maybe he'd underestimated the intrinsic need his shifter side had for his mate. It worried him that this need within him would force him to rush Regan when he knew she would need time to know him before forming an attachment to him, that would hopefully grow into love. He firmed his resolve as he made his way to the buffet, he would give her time despite his wolf's need to bed and mate her.

After filling his plate with succulent roast beef and oven baked vegetables he made his way to her table noting the intense conversation between her and young Ben Duncan. The moment they became aware of his approach they stopped talking and leaned back in their seats. Ben as usual ducked his head and shyly acknowledged Rafe's greeting before continuing to eat, avoiding any eye contact.

Rafe had been racking his brain all morning trying to come up with plausible reasons for Regan to stay at Eden's Retreat longer than the few days she'd agreed to. But apart from involving her in some scheme to trap her father he'd come up empty. To put his mate deliberately in harm's way went against his every instinct. There had to be some other way of tying her to their community that wouldn't risk her being hurt.

He knew a couple of days wouldn't be enough time to break through her reserve and the shell she had built around her emotions. Behaviors she'd developed over years of self-protection weren't going to change in a couple of days.

"Between Steph and the library you must be feeling overwhelmed with information," he stated casually as he sat down.

Regan inclined her head, "Some of it helped me understand why I never felt like I fit in anywhere. The history is good to know. But I feel some of it is almost fanciful – they just can't be as good as the books make shifters out to be," she challenged.

Instead of disagreeing Rafe nodded, "Some of the books do simplify our society – as you've seen for yourself we have problems like any group. But I think we do a better job of looking after each other than most societies," he added.

Regan scoffed at that – just look at her and Ben, no one had looked out for her, Ben was right under their noses, and still he was suffering neglect. No, more than neglect, he suffered emotional abuse that had convinced him he was unlovable. "You keep thinking that."

"Maybe before committing to such a judgment regarding us, you should take more than an afternoon hidden in a library to form your opinion," he chided softly. He hoped her sense of fair play would rise to meet his challenge. He knew she was blocked off emotionally but from his research, he also knew his mate had a strong sense of justice and was fair-minded. He believed if she stayed long enough she would witness the genuine care shifters held for their community. It was something humans could never sustain. Their sense of entitlement and self-worth was stronger than their concern for their neighbor.

"Point," she nodded. Her gaze strayed to Ben who was still head down and methodically working through his food. Although the boy was doing his best to avoid attention, Rafe could tell he was riveted to the conversation. Rafe wished he were better positioned to read the expression in Regan's eyes as she gazed at the young cub, but his wolf was paying attention to the boy when before it had always ignored him. He drew in the cubs scent and he could feel his wolf's curiosity aroused. It wasn't in any threatening way, more inquisitively wanting more information about the boy. The thought came to him that maybe he should even consider moving him under his protection, which was strange; his wolf had never shown any interest in kids before. Perhaps now his mate was near he was ready to father some pups of his own and all children were of an interest to his wolf.

Over the years, Rafe and his wolf had settled into one entity, but Rafe would never claim to understand his wolf fully. Usually they were on the same page; both were dedicated to the protection of shifters. Neither was cut out to be the alpha of the pack – neither of them were interested in the bullshit you had to deal with as the leader. Both were happy to be the beta where they could go out and fix problems not talk them to death. The number of meetings his alpha, Byron had to deal with would make him hang himself. No he was a happy wolf in command of the Sentinels and answerable only to Byron and the other nine alphas who formed the committee that governed all shifters in America.

"If I'm going to stay here any length of time I'll need somewhere private to retreat to exercise and train. I'll struggle living with this many people, I know if I'm to stick it out for any length of time I'll need somewhere private ."

Rafe thought a moment "There is the Sentinel's old training gym. It's down in the basement but it still has some old equipment and no one would bother you there. Eden's Retreat has an excellent gym for the general populace and the Sentinels have a new gym where we train. It was opened a month ago and the old space hasn't been allocated for any other use yet." He held up his hand at her obvious interest "It's not pretty, but if being alone is more important than comfort it should suit. I'll show it to you tomorrow if you like. When you've finished eating if you're agreeable, I'll show you to the unit that's been allocated for your use while you're here.

Regan didn't overly want to be alone with Rafe, the man unsettled her like no other man ever had. Sitting here with him, she constantly had to stop herself from reaching out to run her hand over the delineated muscle of the forearm he rested on the table as he ate. What was that about? Surely even amongst shifters, this wasn't normal behavior, because it certainly wasn't for her. But the temptation to touch Rafe had pulled at her continuously since he sat down beside her, his arm resting only inches from her hand as she ate from her plate. She wanted to rub along his arm and feel the heat of his skin, the roughness of his hair against the sensitive pads of her fingers. She was aware her heart was beating faster than normal and her breathing was shallower than it should be, almost a pant. The smell of musky male was divine. Drawing in a deeper breath, she savored the scent that was Rafe McIntyre. Idly she wondered what his skin would taste like, would the texture be rough or smooth, how hard was that muscle under his tanned skin, would he allow her to sink her teeth into his muscled flesh?

A gentle nudge from Ben's foot stopped her musing, "Yeah sure, that would be great." She cringed at the husky tone in her voice, clearing her throat; she organized to meet up with Ben the next day at the old gym. After finishing their meals, she escorted Ben back to the library where the staff afforded him some protection from the other kids until he headed home, before continuing with Rafe to her accommodation.

Rafe seemed content with the silence as they walked along, Regan would have preferred a chatty wolf; the conversation would have distracted her awareness of the prime male striding along beside her. Her eyes continually returned to slide over his lean frame no matter how many times she dragged them away, he radiated confidence, head held high, broad shoulders, he moved with a fluid animal grace. "Hummm," she almost purred.

"Pardon?" he shot her a smirk of a smile obviously well aware of her perusal of his form.

"Darn it! Did I say that out loud? What is wrong with me?" she berated herself. Heat stung her cheeks, "Ahumm. Just clearing my throat."

"I hope you're not catching a cold," his grin, with both dimples in play belied his concern for her health.

She shook her head, "*Where's the justice in the world that with his good looks he also gets the dimples?"* she muttered under her breath.

Once assured he was looking forward her gaze was again drawn to him. His body language shouted pride, confidence, surety, this was a man who had faced danger and prevailed. It wasn't a brash false confidence seen in some who had done the training but had yet to deal with violence at its most base level. This man had dealt with brutality on his own terms and had gained confidence from the experience. He had the scars of a soldier on his body but in his eyes she had seen the knowledge of the perversion some held in their souls. He had witnessed the trauma of the victims, not just the physical, but also the higher emotional cost. She was sure the victims haunted this man, not the viciousness he himself employed to destroy shifters who were twisted and malevolent.

During her reading Regan had covered the *Sentinels* and any information she could find on Rafe. So what if she had spent a fair portion of her time researching him, it was just natural curiosity, she assured herself. It was sensible to find out about the man offering to protect her from her father. This man planned to go up against her father and if she was reading the situation correctly, intended to kill him.

When she had first realized the punishment for her father's actions would be his death her breath had frozen in her lungs. Her muscles had quivered with tension and her stomach had sunk, she'd forced herself to breathe, once, twice. Then she had realized that her tension was for *Rafe* - not her father. When she had forced her thoughts from Rafe to her father she had felt . . . . . . nothing. Slowly that had turned to satisfaction then to anticipation. Nope, there were no conflicting emotions on that front. No "Oh no he's my father you can't kill him," for her. No that man unfortunately may have contributed to her genetics, but he had long ago killed off any feelings she had for him except hatred. Now the thought of his death brought about a sense of justice finally being served. It was an affront that that piece of garbage lived, while her exquisite mother lay buried in the ground.

No her instinctive anxiety had been for Rafe. Obviously, the man knew how to take care of himself, but had he ever gone up against the cunning viciousness that was her father? That her father had survived this long without attracting the attention of the Sentinels showed his ability to plan the finest details and cover his activities. Rafe had no idea what type of insidious creature he was now hunting.

CHAPTER 6

They crossed to one of the residential buildings. Like all the other structures at Eden's Retreat, it was built of wooden logs and drew its design from frontier pine log cabins; however, it was built on a far larger scale. Standing three stories high, its logs had been stained with dark oil. Each level had a massive balcony almost as wide as the building itself.

They entered through the front door into an open area much like an overgrown lounge room. There was a massive flat screen television with lounges grouped around it at one end of the room, and a play station at the other end with reciprocal lounges. At the halfway point in the back of the room was a fully stocked bar, a high-end coffee machine and pantry. The furniture was large and comfortable looking. There were coffee tables and chairs tucked into some of the corners; the tables were covered in magazines. It looked like a room that was well used and inviting, this was definitely not a formal gathering area.

Rafe led her across the room to a circular wrought iron stair well placed on the opposite side of the room to the front door.

“Your unit is on the first floor.”

Rafe indicated they should turn left after they climbed the stairs to the first level. After opening the second door down the wide carpeted hallway, he held out the set of keys for Regan. Regan’s eyes shot to his as their fingers brushed in the exchange, effervescent energy tingled along her nerve endings. Unsettled she moved away from him and further into the room.

She glanced around, the small living area was made light and airy with the use of windows and soft off white décor, broken up with splashes of aqua blue. There was a two-seater lounge and a small entertainment unit along the opposite wall, as you entered the unit, a small galley kitchen was to the right. Regan moved down the short hallway to the left and found a bathroom and laundry on one side and a bedroom with a sliding door that opened out onto the communal deck that ran the length of the building.

She backed out of the bedroom and entered the bathroom ostensibly to wash her hands but really, it gave her another few minutes before facing the unsettling male who was now clanking around in her kitchen. The familiar scent of her favorite soap made her take notice of the shampoo and conditioner in the shower stall. Someone, and she'd bet it was Rafe, had been back to her house and retrieved her personal toiletries. Opening the cupboard under the sink, she found her moisturizer, brush, hair bands, and her small collection of makeup. Everything she would need to make her stay more comfortable. Regan went back into the bedroom and opened the wardrobe; it was full of her clothes.

What sort of man thought to bring a guest her clothes and toiletries? His consideration touched her; no one had gone out of his or her way to make her life easier since she was a child. Although the clothes Steph had brought her were more than adequate, she was grateful to have her own things to wear. He'd even brought the novel she was currently reading which had been sitting on her bedside table.

It was nice to know, as she moved through this strange new world, that tomorrow she would have the comfort of her own clothes to shore up her confidence. Regan had a feeling Rafe had known this when he'd collected her things for her.

"Hey Regan, I've heated up some brandy snaps for dessert, would you prefer whipped cream or ice cream with yours?" His deep baritone caused a pleasurable shiver to race over Regan. Licking her suddenly dry lips, she moved back into the living area and crossed over to the kitchen.

"If you're going to the trouble of cooking a dessert it has to be cream. You didn't have to do this," she added, not sure that she liked him making himself at home in her unit.

Smiling at her over his shoulder, Regan could physically feel the caress of his eyes as they ran over her, pausing briefly, where her breasts strained against the material of the T-shirt Steph had given her. Her nerves quivered as she read the interest that flared in his eyes. Anticipation fought with unease within her. Nervously she tucked a lose strand of hair behind her ear, looking about for some way to ease her tension.

Rafe turned back to the cook top, "It's no biggy. We had to celebrate you being up and about for the first time in five days. How are you feeling after being on your feet all afternoon?"

Regan shrugged, feeling awkward at his interest in her wellbeing. "I'm OK; I ache a bit, but nothing like when I first woke up," she added.

Rafe turned to see Regan standing on the other side of the kitchen bench looking lost as she stood with her hands thrust into the pockets of her jeans, a slight frown pulling at her fine brows. Her small white teeth nibbled at her pillowy bottom lip, causing a kick of desire to punch at him as he imagined sucking on it.

"Can you grab some cutlery and the cream out of the fridge? These are ready to eat," he turned back to the job at hand and slid the brandy snaps onto two plates, hiding the desire that no doubt showed on his face. His mate was already skittery enough, without adding to her anxiety at being alone with a man she barely knew.

"Sure," Regan was relieved to have something to do with her hands.

"I've stocked up the pantry with the bare basics. I'm not sure if Steph showed you, but we have a small general store here. If there is anything you would like that they don't have just let them know in the morning, and they'll usually have it for you by the afternoon."

"Thanks for that. How much do I owe you?"

"I left the receipt over there," he indicated with a nod of his head towards the other end of the kitchen. "But you don't owe me; I set up an account for you at the store. Just pay them at the end of each week."

Rafe carried the plates to the bench and sat on one of the two stools the unit was furnished with.

Taking a small forkful of the delicate dessert, Regan closed her eyes to savor the sweet taste of the pastry and the burn of the brandy. "This is delicious." Opening her eyes, she found him watching her intently.

Sensing that he was making her uncomfortable again, Rafe lowered his gaze and attacked his dessert, wishing he could savor the heady taste of his mate instead.

Regan spoke in the silence, “Did you organize for my belongings to be brought here?”

Rafe lifted his gaze back to her, “Did I forget something?”

Smiling Regan shook her head, “No I just wanted to thank you, it was very thoughtful.”

Shrugging his broad shoulders, “It was nothing, I wanted to go over there and make sure the cleanup crew had done a thorough job and that the window I smashed through was fixed,” he added with a wry smile.

“It seems I’m moving further and further into your debt.”

“I’m sure you’ll think of some form of payment,” he said suggestively.

At Regan’s questioning look he muttered to himself, “Or not.” He resettled himself on the bar stool, trying to find more room in his jeans for his growing erection without being too obvious about it. It seemed he’d need to accustom himself to being rock hard whenever his mate was near; maybe he should look at buying the next size up in jeans for the extra room. Being this close to his mate had a powerful effect on him, and his wolf constantly urging him to seduce Regan wore at his control. If he could convince his other half to give him some time it'd help, but his wolf wasn't listening to reason. Clenching his knife tightly in his fist, he tried to force his wolf and body to calm down.

Trust, is what tonight was about, building Regan's trust in him, *not* seduction.

"I know my father escaped, but what happened to the other two men at my house, were they both killed? It's all a bit hazy in my memory."

"I killed one; the other took off through the back door when I crashed through the window."

"Oh." Regan paused as she assimilated that, "It's a wonder the police allowed you to remove anything from my house with a dead body there. How have you kept them away from me today? They'd want my statement as soon as possible I imagine."

"Ah, well that would be because there was no dead body or blood left by the time the police arrived. I had my Sentinels do a quick clean up and remove any evidence of the failed abduction. Two of them hung around for the police when they finally responded to your neighbors call about gun shots, and fed the police false information about hearing shots coming from the bush land behind your property."

Regan stopped chewing as he spoke and stared at him.

"You lied to the police? Why? What'd you do with the

body?" Standing, she shook her head, stepping away from him, "I'm not going to jail for accessory after the fact for you, no matter how nice you've been to me."

Rafe slowly set down his cutlery and held his hands up, "Hold on Regan. I am the police. Sentinels police shifters. The attack on you was led by a shifter against another shifter. That falls into my jurisdiction. I have the authority to kill. If I had not shot that man, he would have shot me. I would have preferred to have taken him alive to question him, believe me. We are desperate for information about *Titan*. As to what we did with the body, we left it where no one from the public would stumble across it and anonymously notified the police as to where it was. That way if the police can identify him, his family won't be left wondering where he is."

Regan had stopped to listen, she supposed if you accepted shifters had the right to police themselves, no real moral law had been broken. Those men had brought the fight to the shifters, not the other way around.

"But the police will waste resources trying to find that man's killer," she argued.

"It's regrettable, but if you and I go the police with the bare facts that three men including your father attacked you for no reason and I killed one of the attackers in self-defense, how many more hours will be spent investigating our statements? No doubt they would prosecute me for manslaughter at the very least; our lawyers would have the public prosecutor's office running around for years and all because I came to your aid? What would that achieve? It is better for the Sentinels to take care of this, we know why you were attacked, but can't reveal that to humans."

"But society must have laws that are followed; you can't just go around killing people and answer to no one."

"But I do answer to someone, I answer to our Alpha. There is also an elected panel of eleven alphas that govern all shifters in the United States, Byron will report my actions to them, and if they deem them unlawful, I'll be punished. In this case, that won't happen; the man attacked a shifter and was killed in self-defense. If it eases your concerns any, we have to follow all human laws, except where they clash with shifter laws, and the necessity of hiding our presence from humans."

Regan sighed, she could see his point, but she was uneasy at how shifters seemed to have a get out of jail free card.

"Come, sit, and finish your dessert; as you get to know more about our society you will see there are checks and balances to keep us under control," he coaxed.

Regan resumed her seat at his urging. She did have a lot more to learn before she could pass judgment and she wasn't going to learn it all tonight. As they both focused on finishing the sumptuous pastry, Regan became increasingly aware of the male sitting next to her. Rafe was a large man with a powerful body and he took up a lot of space in her unit, but it wasn't just his physical size, his presence seemed to take over the room. He had a charisma that drew her; she was constantly fighting the need to watch him. Again, she studied his tanned face covertly, he was gorgeous, and there was no denying it, with his broad forehead and slashing brows - the same russet brown as his shaggy hair. His high cheekbones and straight nose drew the eye to his mouth with its full sensual lower lip and strong jaw.

She judged him to be around thirty-five, by now he'd be experienced sexually. Regan wondered idly as she sucked the last of the brandy sauce off her fork, what it would be like to kiss such a man. It was so unlike her, this curiosity. Why him? Why now? What could he teach her about kissing? Would he be commanding, ravenous, or tender and loving? Would he rush her and overwhelm her with a frenzied passion, or lead her slowly, building a delicious burning need in her that would never go out?

Self-preservation raised an alarm within her. She had an eerie precognition, if she allowed this man to enflame the ember of passion which now burned within her, she would never be able to extinguish the fire, and she would always burn for this man. It unnerved her.

Her curiosity would have to go unanswered. She was torn

between wanting to see him gone and not wanting to be on her own tonight. She was used to her own company, chose to live that way and the majority of the time she could ignore the loneliness, but some nights it was hard to push that feeling of desolate isolation away, and tonight was going to be one of those nights.

If left to her own devices, she knew she'd have a tough time drawing her mind away from the bleak realization that her father was trying to sell her to men who would hunt her down and shoot her for sport. She knew her father was evil and hated him, but it still shook her that he would do this to her. Did he do it for the money or did he gain a sick pleasure from selling his daughter? She didn't want to think about him, it depressed her to think that even after all these years he still had the power to hurt her.

"How about I help you clean this up and then we can have a game of cards?" Rafe suggested when they both finished eating.

Regan tilted her head considering, which would be worse, spending time with this unsettling man or to be left alone with her morbid thoughts? *Fuck that*, she could handle this man. *Grow a spine girl,* she castigated herself.

"I only really know poker; you want to play for stakes?"

Rafe narrowed his eyes at her easy capitulation; he'd been prepared for an argument as to why he should leave, maybe

Regan was more unsettled by today's revelations than he'd thought. She hid her emotions behind an impenetrable wall; even his wolf only sensed brief flashes before she shut them down again. She showed the world such a cool front, it had fooled even him. She had to be shocked to her core to learn she was a shifter, and that a panther shared her being, and then on some level she had to be shattered at her father's betrayal, no matter how much she hated him. Of course, his mate would need companionship tonight. To know she was not alone in the world, but how to convince his gun shy mate to let him stay?

"How about we play the best of seven hands, the winner gets to make a request of the looser?"

Regan paused in the process of squeezing detergent into the sink, "I'm not playing strip poker or having any sort of sexual stakes," she stated in a flat voice.

He held his hands up, "The thought never crossed my mind," he assured her, his big brown eyes open wide, his face a beacon of innocence.

Regan snorted at the act, "Yeah right. I know the difference between a wolf and a pup. It doesn't matter how innocent you act, that wolf is still staring out at me from your eyes."

He chuckled, "Astute thing aren't you. Let's finish this, there should be a pack of cards and a few other games under the entertainment unit and I promise if I win my request will not have anything to do with sex, if you win however feel free to use me any way you want," he shot her a cheeky grin.

Regan rolled her eyes at him; really, those dimples should be outlawed. It was hard to stay firm with him when her heart was going pitter-patter, like a teenage girl in the throes of her first crush.

They played cards for over an hour, Rafe unfortunately for Regan, was the better player. She was fairly sure he'd let her win her meager two hands. Tiredness was pulling at her as he laid his final winning hand down. He'd been a good distraction for her tonight but her body was demanding sleep, her healing ribs were a dull ache and her head now throbbed.

"So Miss Reynolds, ready to hear the winners request?" he twitched his eyebrows playfully.

"Yeah, yeah, bring it on, what's the big bad wolf want?"

"Let me sleep with you..."

CHAPTER 7

Regan cut in, "No," she shook her head as she jumped up. "That's not going to happen. I made it perfectly clear there was to be no sexual payment for losing before we started." Regan tried to ignore the sharp stab of disappointment, she'd believed he'd behave decently if she let him stay and now here he was proving her judgment wrong. She should have shown him the door as soon as they'd finished eating.

"Hey get off your high horse lady. I don't need to trick or push unwilling women into having sex with me. That's really offensive Regan. If you'd let me finish, I meant let me sleep in wolf form at the bottom of your bed. You've had a lot thrown at you today, I just wanted to keep you company through the night."

"Oh." Regan sat back down and picked at a chipped nail. Now she felt like an ungrateful bitch. Rafe had shown her nothing but kindness and she'd offended him with her misjudgment of his intent. "Sorry. I don't have a lot of faith in people and expect the worst from them."

Rafe's expression softened, "Well hopefully after spending some time with us you'll realize not everyone is an asshole. Come on," he stood up, "I can see you're ready to drop. By the time you change and brush your teeth, I'll be settled on the bottom of your bed. You can relax and sleep, my wolf will watch over you."

Regan couldn't deny the thought of his wolf curled up at the bottom of her bed appealed to her. She'd never allow Rafe the man into her bed, but while the man unsettled her the wolf soothed her.

"Alright, I'll see you or rather your wolf in there in a few minutes."

Regan grabbed an old T-shirt and some soft shorts to wear to bed; she didn't actually own any pajamas per se. As Regan brushed her teeth, she questioned her decision, what was to stop the wolf changing back into a man? She would be vulnerable in her sleep; he could have her pinned down before she could defend herself. Yes, she had no doubt he didn't have to force women to have sex with him, but for some men they got a charge from dominating a helpless victim. What had she been thinking, agreeing to this? She re-entered her room determined to tell Rafe he couldn't stay, but stopped short and stared at the wolf laying curled up at the foot of her bed. He lay with his bushy tail over his nose and paws, as she'd entered he'd opened his eyes and now stared at her with his rich chocolate eyes.

The agitation drained out of her tense body, as she stared into his knowing eyes. A soft whine emanated from him as if he could sense her upset and it pained him that she was distressed.

She walked over and ran her hand through his ruff, "It's OK big guy, I'm just not used to sharing my space, it freaks me out – but I'm OK." She continued stroking her hand down his back; she smiled as the wolf closed his eyes and groaned with pleasure. "You're not going to hurt me are you fella?"

He opened his eyes and stared at her sadly, she sensed the sadness was for her and the harsh lessons she'd endured, which made her uneasy around others.

"Don't worry, I'm OK," she gave him a wobbly smile.

He nuzzled his broad snout against her thigh where she leaned up against the bed.

"Alright you can stay, you I trust, your human half, not so much."

Regan climbed into bed and settled down enjoying the comfort of the heavy weight at her feet. Strange, the dichotomy she felt for Rafe and his wolf, and the strange affect they both had on her emotions. With a sigh she let sleep sweep her away from her concerns. They would be waiting for her tomorrow.

~~~

Regan blinked her eyes open to the soft light of dawn. She angled her head to look at the wolf sleeping at the foot of her bed; she sucked in a breath - that was no dog laying spread out at the bottom of her bed. Rafe lay sprawled on his back, one arm resting by his side the other slung across his chest and legs slightly spread, sound asleep.

Regan's eyes were drawn to his penis, which was lying across his left hip semi-erect. She tried to draw her eyes away, but having never seen one in real life, she was intrigued – at least that was the excuse she was giving herself for not turning away. She swallowed dryly as she studied the size and the bulbous head with the crease in the center, from where his semen would gush as an orgasm flooded through his body.

Sitting up slowly so as not to awaken him, she ran her gaze over his whole body, God he was beautiful. Slabs of muscle sculpted his pecks and abdomen. His chest was tanned and nearly hairless but a dark trail of course hair started below his navel and led down to his dark pubic hair. His thighs were muscled but not overly so, she imagined he ran a lot, his calf muscles were well defined, and his long feet even seemed sculpted by a master craftsman, and perfectly proportioned for his body. Her eyes were drawn to a thick
~~~

scar that ran from his hip down the side of his left thigh, it was puckered and raised, whatever had caused the damage had torn his flesh, not cut it. She remembered feeling the hard scar tissue yesterday when she'd petted him in his wolf form.

She leaned forward, her hand draw to trace over it as she'd done to the wolf. With the pad of her forefinger, she softly traced the raised tissue over his hip and down his thigh. Flinching her hand away, she sat back as Rafe moaned in his sleep, she watched his face intently, but he didn't waken. Anticipation tingled along her nerves as she studied his face, morning stubble coated his strong jaw, that full bottom lip that so intrigued her was slightly parted from the thinner, firmer, top one as he breathed deeply in his sleep.

Her inner core flexed as she imagined kissing him, she breathed in his delicious earthy scent and it reminded her of the smell of a rainforest. If she didn't know it impossible she swore her inner cat stretched sensuously, rousing itself from slumber at this man's scent. Need started building in Regan, a need to touch and be touched, she fantasized about cupping his tight testicles in her hand as she ran her mouth down his chest and stomach before lapping at his erection, savoring the salty taste of his smooth skin.

A soft sound, almost a purr left her throat; she couldn't resist tracing her nail over the nubbin of his nipple. She wanted to rub her body against his, mingling their scents. Closing her legs tight, she tried to relieve the tingling ache between her legs. Her head fell back at the delicious sensation. Never had she felt this way. As if she wasn't in control of her own body, she didn't understand why she could react this way when she'd never done so before. Her blood heated her body, dampened in yearning, for the first time preparing itself for penetration. She yearned for something, uncertain what would appease her hunger.

Her eyes dilated when she looked back down to see Rafe's dark eyes watching her reaction, his nostrils flared as he drew in her scent. His hand rose slowly to tangle in her hair as he drew her mouth down to his. He watched her eyes carefully, searching for any resistance. He raised his head the final inch to brush his lips across hers, questioningly. Any thought of resistance melted from Regan at the first delicate contact. He nibbled along her lower lip to the corner of her mouth before slipping his tongue briefly into her mouth for a taste. A delicious shudder coursed through her at the first taste of him. He closed his mouth over hers, inviting her tongue in to explore his mouth. Regan surrendered to sensation, lost in his taste and the rough texture of his tongue as it tangled with hers. Lust surged through her, a purr of pleasure mingled with his growl as urgency entered their kiss. Rafe rolled them over but rather than settling his weight onto her, he withdrew and returned to gentle sipping kisses. Slowly, gently, he brought them back down, easing the painful lust but leaving them both unsatisfied.

Eventually as their breathing returned somewhat to normal, he lifted his head. She opened her eyes and shame filled her, she had lost control, she had led him on and it was Rafe who had the self-control to stop.

“It’s alright Regan, it was a kiss between two consenting adults, it doesn’t have to lead to anything else, although I hope it does,” he smiled teasingly before stealing another quick hard kiss.

“Go grab a shower and I’ll start breakfast,” he offered, allowing her to escape and regroup.

Rafe smiled to himself as she almost sprinted from the room. Once he heard the bathroom door shut, he lay back and threw an arm over his eyes.

“Holy shit,” he muttered, he didn’t think he could do that again. Not only was he fighting his own need, his wolf was wild to have his mate. Even now, his wolf howled in frustration and outrage at letting her go. She’d been there in bed, wet and wanting him. The brutal urgency to possess her was overwhelming. He wondered if next time he’d find the strength to stop. He ground his teeth as he fought his body back under control.

He'd stopped because he wanted Regan to trust the man as she did his wolf. But, no matter how much he rationally knew he shouldn't rush Regan, he didn't think he'd be able to hold back the mating for long. The heat between them was too strong for either to resist. The primitive need was desperately powerful and surged between them white hot. If his wolf would try to hold back maybe, he could slow down their courtship, but he couldn't fight both his wolf and the blazing need creating by the mating bond.

Rafe had coffee ready for both of them by the time Regan reappeared showered and fully dressed in jeans, sneakers, and an old baggy T-shirt.

"Coffee is waiting for you in the kitchen; can I grab a couple of slices of toast before I head off to work?"

If Regan was trying to downplay her looks she was failing miserably, her freshly washed hair was brushed back off her face, highlighting her feline features, accentuating the tilted up corners of her eyes. The soft material of her T-shirt molded her high firm breasts, making Rafe's mouth water for a taste. As she walked past him to claim her cup of coffee, Rafe's appreciative gaze noted how her worn in jeans hugged the globes of her ass, making him groan as his erection surged back. Christ, he'd only just gotten the damn thing to settle down, now it was back and ready to party.

Opening various cupboards to locate the bread and toaster

Regan busied herself, still feeling self-conscious about the *bedroom incident* as she was referring to it. Man if she had felt unsettled around Rafe before, now she felt totally disconcerted. Why had she behaved like that? Worse still, she was still aroused, her skin was sensitive and even after her shower she was still damp between the legs. If she was honest with herself, she was actually feeling pissed off with the man because she felt unfulfilled and edgy, and it was his fault. This was all new to her and she didn't know how to handle it. She should be able to lock all these feelings away like she always did, but the physical hunger wouldn't stop and she didn't know how to shut it down. One moment she felt like rubbing herself all over him, the next instant she wanted to take a swipe at him like the cat she was purported to be.

Thankfully, Rafe filled in their breakfast with idle chatter, they arranged to meet outside the Sentinels offices at 5 o'clock, and Rafe would show her the gym they'd discussed the previous evening.

Regan spent the day watching the shifters and the way they interacted with each other. She walked the pathways, watching the antics of the wolves at play; the wolves seemed to dominate in numbers, from what she'd seen so far, it seemed that around 60% of the pack was made up of wolves. Shaking her head, she watched a lion stretched out sunning itself, with two female lionesses grooming him as he idly flicked his tail back and forth as if this was his due. Regan wondered how that all worked when they turned back into human form.

There weren't as many shifters about today; being a Monday, obviously the majority were at work. She noticed when in human form the people of Eden's Retreat inevitably stopped whenever they passed each other. There was a lot of hugging and smooching involved; Regan noted the same tactile behaviors was true for both males and females. Men were just as physical with each other as they were with the women. She was eternally grateful that people just passed her with a friendly wave or smile, and didn't try to stop her as she passed them. She didn't know if she had Steph and Rafe to thank for that, or if shifters were somewhat reticent around strangers.

She also pondered her immediate future, she was determined to improve Ben's situation. Something in her just wouldn't let her walk away from him; it really irked her that the adults here were ignoring him. She also needed to come up with a way to help Rafe capture her father. She refused to go on the run, and forever be looking over her shoulder. She didn't think Rafe yet fully appreciated the cunning her father possessed, and if he now had money backing him in the form of *Titan*, he would be a relentless adversary.

She spent the afternoon walking the trails in the forest that covered most of the shifters holding. She had a quick shower before heading over to the Sentinel's office, looking in the mirror she noted her facial bruising was nearly gone, just a faint yellow tinge here and there, her ribs ached as if bruised, but astoundingly the sharp pain of the break was completely gone. The only real symptom she had left was her head ached when she was in bright light, but dark sunglasses and avoiding bright lights alleviated the worst of the pain, leaving her with a dull ache that she could live with.

At 5 o'clock, she was waiting in the hallway outside the Sentinel's offices, determined to keep her interaction with Rafe at a friendly distance. She didn't know the woman she'd been at breakfast this morning, and she hadn't enjoyed feeling like a cat in heat. It was a rational decision to keep some distance between them, once he'd shown her the gym, she'd go out of her way to avoid him for the remainder of her stay at Eden's Retreat. She shored up her resolve as she watched him exit his office and walk towards her. She refused to acknowledge her heart leaping at the sight of him, or her blood warming as he neared her.

Rafe placed his large hand at the small of her back as he directed her through a doorway, just along from the Sentinel's office and down a set of stairs into what was obviously the old gym he was offering her the use of. Regan tried to ignore the anticipation bubbling through her system, and instead focused her attention on the room they'd just entered.

He flicked on the lights and a smile tilted Regan's lips; this would be perfect for her and Ben. Obviously most of the equipment had been removed, but there was still a full set of free weights, some old punching bags, and a boxing ring. That would be perfect for the style of fighting Regan would be teaching; the floor was slightly rubberized to soften the landing when you hit the deck. There was even a treadmill and the requisite skipping ropes.

"Perfect. Is there somewhere close by where I can purchase a couple of fit balls and medicine balls?"

Rafe waved the question away "Don't worry about it, I'll bring some back from the new gym. They won't be missed."

As she moved over to the boxing ring Regan could feel Rafe's gaze following her, it made her feel edgy, her senses heightened as she tingled with anticipation. Again, he unsettled her. Rubbing her hands restlessly down her thighs, Regan felt arousal seeping in, mixing with the anticipation thrumming through her. *Did the man have to be so sexy?* It was playing havoc with her libido. A libido she wasn't aware she possessed until she met him. *Ignore it Regan.*

Glancing at him from beneath her lashes, she felt the raw sexuality that radiated from the man. No wonder she was aroused for the first time in her life, if any man was going to wake up her latent hormones, it was this one. She ran her eyes over his body, God he was stunning.

Rafe's lips tilted up as he contained his smile, he'd been enjoying her perusal of his body, but the slight widening of her eyes and the way they were now glued to his straining cock made him want to laugh. However, the tempting smell of his mate's arousal caused his own desire to flare aggressively. His wolf howled and tore at his control, desperate to claim his mate here and now, but the man knew he had to wait, the internal conflict grated. His little mate needed enticing and a small taste of the wild passion mates enjoyed, not the rough frenzy of his frantic wolf. He would not force a mating on her, she had to come to him, but he intended to tempt her with what she was missing, he desperately hoped her panther would continue surfing enough to increase Regan's own urgency and bring her to him sooner. He honestly didn't know how long he'd be able to restrain himself.

A mate claim involved two parts, the sexual claiming, and the verbal pledge, which could be recited by either of the pair or both. Once both had taken place, a thin blue band would mystically appear under the mated pair's skin around their wrists. It would remain for the rest of their lives proclaiming them mated. Traditionally the ritual words were recited in front of the clan, similar to a human wedding ceremony and celebrated as enthusiastically after the ceremony, as any human reception. After the ceremony had been completed, the sexual urgency that tormented the pair would slowly fade over time to more manageable hunger for each other.

It was time to begin coaxing his mate to his bed. Rafe moved across to Regan and used his body mass to guide her back a couple of steps until her back came up against the wall. She raised her palms to his chest ready to push him back when he leaned in and inhaled her luscious scent from the junction of her neck and shoulder. Nuzzling her hair to the side, he used his rough tongue to lick her skin, savoring her taste. A soft growl rumbled in his chest, she tasted sweetly tart; the flavor of her skin reminded him of nectarine and made his mouth water as the succulent taste flooded across his tongue. Regan paused in the act of pushing him away; he felt the shudder that coursed through her when he again growled, this time in rebuke at her attempt to push him away.

He pressed his hardened cock up and into her heat. The scent of her musky arousal filled his head, as her body's honey seeped from her moistened labia; it teased him with a stronger scent, arousing him further. He dragged his lips up and along her jaw, softly rubbing back and forth across her plump lips. Once. Twice.

"Open for me," he demanded before claiming her mouth in a heated kiss. His tongue sought hers, tangling before encouraging her into his mouth to sample his taste.

He hummed his approval as she came into him. Heat blazed through his blood. Running his rough hands down her back learning her shape, he massaged her lush bottom. Before lifting her feet from the ground, he fitted his lean hips in the cradle of her body. Wild fire raced through him.

"Let me touch you my beloved," his voice rough with desire. Using his powerful body to anchor her to the wall, he undid her jeans, allowing his questing fingers to separate the folds of her femininity. Slick heat smoothed the path as he ran the rough pad of his thumb over her engorged clitoris. Liquid gushed to meet the fingers, gently pushing apart the lips of her genitalia. Once he had her fully opened, he rested his hand there and applied more pressure, this time his thumb circled her clitoris. Gasping she tore her mouth from his.

Regan threw her head back gasping for air, pleasure ripped through her, brutally overwhelming all common sense. Mindlessly she thrust her hips; caught in the moment with no control, a vortex of pleasure whirled through her body, whipping her mind away as sensation rode her. Before she could take more than one breath, Rafe moved to claim her mouth again, grinding his palm between her legs. She needed release, the pressure agonizing already. Urgency pushed her. She ground herself against his broad palm again and again, twisting her head, she tried to gain a breath of air, but he dominated her, moving with her, not allowing her to breathe without him. Sensation raged, heat consumed, her nerves over stimulated, urgency gripped her, and she needed release.

Whimpering she surged against his now probing fingers. More, she needed more, straining she pushed her shoulders back against the wall and held herself wide open to him. He rewarded her by roughly pushing two fingers into her and rubbing his thumb back and forth over her clit. Groaning, she opened her eyes and gazed into his, so close to her that she saw his burning need as he stared into her bared soul. That must have been what he wanted, as with a grunt of approval, he increased the pressure on her clit, roughly withdrew, and then pushed back in with his fingers. His eyes intently watched as the building pressure whirled her away.

Orgasm erupted through her. She arched back impossibly further, every muscle straining to the limit, and still he ravaged her mouth, her body held open to his. It was his to take. Darkness edged in as finally her muscles began to relax, pulses of orgasm racing along her nerves. Her inner muscles clenched and flexed around his fingers still buried in her body. His kiss gentled as he brought her back down.

Rafe continued to gently kiss and nibble on her lips, occasionally softly brushing his thumb across her over sensitized clitoris, his fingers still inside her clasping vagina. Sucking in a rough breath, he slowly slid his fingers from her body, bringing his fingers up he ran them over her lips before kissing the moisture away, savoring her exquisite taste. He then sucked her honey from his fingers, relishing the succulent taste of his mate's sex. Regan licked her lips taking in the residual taste of her body; Rafe kissed her deeply, allowing her a further taste from his own mouth.

"Hmmm, delicious," he allowed her legs to slide to the floor before zipping up her jeans. At her questioning look, he grinned at her. "Don't worry love, we will be doing a lot more than this, but today was just an appetizer for you."

Regan lowered her eyes from his, embarrassment, and shock at her body's reaction warring within her. She was out of her depth; she didn't know how to behave towards Rafe after exposing herself this way.

With her body sated there was a warm comfort standing there leaning against his strength, feeling all that hard muscle holding her up against the wall as they got their breath back. She could literately feel her body absorbing his heat; it warmed her soul, always so bleakly frozen before this man. He gave her comfort, eased the eternal ache always within her. The raw jagged wound that had never healed after her mother's death, eased with touch. A drowsy peace crept in to replace gray misery, until now she'd never realized the burden she carried within her. How crippling it was to carry such pain. Could this man help her heal? This was the second time in a matter of days she had felt serene, and both times had been when this man held her.

She needed to explore her options. Was it just this man who could help her attain a sense of contentment, or was it as Rafe had stated earlier, shifters craved contact with their own kind? The hollow black wretchedness that seared into the center of her being wasn't entirely twisted around her mother's brutal murder, but some of the cold darkness within her was because she had no contact with fellow shifters.

Whatever the cause of her crippling pain she didn't want to return to that state. There was a certain level of comfort staying isolated as she was, it was debilitating and draining but she knew what to expect, knew she could cope, to risk change was unnerving, the uncertainty frightening. Instinctively she knew the man holding her had the power to hurt her in ways she'd never been hurt before. She wasn't a coward; if she needed to live amongst shifters to thrive, she would learn to do so but at the same time, she would keep a protective wall around herself. After the high Rafe had given her, she was starting to feel weary.

Rafe could feel the confusion in his mate but he also felt the tiredness pulling at her. This was only her second day out of her sick bed and now was not the time for major discussions. Moving her gently in his arms, he turned them so their backs were against the wall. He slid down pulling her unresisting body with him and settled her across his lap with her head resting in the crook of his neck. His arms supported her back. He let her drift into a light doze; her body still healing the injuries dealt by her father. His little mate needed some peace and time to heal. He lowered his head over hers protectively, and pulled her closer. She was his to protect.

Before she had tumbled into sleep, his wolf had sensed the agony she lived with. The drive to ease the searing pain she held within was now his priority. He would do his job, but his mate would always come first, her needs where now his. His plan to win his mate was now four pronged.

1. To seduce her. 2. Spend time with her and win her trust. This was essential to do before she found out that her childhood hell was his fault. That he had deliberately left her with that madman. 3. He needed to involve her in the shifter community at Eden's Retreat. He needed her to form friendships that would tie her here. This would also help her cat heal and become strong enough to enable Regan to shift forms. Plus, he wanted his mate happy, and friends she could trust were a vital part of that. 4. Eliminate the threat against her. If her father had given up her name to the hunters from *Titan*, they all had to be eliminated, including her father. That sort of threat to his mate was unacceptable.

CHAPTER 8

Regan settled into life at Eden's Retreat with relative ease. That wasn't to say she was a *normal* shifter. She still cringed whenever anyone touched her, she felt edgy when people stood close to her and the shifters could sense it. Thankfully, word had gone out and in general people refrained from hugging or petting her, which she appreciated no end. She could see it wasn't natural for them to withhold their touch from her and that it made some uneasy when with her. She couldn't undo a lifetime of wariness in days. She had trust issues and probably always would.

Over the last week, she had noted how tactile they truly were. When talking they would constantly touch, whether it was by leaning against each other or running a hand over another's arm or back, they'd play with each other's hair, although she had noted the males didn't do this to each other. It was so weird seeing men hugging and casually rubbing their hand across the others shoulder as they spoke. If she'd seen men behave this way outside Eden's Retreat, she would have assumed they were in a relationship, but here there was no sexual vibe at all.

She was now fully healed from her attack, and working Ben and herself as hard as she could in the gym. Ben's commitment never faltered, no matter how hard she pushed him. Her pride in the kid grew with every day she spent with him. He never complained, he worked until his muscles failed him. With Ben, she was able to let her guard down, he was no threat to her.

Strangely, she found herself constantly reaching out to pat him on the shoulder or pulling him in for a quick tight hug. At first, he'd either moved away as if he hadn't noticed her reaching out to pat him, or stand passively under her touch. Then earlier today he had given her a quick squeeze back before moving away from her. Just now, he'd given her a high five after completing 20 chin-ups for the first time, while flashing a smile full of life and enjoyment at the achievement. Exaltation caused her eyes to tear up at seeing the change in him, and she'd cleared her throat before directing him in his next set of drills.

His mother had apparently given her blessing for Regan to train Ben. When she had asked Ben if his mom had wanted to meet with her Ben had shrugged "Nah – she's happy to have me out of the house. Don't worry about it; she's not interested in meeting you."

Too bad, Regan was very interested in meeting her. Regan had quite a bit to say to the woman. Nevertheless, before she upset that apple cart she had to get her own house in order. If she was going to interfere in Ben's home life, she had to make sure she was going to be here to support Ben. No doubt, there was going to be some volatile encounters between Regan and his mother, before such entrenched behavior towards Ben could be changed. Maybe the woman didn't have any maternal instincts at all for Ben. Although how you couldn't love Ben, was beyond Regan's comprehension. There wasn't a mean, dishonest, calculating, vindictive element to his character. That he wasn't bitter and angry towards the world amazed Regan.

Over the last week, Ben in passing had revealed the treatment he was subjected to at home. His tone was never bitter, just matter of fact as if it was normal for a mother to belittle, and denigrate her child at every opportunity. It wasn't that he wasn't traumatized he was, he was withdrawn and he'd already learned to shut down his emotions. It was better to feel nothing at all than to feel the pain of rejection. His mother knew he was bullied and did nothing to support him or intervene on his behalf. She also knew some of the kids made eating at the food hall a torment for Ben, yet she refused to feed him herself or ensure he was eating enough.

Regan could see she did just enough, that the other residents of Eden's Retreat didn't feel it necessary to interfere.

Regan knew given time she could form a strong bond with Ben, it would take commitment and that was why she needed to get her own situation sorted. The need was growing within her to fix Ben's problems; she had to make his life better. She couldn't look the other way, in her heart he was hers to nurture.

It would be easy to love him, and she had the patience to bring him out from behind the walls he had erected. She also knew that she couldn't take him away from this community, he was a shifter, and he needed to be around others of his kind. To take him away would cause more damage, more loneliness, pain, and isolation. Regan needed to meet his mother and see if she could love her son eventually or if it would be better to remove Ben from her neglect and bitterness and look after him herself. Maybe with separation and intervention, his mother might come to see that hurting Ben would never help heal the wound left from being attacked all those years ago.

Before she confronted his mother, Regan needed to organize a job. She planned to sell her house and buy something here. Ben needed to *see* she was staying; words were not going to be enough to convince him to trust her. She would love him, support him, help him negotiate life's obstacles and maybe together they could find trust and a safe place where they didn't have to be constantly on guard from emotional hurt. A safe place, somewhere just to be, their home would be a safe zone for them.

She would interact with the residents of Eden's Retreat, she would make sure Ben had the opportunity to form friendships and become a part of the community. To that end, she now had a strange collection of people who ate at her table in the food hall on a regular basis. Regan made sure she ate breakfast and dinner at the hall every day. This ensured Ben ate at least two healthy meals each day. She could already see the benefit regular meals was having, he was already putting on much needed weight.

Regan watched Ben as he lifted weights and thought back to the second morning they'd shared breakfast. They had been discussing one of his homework projects when a female shifter had stalked over to their table. She was around 5' 10" leanly muscled and wearing the black cargo pants and long sleeved black T-shirt uniform of a Sentinel. Her sable colored hair was cut into a sleek bob, short at the back while the front came to the bottom of her jaw. Regan assumed she chose that style to help cover the harsh scar that ran across her cheekbone to the left side of her lip. It was an old scar gone white with age, but it was the new comer's eyes that held Regan's attention. They were dark grey and blank of all emotion, she ruffled Regan's fur the wrong way.

"You gotta problem with me sitting with you and the pup?"

Before Regan cold tell the surly piece of work that she did in fact have a problem, Steph appeared out of nowhere, Regan still couldn't figure out where she'd come from.

"Of course Regan doesn't Jen. We'd love for you to join us," she added as she sat her bowl of cereal down between Regan and Ben, indicating Jen should take the seat opposite her.

Regan shot Steph an *Are you kidding?!* look.

Ignoring Regan, Steph smiled brightly at everyone as Jen scraped her chair back and sat down, staring at Regan the whole time, daring her to object.

"Well isn't this lovely?" Steph enthused into the sullen silence of the table.

Regan shot Steph a look of disbelief, Ben put his head down and focused on eating his scrambled eggs.

Jen moved her gaze off Regan, "Yeah Steph, this is great, let's all go clothes shopping next, then spend the afternoon painting each other's nails, by tonight we'll all be BFF's," she replied in a *put on* high pitched girly voice full of fake enthusiasm.

Regan snorted a laugh, this bitch was the first person she'd come across to give Steph some shit. Everyone else loved the girl and bent over backwards to ensure she was happy.

Steph dunked a finger in her cereal and flicked milk at Jen, hitting her right in the eye.

"Very mature Steph and a great example you're setting for the pup here," Jen nodded at Ben who was now openly watching the by-play between the three females.

Steph had gone on to fill their breakfast with her idle chatter and since then Jen had joined Regan and Ben for every breakfast, and as often as not appeared during their dinner. She'd sit herself down with a brief acknowledgement, eat her meal, and leave. Why Jen continued to seek them out, baffled Regan. It was only when Steph joined them that the woman would talk, and then only in monosyllabic answers to Steph's direct questions. It actually made Regan feel great, if she had problems socializing with these people it was nothing compared to how taciturn Jen was. In comparison to Jen, Regan was an extrovert. If these shifters could accept Jen into their community, then Regan expected they'd accept her too.

The other regular to their table was Jordan the fox. On Regan's first day exploring Eden's Retreat, Steph had introduced him as Rafe's right hand man. The attractive Sentinel often joined them for dinner, especially if Jen was there.

It was interesting watching the two Sentinels interact. If Jordan gave Jen a direct order or requested a verbal report, Jen was professionally articulate in her response to him, but as soon as the topic was not work related, she retreated into monosyllabic answers and cut all eye contact. On more than one occasion, she'd watched Jordan grind his teeth in frustration with the reserved female.

Last night Regan had actually ground her heal into Jen's foot under the table, when she'd cut the poor guy down again. Jen's head had shot up as she glared at Regan.

"Gees Jen throw the man a bone would ya?" she'd whispered.

Jen had stared at her questioningly.

Regan had rolled her eyes, totally clueless! "Would it kill you to be nice to Jordan?" she'd asked softly.

"Hey if he wants nice he can chase after any number of light hearted, light skirted females here or in the city, as he's done on numerous occasions in the past," she'd growled, before returning her attention to her meal, cutting her steak viciously with the razor sharp knife she held in her right hand.

Regan had been taken aback at the raw emotion in Jen's response, *Huh, she does suffer from emotions like the rest of us, there ya go.*

She'd looked back to Jordan and shrugged helplessly, obviously the man had a lot to make up for in Jen's book. Jordan had smiled at her appreciatively before turning his attention to Ben.

Regan actually found it easy to talk to Jordan, he was a skilled conversationalist and adept at drawing people out, quick intelligence alive in his eyes as he listened attentively to whoever was talking. Regan warmed to the guy even more as he worked away at Ben; patiently drawing Ben more and more into their conversations as the days went by. There wasn't anything fake about his interest in Ben; Regan would sense that kind of deceit. With Jordan's intelligence, it would be easy for him to be condescending, but he never was, he was openly curious about people, and what they thought about any given topic.

Rafe would also join them whenever he could but he was working grueling hours traveling all over the country supporting his Sentinels in their investigation of Titan while still carrying out the normal policing of shifters throughout America.

They made up strange dinner companions, with Steph the golden girl who couldn't stop talking, Jen, who'd obviously prefer to be on her own but for reasons unknown continued to sit with them, Jordan, who's innate inquisitiveness and genuine interest in people made him hard to resist, Rafe, who always managed to seat himself next to Regan and Ben, who watched them all as if he was at the circus.

As Regan continued to watch Ben train she turned her thoughts from her dinner companions to her father, she needed to remove the threat he posed. His attack on her proved that she wouldn't be safe until he was dead. That he could find her through his paternal bond with her meant she couldn't hide, so that left confrontation.

Rafe and his Sentinels were working day and night to track him and the people of *Titan* down. Jordan was pulling together the names of people who were financially capable of conducting an undertaking like this and keeping it quiet. Once Jordan had a potential name, Sentinels were then sent to observe them and discern if they were capable of hunting and killing shifters. Sentinels were flying all over the country observing these mega rich people, trying to ascertain if they could be linked to the hunting pack Justin described. In the end, it would be a small group who held no sanctity for life, who believed the law did not apply to them. Hopefully, their sense of entitlement would lead to a mistake, allowing the Sentinels to identify them.

Regan knew from listening to the residents of Eden's Retreat that the Sentinels were spread thin and wouldn't be able to maintain the travel and hours they were exerting, in their attempt to unearth the members of *Titan*. They needed something to crack so they could pry open the rotten core that was *Titan* and spill out the twisted souls who hunted and terrorized people for pleasure. If they could just find a thread to follow, they'd be able to rip the organization apart and maybe she was what they needed. Maybe she could bring her father out into the open.

Rafe could use her for bait and set up a trap around her. If they were successful, not only would they have her father but also any associates he brought to capture her. He hadn't been alone when he tried to kidnap her so there was no reason to believe he'd be alone when he next tried. That would give the Sentinels more people to question.

~~~

Strong hands grasped her hips and pulled her back into the tall muscular frame she was coming to know intimately. Rafe was very unsubtle in his pursuit of her. It mattered not to him if they were alone or in public, he would steal every opportunity to touch and kiss her. Regan wasn't sure how she felt about his interest in her. No that wasn't true, her body was enraptured, for the first time she was sexually interested in a male and it was a heady feeling. Her body pulsed and burned for him. She often found her mind drifting to thoughts of him. Wondering what he was doing, who he was with, if he was happy, angry, frustrated, or if he was thinking of her.

She had never been infatuated with a boy during her teenage years, and now found herself for the first time obsessed with a male, it was disconcerting. She had assumed her childhood had damaged that part of her psyche and she was unable to have a relationship with a male. With her trust issues, it had
~~~

never bothered her. Now she found herself aching to be with this man, and maybe she could relax enough with him to let it happen.

They weren't mates so what he was offering was only short-term, which she assured herself, was what she wanted. She had too many issues and couldn't see herself dealing with a long-term relationship and the emotional, as well as mental, intimacy required. Rafe's warm breath on the back of her neck as he nuzzled her hair aside brought her back from her rambling thoughts.

"Hi sweetheart. Want to come for a walk with me. I have a spare half hour before I have to head out with the team," he dragged his lips down the side of her neck suckling softly on the sensitive skin at the juncture of her shoulder and neck. A shiver of arousal ran up her spine as she tipped her head to the side allowing him greater access.

Ben sent her a smirking glance, "I'll be fine, I know the drills well enough. I'm sure I can cope for half an hour while you two go for a *walk*." The inflection he put on walk assured Regan that he believed they'd be doing a lot more than that.

Rafe sent Ben an appreciative smile. "I'm really beginning to like that boy," he commented as he pulled her from the gym by entwining their fingers together.

Regan flashed a smile at him as they exited the building and headed towards the forest.

"He's a great kid," she assured, "I'm enjoying my time with him." Rafe pulled her close to his body, his hand resting on her hip as they walked along one of the narrow paths heading deeper into the trees. He matched his step to hers, anticipation hummed through her as they walked.

Rafe yanked her off the path as a wolf barreled past them, tail held high in delight. Before Regan could step back onto the path a lioness tore past them, her lips curled back revealing deadly fangs, her yellow eyes narrowed on her prey. Regan stood still for a moment watching as the pair disappeared round a bend in the path.

"Umm shouldn't you go see if the dog needs some help?" Would she ever get used to wild animals racing through these woods?

Rafe laughed. "Nah Ethan can take care of himself. No doubt, he deserves the pummeling Alana will deal him if she can catch him, but Ethan would have to allow her to catch him. Wolves can run for hours, whereas the lions are too heavy to sustain that pace for long. Ethan is Alana's mate's younger brother and he torments her endlessly, but she won't do any permanent damage to her brother in-law."

"Every time I come in here I see more shifters in their animal form rather than their human, why's that?"

Rafe shrugged as he tucked her back under his shoulder as they continued, his fingers rubbing back and forward across her hip. “It feels good. We have freedom when in animal form that we can never attain while in human form. Cares and worries recede while you live in the moment. Once you’ve changed for the first time you’ll understand,” he smiled down at her.

“Well that’s not likely to happen any time soon so I’ll take your word for it.”

His gaze slid away from hers as he changed the topic, “You’re having a positive influence on Ben.”

“He needs someone to take an interest in him, to make him feel valued.”

Rafe’s hand drifted from her hip to rest on her waist with his fingers spread his thumb rested just below her breast.

Her breath hitched as he slowly rubbed his thumb back and forth under the weight of her sensitized breast. The more time she spent with this stunning male, the quicker her body was to respond to his. Everything about him seemed to arouse her desire. Her mind enjoyed his clever wit, the way he eased her into a variety of conversations, listening intently to her opinions. Her body responded to his with a burning intensity. Her erotic dreams of his powerful body taking hers and pushing her body into a frenzy before she awoke writhing on her bed in orgasmic bliss, occurred night after night. Now a mere touch had her body purring in anticipation.

Turning her into his muscular frame, he widened his stance to settle her between his thighs ensuring she felt the hardness of his erection pushing against her lower stomach. He bent to nuzzle under her jaw, tilting her head back exposing her throat to him. She moaned as he trailed his lips up to her ear before gently taking her tender lobe between his teeth and biting softly. The embers of her passion burst into flames at the feel of his teeth on her skin and the sense of vulnerability with her throat exposed submissively caused a delicious heat to course through her.

With his hands on her hips, he pulled her tighter against him as he moved to take sipping kisses from her lips, coaxing her to open for him. Moisture gathered in her mouth in anticipation. Unwilling to wait for his teasing lips to take full possession of her mouth; she reached up and grasped handfuls of his thick hair to bring his mouth fully against hers.

She felt his smile against her lips before he took control and covered her mouth fully. Cupping her bottom, he raised her onto her toes to rub against his straining shaft. His tongue swept against hers, then coaxed her into his mouth. One hand held her frame clasped to his as he ground into the junction of her body, his other swept up under her shirt. His rough palm trailed up her spine savoring the texture of her soft skin.

He groaned his approval as she enticed his tongue back into her mouth to suckle greedily. She swept her hands over his broad chest, savoring the hard muscles before running them over his tight abs, to drag them back up and over his broad shoulders. She needed to be closer, to feel his skin against hers. She felt elemental, powerful; she nipped at his lower lip as she tried to pull his shirt out of the way of her questing hands. Exotic heat traced a path directly to her inner core. She burned there; she needed him to fill the emptiness. Moaning in frustration, she ground herself against him.

Rafe broke the kiss. "Baby you're killing me here," he groaned as he rested his forehead against hers.

"I need," she demanded, disliking that he was pulling away, again.

"Stop teasing me like this," she hissed, when he refused to take her upturned mouth in another kiss, her nails sank into his shoulders in frustration.

When he didn't, she tried to shove him away from her but he held her tight to him.

"I'm sorry baby I didn't mean to get so carried away," he rubbed his chin back and forth across the top of her head trying to sooth her. With a frustrated sigh, she settled back against him. "When we make love for the first time it will not be a quickie because I have to catch a plane headed to the other side of the country," he kissed her sulky lips before turning them back towards the nearest exit.

Rafe grimaced as he shortened his stride to Regan's; he understood her frustration. The burning drive for sexual fulfillment the mating induced between them was a constant torment now; it was like nothing he had ever experience before. The need for her was painful in its unrelenting intensity. If people's lives weren't on the line, he'd ditch his latest investigation to fulfill his mate's needs, satisfying his own at the same time.

Trying to distract himself from the exquisite smell of his mate's arousal, he focused on his work, "I'll be gone for three or four days. We have isolated a small group of men who fit the profile of the men hunting us."

Regan listened as Rafe talked of their attempts to track the killers. This group he was investigating got their jollies hunting and killing animals on the brink of extinction. They loved the idea of being responsible for the end of a species. It gave them a sense of power. It thrilled them to do something that their peers would never have the audacity to do.

The psych evaluation showed the people Rafe was hunting would be wealthy with a sense of entitlement. Everything they ever wanted was given to them; their wealth would make any legal issues disappear. They would never have faced consequences for their actions. They were disconnected from other people, true sociopaths, with no empathy for others. No laws or morals would stop them.

They wouldn't need to brag about what they were doing, that they had discovered shifters existed or that they hunted them for sport. Their sense of superiority didn't require acknowledgement from others. But that was OK, because the shifters wouldn't be playing by human societies' rules either. These men would be hunted down and killed as they had hunted and killed.

In the mean time, it would be more of the same for both of them. Tormenting arousal, unfulfilled need, and restless sleep filled with erotic dreams that left them both burning with need. He was determined to claim her when he came back from this trip. Her need was as elemental as his now. He'd given them as much time as he could, her panther was rising closer to the surface each day; he wanted her as addicted to him physically as he was to her, before he was forced to tell her about being mated to him. He needed her tied to him in as many ways as possible.

~~~

Regan had changed into a pair of running shorts, a sports bra, and tank top, and was heading back to the forest to run off some of her sexual frustration. She figured a good hard five-mile run should take the edge off, hopefully allowing her to sleep that night.
~~~

She'd just left her building when she literally ran into the stunning doctor who'd helped her recover. She should feel gratitude towards the doctor, instead the hair on her arms and the back of her neck rose in hostility. She was tempted to take a swipe at the perfectly made up woman. Her makeup was done subtly emphasizing her dark chocolate eyes and high cheekbones, her hair done up in a perfect chignon. It was the end of the day for God's sake and she still looked as perfect as she'd no doubt looked this morning when she'd left for work. Here Regan was in her baggy old running gear and Dr. Warner was in her high heels, knee length pencil skirt with matching jacket of dove gray over a rose pink camisole, looking like she'd just stepped out of the pages of a fashion magazine.

Regan dredged up a smile that quickly faded as Dr. Warner ran her eyes over Regan; it was obvious Regan had come up short in the doctor's assessment.

"I see you're recovering well. Do you have any lingering symptoms I should know about?" she asked in her husky voice that set Regan's nerves on edge. Mind you, Regan acknowledged to herself everything about this woman set her nerves on edge.

"Nothing for you to worry about."

"Good." The other woman started to leave, but turned back, "I hope you appreciate the chance Rafe and Byron have given you by allowing you to stay here. You'll find shifters more open and caring than the humans you've lived among up till now."

Regan already on edge, moved straight to offended, at the lecturing tone the doctor used.

"I hope you don't think it's perfect here, this place isn't really 'Eden' you know."

"Not 'Eden' no, but certainly shifters in general are honest, and look out for each other. I'm just saying you will need to make an effort to mix and help others if you want to belong here."

"From what I've seen so far, you guys aren't that much better, if at all." Regan was thinking of her father and the neglect Ben suffered as all the *caring* shifters of Eden's Retreat looked the other way.

Shrugging her slim shoulders in dismissal the willowy brunet stepped around Regan, "Well your loss if you don't want to stay."

Regan watched with narrowed eyes as the other woman sauntered off with a catwalk model's grace. Crap, the doctor got under her skin, muttering to herself she headed for the forest, maybe she would need a ten mile run. Regan bent her neck from side to side, as she walked trying to release some of her tension. It was just as well all shifters weren't like Dr.

Warner, if they were it would be intolerable here.

CHAPTER 9

"I've been looking for you." The rough voice at her ear pumped adrenaline through Regan's system.

Instinctively she jabbed her elbow backwards into his midriff before ducking low avoiding retaliation. She spun into a defensive position, arms up, perfectly poised to counter any attack.

Rafe sidestepped her jab and raised his hands in peace. "Whoa there gorgeous," he laughed. "I didn't mean to startle you."

She stared at him, pissed that he'd been able to sneak up on her. She was so frustrated sexually she was ready to scream. Regan acknowledged she was in a bitch of a mood and if this man wasn't careful, he'd be finding out just how frustrated and vicious she was feeling. The last three days had been hellish; she constantly burned with arousal. Her clit was so sensitive she couldn't even wear jeans and it was entirely this idiot's fault.

She was vacillating about entering into a relationship with him or not. She hated feeling like this, as if she no longer controlled her own body. She didn't want to become dependent upon him easing this ravaging desire that ruled every moment of her life. Did she want to be involved with him or was it better to avoid him and hope this constant arousal would die down?

From listening to others conversations, she knew Rafe was well respected and liked by both the males and females of Eden's Retreat. He obviously worked long hours and was dedicated to protecting his people. The respect in the Sentinel's eyes as they spoke of him spoke volumes of their regard for their esteemed commander. Even Jen put together more than two words when Regan had asked for her opinion regarding Rafe. In fact, she'd waxed lyrical about how fantastic he was, her face alight with reverence.

Regan had met admirable men before who were visually attractive, but never had she been the least interested, so why this man? She didn't know how to behave, didn't know what she wanted.

On one level, she longed to rub up against him, to stroke her cheek along his shoulder, and across his powerful chest, to burrow into his heat. But, her inbuilt caution prevented her from following her instinct. She had no experience with men, obviously, he expected to have sex with her, but she didn't know if she could let go of her control. Yet after her reaction to him in the gym that day, maybe she could lose herself in the burning passion that sprang between them. But did she want to?

Her mind had circled around and around for the last three days and the vacillation was sending her nuts. Did she want to have sex with Rafe? Could she let her control go, allow that level of vulnerability? Did she trust him enough? Wouldn't it be easier to go back to how she'd been before meeting him? She wanted the comfort back of being disconnected from all these raw emotions tearing at her. It would be a relief to retreat back within herself. When she was away from Rafe, she often felt resolved to cut off all contact with him, but when she was with him that resolve dissipated like morning mist under a hot sun.

"So, alone at last," he murmured as he approached her, he'd been relieved to find Ben absent when he'd tracked her scent to the gym and found her exercising alone. He lowered his head to nuzzle her behind her ear. "I've missed you," his rough whisper sent shivers along her spine. Slowly he shifted his large frame into contact with her softer body, with his head bent protectively over her.

Regan couldn't resist leaning into his strength. His warmth invaded her, his musky masculine scent as soothing as it was arousing. She rubbed against him, savoring his leashed power, to stay still was impossible. Moving her head to the side, she allowed him better access to her vulnerable neck. He ran his rough tongue along her pounding pulse before blowing gently on the moisture. A small sound of pleasure escaped as she nuzzled aside his shirt to rub her cheek against his hard nearly hairless chest. His rumble of pleasure sent molten heat thrumming through her body.

"I need to talk to you," she whispered.

"Mhmm?" he nibbled an erotic path along her neck to bite her shoulder lightly. Her womb clenched in response, she reflexively rubbed herself against his firm erection. His rough jeans added friction, increasing the sensation washing through her. She continued her own nuzzling until she found one of his flat nipples. Entranced she ran her lips back and forth, learning the texture. She watched as it tightened from her attention, then leaned back in to taste, running her tongue around the nubbin for a tantalizing taste before using the broad flat of her tongue to lick across the disk. Again she pulled back to look at his bodies reaction, before leaning in to grasp it gently in her teeth and pulling.

His growling response was to wrap his arms around her and lift her firmly against his erection, inundating her with sensation.

Drawing her alluring scent deeply into his lungs he

grumbled, "You want to talk to me about something? If so, you'd better talk quick, because if you keep that up my brain is going to fry."

"Hmm, yes I need to talk to you," she murmured as she nuzzled her way across his chest to his other hard nipple and continued her investigation of his body. This time when she tugged on his nipple, he threw his head back and ground his heavy erection into her wet softness.

Rafe was losing his control, he'd intended a little nuzzling and some hot wet kissing, but his body's reaction to his mate's interest was like wildfire. Heat pounded through him. He wanted to bend his mate over the weight bench and pound into her from behind. The scent of her arousal made thinking impossible; instinct was to take what was his. Shuddering, he tried to remember his big plan, to seduce her slowly. Turning her over a bench, ripping down her sweats and fucking her to oblivion, was unlikely to help with his plan, but holy hell, the temptation of his mate's sweet scent drove his plans into the stratosphere.

Taking her lips in a ravaging kiss Rafe swept his tongue into her mouth exploring ruthlessly, taking her taste into him. As he did so he lifted her so he could grind his hard cock against her center, the need to possess her consumed him.

She tore her mouth from his gasping for air and mumbled, "Need to capture," she gasped, "father."

Huh – her father? Here he was about to explode in his pants and she was thinking about her scumbag father?

"What about your father?" he muttered before capturing her mouth again. Pleased as she angled her head so he could deepen his kiss. Her hands clenched at his shoulders, sharp little nails piecing his skin, his wolf rumbled in pleasure at her scratching his skin.

Dropping her had back out of his reach she gasped for air. He took the opportunity to suckle on her exposed throat, marking her creamy skin.

Hmm better, he reveled in her abandoned response.

Gasping she continued, "Use me for bait to catch my father." With her eyes closed as she savored the sweet sensations coursing through her, it took a moment to realize Rafe had stopped suckling her throat and wasn't moving at all. Opening her eyes, she saw his eyes had changed from dark chocolate to hard uncompromising gold.

Slowly releasing her, he ensured she had her balance before moving his hands to her hips holding her still, waiting until the fog of desire cleared.

"No."

"That's it? Just 'No,' she deepened her voice to imitate his. "What about – 'I don't want to do that, but let me hear your idea Regan before I make up my mind,'" she glared up at him.

“OK – let’s hear your idea, then I’ll say, no,” his arms crossed uncompromisingly across his chest, his face closed.

Regan narrowed her eyes at him. If she didn’t need his help with her father she’d just give up now and walk out without even trying. A more closed off response she had never seen. But if she was going to help Ben she needed to stay here, and she couldn’t stay here when her father could track her through his familial bond with her. Pity that bond didn’t work both ways. If she could track the fucker, she wouldn’t need Rafe’s help. If her father found Eden’s Retreat, he’d sell them out to *Titan* before the day’s end. How Rafe could be blind to that danger bewildered her. Licking her lips, she began listing off the facts as she saw them.

“OK bear with me here,” she held up her hand signaling for patience. At his nod, “Here’s how I see it. A) My father is spotting shifters for *Titan*, who then with his help, captures, hunts and kills them. Without the help of my father, *Titan* will not be able to find shifters to hunt.

B) My father has a paternal bond with me, which allows him to find me no matter where I hide.”

She waited for his nod of agreement before continuing. “C) My father will eventually find me here. Once here, he will realize he has found a shifter compound and he’ll be able to pick them off one at a time to hand over to *Titan*.” As he opened his mouth to argue the point, she quickly continued so he'd have to talk over the top of her.

"D) You've been trying for weeks to get a toe hold into *Titan* or a lead on my father and have come up with nothing yet." His mouth tightened at that, but he refrained from butting in.

"E) Time is running out, because my father could turn up here any time. I'm fully recovered from our last encounter and so, no doubt is he. He's out there looking for me right now, coming ever closer to here.

F) If you don't capture him and someone from here is taken, it will be my fault for staying instead of moving like I always have before." She pleaded, "I couldn't bear it if someone was murdered because I stayed here too long. What are you going to do if he tells *Titan* where Eden's Retreat is? Can you protect everyone? Can you ensure everyone's safety when they leave here to go to work or go shopping?"

The haunted look in her eyes drew a groan from Rafe as he ran his hands through his hair in frustration. "Regan you are not saying anything I haven't thought of," he stalked away from her. "Why do you think I've run my Sentinels into the ground trying to find these people?" He scowled over his shoulder at her, "But to ask me to use you as bait," he shrugged helplessly as he turned to face her. "I can't. It goes against everything I am."

She couldn't understand that as his mate his overriding primal instinct was to see to her wellbeing and happiness. To put her in danger deliberately, was abhorrent to him. He fought to exert control over his wolf; its repugnance at the possibility of putting their mate in harm's way was straining his ability to control his animal.

His wolf wanted to cover his mate and dominate her into submission, but Rafe had enough reason left to know that their woman would not yield to such domination. She would want equal status; she was looking for a partner in all things, not a master. Having witnessed her mother's subjugation to her father would make it intolerable for Regan to submit in such a way to him. Her founding character had been formed in hell, she would associate any form of domination in their relationship to her brutal father. But to expect him to deliberately place her in danger, neither he nor his wolf could tolerate it.

"Regan – I can't place you in jeopardy. Ask anything else of me but not that," he demanded.

Regan studied his face. He truly looked tormented at the thought of her in danger. It warmed her to think he cared deeply for her, where no other did. But she couldn't live with herself if someone was taken because she hid like a coward behind these walls.

"Rafe, I can't stay here if my father is on the loose. How

could I live with myself if someone was killed because I led *Titan* here?" she implored for his understanding.

"You think I can't protect you?" he snarled, offended to his very core.

Palms up in a placating gesture, "You're not listening. I trust you to keep me safe. That's why I offered to use myself as bait. I trust you *that* much." Seeing he'd settled somewhat, she continued, "I know by now you've learned all you can about my father and in doing so you've looked into my past. You know of my childhood and my trust issues."

She raised her chin defiantly; knowing his people had dug through her past was a violation. On one level, she understood why they had done it but it was still a violation, she hated that they knew of her past, it made her feel exposed. They needed to know their enemy, to find any weakness; unfortunately, she meant nothing to her father and couldn't be used against him. Regrettably, knowing they knew her past increased her discomfort around the Sentinels. Who wanted to be around people who knew the humiliation of her childhood, of her agony and isolation after her mother's murder, her failure to cope? They had poked and pried open everything she wanted buried in the dark.

Rafe walked back to her when he recognized the humiliation haunting her now downcast eyes. He cupped the side of her face, drawing her eyes to his, "You know we investigated you?" he softly asked. His heart turned over as he read her discomfiture, what he didn't see was resentment, which was what he thought he'd have to deal with when she realized they had dug through her past. "I don't know if this makes it any easier, but the only people who know of your childhood are Jordan, as he did the research and Kylie, as a trusted friend and doctor. I asked her advice on how to help you fit in here."

A slew of emotions attacked Regan at that revelation: relief that they all didn't know, acceptance of Jordan, he always met her gaze head on and treated her as he did everyone else. He was warmly welcoming of her and ate at her table regularly; he always stopped to chat if they met in passing. Jordan's love of life was contagious, after talking with him, she always felt lighter, more optimistic. She couldn't find it in herself to resent him.

Opposite to that reaction, was her response to Kylie; the doctor treated her with cool remoteness and Regan's hackles rose whenever the woman came near her. Why Kylie affected her in such a way, she didn't understand, but the thought of Rafe sitting down and having a lovely old chat about how poor Regan was abused as a child stuck in her craw. Kylie would now know how weak she had been as a child, Rafe had told Kylie how Regan's beautiful mother had died while Regan watched, and it felt like the deepest of betrayals.

She'd believed she could trust him but for him to talk to that woman and reveal Regan's soft underbelly was nauseating, it triggered her temper. Animosity boiled out of her. Uncontrollable, the seething force making her shake as she jerked away from him. "If you're going to tell *her* why not everyone?" she snarled.

Rafe narrowed his eyes as he studied her. Now this was the reaction he had expected when she found out they had invaded her privacy, but why this antagonism over Kylie knowing her past, and not him and Jordan? Watching her, he realized it wasn't just antagonism, her eyes blazed with feral rage and betrayal. His mate felt he had betrayed her and it made his chest ache. He rubbed at it absently as he listened to his inner wolf that'd gone from crazed at the thought of placing her in danger, to silence at the scent of her pain bleeding through the anger and betrayal. How to comfort her? The scent of her pain was intolerable to both of them.

Trying to reassure her he explained, "Kylie wouldn't tell anyone else, if that's concerning you." Her look of resentment told him that wasn't the problem. He tried again "Kylie is a wonderful person; she's been my friend since grade school. I trust her implicitly. She would never want to hurt you."

Her face went red as she stopped pacing to glare at him as if he was an imbecile. He didn't need his wolf's senses to realize he was fucking up here. Every time he opened his mouth, his mate's fury increased. She now looked like she was going to explode, the only relief was that the scent of pain was gone, just rage and betrayal now. Yep, he was doing a bang up job here. Where was his wolf's intuition when he needed it? He ran both hands through his hair in frustration at his ineptitude.

"That's fantastic, I'm happy for you and Kylie. Nothing like having a great *friend* like that," Rafe winced at the derision dripping from her voice.

It was the emphasis on *friend* that finally gave him a hint. He lifted his nose and drew in deeply and there it was, mixed into the rage – jealousy. His mate was jealous of Kylie, and felt betrayed that he'd discussed the most private degrading details of her life with a perceived rival. Relief she cared enough for him to feel jealous warred with caution over how to fix this. The misplaced jealously didn't negate the betrayal she was feeling.

"Regan, Kylie is a friend – nothing more. We have never had a physical relationship."

"You owe me no explanations," her voice was wooden as she tried to reign in her emotions.

"I do, I want to have a relationship with you. I don't want you misunderstanding my friendship with Kylie. Your sense of betrayal is so strong it is hurting me. How you can tolerate it without screaming is beyond me."

"Pain is life, my fault for opening myself up to the hurt." Her sharp laugh grated his senses. "You'd think I'd know better," still she wouldn't look at him; instead, she focused on the door obviously wishing to leave.

Rafe knew she was pulling away from him; she was closing herself off from him. He took her hand in his, rubbing it, "It's true that caring for someone can cause pain, but if you choose carefully the joy far outweighs the pain." He squeezed her hand gently, "In this case the cause of your pain was a misunderstanding, and you felt I'd betrayed you to a rival, but it wasn't like that. And in the future I will be careful around Kylie until you truly come to believe there is nothing between us but a platonic friendship." He ducked his head down so he could meet her eyes "You can trust me Regan; I would never deliberately hurt you."

Rafe held his breath as he waited. She was so fragile emotionally, would she let him in? Take a chance? He subtly moved his body closer offering his heat, his protection, his shear body mass to stand between her and the world.

"I'm struggling here Rafe." She glanced up before looking away again. "Half of me wants to run. My brain is saying go, but something inside is stronger and wants to stay to see what happens. But don't rely on me staying. I'm trying to change and let people in, but it is not easy changing the behavior of a lifetime. To be brutally honest, it's an uncomfortable wretched process and I'm not sure if it's worth putting myself through this."

Rafe puffed out a breath, thank heaven for the mating bond. Admittedly, the influence of the mating helped hold her here, but his brave little mate was battling her ghosts and fighting her way towards him. His relief sank again when he thought of the devastation she'd feel when she discovered it was his decision to leave her with her abusive father. That same decision had led to her mother's death. It could all be laid at his feet. Would his emotionally fragile mate be able to come to terms with that betrayal, when just the thought of him and Kylie being together was enough to make her want to run? He desperately needed more time to build her trust and strengthen her bond with him. So when he revealed his betrayal their bond would stretch but it wouldn't break.

She tucked a stand of hair that had come loose from her long ponytail as she met his gaze "But Rafe I can't stay if I'm endangering the people living here. We have to catch my father. You have to use me."

Grimacing he ran his hands back through his already disheveled hair in agitation, "You want me to place you in danger?"

Shrugging she replied, "You do so with Sentinels every day, some of them are women, so it shouldn't be so hard." She regarded him quizzically as she waited for his reply.

'Yes but none of them are my mate!' he wanted to shout. "They are trained warriors not a civilian." How could he explain endangering her went against his every instinct, without revealing they were mates?

Her clear blue eyes narrowed as she assessed him from head to toe. He watched with a sinking feeling as she mentally ran through different arguments. Nodding her head, as she obviously came to a decision, "OK, how about I go toe to toe with one of your Sentinels? If I win in weaponless combat, we work out a plan to draw my father out. If I lose you have more time to find him your way, before we revisit this discussion."

Oh yeah this was great, now he had to pick out a Sentinel to pound on her, so that he wouldn't have to risk placing her back in her father's brutal hands, boy was this his lucky day or what? He'd come in here hoping for a little hanky-panky, have a little fun with his mate, and warm her up towards him. How had they ended up with him picking someone out to fight her?

Regan watched as Rafe's eyes melted from gold, back to molten chocolate, he tilted his head to the side, assessing her as he slowly closed the distance between them, gently pulling her into the shelter of his body by placing his hands lightly on her hips. She closed her eyes as she breathed in his fresh, rainforest scent. Just for a moment, she would rest against his strength before continuing their argument.

She could literally feel her cat rise inside her as the temptation to arch her back and needle those spectacular peck muscles with her claws.... no. She meant nails. She had nails not claws; she shook her head at the mistake. She'd have to talk to someone about how much influence their inner animals had on their thinking. She'd thought that for females it was minimal until they met their mates, but maybe it varied from person to person. She'd think about it later, right now she intended to take a couple of minutes to snuggle up to this spectacular male. She felt like purring as she nuzzled her nose under the edge of his shirt where he hadn't buttoned it all the way to the top and rubbed her cheek along the firm muscle of his chest. His warm breath disturbed the sensitive hair at her nape as he leaned over her. "Hmm" she smoothed the sensitive pads of her fingers over his biceps. She could lose herself in the enticing pleasure.

What had they been discussing anyway? She jerked back out of his reach. "Nice try hot shot," she held her hand up warning him to stay back.

He grinned unabashed, "A wolf has to try. Putting his woman in harm's way," he shook his head "is just not right.

You don't understand what you are asking of me."

"I'm not your woman and I'm trying to give us a chance to be together. If my father isn't caught soon I have to leave here," she tried to suppress her frustration. Getting angry wasn't going to win Rafe over; she had to be logical.

"You're in a relationship with me, therefore you are my woman. And I'll get your father without using you as bait," he lifted his chin dogmatically.

Breathing deeply she reminded herself to stay calm, even if he was starting to piss her off. She'd let the "*You're in a relationship with me*" comment go for the moment, her father was the bigger issue here. "How many shifters could be hurt while you are searching for him? You can't lay that guilt at my door Rafe. Let me show you I can hold my own in a fight. I won't be a liability to your team."

"You've only just recovered from you last run in with your father. How can you expect to hold your own Regan? The man would have kidnapped you if I hadn't been there." Just as well, there was no condescension in his tone or she'd be tempted to take her frustration at his bullheadedness out on him.

His lack of faith in her ability to defend herself pinched at her pride. Hey, give her some credit there had been three of them that night. "Set up a match with one of your Sentinels Rafe. Then we will come back to this conversation. Get someone down here now. Once you see for yourself I can hold my own maybe we can get on with catching my father."

Frustrated that she was persisting with this Rafe grabbed the radio off his belt and called Chris. Chris was a massive man, over 6' 5" with hard muscles from years of training. His biceps were the size of Regan's thighs, his chest so thick Regan would have a hard time putting her arms around him, but for all his size, he was still lethally fast. His sheer size would allow him to overpower Regan quickly and put an end to this. Once Regan realized how quickly she could be trounced, maybe she would leave off this notion of using herself as bait. Walking from the room, he filled Chris in on the situation as the large shifter made his way down to the gym.

"So you've got trouble with your woman already," the big man grinned at Rafe as he walked up to where Rafe was waiting outside the gym. The Sentinel had dark brown hair that faded to a lighter caramel color at the ends, even though it didn't go past the collar of his shirt. His sherry brown eyes held laughter as he gazed down at Rafe, his broad features gave him a handsome ruggedness, the look enhanced by the perpetual five o'clock shadow along his square jaw line.

Clapping Rafe on the shoulder his voice rumbled from his deep chest, "Come on let's get this show on the road."

Grabbing hold of the big man's forearm as Chris went to

enter the gym, Rafe warned him "Subdue her as quickly as you can but if you hurt her you'll be answering to me."

Chris couldn't help but laugh. He'd never seen his boss in such a lather, and all over a mate nature had ensured could never walk away from him. "Man just tell the woman no." He faced his friend still unable to wipe the smile off his face, "Here follow me, we'll practice together before you go back in there." Enouncing the words slowly he encouraged Rafe to join in with a wave of his hand, "No Regan you cannot help capture your father." He grinned at Rafe, "See that wasn't so hard was it?"

Gritting his teeth Rafe growled at the clown, "I can't wait until you find your mate. Just get in there and do as I've asked, will ya?"

CHAPTER 10

Regan nearly laughed as the behemoth Rafe had selected to fight her ducked his head to enter the room. For God's sake, the man nearly had to turn sideways, his shoulders where that wide. "What the hell are you?"

He grinned wickedly showing off a great set of white teeth, but she noticed that the lines caused from laughter were much deeper than the frown lines on his face, indicating he found fun in most situations. She guessed his was in his late 30's, a man in the prime of his life. As he moved towards her, she could see he was at ease with his hulking size and had an innate sense of balance. "Grizzly bear," he held his hand out "Chris York at your service."

Rafe watched Regan take Chris' measure as she shook his hand, she didn't seem at all worried about his size. Dressed in black cammo pants, shit kicker boots, and a grey T Shirt that stretched across his massive shoulders, he towered over her. Most people found him intimidating but Regan seemed oblivious. Chris and Rafe had been friends since childhood and both had joined the Sentinels together. If Rafe had to trust his mate's delicate body to anyone, it was Chris. He was immensely strong but was always in total control, knowing how much harm he could unintentionally cause.

Regan assessed the reach Chris would have during the fight with those long arms and heaven help her if he got in an unimpeded strike to her head with one of those hams he called a hand, it would be lights out for her. Although an experienced fighter, he would still be slower and less maneuverable than she would. He'd also tire quicker than she would; he was all about brute force while she was all about speed and endurance.

Regan indicated the sparing area, "Shall we, Fozzie Bear?" her lips kicked up as his eyes narrowed at the Muppet reference.

With a good-natured wink, Chris replied, "Yeah, why not. I promised the guys I'd be back within five minutes," he ribbed. Regan's lips quirked up as she read the humor he found in the situation in his gleaming eyes.

Chris had to admit he found it comic watching Rafe twitching at the thought of his mate being hurt. The man was in a bad way and the fight hadn't even started yet. He loved seeing his usually unflappable friend about to have a tizzy fit because his girl might sustain a bruise.

Regan smiled back at him from the center of the mat as he moved to join her after removing his boots, “I’ll see if I can accommodate you.”

Chris’ eyes widened as she struck out swiping his feet out from under him while he was still walking towards her. Before he could register her move, he found himself dumped on his ass. Regan stepped back out of reach and watched as Chris gave Rafe a “What the fuck?” type of look as he sprang agilely back to his feet.

“OK hot stuff; try that again, now I’m ready.”

Trying to look put upon, Regan rolled her eyes and sighed, “Ready?” But seriously, it was hard to keep the smile off her face, it had been ages since she’d sparred with someone who had skill and she assumed Rafe had selected one of his more skilled Sentinels in the hopes of taking her out quickly. Before Chris could counter more than two of her attacks, he found himself flat on his ass, again.

“Tricky female,” he grumbled has he jumped back up. With a come here wave of his hand, he let Regan come at him again.

This time it was more of a contest. Regan couldn’t use surprise on him, but although he was stronger and had a greater reach, this was what Regan had trained for all her life. She was always going to be smaller and lighter, therefore she had to be faster, more subtle, and able to flex her body to maneuver out of reach, and her strikes had to be timed to deliver the most power. She simply did not have the brute strength of her opponents. Her other advantage was her father had started her training as soon as she could walk. While Chris was off playing with his friends, Regan was doing drills with brutal punishments from her father if she failed to please him. Her tolerance of pain had begun in childhood and her father had kept pushing her through all boundaries. She could take punches and kicks without breaking her concentration or veering from her own attack. So unless something was broken, she'd fight through pain that would cause others to falter.

Chris was fascinated, he was no longer pulling his punches, but few landed on Regan and those that did slid off as she moved with the punch. She was fluid, seemingly always to slide away at the last instant so his punches glanced off her, causing no real damage. She however, seemed to land endless blows on him, his lip was split, one eye was in the process of closing up and if she jabbed him in the kidneys one more time he'd be roaring with frustrated pain.

He rushed her swinging his elbow as he passed, aiming for her temple in an attempt to stun her, again she arched back with inhuman agility maintaining her balance, then as he passed she used his own momentum against him and swept his right foot out from under him just as he put his weight on it. Before he could regain his balance, she pivoted and snatched his left foot up causing him to face plant the floor. Rather than spinning into retreat as before, she unexpectedly landed on his back with her knees driving him to the floor. Before he could fling her off, she wrapped her right arm across his forehead and used her left to push at his jaw in the opposite direction, in that position she could snap his neck.

“Enough?” she panted to Rafe.

At his nod, she leapt back and away from Chris. Rafe’s pride knew no bounds. His mate was a fighter, not only a fighter but also a fuck’n fantastic fighter. She moved like the panther she was, all sinew and grace, flexibility and power. Striking with speed and lethal mastery, only to leap back out of reach, constantly in movement, she never provided a stationary target. My God she was magnificent and she was all his.

Panting for air, Regan watched as Christ surged to his feet, some men didn’t react well to losing to a woman. But the broad smile on his face showed no hard feelings.

“Now that was just plain mean spirited of you, to show me up in front of the boss like that.” He wiped his arm across his face, removing the sweat tracking down his forehead. He used the sleeve of his T shirt to dab the blood from his lip, although it was already healing with the help of his shifter metabolism. He huffed out a rough laugh, “Tricky female, you paid me back for that five minute comment didn't you?"

Regan couldn't help the cheeky smile that spread across her face, unknowingly lighting up her features and arresting both men with her exquisite beauty. Rafe's soft growl caused Chris to start. "You can't blame a guy for looking," he shrugged at his friend helplessly.

Regan, catching the byplay tipped her head back and laughed. It was spontaneous and felt wonderful, she felt vibrant with life, endorphins giving her a natural high. A secret part of her was flattered by their attention, what girl wouldn't relish admiration from these two prime males?

"OK hot stuff, what military group trained you? You sure as hell didn't learn how to fight like that at a local martial arts class or kick boxing studio," Chris gave her an affectionate hug, and kindly pretended not to notice her flinching away from him or Rafe glaring at him.

Losing some of her euphoria from the match, she looked at Rafe, "No military training, mostly my father when I was a kid. Then I augmented what he taught by studying any kind of combat I could find time for since then." Shrugging self-consciously, "I'm an apt pupil and seem to pick up techniques quickly. I've worked hard to ensure if I ever met my father again I would not be a victim."

Sighing in defeat Rafe nodded at her, "OK we'll work something out. Why don't you go shower, then meet me in my office in half an hour?"

Rafe nodded to Ben who was standing just inside the door as he and Chris left together, he was aware the boy had shown up during the match. He noted as he left that the kid had finally started putting on some weight, he was all sinewy muscle and if Regan was training him to fight as he assumed, the kid was going to shock anyone stupid enough to take him on. About as much as he and Christ had just been, his lips quirked as he remembered the look on Chris' face the first time he'd hit the mat, no doubt his own face had looked just as ridiculous.

"Laugh it up wolf boy," Chris nudged him with his shoulder containing his own laughter as they ambled down the corridor. "That's your woman," he hitched his thumb back towards the gym, "most of us only have to worry about a pot beaming us in the head when we anger our mates. Yours can take you out with her bare hands without raising a sweat and you won't even see it coming."

Rafe grimaced at the thought.

"Yeah, not so funny now is it Mr. Chuckles."

~~~

"That was awesome!" Ben enthused when the two Sentinels left. Regan smiled as Ben bounced on his toes full of zeal. "I can't believe you took Chris out! He's one of our best
~~~

fighters. No one ever beats him in the ring and you did it."

"He wasn't trying to kill me or permanently incapacitate me, so he had to hold back. In a real fight I'd be lucky to hold my own," she cautioned.

"Yeah but you were holding back too. You didn't hurt him either."

Regan laughed at his loyalty, hugging him tightly to her, her heart warmed when he hugged her back. They were both coming along when it came to touching and being touched. There was hope for them. They would never be as open as other shifters, but they didn't have to be as neurotic as they had been either.

"I'm so going to flog Peter's ass!" Ben exclaimed as he leaped, punching his fist into the air. Regan could see the belief in him now. Before he'd been going through the motions but his self-belief had been absent. Now he'd witnessed a smaller opponent take down a larger one. Her impromptu battle with Chris was bearing more fruit than she'd anticipated.

Smiling at his enthusiasm, she instructed him, "OK scamp – muster all that energy for your circuit. This afternoon I won't be here to watch you, so use the mirrors to make sure your technique is correct. You can do the same one that we did this morning since that's fresh in your mind. If you're unsure, drop it out of the circuit. I don't want you picking up bad habits. After you've done the circuit three times, hit the treadmill. Do five miles. I should be back by then. Any questions?"

"Nope, I'm all good. If you don't make it back by the time I finish, I've got homework to do until you return." He held his hand up for a high five, which she slapped as she walked past him to leave the gym.

Thirty minutes to the second, Regan tapped on Rafe's office door. Rafe opened it and it took Regan no small effort to drag her eyes away from his ruggedly handsome features and acknowledge Chris and Jordan, both were lazing at opposite ends of the large lounge pushed up against the far wall. The office was as big as Regan's living and kitchen area combined, the wall Chris and Jordan sat against had a bank of windows allowing natural light in.

As Regan entered the large airy office, she had the choice of the other lounge, placed along the wall to the right of the door, or moving one of the plush chairs sitting in front of Rafe's desk on the left. Rafe obviously wasn't into clutter. His mahogany desk had his computer and a closed file on it. His filing cabinets were all closed, his bookshelves all stacked neatly, even his garbage bin was empty. Regan's lips quirked, *"OCD or what?"* she thought as she sat in the corner of the lounge at the end closest to Jordan and Chris.

Her humor fled when Rafe sat next to her, his hard thigh

rubbing against her as he settled back into the plush leather. His broad shoulder caused her to lean away from him or have her mind scrambled, as her body started heating up in response to his proximity.

"Are you right there?" she muttered at him sarcastically.

Chris didn't even try to hide his snicker, as Rafe in the process of resettling himself managed to take up the small space Regan had created between them by wedging herself into the corner.

Rafe turned innocent eyes on her, "Just fine, and you?" he asked politely.

"Well since you asked, I'm a little squashed here," she waved her hand at the space on the other side of him, and then leaned awkwardly against the arm of the couch.

"Well move over here then, no need to hide in the corner," he reached his arm around her and pulled her up against his side, the warmth of his big body wrapping around her immediately. His hand rested casually on her ribs; if he moved his thumb at all, it would brush against the underside of her breast. How was she supposed to concentrate when she was surrounded in his masculine warmth? Her heart started its pounding reaction to his nearness. Anticipation rolled through her. Now that she was in his presence, she wanted nothing more than to snuggle into his large body and lose herself in the powerful arousal that flared between them.

"So Regan, what ideas do you have on how to draw your father out?"

Jordan's question pulled her partially out of the web of arousal she was snared in. Clearing her throat, she tried to collect her thoughts, "Well, it would be best if I moved back into my house and tried to draw him there rather than here. We don't want him discovering Eden's Retreat." She felt Rafe stiffen in rejection of the idea. "Hold on Rafe, I'm not saying I'd go there unprotected. We can work out security for me. I selected that house because it's easy to defend, and with the forest right out the back door, there are many escape routes if necessary. If we set this up right we can capture him and find out who's behind *Titan*, and you can put a stop to the hunting."

Rafe surged to his feet rubbing his hands through his hair in agitation as he thought of all the things that could go wrong, one horrific scenario after another tormenting him as he paced around his office.

"Rafe you have to pull back and look at this logically," Jordan pulled his attention back to the people watching him, Chris and Jordan with a certain level of sympathy for his position, Regan he saw had no understanding of what she was asking of him.

He watched as Regan glanced at Jordan in surprise. She'd obviously assumed she would have to convince all three males to use her to draw her father out.

"We don't have a solid lead on this organization," Jordan continued. "We've got every available Sentinel chasing ghosts. We've been searching for months and we have nothing. This is the first opportunity we've had to find out who is behind these attacks. We just need to find a way to do it that keeps Regan safe."

"That's just it," Rafe huffed in frustration "how can we guarantee Regan's safety? These bastards are professional or we'd have found them already."

"No one is infallible Rafe; trust us to guard your m... muffin here." Jordan flashed Regan a quick smile.

Regan raised her brows at Jordan "Muffin?" she mouthed back at him, and then mimicked hanging herself.

Chris who'd been watching everyone from his sprawled corner of the lounge tipped his head back and laughed, "Oh girl, you've just earned yourself a new nick name. Never react like that around shifters, we can't help but toy with someone who reacts like that."

"Great," she rolled her eyes in disgust, just what she wanted a bunch of fun loving shifters calling her muffin. She had no doubt that she'd be hearing it an awful lot by the laugher gleaming in Chris' brown eyes.

Rafe sat back down next to Regan; putting his frustration on the back burner; he was pleased to see Chris and Jordan's acceptance of Regan. He felt his optimism rising, maybe she would want to settle at Eden's Retreat. Her barriers weren't as high as they had been when she'd first arrived. She was still reserved for a shifter, but for Regan she was as open and as interactive as he'd ever seen her. Her body language was open, her face lit with amusement as she responded to Chris' teasing. Even more importantly, his wolf could sense her happiness at being teased, and made to feel a part of the group. It showed him the resilience of his little mate, here they were discussing using her to trap her father, yet she found joy in the moment instead of fear. Instead of retreating further behind her barriers, she was stepping out from behind them.

Tipping her chin up at a haughty angle, she retorted, "Apparently I'm a noble, powerful, panther. Muffin seems vastly inappropriate for such an elegant creature."

"Regan – be quiet." Jordan shook his head at her, happy to see the little cat at ease amongst them. Knowing her background, he understood how hard it was for her to relax in their company enough to play with them. Over the last weeks, he'd made sure to take time out of his schedule to spend with her. It had taken patience to move her to the stage where she wasn't constantly scanning for attack while he distracted her. At first, she obviously couldn't attribute any other reason to his wanting to talk with her.

He wanted his friend's mating to run as smoothly as possible, considering Regan's background. He figured the happier Regan was at Eden's Retreat, the more open she'd be to staying here and mating Rafe. He'd grown to like and respect Regan, she'd gone through hell, and wasn't bitter or angry, just very gun shy of people, and hey who wouldn't be after her childhood?

He realized the community in general would see her standoffish behavior as rejection of them, and in turn wouldn't continue to try and befriend her. But, they didn't know what her childhood had been like, how cut off and isolated she'd been. His heart had bled for the little girl she had been, during his investigation of her past. His admiration for her ability to function at all knew no bounds, for a shifter to be cut off from their own kind as she had been, was the equivalent to a human losing their sense of wonder in the world. She would have felt as if some part of her was dying, but have no understanding of why.

Now when she saw him walking towards her, there was warmth and pleasure in her eyes not wariness. She no longer held a defensive position, although she still constantly scanned her surroundings, no doubt, she would still be doing so when her hair was grey and she was watching her grandchildren play.

Leaning back, he stretched his jean-clad legs out straight, his amber bright eyes studying Rafe. Jordan figured if he could make progress with Regan he had no doubt Rafe could, although he didn't envy his friend the task of taming Regan's panther. Surely, she would give Rafe's wolf a run for his money. That part of the courtship was going to be fun to watch. Before Regan was finished with him, Rafe's wolf wouldn't know which way was up, the thought brought a crooked smile to his lips.

"The more you protest, the longer he will continue to call you muffin, and the more he will encourage others to do so."

Regan rolled her eyes at the two lethal men grinning back at her. Jordan with his vibrant red hair, and Chris with his shaggy bleached brown hair towered over Jordan, even with both of them slouched in opposite corners of the lounge. She'd have to find something Chris hated just as much and make sure to call him by it at every opportunity. "Remember pay back's a bitch," she warned.

"Oooh," Chris mock shuddered as he turned to Jordan "the little panther is starting to show her itty bitty claws."

"Hey, I wouldn't piss her off too much. From what you told me, the itty bitty pussy cat dropped you on your ass no less than three times."

Chris rubbed the side of his nose closest to Jordan with his middle finger raised in response to the gibe.

"Hmm, speaking of fighting, how are we going to catch daddy dearest?" Regan asked, bringing them back to point.

The three men started tossing ideas out, pointing out weaknesses in different scenarios. Regan was relieved to see Rafe was wholly on board now, although she noted he was shooting down some good ideas his Sentinels were proposing. He was trying to come up with something, so she sat back and tossed in anything she thought might help.

After hours of planning, counter planning, and numerous pots of coffee, it was agreed.

Regan would stay at Eden's Retreat during the days where she would be safest. At night, she would return to her house. Two Sentinels would shadow her home in case someone started following her and to ensure her safety if they tried to abduct her out on the street. Another Sentinel would be dispatched to her house now; they would scout the surrounding area before entering the house to ensure no one was waiting to ambush her. The three Sentinels would then retreat and set up watch on the house. Someone would guard the house 24/7 from now on.

Chris would drive Regan to the house and back, staying overnight with her to provide extra security. He would also ensure no one followed them to Eden's Retreat in the mornings; the last thing they wanted was to lead the enemy to Eden's Retreat.

They hoped her father would attack her at her home, where there were the least variables and they had a higher chance of capturing her attackers for questioning.

Regan was also informed during the meeting that the Sentinels had found listening devices in her house, and had decided to leave them in place so they could be used to provide misinformation. Regan would need to be vigilant regarding her conversations with Chris conscious not to give out information that would help her father or *Titan*.

With their plans set, the meeting broke up. Rafe walked alongside Regan as she headed back to the gym and Ben. As always, the heat of arousal pulsed with every beat of Regan's heart when Rafe was near. Boy he made it hard to think when he was around. "I need a job here at Eden's Retreat." She blurted out trying to break the sexual enthrallment surging between them. Rafe threw her an amused glance, but played along.

"What did you have in mind?"

Rubbing her hands up and down her arms, trying to rub away the prickling awareness, "I was thinking of some type of gardening or grounds work. I like the outdoors."

Rafe tipped his head considering, he could see the solitude of the work would appeal to her, but he thought her mind spun too quickly to be satisfied.

"You sure? After your demonstration today, I was wondering if you'd take on some sort of roll in teaching self-defense. Obviously, I haven't thought the idea through but I was thinking along the lines of training kids to start with, and then opening it up to adults. I know in the past you've volunteered at women's shelters and trained women in self-defense, so I assume you find satisfaction in the work." Rafe hid his disappointment when she shook her head immediately in refusal at the idea. Did she not want that sort of commitment to the community? It was easy to walk away from a gardening job, not so easy to disappoint people who love your class, especially the kids. "You sure? Ben seems to be benefiting from the training you're doing with him. It's easy to see he has put on muscle and grown in confidence since you've taken him under your wing."

She tipped her head considering his idea before giving a firm shake, "No, I'd prefer to just work with Ben for now. I'd also appreciate it if you wouldn't mention to anyone that Ben's training with me."

He lifted his brow at that request. At his questioning look, Regan debated telling him of Ben's troubles and asking for Rafe's silence and non-interference until Ben had a chance to solve the problem of the bullying himself. Did she believe in Rafe's integrity, that if he promised his silence he would maintain it? She didn't think Rafe would have a problem with Ben sorting out Peter using force. He was a wolf after all; he'd understand that if Ben didn't stand up for himself, he'd never have the respect of his peers. So it came down to, did she believe he would keep his word and keep silent? Huh... surprisingly enough she believed he would. What do you know, she trusted him in this.

Wow aren't I coming along in leaps and bounds. She'd formed a tentative friendship with Jordan and Steph and then there was Jen, she wanted to care for and protect Ben and now not only did she lust after Rafe, she trusted him. She hardly recognized herself these days. She still found herself craving the solitude of her former life, yes it was isolated and she often felt lonely and desolate but there was comfort in those feelings too. It felt normal to her and there was assurance in knowing what each day would bring; now this involvement with others made her feel indecisive, uncertain, and anxious - it was stressful. She found it hard not to focus on these negative feelings when she was alone and talk herself into leaving. If she left, she wouldn't have to deal with all these emotions and see how inadequate and lacking she was.

When she watched other shifters meeting she saw the joy they felt seeing each other and the comfort they gained from touching. When she met up with Jordan or Steph, she did feel a small amount of anticipation and joy, but she still felt uncertain and anxiousness when talking with them, she was sure she would say something wrong and they'd give up on her. She overanalyzed the conversations and what she'd said, it was exhausting.

But she wasn't a coward, yes she was uncomfortable here, facing her inadequacies, but she would not walk away from Ben. She would improve herself and her people skills so she could model appropriate behavior for him. She didn't kid herself into thinking she would ever be gregarious, but she could be more than an introverted hermit.

Continuing with her resolution not to be a coward, she wouldn't run from the storm of feelings Rafe aroused in her either. Yes it was frightening to feel the rip tide of passion Rafe caused, when she'd never felt even a twinge of awareness prior to meeting him. Once again, she refused to run, she might be singed from the explosive passion between them, but having never felt sexual awareness before, she wasn't willing to walk away, as she might never feel this way again. She didn't want to look back later with regrets, she would experience all there was to be had between them. And, if she was being truthful with herself, unless she ran away from Eden's Retreat and cut all contact with Rafe, she was going to end up in bed with the man anyway, why fight the inevitable? She lost all common sense around him; the urgency was undeniable.

Rafe walked patiently beside her, not pressing for a response to his unasked question about why she didn't want anyone to know she was training Ben. But when she started to explain about Ben being bullied and generally ostracized by the other kids, he was fascinated to hear the protectiveness in her voice. There was more here than someone trying to correct an injustice. Regan was emotionally bonded to Ben. His wolf could sense her connection to the boy. If his mate was forming a familial link to Ben, it would explain why his wolf had taken such an interest in the young man. His wolf had already sensed that Regan was bonding to Ben, that the boy would be an integral part of their family, and would be coming under his care.

If he were in wolf form, he would be wagging his tail in delight. His little mate's heart wasn't totally frozen, it had melted enough to take a misfit under her wing and to champion his cause. If she took Ben fully into her heart, she would be a fierce defender of his rights. Ben's life was changing for the better and it was because Regan had entered it. He hoped that when she found out about his abandoning her as a child that she wouldn't run, that she would stay and fight with him. Yes, he deserved her condemnation but he hoped she would eventually forgive him. He would carry his guilt and remorse to his grave, but he was a selfish bastard and wanted Regan in his life and her forgiveness.

When they entered the gym, there was no sign of Ben. Regan crossed the floor and picked up the jumper she had left there earlier. Rafe, who'd been following close behind her still wrapped in his thoughts, didn't realize she was going to stop until his erection that he was never without these days pushed up against Regan's round plush bottom, causing Regan to lose her balance. She put her hand out on the weights bench in front of her to stop herself from tipping over.

Rafe looked down at his mate bent over at the waist, bottom up in the air and hands flat on the low bench for balance. As she went to stand back up, she pushed back and rubbed against the erection pushing painfully at his zipper. He couldn't help himself as he grabbed her hips and rubbed her softness against the aching ridge of his erection. Bending his knees slightly he made sure his shaft slid between the cheeks of her ass and groaned as she pushed back against him adding a gentle twist to her hips.

He couldn't wait any longer.

CHAPTER 11

Her arousal, as instant as his, they were like a match to petrol, explosive in each other's company. The need to claim her and make her his, was overwhelming. She belonged to him; he had to have her now, it was impossible to stay still, the need to grind against her compulsive.

He urged her forward and bent her over the weight bench, the vulnerable position left her bent over on all fours, but with the bench under her stomach, her bottom was up in the air and very available to him. Going down behind her, he laid his weight across her back, holding her in place as he nuzzled the hair away from her sensitive neck, and scraped his teeth across the exposed skin.

"Turn your head to me," he growled. When she complied and turned her flushed face towards him, he reached over her and closed his mouth over hers in a claiming kiss. There was no room for gentleness; the need to posses overwhelmed his good intentions to woo her slowly.

He continued to grind his cock into her as he kissed her voraciously. It wasn't enough, as he continued his invasive kiss; he stripped her yoga pants and panties from her, and then nudged her knees apart to make room for him. He could feel her damp heat through his jeans and groaned into her mouth, but refused to release her. His tongue surged into her mouth, he moved one hand down between her legs and ran his rough hand over her labia, slick liquid met his palm as he rubbed her roughly with his open hand. Using his fingers, he separated her soft folds to find her entrance. He had enough sense left to stretch her somewhat before thrusting into her. He pushed one finger into her tight heat, rubbing her clitoris at the same time with the pad of his thumb. She pushed back at him trying for more penetration; he pushed and withdrew a time or two before withdrawing completely to enter her with two fingers. He used his free hand to pinch her clitoris, making her writhe against the seat. She'd thrust forward searching for more friction, before thrusting back seeking further penetration, silently demanding more of him.

Releasing her mouth, he clamped his teeth to her shoulder and used the weight of his chest to keep her in place; he removed his fingers from her warm clasp and dragged them across her lips.

"Lick them," he rumbled in her ear. He held them to her mouth, at the first instant, she was resistant, but then the scent of her own sex must have aroused her curiosity enough for a tentative lick. "Suck them," he growled, leaning forward and to the side so he could watch his fingers enter her mouth. After letting her sample her own erotic taste, he turned her head to sample the juices he'd smeared on her lips and cheek. He hummed his appreciation of her exquisite taste.

He released his erection from his jeans and pushed them down enough so they were out of his way. He came up over her again, settling his heavy body over her; he used one hand to pinch her stiffened nipple, the other he used to rub the purpled head of his cock through the silken folds of her pussy, gathering the slippery moisture of her arousal over the head and shaft of his erection.

He used her own honey to rub the sensitive nerves above her entrance; he had her writhing beneath him moaning her torment, unable to reach her climax without his help.

"Do you want me pretty Regan?"

She moaned her reply and tried to push back against his erection, which he now had lodged just inside her entrance holding her open, but leaving her hollow and wanting.

"Say it. Say you want me," he rasped, it took everything in him not to thrust into her.

"God yes!" she yelled. "I want you. I need you in me now," at her capitulation to him, he surged into her, straight through the barrier of her innocence. Pushing into untried muscles, once fully seated, he held still briefly, to allow her to adjust to the feeling of being penetrated. But, the urgency of the mating wouldn't allow him to hold still long, he rubbed her clit once, moved to gather more of her juices then rubbed again at her sensitive nub. At her tentative move in search of more, he dragged his erection out of her body then pushed back in; at the same time, he pinched the bundle of nerves hidden in her folds. She pushed back against him searching for more and he lost himself in the mating.

Heat blasted through him from his toes to his scalp. He pulled out, plunged back inside her clasping body, and lost it. He grasped her by the hips and thrust into her again and again, he couldn't get close enough, and he wanted to grind into her. He slammed into her, gritting his teeth, he could feel his climax boiling up through his balls, he rubbed her clit frantically, and then pulled her head back by her hair so he could claim her mouth in a ravaging kiss.

"Come for me," he growled against her soft lips and he felt her hot inner muscles grip his erection as her climax ripped through her. He released her mouth and tipped his head back to roar his own release. His body surged into hers and he pressed as deep as he could go. His lungs worked like bellows as he tried to regain his breath. He rested his lean body over hers, drained for the moment.

Regan collapsed back down on the bench and he settled himself onto her back. Gently he nuzzled her hair aside to rain gentle kisses along her neck; the ripples of climax ran through them as they slowly came down from their high.

He waited until she had recovered her breath, then began to gently stroke around her clit, not yet touching the over-sensitized bundle of nerves. He gathered some of their combined fluids from where they were still joined and rubbed them over her outer folds and around her nub. Turning her head, she looked at him in confusion.

"Again?" she asked.

"Again," he confirmed. "But this time gently, as I should have done for your first time. I should have taken my time to arouse you fully and taken you as tenderly as you deserved."

Her lips quirked into a smile as she looked at him over her shoulder, "Don't sweat it Rafe, I'll take what we just did any day of the week. I don't feel cheated, trust me."

"Hmm," he kissed her sweetly, and then ran his lips along her cheek, down to where her neck joined her shoulder and lightly nipped at her. "Let's try slow and easy, and then you can decide if you were cheated."

He dragged his erection out of her slowly until just the head was wedged in her opening, then slowly pushed back in with a roll of his hips and a gentle squeeze to her clitoris. He held deep inside her as he used his fingers to pluck open her outer labia, and then ran his fingers around the base of his erection that extruded from her body. He pulled back slightly, then surged gently back in, this time he used her pubic hair to tug at her lips.

"Bring your hand down and feel how I'm filling your body," he encouraged. "How your skin is stretched to accommodate me." He sucked in a sharp breath as she felt around their joined bodies. Her questing fingers then searched out his tight balls, squeezing gently, and then plucking at the rough hair causing him to surge into her further in reaction. Tingles shot up his spine.

"Straighten up and feel the difference inside you," he urged.

Her muscles clamped and released him as she raised herself up to rest the back of her head against his shoulder. Again, he rubbed his fingers through their combined juices and spread them over her nether lips. He held himself tight in her as she slowly rotated her hips, savoring the sensation of his hard shaft inside her untried body. The ripples of the muscular contractions of her vagina told him his little mate was enjoying herself. His balls tightened against his body, it was all he could do to hold still but this time was for Regan.

He ran his rough hands up her belly pulling her shirt up as he went, then off over her head. He then gently extracted her pert breast from the lace bra cup so it jutted out, held up in place by the lace underneath. He did the same with the other breast until they both were held up and out in an offering to his visual pleasure. He carefully pinched both nipples until they darkened to a deep berry color and hardened into tight little buds.

"Look into the mirror," he husked into her ear and watched her reflection as she opened her eyes to see herself kneeling there with her breasts thrust out and his hands rubbing across her flat stomach, then down into her pubic hair. He slowly drew her labia back so she could see them joined, see her flesh flushed, covered in their mingled fluids, and see how thin her skin was stretched around his wide erection that was lodged up into her body.

She moaned and undulated at the sight of their joined bodies. He rasped out of her, and then pushed back through her folds, not quite entering her so she could see the dark engorged head of his cock pushing out between them. He adjusted his angle and then slid back into her tight depths. Her avid gaze watched as he reentered her body, the whole time he held her wide open to their transfixed gazes. She moaned and writhed against him pushing back, jerking her hips as an orgasm washed over her. The clasping of her vagina caused his own release to course through him and he jetted his semen into her, helplessly thrusting again and again. As he regained his senses, he held her close to him until his softening erection slid from the warm clasp of her body.

Regan came back to her senses when she felt Rafe move away, the cool air on her overheated flesh caused her to shiver. She opened her eyes to see herself still kneeling on the floor in front of the bench, her hair tousled, her breasts still pushed out over the top of her bra cups, the nipples still pebble tight and flushed. Except for the bra, she was totally naked; in comparison, Rafe was once again fully dressed and buttoning up his jeans even as she watched. She realized he hadn't even bothered to undress before taking her from behind in the heat of their passion. Her unclothed state made her feel vulnerable and she quickly tucked her sensitive breasts back into their cups then dragged her T-shirt back on. She nearly jumped out of her skin when she felt Rafe's hand between her legs.

"Steady, I'm just cleaning you up," he husked in her ear.

She realized he was using his hanky to clean up the excess fluids seeping from her body. Embarrassment twisted her stomach, she might have been ready to have sex with Rafe, but she didn't know how to act, what to say, or even how she felt at the moment. She didn't know if she wanted to run from the room and collect herself in private or if she wanted him to fuss over her.

Regan tried to untangle her thoughts, leaving seemed the

best option. She hadn't expected sex to be so explosive. She felt overwhelmed; her emotions seemed to be blown wide open. She was close to crying and she didn't understand why. If she didn't get away from Rafe soon and calm herself down, she felt as if she was going to crack wide open and all the grief, crushing loneliness, betrayal, loss, and rage she'd experienced at her mother's death were going to come boiling out, shattering what remained of her soul. She struggled to breath, the weight on her chest was preventing her from getting enough air, she felt panic seeping in, if she lost control now she'd have a full blown panic attack, she hadn't had one of those in years. She was adept at locking down these feelings; she'd built strong walls to prevent this. Head down she dragged in blessed air, life-giving air. She concentrated on breathing the sweet air slowly, counting back from ten again and again, willing her heart to slow its racing.

On some level, she was aware of Rafe turning her and seating her on the bench. He was in the process of handing her panties to her when a voice swung all those volatile emotions Regan was barely controlling towards her. They morphed from grief and crushing loss into black rage. *What is she doing here?*

"So you took my advice and fucked her? Maybe you'll be able to get her out of your system now, as you hoped." The words were spoken as if the owner only had the mildest interest in the scene before her.

Rafe turned to face Kylie, fury pulling his mouth tight. *What the hell?* The Kylie he knew would never try to embarrass or humiliate someone as she was doing to Regan. There was no excuse for this. She knew Regan's past, how hard it was for her to trust and form connections with people. Kylie was deliberately trying to sabotage his relationship with Regan. She made it sound as if he and Kylie had sat down and cold bloodily talked about how he should go about seducing Regan, as if it was a game. It was cold and deliberately done to humiliate his mate.

Kylie raked her gaze over Regan sitting half naked behind Rafe who had moved to stand protectively in front of her. Kylie took a long look knowing the scene would be imprinted on her memory forever, Rafe staring at her in unforgiving anger. Regan, oh she wasn't detached now, rage burned in those blue eyes. So, she could feel emotion, she just chose not to. Neat trick, Kylie wished she had that ability. With one last look, she turned and left the couple.

CHAPTER 12

As she walked down the corridor, Kylie already regretted her harsh words, but she'd been blindsided when she'd walked into the room. She'd followed Rafe's scent there, but hadn't noticed Regan's scent was there too. She had been totally unprepared for the sight of Rafe tenderly seeing to Regan's comfort after having sex. Betrayal and jealousy had rammed into her and the venomous words poured out before she could sensor them. She'd known how to hurt Regan and hopefully, sever any feelings she'd formed for Rafe.

Head down with shoulders hunched, Kylie knew she had no right to her feelings of betrayal. Her secret dream of marrying Rafe even though they weren't mates had been brutally crushed when she'd walked into that room and she'd lashed out viciously in response to the pain.

Damn it, she needed to get out of here for a couple of days and get her head together. If Rafe caught up with her now she'd say something that would shatter their friendship forever, if she hadn't already managed that with her rash words. She'd go into the city for a couple of days; she'd need to organize someone to cover her at the clinic too.

Kylie came to an abrupt halt as someone broke into slow applause as she neared the short set of steps that led up and outside. Looking up Kylie saw she was nearly abreast with Chris, who was leaning his shoulder against the wall at the bottom of the stairs. Being such a large man positioned as he was, he blocked the exit.

"Well done precious, you just managed to hurt a woman who's as fragile emotionally as an abused puppy, and at the same time lose the friendship of one of the best friends you'll ever have. Classy Kylie, very classy," contempt roughened his voice.

"I don't need this right now Chris." Squaring her shoulders, she looked up into his face reading the derision in his sherry brown eyes. Where had she and Chris gone wrong? They'd been friends since they were kids, but over the last couple of years he'd become more distant and abrasive towards her. Their easy friendship destroyed by the barbed comments he often threw her way. She was at a loss to understand why his feelings of friendship had turned to animosity; Kylie only felt discomfort around him now days and avoided him wherever possible.

"You might not want it but you deserve it. Maybe now you'll pull your head out of the sand and realize Rafe was never going to marry you. It's past time you got over your teenage crush and started acting like a woman. If you're not careful you'll lose your mate because he's sick of waiting for you to grow up." Chris straightened against the wall, turned to walk up the steps, and out into the daylight.

Kylie went to grab his arm intending to halt him, but he jerked his arm out of her reach shooting her a dark look.

Dropping her hand she asked, "What do you mean by that?"

Walking away from her, he tossed mockingly, "Work it out yourself, doctor."

Kylie stood alone in the dark corridor feeling as if she'd lost more that Rafe's friendship today.

~~~

Regan's rage cooled to a solid lump of resentment towards the man in front of her, still staring after Kylie. Woodenly Regan pulled on the rest of her clothes. Rafe had lied to her. Obviously, something was going on between him and Kylie. The woman wouldn't act like such a bitch towards her without reason. It was Regan's own fault for letting her emotions get involved. It had obviously just been sex for Rafe and really, that suited her just fine. She didn't want any more emotional entanglements with this community. She
~~~

wouldn't abandon Ben, but she could make sure to keep others at a distance, especially Rafe, she wasn't going to open herself up to more humiliation or rejection. Rafe had the power to wound her deeply, but only if she allowed him. She needed to concentrate more at keeping him at a distance. Sure, they'd had sex, but that didn't have to mean anything. Lots of people had casual sex, she could do that too. All part of rounding out her character, she assured herself.

Rafe waited for Regan to meet his eyes and nearly flinched at the cold emptiness he saw there. Gone was his passionate mate, in her place was a shadow of the woman she was. Totally cut off from him, detached, her armor back in place.

"I don't know what's got into Kylie. She normally doesn't have a mean bone in her body."

Regan shrugged total indifference in her blue eyes as she met his gaze. "You don't have to apologize for your friend. You are not responsible for her actions, only your own. And as such, I prefer you refrain from discussing me with your friends unless it pertains to the capture of my father."

"It wasn't like Kylie made it sound," he began to explain only to stop as she raised her hand to stop him.

"Seriously, I don't care," the disdain in her voice towards him made him cringe inside. *Oh boy, she did care; otherwise, she wouldn't be reacting like this.*

"Regan, you have to let me explain," he tried again.

"No I don't," she cut him off. "I'm going to head home; I'll wait at the front gate for Chris to take me home."

Rafe stared into her eyes, trying to see past the lifeless washed out blue and into the emotions behind her wall. But she had retreated from him totally. There would be no talking to her in this state. She wouldn't hear him. He sighed in frustration, he'd give her time to settle down, and then he'd talk to her. He'd felt her pain before the detachment.

"OK, but understand this isn't over between us, it is just beginning. And I won't always accept you locking me out as you're doing now. You're hurt and pissed and you have every right to be. But next time I see you, we will deal with this, for now I'll give you the space you want." Turning towards the door, he ushered her from the room. "Come on I'll walk you out." He pretended not to notice her stiffening at his touch and her subtle shift away from the hand he'd placed at her back. Running a hand through his hair, he felt like roaring his frustration. If he ran into Kylie now he'd ring her neck. It looked like he was back to square one with his little mate because of her.

Regan ditched Rafe, collected her purse and keys from her room, and then walked to the front gates to await Chris, who'd escort her home. She tried to analyze why her emotions were punching at her walls threatening to crack them wide open. They swirled a hurricane of volatility, blowing up out of nowhere, only to drop away, leaving a dark vacuum.

She had believed she was making progress with her emotions since moving to Eden's Retreat. She felt protective and committed to Ben; she felt a tentative friendship towards Jordan, Steph, and Jen, and could see the potential for the same with Chris and his humor. For Rafe she'd felt longing and desire, her heart lifted every time she caught sight of him. There was trepidation too, the urgency to be with him scared her. Maybe what was between them was too strong, too volatile for her to handle?

Even as she contemplated ending her contact with him, she could feel bleak depression settling over her. She hated thinking of a future without him in it. What was best? What should she do? Cut off their contact or slow things right down so she could cope? She couldn't handle being out of control; she would drown in the cesspool of rage and injustice she locked away deep inside. The earlier panic attack worried her; she'd thought she'd outgrown them.

One thing was a given, she had to keep an emotional distance from Rafe. He'd lied to her about his involvement with Kylie. That jab Kylie had made at Regan wasn't out of general bitchiness; it was from a woman who was hurt and lashing out. Rafe's assurance that there was nothing between him and Kylie had been a lie. He needed to clean house before there could be a physical relationship between them. If there were to be a physical relationship, it would be best if she had no expectations where Rafe was concerned.

"Hey you ready to go?" She watched Jordan walk towards her with the loose-limbed grace inherent to all the Sentinels. The searching look he gave her clued her in that Rafe had opened his big blabber mouth about earlier. "You want to talk about it?" he offered.

"No."

"Are you sure, foxes are good listeners. You have to trust someone."

"I tried that, it didn't work out real well, so no I'm not interested in talking."

Jordan winced at the finality in Regan's tone. Rafe was in for a rough time here, what the hell had gotten into Kylie?

"Hey I won't butt in where I'm not wanted but think about this, if you shut Rafe out you'll be hurting yourself as much as him."

"Will I? Or will I be saving myself from more future pain?"

Jordan rang a finger down her cheek, "Yeah, trust me, if you don't take a chance with Rafe you will be hurting yourself as much as you'll be hurting Rafe." He turned away as Chris pulled up in one of the Sentinel's black 4WD's. "Come on, let's get you tucked in for the night. Rafe and Byron have organized with Paul the head groundskeeper for you to start work tomorrow at 8:30. Paul will meet you at that shed over there tomorrow morning," he indicated a large wrought iron shed 100 yards to her left. "Questions?"

"Can we stop on the way to get some food? Everything I had in the house will be rotten by now."

"No need," he assured, "Rafe has taken care of everything for you. He had your window repaired and perishables removed while you were recovering. By now the kitchen will be stocked with enough food to keep Chris fed. He didn't think it fair for you to fork out the money it takes to feed him. You'd think he'd have slowed down over the years but he still eats like a teenager who hasn't seen food for days. I keep telling him he's starting to get fat, but he won't listen," he grinned at Chris who'd pushed open the door for Regan from inside the cabin in time to hear the end of Jordan's conversation.

"Hey dickhead it's all muscle," he growled, Regan could easily see the bear was irked at Jordan's teasing.

Regan had to pull herself up into the 4WD, it had that much clearance from the road, it was more an all terrain vehicle, than an ordinary 4WD you'd normally see on the city streets. She didn't know whether to be pleased or pissed at Rafe and his interference, after a second of contemplating going through her fridge and throwing out rotten food, she decided to get over it. Now she could go home, have a shower, something to eat, and work out what she was going to do tomorrow about Rafe.

~~~

The next morning Regan headed over to the shed Jordan had pointed out to her the previous evening, to start her new job as a grounds keeper. As she approached the open double roller door, she heard someone moving around inside.

“Hello!” she called as she tapped on the outside wall.

“Hold on a sec,” a deep voice issued from the dark interior.

The voice had a smoky husk to it that sent a shiver down Regan’s spine. Regan breathed out in appreciation as the owner of the voice walked out of the shadows into the morning sunlight. Her first impression was that of a fallen golden angel. He was too earthy to be a divine entity. His hair shone in the light with metallic shades, from deepest copper through gold, with streaks of silver highlights. His skin too was burnished gold; his black brows and luxuriant eyelashes highlighted the gilded gold flecks in his light brown eyes. High cheekbones and strong jaw line stamped his masculine face. Regan had honestly never seen a more stunning man. His khaki shorts rode low on his lean hips and he’d already discarded his shirt, Regan couldn’t prevent
~~~

her eyes from running over his sculpted body.

"You must be Regan," he enfolded her shorter form in a warm embrace in a shifters way of greeting. He leaned down and sniffed the side of her neck breathing deeply of her scent; Regan stepped back out of his embrace. *Icky!* She hated it when they did that whole sniffing thing.

"Byron called me last night and said I'd have extra help, but he failed to mention how gorgeous my new grounds keeper was," he flashed her a charmingly lopsided smile.

"You can turn down the charm Romeo," Jen commented in her usual flat voice as she and Steph rounded the corner. "Your BS won't work on Regan." Dressed in her usual black Sentinel fatigues and T-shirt, she ran her grey eyes over Regan, "You OK?"

"Sure," Regan nodded.

Jen gave a derisive snort but didn't say anything else; she just folded her arms over her chest and leaned back against the shed subtly distancing herself from the group.

Paul hadn't taken offense to Jen, sending one of those breathtaking smiles at the reserved Sentinel, "And good morning to you too Jen, lovely to have your sparkling personality here to brighten up our day."

Jen's flat stare didn't seem to faze him at all.

Turning to the surprisingly quiet Steph, he pulled her into

his body for a squeeze before rubbing his knuckles across the top of Steph's head in brotherly affection.

"So what are you doing here pip squeak?"

Steph pulled away from Paul to hug Regan. Regan had given up asking her to stop doing that and gave an exaggerated sigh as Steph linked her arm though Regan's before turning back to Paul, "We just wanted to nail Regan down for lunch today."

"Typical female, organizing her social life before she's even done any work." He took the sting out of the words by tossing Regan a smile. "When you're ready come in the shed and we'll get you sorted out." He waved at Jen and ruffled Steph's hair before walking off with long limbed grace.

Steph gritted her teeth at the treatment.

"Give it up Steph, he's too old and too experienced for you to cut your teeth on," advised Jen.

"You know I liked you more when you never said anything," Steph replied tartly.

"You should have thought of that before you decided I was one of you special projects and couldn't be left in contented solitude," came the dry response.

Regan huffed a laugh at Steph's exaggerated look of affront.

"You weren't content, you were lonely! How many times do I have to explain this to you?"

Jen rolled her eyes.

Pushing off the shed, she asked Regan, "Are you free for lunch at 1 o'clock?"

"I can't see why not," Regan watched as the two women headed off shaking her head as Steph bounced around Jen like a young pup trying to gain an adult's attention, while Jen moved with the lethal grace of a veteran soldier. The two women couldn't be more diametrically opposite, one short with a fragile build, the other tall and honed for battle. One filled with an open joy in life and people, the other scarred inside and out, with a closed in personality, and an aversion of people.

~~~

The next few days fell into routine for Regan. Paul was flexible with her hours; giving her a list of jobs to do each evening for the next day, as long as they were done he didn't care how long it took or when she did the work. That attitude allowed her to spend a couple of hours each day training Ben. The physical labor of her work and the training ensured she was exhausted by the time her head hit the pillow. Of Rafe, she'd only seen him once briefly, when he'd sought her out to let her know another shifter had been kidnapped off the streets of Salem this time, and he was headed out to Oregon to see if he could pick up a trail. He'd given her a chaste kiss on the lips before jogging off towards
~~~

the car park.

She'd heard others talking in the cafeteria that morning, the victims mate had confirmed her husband's death. Her bond to him had been severed; the only cause could be his murder. The somber mood at Eden's Retreat affected Regan more that she'd anticipated. Even though she wasn't overly involved in the community, apparently her panther could sense and react to the other shifters' misery. She'd broached Chris about how the atmosphere was pulling her down in a way she'd never experienced before. He'd reassured her that her panther held more influence over her because for the first time in her life she was amongst shifters, and her cat was responding to that.

It was still so strange realizing she had an inner animal, which would and could affect her emotions and senses. Since coming to Eden's Retreat, she was aware of her own senses strengthening, as if her cat was coming awake. She could see better at night, her hearing was incredible, her sense of smell was developing, and she could now distinguish some people by their scent. Her ability to know when someone was near was developing. It was a relief to know she had these abilities because she was a shifter and not because there was something wrong with her.

She spent time each day actively developing that skill. She would sit in the park and put music on her iPod, close her eyes, and try to determine when people approached her, before her other senses picked them up. It seemed to be like any other skill, the more she practiced the better she became at it.

She was also becoming aware that her cat was a hussy, a hussy fixated on Rafe. Boy she now knew how a cat felt when it was in heat. It took all her control not to rub herself whenever her thoughts drifted to Rafe. This constant arousal had to be her cat; it wasn't normal – unless she had suddenly become a nymphomaniac. But, it wasn't that because the thought of any other man touching her was as abhorrent as it had always been. Every night she dreamed of doing things to his muscular body that she'd never thought of before meeting him. She wanted to touch, taste, and devour him. Her stance on keeping distance between them was crumbling under the sheer unrelenting need for him. Somehow, she had to guard her heart.

She needed to talk to Jordan or Chris about what was happening to her, Steph was too young and Jen... Regan shuddered at how stilted that conversation would be. No thanks. She had to know what to expect from her cat, how prominent would it become? It was already affecting her personality; she now sought out Jordan and Steph's company, and often found herself instigating contact with them. In addition, this constant sexual craving for Rafe wasn't her; she was at the stage now where she had to bring spare panties to work, as hers were always damp, her mind always drifting to him.

Although she had come to terms with having a physical relationship with Rafe, she was determined to keep her emotions separate. Her meltdown after their first time together was warning enough; she was ill equipped to cope with betrayal or rejection. She would be a mature adult and have sex with the man without attaching sentiment to the act. They weren't mates so it made sense to keep a certain distance between them, because when his mate came along he'd drop her like the proverbial hot potato, if they even lasted that long. Their time together was finite and she had to protect herself.

~~~

Regan jerked awake, her heart racing, the door clicked open and Chris slipped silently into her dark room.

"Good you're awake," Chris whispered. "Get dressed we have company coming. The two Sentinels on duty have fallen back in behind him."
~~~

CHAPTER 13

Regan slid from her bed, went to her chest of draws and pulled out some black yoga pants, a black long sleeved T-shirt and sport bra silently from the drawers. Crossing back to her bed she was about to pull the oversized T shirt she slept in over her head when she realized, if she could vaguely make things out in the pitch black of her room, Chris would be able to see substantially better than her. She used a finger in a circling motion to signal that he should turn around.

"What no free show?" he complained, as he obliged her by turning away.

As she dressed, he quietly explained that they planned to let the intruder into the house and make his way into the living room where Regan would flick on the lights for an instant ruining the intruder's night vision. Chris would then take him down and they'd finally have someone to question. The other two Sentinels would remain outside to ensure there were no others coming for Regan.

"You let me take this asshole out Regan, no heroics from you tonight."

"Yes, yes I know, you're the man, I'm the helpless woman," she huffed as she waved him to the far side of the living room. Honestly, she may never have worked with them before, but she wasn't a complete idiot. There was a plan, Chris was the leader, and she'd follow directions. Chris wasn't going to be hurt because she refused to obey his orders.

They both settled in to wait, silent shadows in the dark of night. Regan consciously calmed her breathing so she'd be able to hear the slightest of noises, indicating the intrusion of her home. She concentrated on her new awareness of others around her; she could feel Chris' vibrant presence and found it hard to work past that to perceive anyone else. It was frustrating, she felt she should be able to sense the intruder, but she just didn't have the discipline to move past Chris. Before she could feel the intruder she heard her back door click open, she looked to Chris waiting for his signal to turn on the lights. Her night vision was strong enough that she'd see when Chris waved at her.

Her assailant crept into the room on silent feet. He moved straight towards Regan's bedroom, it was obvious he knew the layout of her home. Chris signaled Regan as he soundlessly moved behind the intruder. Regan closed her eyes then flicked the light on briefly, blinding the intruder.

The man was obviously trained, as soon as the light went on he dived to the side, trying to give himself time to form a defense, but Chris had the advantage of his animal reflexes, no matter how fast the man had moved he would be no match for Chris in this situation.

Regan's faith in Chris was upheld as the Sentinel flowed after the trespasser, all animal grace. When the man rolled to his feet, Chris smashed his fist into his jaw. He managed to flinch back enough to avoid full impact, but he staggered, backing into Regan's lounge and went down on one knee. Chris lashed out ruthlessly with his foot, which the man was unable to deflect; the connection of boot to head tossed the man onto his back in an unconscious sprawl.

"And that boys and girls is how it's done."

"Well I hope you didn't break his jaw. We need him to talk remember?" she pointed out as she turned the lights back on.

"Nah. Didn't kick him that hard," Chris tipped his head to the side contemplating the man for a second before using his boot to roll his unconscious victim onto his side and into a recovery position. "Mind you we don't want the bastard to go and choke on his own vomit either," he muttered. He motioned Regan over, "Are your senses acute enough to hear his heart beat?"

Regan cocked her head and listened, soon enough she could hear the slow, but steady beat, she nodded.

“OK when he starts to wake up his heart will pick up, it doesn’t matter how good an actor he is, he can’t stop that anatomical response. I’m going out to call in the transport; we’ll take him back to Eden’s Retreat but leave some sentinels here in case any of his pals show up looking for him. The more we have to question the better. If he starts to wake up cuff him.”

“No worries.” As Regan accepted the cuffs from Chris, she saw approval in his eyes.

Regan was a star as far as Chris was concerned. She followed instructions to the T; there was no fussing about a bit of blood on her carpet. He could hear her pulse and her heart was rocking along at a solid eighty beats a minute. His boss was a lucky man, scoring Regan as his mate. Sure, she had some social issues, but he’d take a mate that was cool under fire and could handle herself in a fight over the scholarly type, any day. Chris could only hope his own mate would step up one day.

After Chris left the room to organize his troops, Regan crouched down in front of the man on the floor. Her mouth turned down in a grim line as she recognized him as the first of the two assailants from her father’s failed abduction attempt. His broken hand had obviously had time to heal.

Regan frowned, this didn't make sense, why use three men on the first attempt and now when she was on her guard only one? Noticing the man's increasing heart rate she rolled him onto his stomach and cuffed his hands behind his back. She then went to her hall cupboard and pulled out a duffel bag full of neat things including flexi cuffs. She quickly returned to the now moaning man and used the flexi cuffs to bind his ankles together then used her foot to roll him onto his back.

She noted her captive was in his early thirties, average height but leanly muscled with a few small scars on his face and hands, by the look of them they were probably from brawling. His features were average; there was nothing about him to make you remember him until he opened his eyes. They were a soulless ice blue and filled with bitter animosity.

Regan smiled down at him as he tested his bonds. "Hello, where's your friend from last time?"

"Don't play innocent with me you stupid bitch. You know you killed him," he snarled through clenched teeth as he continued to struggle against the cuffs.

Regan held up her hands in a show of innocence. "Wasn't me pal. But you can't complain if something bad happens when you enter someone's home and try to abduct them. Surely they have the right to defend themselves?"

"You animals have no rights! You're not human; you have no

right to expect human laws to protect you."

Regan raised her brows at his malevolence. Boy, this guy had some anger issues, but hey it made it easier for her to provoke info out of him. This angry he wasn't going to be guarding his answers.

"So if we're that bad how is it you take orders from my father, he is after all just an animal like me. It must stick in your craw being told when to jump and how high to jump by a dumb old alley cat. Must suck to be you, huh?"

The man's face twisted with fury, he writhed on the floor kicking out wildly trying to break the flexi cuffs. Regan backed out of his range in case one of those wild kicks connected with her shins.

"Why do you think I'm here without backup?" spittle flew from his mouth. "Your oh so clever father said this house would be a trap and the coward refused to come here or order an attack. He refused me assistance when I demanded backup for tonight. If that coward had listened to me you'd be cuffed and on your way to the park to be hunted like the animal you are." Hacking deep within his chest, he spat at her.

Regan danced out of the way of the glop of phlegm. "Hey don't do that in my house! That's just gross!" Regan saw the man's venomous gaze shift from her to Chris as he reentered the room. She tried to follow the expressions racing across his face: shock, fear, resentment, and finally resolution. For the first time since he'd come to, he seemed to gain control over his anger.

"So the bastard was right, this is a trap," his lip curled in disgust. "You won't get any information from me," he ground out.

Chris walked over to the prone figure. "Sure we will dickwad," he smiled down at him. Regan thought it was one of the most evil smiles she had ever seen, it seemed as if Chris had let some of the bear out of its cage and it sent a shiver down Regan's spine to see it.

"You get nothin' from me."

Regan frowned as she noticed his face was changing from flushed to a sickly pasty white. Sure Chris was a big bastard and right now with the grisly close to the surface, he was menacing – but he hadn't even made any threats let alone caused any pain. So why had this moron gone so pale, and was that foam at the corner of his mouth? Regan leaned forward, drawing in her breath, trying to assimilate the changes she could see happening.

The man turned his head towards her, "Your father will capture you, and they will hunt you down and shoot you like the animal you are." He gasped trying to draw air through obviously constricted airways.

"Oh you stupid prick." Chris dropped to his knees at the man's side. "What did you do?" Chris shook him. "What have you taken?"

But Regan could see the man was already losing consciousness, his breath, already laboring stopped as Chris rolled him over to release the cuffs. When he rolled him back over to commence CPR, Regan heard the last beats of his heart slow to a halt.

Regan knelt down beside Chris and they worked as a team. For fifteen minutes, they tried to revive a heartbeat, but whatever he'd taken defied their efforts.

"Shit! Shit! Shit!" Chris sat back on his heels, signaling for Regan to stop. "Such a rooky mistake," he rubbed his face in frustration. "Rafe is going to fuckin' have a fit."

"What for?" Regan asked, still bewildered by what had just happened.

"The stupid prick poisoned himself somehow. I should have patted him down when he was unconscious. I just didn't think they'd be fanatical enough to kill themselves, rather than being captured." He reached over and pried open the dead man's mouth seeing nothing he took one of the man's hands in his, turning it over to look at both sides. He did the same for the other hand, "Huh – here it is. God these guys must think they are the secret service or something. See his ring; it has a false front and a small needle inside. All he had to do was flick it open and jab himself." Chris flung the hand down in disgust. Due to his incompetence, they had lost their first real break.

"I don't suppose he gave you any useful information before committing hara-kiri?" he asked as he pulled his phone from his pocket preparing to call Rafe.

Regan shook her head, "Not really. I think he was acting on his own. He did say that my father thought me being here was a trap. So we will have to reevaluate what we are doing here. It doesn't sound like he's going to take the bait until the odds are more in his favor."

~~~

The mood in Rafe's office was somber. He'd only flown back in from Salem a couple of hours ago after wasting days canvassing the street John had been abducted from and going over the investigation his Sentinels had conducted. He desperately wanted to find a lead to *Titan* without continuing to use Regan as bait. Right now frustration seethed within him, his temper riding him hard. His mate had been attacked again and instead of being there to protect her, he'd been thousands of miles away chasing his tail. And thanks to Kylie his mate didn't even want him touching her.

Chris stood near the door refusing to sit with the rest of them, his massive frame stiff with self-condemnation. Jordan sat slouched on the sofa under the bank of windows.
~~~

Regan perched on the edge of the lounge she'd sat in last time the four of them had met. Rafe had scented her relief when he'd dragged over one of the office chairs and sat on that rather than next to her, and the rejection pinched his heart.

"So in summary his fingerprints aren't on any data base known to mankind, he had no ID on him and his phone is encrypted and you haven't been able to hack into it yet." Rafe huffed in frustration; these fuckers just couldn't be this good. They had to make a mistake soon.

"That's about it," Jordan stretched out, tipping his head to the side cracking his neck. "As soon as we finish here I'll get back to it. I'll be able to hack into it, it's just a matter of time."

"Which we are getting short of," Regan pointed out. "My father must have recovered from his injuries by now, it won't be long before he tracks me and if I'm here then everyone at Eden's Retreat will be in danger."

She turned her gaze to Rafe who was staring at the floor between his feet.

"Rafe we don't have any choice we have to make abducting me more attractive. My father knows the house is a set up. We have to let them think they can grab me."

Rafe hissed out a breath, animosity riding him. It was like

chasing ghosts; he'd hardly slept in the last three days, chasing leads down all over the country and still coming up with nothing. Thankfully, the shifter community in Salem was small, and even now relocating, preventing *Titan* from abducting anyone else from the clan.

Rafe had personally interviewed the witnesses, but apart from vague descriptions of two average men, a white van with no distinguishing features, and conflicting views regarding the model and partial plate number, there was nothing to follow up. The investigation was thwarted at every turn.

He'd spent countless hours canvassing the street trying to find more witnesses; the only thing he'd succeeded at was to piss off his Sentinels, who now believed he didn't trust them to do their jobs. He'd also spent time with Sonya, watching the hope fade from her eyes as the days dragged by. At least she didn't blame him; her husband's family wasn't as understanding. They'd questioned his abilities, his commitment, his competence, bluntly suggested someone else should take over, as he was proving to be useless in the hunt for *Titan*.

It was hard to dispute them, but his Sentinels knew the lines of communication were open, if anyone had any ideas they brought them to him. Everything was being done that could be done, all resources were being utilized, everyone was working exhausting hours investigating even the smallest of leads. They were analyzing the mega rich, covering large tracks of land where the hunts could be taking place, but it was a big country, and there were thousands of people to be investigated, and more still to be tracked down who were hiding behind companies and trust funds.

And then there was his mate, who, by the way she was keeping her distance from him and the closed off expression in her eyes whenever she met his gaze, was obviously still under the misapprehension that he'd lied to her about Kylie. One thing he was going to fix after this meeting was the misunderstanding between them. He would not stand for the wall she had built back up between them.

He felt his phone vibrate in his pocket and drew it out, his heart turned to stone as he read the message. "Shit," he closed his eyes so the others couldn't see how close he was to losing it. When he got his hands on these fuckers, they were going to die a slow painful death.

"What is it?" Jordan sat up.

"Sonya committed suicide."

The atmosphere went from somber to miserable as they each retreated into their own thoughts. Everyone knew Sonya would probably choose to follow her mate into death, but the reality was a slap in the face.

"That's enough, we have to set up something to catch these monsters," Regan looked to the others, noting the anger mixed with their sorrow. These men felt the loss of John and Sonya, it wasn't just a job for them, they felt committed to protecting their own, and at the moment, they were failing.

Rafe turned to look at Regan, although she had never met John or Sonya, she was hurting for them and their family. She wasn't as disassociated as she thought. She was becoming entwined into the shifter community, and what hurt one, hurt them all.

He was backed into a corner with regard to using Regan as bait. People were dying and he had no other ideas about how to find these pricks. With time, he knew he could uncover them, but they didn't have time, so that left Regan. Time was a factor on two fronts: more shifters could be abducted, and Regan's father could find Eden's Retreat if he tracked Regan here.

"Shit, OK let's pull this together," Rafe glanced at his watch. "It's two in the morning now," looking at Jordan, "you have today and tonight to crack into the encryption. Tomorrow we will put Regan out there in such a way she's irresistible to them." He looked over at Chris who was still standing by himself next to the exit. "Chris get your ass over here," he ordered. "Yes you fucked up, but it's a mistake any one of us might have made. Don't wallow in self-pity, get your game face on, and help fix it. We don't have time for you to sulk."

"I'm not sulking, I missed something so basic I don't deserve to be in here," Chris growled.

Rafe's eyes narrowed on Chris and some of the anger he was feeling seeped into his voice, "Get over yourself. You're not perfect, grow up!" he snapped. "I don't have enough time, energy, or inclination, to baby you. Either get in or get out," Rafe locked eyes with Chris, his changing to gold as he allowed his wolf closer to the surface.

Yes, he was pissed that Chris had missed something so basic and ruined their best chance to find these bastards. His oversight also meant Rafe now had to place Regan in more danger than before. Yes, he wanted to take Chris down right now and belt the living shit out of him. He was struggling to control his wolf as well as his own resentment at the situation he found himself in, and Chris was a prime target for his anger. His wolf wanted to go for Chris's throat because now Regan was going to be placed in a position fraught with danger.

Rafe had enough control to know that although going a couple of rounds with one of his best Sentinels might make him feel better, it wasn't going to help solve this situation, and Regan was more important than venting his frustration.

Chris eyed Rafe as if he wanted to keep arguing, but he must have sensed how close Rafe was to losing his grip. As Rafe had said he either got out of their way, or helped fix it. With a stiff nod, he stalked over and sat next to Jordan.

"Right, let's get this organized, here's what I suggest, jump in with ideas and concerns. I want this operation as tight as possible. We are not going to lose Regan." He laid out his rough plan: they knew *Titan* had placed listening devices in Regan's house, Regan and Chris would have an argument at her house the following afternoon leading to Regan demanding Chris leave. They all agreed it was too dangerous for Regan to return to Eden's Retreat. It would require the complete evacuation of the community if Thomas tracked her there. So, until her father was flushed out, she'd stay away.

If her father believed she was breaking away from her protection hopefully, he'd come after her at her house. To ensue she looked vulnerable, the Sentinels would pull back further from her house; her father would not be able to sense them. Regan would be hooked up with a tracking device for the worst-case scenario, and an earwig so she could communicate with them while out of their line of sight. They had to be far enough back that her father wouldn't be able to sense them, but not so far, that they couldn't foil the abduction when it took place. It all had to be fluid and mobile as the abduction could take place anywhere. They agreed if Thomas didn't come after her tomorrow night, Regan would call a cab the next morning and head into the city, hoping to drag them out in the open that way.

When they believed they had covered every contingency, dawn was a hint on the horizon. None of them were getting the sleep they needed and wouldn't be in the coming days. As they filed out, Rafe held Regan back by placing his hand on her arm.

"Come over to my place and have breakfast with me."

"You honestly look like you need sleep more than company."

He smiled wryly, "I'm not denying some sleep would be good, but it's more important to me that we straighten out things between us. Once that's done I'll catch enough shut eye to keep me going," he ran his hand down her arm lightly and taking her hand, gently tugged her towards the door.

"I'll come, but I don't think there is too much you can say, Kylie's reaction to seeing us together wasn't that of a platonic friend."

Rafe pulled her out the door and led her across the wide lawn towards his housing block. "All I ask is that you listen with an open mind."

They followed one of the winding paths that led to his building, Regan breathed in the fresh air of early morning. As they approached Rafe's building, Regan could see around twenty shifters gathered on the wide verandah on the second level preparing an early BBQ breakfast. She shook her head, these people took living together to a whole new level. Regan hated having people walking along the deck outside her unit whenever they wanted, and looking in if she didn't have the curtains drawn. There was no privacy and it gave her the creeps.

Rafe noticed Regan eyeing wide decks with aversion; he supposed it would be off putting for a loner to live in such an open environment. The three residential buildings were designed for easy mingling, and shifters loved dropping in unannounced. Privacy was not a highly sought after commodity. He'd have to look into the availability of one of the cottages scattered around Eden's Retreat, they lent themselves to more privacy and would suit Regan more.

He ushered her into the elevator, rather than taking the stairs as he usually did to his third floor apartment. He absently rubbed his thumb back and forth over the hand he'd refused to relinquish as he waited for the lift doors to open, and smiled to himself as he felt her shiver in response. Thank God for the sexual chemistry between them. If they didn't have that urgency pushing them together, he didn't think she'd give him the time of day.

It had killed him to stay away from her and give her time to cool down. She would have realized by now that even though she was angry with him she still wanted him. Her cat would have ensured that. His wolf could sense her rising closer to the surface, and she would want her mate as much as his wolf wanted her. Regan's cat would not be interested in misunderstandings, and she would be using her influence on Regan to ensure she had her mate.

It was common knowledge in the shifter community to give new mates privacy for those first few weeks, when the female shifted for the first time. Their sex drive was nearly insatiable. Many male shifters proudly proclaimed their mates nearly killed them during those first intense weeks. It was not uncommon for the male to come out of those weeks a few pounds lighter than they went in. But, no one ever complained of the hardship. Rafe's mouth watered with anticipation of his own weeks following Regan's first shift.

When they reached Rafe's door he ushered Regan in with a hand low on her back, "Have a look around," he invited, "I'll make some coffee and toast."

Regan absently acknowledged him as she walked through the living area; she was surprised at the size of his unit. High raked ceilings increased the sense of space, allowing him his oversized lounge and chunky furniture without making the room feel cramped. Rather than ultra modern, which she'd picked as his style, it had a rural feel to it. Two large dark leather lounges dominated the center of the room, with one placed to face the view out the floor-to-ceiling windows and sliding doors, the other placed to take advantage of a plasma panel attached to the wall.

The square kitchen table could comfortably seat eight, was made from oak, and was either an excellent reproduction or an antique. Regan wasn't able to tell the difference, never having had the time or money to get into antiques, although she liked the history attached to old furniture, rather than the mass-produced, flat packed furniture of today.

The kitchen was divided off from the living dining area by a large wooden bench, which had stools placed along the living area side, inviting guests to sit and talk as the owner prepared meals. The overall atmosphere was one of homely comfort, although male dominated.

Moving down the short hall she found what was obviously the second bedroom, but Rafe had turned it into his home office. It was as anally neat as his office at the Sentinel headquarters. Boy, he'd have a heart attack if he ever saw her bedroom. While she kept her slothfulness under control in the rest of her house, her bedroom was always a write-off. The bed only ever made the day she washed her sheets and the clothes only ever picked up when she was running out of clean ones and needed to wash.

Ardent curiosity drew her to the master bedroom; this one was on the opposite side of the unit to the extensive balcony that ran along the front of the apartment, affording Rafe more privacy in his bedroom. Once again, the room was generous in size. A massive king bed dominated the room; made from oak, he had a chest of drawers and side tables to match. The quilt was made of geometric lines in royal blue and emerald green. The overall effect was masculine yet enduring; nothing would go out of fashion. Rafe obviously didn't bend to the latest trends. Nothing in the room was transient. Was this an insight into Rafe's personality? Usually bedrooms were a true reflection of a person; take hers for example, a mess that reflected the state of her inner self.

She was so tight emotionally, having never dealt with her childhood. Now that she was dipping her toes into that arena, feelings she had no experience negotiating, were overwhelming her. This was why she needed to keep an emotional distance between her and Rafe. If she didn't, she'd drown, and she wasn't sure she had the ability to resurface.

She didn't have the social skills or emotional experience to deal with the feelings Rafe ignited in her. He made her feel out of control, vulnerable, and exposed; her abhorrence to feeling this helpless was bone deep. If she didn't have this inexplicable, urgent, soul deep need to be with him, she would walk away without a backward glance. But, as much as she had tried to talk herself into breaking away from this, the necessity to be with him had her enthralled, and the thought of ending things left her in searing pain.

Squaring her shoulders, she closed the door to his room, returning to the kitchen and Rafe.

"I was just coming to get you. Would you prefer orange juice or coffee with breakfast?" his searching gaze tried to discern her opinion of his apartment, but she was playing her cards close to her chest again. Her face was expressionless as she thanked him for the toast and requested orange juice. She had retreated behind her walls again. He hoped that after his explanation she would open to him again, he hated the way she shut him out.

Once she'd chosen her seat at the table, he sat at the corner to her so he could read her face as he talked to her. Rubbing his hand up and down his thighs, he contemplated where to start this conversation. *Might as well dive in the deep end, pussy footing around isn't really my style anyway.*

"About the things Kylie said the day she walked in on us: as I tried to explain at the time, I did not sit down with Kylie and discuss strategy on how to seduce you. I wouldn't demean any woman that way, nevertheless you." At her raised eyebrow, he elaborated. "You mean more to me than any other woman I've ever entered into a relationship with." He could read the disbelief in her deep blue eyes. His lips tightened, he was not used to his integrity being questioned, it was especially hard to take from his mate, and it lit his fuse, he could feel his temper starting to smolder. Regan had a right to question his honesty after Kylie's performance but it stuck in his craw that she believed Kylie's vicious jabs over his explanation.

"As I've told you before, Kylie and I have been friends since childhood. We have a history together and a closeness, which I can see would be threatening at first until you get to know her as I do, and see there is no spark between us, never has, and never will be. If I had to describe how I feel towards Kylie, it would be as a brother feels towards his little sister. The thought of having sex with Kylie is just fundamentally wrong."

Regan felt her mood shift at his shiver of distaste. Did she believe him? She was inclined to, but did it really matter if she was going to keep an emotional distance from him? If he had lied to her about Kylie, did it really matter as long as he wasn't involved now? That was what mattered. Right? Right? The vicious bit of jealousy was her answer; she didn't want that woman anywhere near Rafe.

He might have platonic feelings for her, but Kylie's feelings were anything but platonic for Rafe. The woman was stunningly beautiful and Regan couldn't believe Rafe wasn't drawn to Kylie's sensual allure. Just watching Kylie glide across the compound caused Regan to feel awkward and ungainly. Until her dry humor surfaced when she noticed how many men stopped to watch Kylie cross the lawn, their eyes glued to her long legs and the seductive sway of her hips, if they were in their animal forms their tongues would be hanging out with drool and all. Regan wondered if it came naturally, if Kylie was so at ease with her femininity that it oozed from her every pore, or if it was something she practiced, and perfected like a model walking the catwalk. Bringing her attention back to Rafe, she assessed him for a moment.

"Listen, whether you and Kylie have had a relationship in the past or not isn't my business. What I need you to promise me is that you are not involved now."

"But it does matter Regan," he reached out and grasped one of her slender hands in his, needing the connection to her, willing her to believe him. "How can you trust me now when I promise Kylie and I aren't involved, but not when I'm telling you we have never been involved romantically, and that I did not sit down and cold bloodedly discuss your seduction with her?" He rubbed her chilled hand with his rough one. "If I'm lying about the past what's to say I'm not lying about the present?"

Regan shrugged and looked out the windows absently, taking in his view of the manicured gardens and treed parkland further in the distance.

"Rafe I can't give you the answer you want. I'm inclined to believe you, my gut tells me to believe you, but I just don't trust people. Trust makes you vulnerable. If I trust you explicitly, then next comes relying on you, and if you let me down, I'm not equipped to bounce back from that sort of betrayal. I think it's better if we keep this thing between us light and just see where it leads for now."

Rafe ran the back of his fingers over her head, and following the straight flow of silky black hair to her shoulders, marveling at its softness. "You're stronger than you think Regan," he promised. He reluctantly settled for her partial acceptance of his honesty for now. It wasn't something he could force from her. Hopefully, when she spent more time with him she'd see his integrity and trust would follow.

Standing he asked, "OK enough of the deep and meaningful stuff. How'd you like to ditch this place, head out to the Peltry National Park, and go for a hike together? It will blow the cobwebs out, and I need some down time away from the investigation. What do you say?"

Regan couldn't hide her surprise; she'd assumed they would end up in his king size bed. *Now he wanted to go bush walking? Didn't he feel the same burning need that punished her?*

"Uh, sure," she shrugged. "*What are you doing? Didn't you promise yourself this was just going to be sex between you?*" she chastised herself. "I'm a glutton for punishment," she muttered. If she was going to keep things light between them, then she should not be spending *quality* time with him, she should be having sex and then getting out. But the imperative demand to be with him made it impossible to say no, besides, she reasoned, alone in the wilderness surely there would be an opportunity to tempt him. She imagined backing Rafe up to a tree and nuzzling at his neck before licking his tanned skin just below his jaw, absorbing his earthy masculine scent before biting down on the muscle between his neck and shoulder. Hmm, then she'd draw his shirt up exposing that yummy six pack and then his heavily muscled chest, cherishing the freedom to run her hands over all that hard muscle, hers to savor and enjoy.

Rafe's nostrils flared as the scent of his mate's increased arousal softly perfumed the air. Resisting the temptation, he reached for their plates taking them to the kitchen, turning his head as he walked past her, he noted her flushed cheeks and elevated breathing as she gazed out the window lost in her thoughts. He hoped to hell that he was the main feature in her daydream. It was all he could do to move away, he dropped the plates in the sink, and collected his keys and leather jacket from where he'd tossed them earlier on the hall table. He had to get them out of here now.

His own arousal, always present, blazed through him, burning him with urgent lust, while his back was turned to Regan he adjusted himself trying to find some relief in his now too tight jeans. He grimaced in exasperation, here he had honorable intentions, taking his mate for a nice walk, and she was obviously fantasizing about outdoor sex. If he had her full trust he'd be sinking into her welcoming heat right now, but he didn't.

He wanted her trust, not to just bind her to him through sex. Great in theory, but the practicality of being near his aroused mate and not having sex was fucking killing him. He needed her bound to him, he'd thought having sex with her would ease his constant need, but the taste he'd had only made the need burn brighter. Without the ritual binding their souls together, he struggled to resist his wolf instincts to fuck her into submission. Then bind them together without her consent. It could be done, only one mate needed to voice the words that would bind them for life, but it was rare for a mate to force a mating in such a way. Forcing a bond on your mate was a sure fire way of destroying the connection between you, and turning a mystical enchantment into a life of wretched misery. Now he just needed to convince his primitive wolf to wait and let Regan come to them, as the man understood must happen.

Regan followed Rafe down to the garage, admiring the view of his backside nicely encased in his faded blue jeans. Her temperature steadily rose as she followed along blindly, captivated by his easy long legged stride. An involuntary laugh escaped her when he stopped next to a mean looking black and chrome Harley.

You have to be kidding me; she huffed to herself in exasperation.

"*Guess not*," she muttered under her breath. He truly expected her to ride pressed up against him on a bike that was going to vibrate between her legs, and expect her not to ravage him the minute the bike stopped? Her panties were already soaked; she was so horny, it was all she could do not to rub herself to relieve the ache. It wouldn't take much pressure to bring her to orgasm, and she had a sinking suspicion that spreading her legs over that seat and the throb of the engine, would be enough.

Maybe he wouldn't notice if she got herself off while they were riding, she'd be behind him after all. Shrugging fatalistically, she turned her back to him and allowed him to slide on the leather jacket he'd picked up off the seat and held out for her to put on.

Regan was surprised at the heavy weight of the jacket as she settled it on her shoulders and breathed deep of the rich smell of new leather. Regan watched Rafe through lowered lashes as he moved in front of her and zipped her up, before threading the stitched in belt through the buckle at the front pulling it tight around her waist, using enough force to tip her off her balance and into his chest. He reached behind her to tug the back of the jacket down to settle it properly, taking the opportunity to rub her bottom with his broad palms before stepping back.

Without a word, he knelt before her, removed her joggers, and helped her step into chunky boots made specifically for riding bikes. Still without a word, he stood and helped her into a full-faced black helmet with reflective visor. Regan felt taller, more powerful somehow, a knight in modern armor. She swallowed as Rafe pulled his own full-faced black helmet on, with the visor down he seemed unattainable, a big man with broad shoulders and a powerful aura. No one today would mistake this man as anything but an apex predator.

Lust pounded at her as he swung his leg over the pillion and settled on the leather seat, the worn denim of his jeans enhancing the definition of his muscled thigh. A self-satisfied smile pulled at her lips, this virile man wanted her above all others.

“Hold tight,” he advised as she swung on behind him.

CHAPTER 14

He kicked the engine over and Regan gasped as the bike throbbed beneath her. She tried sitting back so the folds of her pussy weren't in direct contact with the seat, but Rafe popped the clutch and she had to cling onto him or fall off backwards. Her sensitive breasts now rubbed against his broad back, her arms were wrapped tightly around his lean waist and her pussy against that damned seat.

For a short time the exhilaration of weaving through traffic, the surging of the engine as Rafe powered around corners, the freedom, and the adrenalin of riding such a powerful machine, distracted her from her little problem. But by the time they left the city behind, the constant throb of the engine between her thighs was driving her crazy.

Breathing deeply she tried to calm the urgency racking at her. She attempted to focus on the changing scenery as the houses petered out, while they followed the highway into the mountains. As they started their ascent, the urban gave way to towering trees whose massive canopies shadowed the road in dappled sunlight. The dense forest grew to the edge of the road; only on the occasional switchback could she view down the mountain range back to the city they'd left behind. The bike easily climbed the steep, single lane road they traveled, after leaving the main road. Unfortunately, the magnificence of the primordial rainforest was not distracting her from the burning ache between her legs.

Heat blazed through her, a small moan escaping her lips, as Rafe leaned the bike into another turn, unconsciously brushing against her sensitized nipples. If she just rocked her hips forward, the vibration of the bike would surely bring her release. She had to do something, the arousal boarded on painful; she was so close now, not to come would be intolerable.

Biting her lip, she slowly eased her bottom back on the seat allowing room for her to tilt her pelvis forward. She eased her thighs wide allowing her clitoris direct contact to the vibration that had sent her arousal spiking uncontrollably. Her breath left her in a rush. *Oh yeah, this is what I need.* Her inner core clutched, she rested her head against Rafe's back, drawing his scent deep into her lungs as she rocked back and forward, trying to keep her movements small, but oh God she needed just a little more. Her vision darkened with the impending explosion. Convulsively she clutched

Rafe closer as she ground her clit against the seat. She threw her head back as powerful waves of bliss ripped through her. She screamed her pleasure as it blazed through her, the wind ripping the sound away. All the colors of the universe exploded behind her closed eyes as she was swept away.

Rafe stiffened. *No . . . Surely not.* His little mate did not just orgasm behind him. But the scent of her satisfaction, that even their speed couldn't completely whip away, confirmed that she had in fact just attained her release. *How is this fair?*

Within minutes, Rafe entered the parking area for the national park.

"Enjoy the trip?" he grinned as he hung his helmet on the handlebars and pulled his jacket off.

Regan, who now basked in the radiant afterglow of her little indiscretion, smiled cheerfully as she whisked her own helmet off and rested it next to his. She followed his lead and shed her jacket.

A smile tugged at Rafe's lips as Regan practically skipped along beside him as he headed off onto one of the many walking trails available. The path was wide enough that she could easily keep pace beside him. This was a side of Regan he'd never seen before, carefree and openly enjoying herself. Being surrounded by shifters was working its magic on her, this was Regan as she was meant to be, not the cautious self-contained woman he'd first met.

"It was fantastic!" she tossed him a smile. Humming under her breath, she breathed in deeply taking in the musty scent of the lush forest they walked through. Avidly she gazed at the massive trees with thick vines hanging from the towering trunks all the way to the ground, an abundant variety of small palms, ferns, and verdant new growth filled the available space between the immense trees. Birds perfumed the air with their calls to each other.

"I bet it was," he smiled self-depreciatively. He'd be due sainthood if he made it through this morning without bending his mate over and taking her from behind, as both he and his wolf craved. The scent of her satisfaction teased his senses, as she sauntered along beside him all rosy cheeked and clueless to his own blazing need. Why wasn't he fucking her right now? Oh yeah, her trust issues. He wanted to build her trust in him. But he could do that and still fuck her senseless. Right? The bludgeoning power of the arousal powering through him, made rational thought nearly impossible. He glanced at Regan, watching the slight sway of her breasts as she sashayed along beside him. He clenched his fists to stop himself from reaching out to test their weight.

He rubbed his forearm across his face to wipe the image away. This wasn't going to work. He should have taken her somewhere with lots of people, not into a forest where they were unlikely to meet another human being.

He could work on the trust issue another day, or maybe if he could just pound some of this burning need into her, he'd be able to think of something besides sex. He might actually even be able to have a conversation with her, but now he was wound so tight, he struggled not to tip his head back and howl in frustration. Everywhere he looked he imagined her naked, with himself thrusting into her tight sheath. His breath shortened as image after image formed with perfect clarity in his mind.

Rafe was imagining how he would position Regan on a tree stump partially hidden from the trail they walked along, when Regan brushed up against him as the trail narrowed. It tipped the balance, without a word he picked her up into a fireman's hold and walked off the track and into the forest.

Ignoring her laughing demands to be put down, he walked into the ever-darkening gloom of the forest until he found a tree stump about three feet high that would serve his purpose. He placed Regan so she was standing on the stump in front of him. Her laughter died as her gaze met his and she saw the arousal burning in his eyes. She licked her bottom lip nervously as he continued to stare silently at her.

"Undress for me," he demanded. He needed some sign of her trust. She may not trust him fully but on some level, she must have faith in him, or she would not have been able to be intimate with him. If she could place herself in a vulnerable position with him, her own actions would help her trust him intellectually, as well as instinctively, and what would make her feel more vulnerable than standing on stage naked before him, while he remained fully clothed?

He hid his relief as she tentatively began undoing the buttons of her shirt. He held her gaze with his, not allowing her to look away. He gave her a nod of encouragement as the shirt fell to the ground and she shrugged her bra from her shoulders before undoing the clasp and allowing it to follow her shirt.

Rafe's mouth watered as Regan's sensual curves were reveled. Her narrow waist dipped in, her breasts surprisingly lush for someone so lean. Her eyes lowered, demurely excited by his dominate nature. When she glanced up, he kept his gaze locked on hers, seeing her nervousness, but he also noted her eyes darkening with arousal. She undid her jeans, toed off her boots, and then shimmied out of her jeans, taking her socks with them. Standing tall before him wearing only her lace panties, she excited him as no one ever had. He waited as she slowly lowered her panties before stepping out of them. Her eyes smoldered with arousal as she licked her lower lip, drawing his attention to her lush mouth and thoughts of where he wanted it, later.

She stood before him, exotic as any wood nymph with her black hair partially hiding the budded nipples of her proud breasts from his gaze; the black hair of her mons hiding the secrets of her femininity from his piercing gaze. Rafe walked around her, studying her as if she were a slave on the auction block. He silently walked behind her and gathered her silken hair so it fell down her back, no longer protecting her breasts from his heated gaze.

Soundlessly, he moved back in front of her and reaching out, he squeezed one nipple between forefinger and thumb. When he released it, he watched the blood rush in, darkening the nipple to a deep berry hue. He moved his gaze from her nipple's reaction to read her eyes, which were half closed, as she absorbed the sensation.

"Harder?" he questioned.

At her hesitant nod, he again pinched her nipple using more pressure and pulling it out, extending the pink flesh as far as it would stretch, before releasing it to spring back into place, causing the flesh of her breast to quiver slightly. Breath rushed from her as she absorbed the pleasure pain of his treatment.

"Look how dark and hard it is compared to the other."

Taking her neglected breast in his hand, he lifted it to his mouth, suckling hard as he again pinched her other nipple. He trailed his tongue from one breast to the other leaving a wet trail for the breeze to cool. He nuzzled against her plum breast before latching onto her abused nipple, alternating his suckling with the graze of his teeth, all the while pinching and releasing the other nipple.

Regan's ragged breaths assured him she enjoyed the treatment. He stepped away from her, raking her aroused form with his eyes.

"Shall we see how aroused you are my love?" With no warning, he pushed a finger up and into her body. Her honey seeped from her inner lips to smooth over his palm as he held his finger deep inside her body. Rafe felt her inner muscles contract around his finger in search of a deeper, fuller penetration. A moan escaped from Regan as her head fell back, her hair tumbling down her spine, brushing her bottom and providing further stimulation to her heated skin as Rafe touched nothing but her inner core. She raised her hands to her breasts needing to squeeze them, but Rafe immediately removed his finger from her body.

"Did I tell you to touch yourself, precious?" he scolded softly.

As she reluctantly removed her hands from her breasts, he rewarded her with a nod of approval, he was in control here.

"OK sweetness on your knees for me," he watched avidly as Regan lowered herself. "Place your knees to the edges of the stump so you are spread wide for me." Again, he walked around her, silently appraising her in this new position, increasing her anticipation of what he would do next. And anticipating she was, her nectar was now flowing from her body. With her legs spread like this, her essence eased from her body and down the inside of her thighs, he could see it and smell it, it was driving him wild to see her so aroused by their little game.

His mate was so responsive, he knew he wouldn't last much longer; the need to be inside her was overwhelming. Soon, he promised himself. He stood behind her and ran his lips from her shoulder across to the nape of her neck, where he gently nipped before trailing his tongue down her curving spine, stopping to tongue the indent above her buttocks. He blew gently on the spot watching the shiver run down her back. He handled each of her cheeks pulling them apart to allow the cool air on her wet heated inner flesh.

She moaned at the sensation, he gently closed her massaging the globs of her delightful bottom gently before moving in front of her. He knelt down in front of her platform, leaning forward he ran his tongue along her inner thigh, lapping at the elixir released by her body.

"Dear God, your taste is as potent as a 100 year old distilled whisky, spicy, rich, and addictive."

Grasping her hips, he tilted her pelvis forward and nuzzled his nose into the hair covering her mons, drawing in her succulent scent before scraping his teeth over the small sheath protecting her clit.

Regan brought her hands to rest on his shoulders, as he bent lower to increase his access to her heated core. He showed his approval by licking the flat of his tongue across her opening, before lapping the sweet tang her body expended on reaction. He nuzzled, licked, and nipped at the pretty lips of her sex. Taking his time, he savored her taste, scent, and texture, probing her entrance with his tongue, relishing the sounds of her pleasure.

Leaning back, he unzipped and removed his distended cock from his jeans.

“Pull your pussy lips apart, sweet,” he husked. He stroked himself as he watched her fingers pull her outer lips apart, bearing her inner core to his view. He licked his lips at the sight of her plump flesh, flushed with arousal. “Lean over and take my cock into your mouth, but keep holding yourself open,” he demanded. He raptly watched the bulbous head of his cock slowly disappear into her hot mouth as she leaned forward to engulf him. He groaned in ecstasy as she sucked him greedily, taking as much of him in as her position would allow. Afraid he would spend himself in her mouth, he pulled back his erection, leaving her mouth with a soft pop.

“Move forward to the edge again,” he rasped, “then insert my cock into you.”

Still on her knees, Regan bit her lip as she shuffled to the edge of the stump; she grasped his slick erection in her hand and directed it to the moist opening of her body. Lifting up on her knees, she angled her hips and lodged the head into her opening. Her breath hitched as she moved further forward so the soft head of his penis could push into her. She held still with him lodged just inside, savoring the sensation as her womb clenched searching for more, stretching, making room for him.

At this angle when she moved, his hard shaft rasped over her engorged clit. She moaned as she edged closer again taking more of him into her quivering body.

"Fuck you're driving me crazy," Rafe growled, holding still as his little mate worked him into her tight little body. Soon he promised himself he'd take control but for now, he let her work him into her clutching pussy at her own pace. He gritted his teeth and arched back, closing his hands around his own ankles squeezing tight in an effort to prevent himself from grasping his mate by the hips and pounding into her uncontrollably. In this position, he could clearly see his cock jutting from his body and entering hers, as she held her pussy lips apart to help with his entry into her body. Inch by slow inch she swallowed him, and he watched captivated, as his shaft disappeared into her.

He groaned as she used her finger to collect her body's honey and spread it over his shaft, easing his entrance. With the next flex of her hips he was seated fully, they gazed at each other as they both knelt there, with him fully embedded in her body.

He watched a shudder run through her, then felt the clutch of her pussy around him as a small orgasm washed over her, Regan tipped her head back moaning in ecstasy. The sound broke his control, grabbing her by the hips he pulled out and thrust back in, it wasn't enough. Changing the angle slightly, his shaft sawed over her nerve center increasing her pleasure. He ran his open mouth up her throat seeking the warmth of her mouth and her exquisite taste. He groaned as she accepted his tongue into her mouth, sucking on it as her body sucked at his member with every thrust of his body.

He ran his rough hand over her smooth back, pulling her as close as possible, rubbing her soft breasts against his chest. He released her mouth in order to breathe, but Regan threaded her fingers through his hair and dragged his mouth back to hers, meshing their mouths together as urgency inundated their senses. Regan met every thrust of his body, grinding her hips against him in a desperate search for release from the tension overwhelming them, dragging them under with an irresistible force; they were caught, their bodies out of their control. They rode the crushing wave as it crested, hurtling them into an orgasm that crushed the breath from them. Light exploded as they shattered into particles of fragmented ether. Rafe roared his release as

Regan arched back, her vocal cords paralyzed as the frenzy took her. When finally the racking ecstasy released her, she slumped against Rafe who cradled her in his strong arms, holding her safe.

As he regained his breath, he rubbed his cheek against her, and then nuzzled her into meeting his lips for a soft warm kiss. Pulling back, he smiled at her ruefully "It wasn't my intention to make love today; I wanted to spend time with you so we could know each other better." He smoothed her sweat-dampened hair gently from her face with the back of his fingers, "You are irresistible to me. Dear God I have no control with you."

What was a girl to say to that? Yes, sex with Rafe took her to the edge, but that he wanted to know her and spend time with her warmed her heart, even when she didn't want it warmed. *Remember – sex only girl. None of this warm fuzzy stuff,* she reminded herself. But she couldn't maintain that line of reasoning, as Rafe returned to her mouth again and again with warm sipping kisses and light nibbles at her lips that touched her to the core.

"Hmmm, let's get cleaned up and go for this walk," he gave her one last hard kiss before pulling himself from her body. Again, he had a hanky out and used it to clean her body of their mingled fluids.

After helping her dress, he took her hand and led her back to the track. “We haven’t been using contraception,” he pointed out refusing to release her hand once back on the even pathway. “I’m sorry, it’s careless of me and has never happened before, but all common sense takes a walk when I’m with you.”

Regan castigated herself, she hadn’t thought about it at all. Running through her cycle, she figured she should be safe at the moment, but she would make an appointment with a doctor this afternoon to organize birth control. “I’m just as responsible. I’ll see a doctor and organize something, but in the meantime we’ll need condoms if we are going to continue this,” she tried not to blush as she glanced at him, but this was all so new to her. It was going to be some time before she could casually talk about condoms without cringing inside. She had a long way to go before she would feel casual talking about sex.

Rafe walking easily beside Regan, tried not to smile at the blush in her cheeks. “I’ll organize the condoms because there will defiantly be a next time. If you’ve conceived a child from our lovemaking I want you to know I’ll be with you all the way and you’ll have all the support you need from me.” Rafe pictured a little girl running around his legs with Regan’s black hair and blue eyes laughing up at him full of mischief. He was eager for children, but he didn’t want Regan feeling pressured by an unexpected pregnancy. If he could reach, he’d kick his own ass for being so careless. He’d make sure he had protection on him at all times from now on.

Clearing her throat uncomfortably, "It should be OK. There are no, ahh, repercussions from the first time we were together," Regan clamped her lips together. She *so* was *not* going to explain where she was in her menstrual cycle to Rafe.

Rafe tilted his head to see her face better. Her blush increased but she met his gaze obstinately. He got the message that this topic was closed. He had to turn away to hide the amusement in his eyes. She looked so darn cute when she was all flustered like this and it was tempting to tease her by keeping the conversation going.

"So have you read any good books lately?" he obliged her with a total topic change.

~~~

Regan had thoroughly enjoyed her morning with Rafe. They had discovered that although they had the same taste in authors, their music preferences were completely at odds. They'd teased each other mercilessly over their varied tastes in television and sports. The two hours they spent hiking was time outside Regan's previous reality. Never before, had she so easily talked and laughed with someone, it had soothed her soul as nothing else ever before had. She felt centered, confident in herself as a person, and as a woman
~~~

who could attract and hold her man.

The time they had spent had been like living in a different reality. Regan was confident, fortified by the way Rafe looked at her as if she were everything to him. She tucked the memory away, to retrieve when her time with Rafe was over.

Both had regretted the need to return to Eden's Retreat, but Rafe had to contact his sentinels and follow any leads they'd come up with. His brief sabbatical had obviously refreshed him, and she could see his determination and resolve were bolstered from the short break away.

She couldn't help feeling self-satisfied that his time away with her had revitalized him. As for herself, she had never felt so relaxed. She had laughed more today than she had in the last ten years. But, what was even better was that she had teased Rafe and made him laugh with her. As she pushed her wheelbarrow across the grounds towards the individual cottages where she'd planned to spend the afternoon weeding the gardens, she marveled at how buoyant she felt, it was all she could do to stop herself from dancing as she hummed a tune.

Movement in her peripheral vision drew her attention, as Ben and a woman she assumed was his mother, walked around the corner of their house coming from the direction of the house's detached garage. Ben's head was down; his shoulders hunched, the picture of abject misery, as he walked along side his mother. In turn, his mother was gesturing sharply with angry cutting motions, as she ranted at the unresponsive boy. Her eyes cut to Regan and noting she had Regan's undivided attention, she quit her tirade and roughly pushed Ben into the house before slamming the door behind them.

CHAPTER 15

If the woman thought, a closed door would stop Regan from interfering she had a bad surprise coming her way. Maybe the woman had a genuine reason for being angry with Ben, but Regan wasn't leaving until she was sure. Regan left her wheelbarrow and approached the house. Leaning up against the house to the side of the large window for the living area without being seen by the house's occupants, she could hear well enough to assure herself Ben wasn't being mistreated.

Although Ben's mother's voice was muffled, Regan could easily understand her. Regan's eyes narrowed. The woman was castigating Ben because he had outgrown his clothes and she had to waste money on new ones or suffer peoples offer for assistance because he wasn't properly clothed. From listening, it became obvious that Ben's mother wasn't stressed because money was tight; she just hated spending it on Ben. The only reason she provided him with shelter and clothing was because she didn't want to lose the communities respect, but she resented Ben for every cent wasted on him and every minute spent in his presence. Her outburst revealed a deep loathing for Ben; it hurt Regan just listening to her.

Regan's fists clenched, at the venom in Ben's mother's voice. Oh no way could Ben stay here, Regan would be removing him from this toxic situation as soon as her father was taken care of. She would approach Ben's mother about Regan taking over his care. Regan might not be at peace emotionally, but at least she admired Ben and would try to look after him. She might not be emotionally free to love him as he deserved, but she sure as hell wouldn't hurt him the way this woman was.

Regan had heard enough and moved towards the door to interrupt the scathing contempt being poured on Ben's head. She would remove Ben until his mother could calm down. No doubt as soon as she realized Regan was there she would stop, since she was so worried about what others thought of her. But she needed time to calm down, otherwise as soon as Regan left she would start up again. At her knock, there was deafening silence within the house.

Ben's mother wore a courteous smile, but her cheeks were flushed and her eyes fever bright when she opened the door, "Can I help you?"

Regan held her hand out even though she felt more like punching the woman in the face. "Hi, I'm Regan. When I saw you and Ben together, I thought I'd introduce myself. I've been spending time with him, teaching him some fighting techniques."

"How nice," she said with clear disinterest. "I'm Moya Duncan." She briefly squeezed the fingers of Regan's proffered hand. "It was nice of you to introduce yourself. I'm sure we will see each other around," she smiled stiltedly, "but if you'll excuse us, Ben and I have things to do." She tried to close the door in Regan's face, but Regan held it forcefully open.

Moya's eyes narrowed at Regan's hold on the door. "Excuse me?" she raised her brow at Regan. "What do you think you are doing?"

Regan could see her animosity rising at Regan's refusal to let the door shut. Heat flushed Moya's skin and her eyes burned into Regan's.

Regan sighed to herself, "Oh well being subtle was never my strong suit," she muttered. "OK Moya. Here's the thing. Ben's a friend of mine and I don't like my friends being abused. Especially for something they have no control over; like the misfortune of being born to you."

Moya's eyes bored into Regan's at the insult. "Why you uptight, self righteous twat. You overhear part of one conversation and think you can pass judgment on me?" she accused, loosing the leash on her temper.

"I know enough of abuse to know your treatment of Ben is wrong. He deserves better than you."

"Is that right? What about what I deserve? Do I deserve a sniveling runt like him?" she glanced contemptuously over at Ben, who stood in the center of the room, cheeks flushed with eyes glued to the floor in humiliation.

"No you don't deserve him." Regan saw Ben's slight flinch as he misunderstood her meaning. "He still loves you, though why is beyond me. You need to think long and hard about how you treat him. He will never hate you but one day he won't care if you live, or not. Think on it, if you die it won't mean a single thing to your own son." Regan paused, hoping her words would have some effect on the woman. She couldn't read what thoughts moved behind those piercing eyes.

She continued, "He has integrity and an inner core of strength that you haven't been able to destroy, no matter how hard you've tried. So no, you don't deserve to have such a treasure, because you're taking out all your anger on him and punishing him for someone else's sins."

Ben's eyes jumped to Regan's, his eyes questioning hers. Had no one ever stood for him Regan wondered swallowing hard. What was wrong with this community that they couldn't see his need?

Her attention came back to Moya when the women leaned into Regan and sniffed at her. Regan leaned away from her, eww she hated when shifters did that.

For an instant fear lit Moya's eyes before contempt raced in. She pulled her lip back in derision as she pushed Regan in the center of the chest, forcing her out of the doorway.

"I should have known someone like you'd be drawn to him," she raked her eyes scornfully over Regan. "Like drawn to like." Moving out of the doorway she turned to Ben, "Get out of here," she snarled at him, repugnance oozed from her as she watched him slip past with his eyes cast submissively at the ground. Turning her contempt back to Regan, "Do not come here again." She shut the door in Regan's face.

Regan shrugged, "Sure thing," she mockingly saluted the door before turning to Ben who'd stopped a couple of yards down the path, a picture of abject misery.

"Wow your mum's lots of fun to be around huh?" she bumped shoulders with him before leading him towards her abandoned wheelbarrow. "Rather than ponder the warped working of your mum's mind and psychoanalyze our response to her comments, why don't we just pretend none of that happened and work our asses off instead?" she asked lightly, knowing Ben was humiliated enough at her witnessing his mom's treatment of him, without her probing the wound like a dentist with his pick.

Ben briefly met her gaze; "Sure," he shrugged with indifference.

Regan gave him a brief, hard hug, "Just try not to take her bullshit on. She obviously has a problem – but it's not you. Unfortunately, she is taking it out on you because you're available, and no one else in the world would take that sort of crap from her."

At Ben's grudging nod, she set him to work raking up leaves as she weeded the garden beds. *Man, that woman was a piece of work. No wonder Ben was so shut off from everyone. If your own mother hated you, how could anyone else possibly like you?*

Regan was going to prove to him with actions and words, that she loved him. *Huh, will you look at that. I just admitted I love someone and I haven't broken out in hives. Boy am I coming along or what?* As she analyzed her response to realizing that she loved Ben, she didn't feel threatened or panicky; no, she felt an untapped source of warmth. She felt strong, confident in her ability to protect Ben, provide guidance, and support so he could fulfill the potential she saw in him. She would not let her own insecurities allow her to fail Ben. She had to learn to fit in here so Ben would fit in, and form strong bonds with these people.

As soon as she was free of her father, she'd work something out with the mother from hell, regarding custody. *I wonder if she'll be happy to have him out of the house or if she'll put up a fight to keep control of him? Hmm wanta bet control? She wouldn't just do the right thing.* Regan yanked out weeds as if she was yanking out Moya's hair.

"Why are you doing all this?" Ben asked as he continued mechanically raking leaves.

"The gardening?" Regan shrugged, "I like it."

Stopping to look at her, "No. Why do you bother with me? I've been thinking about it, and I can't see any advantage for you to spend time with a kid no one wants." There was no self-pity or anger in his voice, just the mildest of curiosity. Regan realized he accepted no one wanted him; he'd obviously come to terms with being alone and ostracized by the community a long time ago. He couldn't understand Regan gaining enjoyment from his company; it didn't fit with his self-image of being defective in some way.

Regan's heart burned in her chest as his question exposed the damage done to his sense of worth. At least for the first twelve years of her life, she'd had her mother's love. Ben had never been wanted. No one had ever done anything for him because they wanted his happiness; no one wanted his smiles, his laughter, and his joy in life. No one had celebrated his achievements, no one encouraged him, – it was a wonder he hadn't curled up in a ball of misery and given up.

Regan's respect for Ben grew yet again. Would she have had the inner fortitude to go on as Ben did, if she hadn't had her mother in those early years? That he held no bitterness or resentment towards others, and was so accepting of his circumstances, showed Regan he was a better person than she was. She knew if their positions were reversed, she would be filled with anger and resentment.

How to convince him that he was wanted, that he was loveable? Time and actions would eventually prove to him that she wanted him in her life, but the words wouldn't hurt either. As Regan tried to formulate a response, she realized that she had the best example of how to love, from her mother. If she could make Ben feel even half as cherished as her mother had made her feel as a young girl, she would be happy.

She missed her mother more in that moment than she had in years. The void left by her mother's death was always with her, but right now, it weighed on Regan heavily. How she wished she could seek her mom's advice on how to handle Ben and prove her love to him. She acknowledged the feelings, paying a silent tribute to her mother as her heart burned, before forcing her attention back to Ben and his needs. Regan focused on the legacy her mother had left behind. She had taught Regan how to love, now she needed to use that knowledge with Ben. She knew what it felt like to be loved and she had her mother's example to follow.

Releasing a breath Regan let her worry slip away, of course, she could love Ben; she just had to follow her mother's example. Moving over to Ben she took his face in her hands and waited until he met her eyes, "I don't know why, but I felt drawn to you the moment I saw you in the library with your nose buried in a book. Then Pete the idiot came along and tormented you, and that tugged at my sense of injustice. I hate cowards who torment people smaller than them. The more time I spend with you, the more I like and admire you." At his skeptical look, she leaned forward and rubbed her cheek against his, brushing soothingly against him, as her inner cat urged.

She was listening to the other entity that shared her soul more and more as the weeks passed since discovering she had an inner cat, and it felt right to Regan. She wasn't afraid of her cat, she was part of Regan, and since accepting her cat she found herself feeling more centered, and her sense of being lost wasn't as strong as before coming to Eden's Retreat and discovering shifters. Her cat sent her urges, but Regan controlled her own actions. It reminded her that she needed to track down Jordan or Chris and ask some pertinent questions. She needed to know how much stronger the cat's influence would become and how to best hone her senses that were strengthening. She hadn't met her mate yet and knew she couldn't shift, but since being at Eden's Retreat her own cat had defiantly woken up and was having an influence. Nevertheless, that was for later, now she needed to start convincing Ben she loved him, and would be in his life forever.

She pulled back and smiled at Ben "I know it's hard for you to believe that someone would admire you, right?"

Ben shrugged, "I don't see what there is to admire."

"Hmm see if you can follow this: although your mother is punishing you for your father's sin, you feel no resentment towards her, you don't act out, you just suck up the injustice, and go on. Your inner fortitude is amazing.

"You've obviously realized that good grades are the best way of obtaining a decent job and supporting yourself. So even though the other kids haven't befriended you and no doubt Peter goes out of his way to make your life miserable, you stick to your plan and obtain excellent grades." At his downcast look and flushed cheeks she knew she was right on both accounts. "Rather than cut school and avoid the situation you front up every day. You've seen past the short-term misery to the larger goal of a career you want. Your maturity is incredible.

"You've never had someone stand up for you, cheer you on, yet you go on. You don't hate, you're not bitter or resentful.

I admire you because if I were in your position I think I would have given up. You're marvelous."

Taking a fistful of hair in each hand, she gave him a slight shake, "Now listen to the important bit. I've come to love you and I'm always going to be in your corner. Because of you, I'm in the process of organizing to move here permanently. Your life is going to change. Soon you're going to flog that idiot Peter into the ground and the other kids will back off. You will have me in your life every day, and if I see you dealt an injustice, I will be stepping in on your side. I'll always be on your side. I will always be here no matter what you do. My door will always be open to you."

Dropping her hands from his hair, she gave him a moment to process her little speech. "Now I know you're not going to believe half of what I just said, so I'll wait for actions to substantiate the words, before I expect hugs and the occasional 'I love you' from you. But trust me Ben, one day that's going to be as natural as breathing."

"Something else you should know is, I know what it's like to live with an abusive parent. My father abused both my mother and me, physically and mentally. I lived under the threat of his fist until the night he murdered my mother. So I know all about shutting yourself behind walls and trusting no one." Swallowing hard she returned her eyes to his. "I understand why you hide and I won't force you out."

Rubbing his back, she found she needed the contact. She so wanted him to believe her and to have hope that things were going to be better. But she knew he'd need time and proof, before letting any of his walls down. With a last pat to his back, she moved back to her garden bed. "How about we put in another hour here, then go and train so you can beat Peter into the ground all the sooner?"

She felt Ben watching her as she tugged out weeds, hoped that he wouldn't be all freaked out, and take off on her. She let out a quiet breath when he reached for the rake.

Regan spent the rest of the afternoon with Ben. During their training session, she spent time showing him more moves designed for a smaller opponent to take out a larger one. She made him practice again and again until the forms were second nature to him and came spontaneously when they sparred. Ben, being a shifter, was incredibly adept at this type of fighting. She only had to show him something once and he retained the knowledge.

As she watched him practice a series of strikes and counter moves around the punching bag, she thought if he continued to progress at this speed, he'd be ready within a week to face Peter. Ben flashed her a grin full of anticipation, when she told him. She couldn't help but laugh; it was the first real smile she'd ever seen from Ben. Obviously, the thought of some payback filled him with delight. Hey, who could blame him? The thought of watching Ben pound Peter into the dirt, filled Regan with joy too.

Later that afternoon, after Ben and Regan finished the landscaping work, he went back home.

~~~

The sun was setting as she climbed into the 4WD Chris was using to drive home in. She decided to take the opportunity to question him about her growing abilities.

"How much influence will my cat have over my actions?" she asked into the companionable silence they'd fallen into.

Chris's sent her a wary glance, "Um, it varies from person to person, how much influence does she have now?"

Regan described the expansion of her sense of sight, sound, and smell, and how she could now sense people approaching before she could hear, smell, or see them coming.

"Another example is this afternoon when I was with Ben, I had this urge to rub my cheek along his and across his jaw and over his hair. I mean I wanted to do it anyway, but the impulse came from my cat."

Chris's brows lifted in surprise, "She obviously feels protective of him. She tried to scent mark him, warning other shifters that he is now under your protection. I doubt she is strong enough yet to do such a thing, but obviously she wants to play a major role in raising him." He popped some
~~~

gum in his mouth and chewed for a moment before continuing, "Which is strange, since he already has a mother and now a new step-father to care for him."

Regan kept her opinion of his parents to herself. "Another example is this need I have to be with Rafe, I actually feel like a cat in heat. She is relentless in her desire to be with him. Is it normal for her to have such a strong influence over me?" Regan struggled to contain her blush, but heat stole into her cheeks, turning to face forward she added "And I'll neuter you if repeat that to Rafe," she muttered.

Chris choked on his laughter, oh, this was priceless, the girl was obviously close to shifting, and his best friend was tangled up worse than a teenage boy tying to get his first date. If Rafe wasn't careful, he'd lose her completely, especially if she shifted before he told her they were mates. This girl had Rafe so confused he didn't know which way was up, and Chris was enjoying watching his best friend tap dance around Regan, trying to win her over. Always before, women had fallen at Rafe's feet, he'd never had to work for anyone's attention, unlike Chris whose size often intimidated the fairer sex, it was cosmic justice Rafe now had to work so hard to win his mate over.

Dark humor lit his eyes, "I think you should raise these questions with Rafe."

"Why?" she asked nonplused. "What would he know about

shifters that you don't?" *For Christ's sake! As if she wanted to talk about this with Rafe. Could it be any more embarrassing? 'Oh hi Rafe, I've got this burning need to fuck you all the time and I'm sure it's mostly driven by my cat. Is that normal? Or do all female shifters respond like this around you?'*

"Well I just don't know the answer to your question, but I've got this feeling that Rafe will know."

Regan's eye's narrowed on him, "Why? What makes you think Rafe would have answers?"

Chris grinned at her as if he knew an inside joke, "Trust me, Rafe is the one to ask."

Regan sighed, "You're not going to tell me anything are you?"

He shook his head.

"Fine, be like that."

~~~

The next morning dragged as Regan tried to fill in the time with work. She caught up with Ben who ensured that everything at his house was as normal, his mother treating him with her usual contempt but nothing he wasn't used to, before heading over to Rafe's office late that afternoon.

Before she could knock on the door, he called for her to enter. Would she ever get used to shifters and their sense of smell? One look at his face and she knew that they were no
~~~

closer to capturing her father. Jordan was lying across one of the couches in crumpled clothes with one arm flung over his face blocking the light from his eyes. He was the epitome of a man who had spent 24 hours straight at a computer futilely trying to crack an encryption code with no success.

Rafe paced the office like a caged animal, Regan stifled the urge to go to him and offer comfort. *Remember it's all about sex Regan – do not make it more than sex or you are gonna get hurt when his mate turns up.* She shoved her hands into the pockets of her jeans to prevent them from reaching out and trying to stroke away his tension. She forced herself to move over to Jordan's prone figure and swiping his feet off the end of the couch, she sat down so there'd be no room for Rafe to sit next to her today.

"Shit Regan, we've come up with nothing." Rafe ran his hands through his hair as he continued, "Jordan will eventually break the encryption on the phone but there's no way of knowing how long that could take. If you're still willing we will put our plan in place tonight."

Regan forced a smile, "Don't sound so morbid Rafe. Either tonight or tomorrow morning, you'll capture my father, some of his men or both. Then you'll be able to close *Titan* down and save countless lives."

"Yes, but putting you in such a vulnerable position haunts me. If something happens to you I'll never forgive myself."

Regan shrugged, she knew her own abilities and felt she could hold her own until the cavalry arrived. “Well there’s no point bemoaning the situation, let’s just get it done. Personally I’m looking forward to seeing my father taken down.”

“You’re right – but Regan, you stick to the plan. If you get hurt because you’ve deviated from the strategy we have in place, you’ll deal with me and you won’t enjoy the experience.”

She snorted, “I’d like to see you try something like that big guy,” she flashed him a real smile this time. “I know the plan, I agree with the plan. So why would I do something outside of the contingencies we’ve discussed? So hand over my mic, ear wig, and tracking device,” she held her hand out in a give me gesture.

Rafe held her gaze for a long moment before moving to his desk returning with the electronic devices. “The mic is voice activated; I suggest you clip it to the inside of your bra so it can’t be seen. Jordan activates the earpiece. So put it in your ear now and don’t take it out.”

As she slid the small device into her ear, Rafe turned her head to the side to ensure it couldn’t be seen. “The tracking device is in this anklet, once again it won’t be noticeable to them if it’s under your jeans.” Rafe motioned for Regan to lift her foot onto his thigh as he squatted down in front of her. When she complied he pushed her jeans up, she shivered as his callous roughened fingers trailed over her skin. Taking his time, he fastened the silver anklet and removed the one she already wore before tugging her jeans down to cover the pretty piece of jewelry.

Rafe had obviously noticed that the only jewelry she wore were her anklets, it was her one frivolous vice. Her collection of anklets was extensive and she felt bare without one on. Had Rafe specifically asked Jordan to make a tracking device out of the exquisite twisted silver anklet? Glancing at Jordan, he gave her a quick wink, while Rafe adjusted the cut of her jeans over her boot.

As she lowered her foot back to the ground he placed his hands on either side of her face, the pads of his thumbs unconsciously rubbing back and forth over her cheeks. He held her gaze, "Know this goes against every instinct I have. You need to take every precaution you can. You *have* to come back to me. Do you understand?"

Regan swallowed, taken aback by his intensity. Looking into his eyes, she actually saw his wolf staring back at her and it was furious. Instinctively she leaned forward and rubbed her cheek against his, gently soothing him and his wolf.

"It's OK Rafe. Nothing will happen to me. I'll be back tomorrow without a scratch. Trust in me, trust yourself, and your Sentinels."

Rafe nuzzled her under the chin before claiming her mouth in a raw open mouthed kiss. “See that you do,” he growled as he let her go. His eyes were still a feral yellow as he struggled to contain his wolf.

“Don’t worry boss, we’ll take care of her.”

CHAPTER 16

Regan chewed at her thumbnail nervously as she waited outside her house for the cab she'd called. It was late; it should have been here fifteen minutes ago. Her nerves jingled and she was on edge. As agreed, after her fight with Chris last night, all communication was cut. She had been unable to sleep, too wound up waiting for an attack that could start at any instant. Regan had nearly cried in relief when then sun began to tint the horizon with color; the endless night was over. A friendly voice would have gone a long way to settling her nerves, but that was impossible with her father's listening devices still in place. Although she knew she wasn't alone, the silence of the night had dragged at her.

She had expected her father to attack in the early hours of the morning. Surely, it would be easier to grab her here in a controlled environment, rather than out on the streets with moving vehicles and the variable of other people involving themselves?

Pacing in front of her house in an effort to release some of the tension she was pulling her phone from her bag to call the cab company again when a distinctive yellow cab rounded the corner. Reaching back with her left hand she reassured herself that her 9mm SIG was tucked snuggly into the band of her jeans at her lower back. She glanced briefly at the driver as she settled into the cab before doing up her seat belt.

"Sorry for the delay lady. Got caught up in traffic this morning. Where ya going?"

Regan's hackles rose as soon as he opened his mouth, she looked up and gave the address they'd agreed on yesterday, it was a coffee shop in the center of the CBD. Her brain caught up to her instinct screaming of danger, at the same moment she realized the prevailing scent in the car was that of blood. She met the driver's eyes in the rearview mirror and was taken aback by the derision there before he moved his gaze back to the road.

Oh shit they were going to grab her now. She needed to give the team the heads up without alerting the driver. Keeping her gaze out the window as much as possible, she furtively sent Jordan at text, "it's now." Within seconds, the device in her ear gave a slight crackle indicating it and the mic were now voice activated. The small sound settled her she wasn't in this alone.

"Is that blood on the dash there?" she asked.

"What?" The driver looked at where she was pointing at the spray of dark droplets across the dash and steering wheel. "Yeah. Nothin' to worry about, I get a bloody nose occasionally."

Looking out the window Regan rolled her eyes, it was all she could do not to snort. They were leaving her neighborhood, but rather than turn right onto Boundary Road that fed into one of the main arterial roads leading into the city, he turned left.

"Hey where are you going? This isn't the quickest way down town."

"There's been an accident on Boundary Road. I'm just going to go around it the back way and then hook up with the main drag into the city further up. Don't worry lady it'll be cheaper than getting stuck in a traffic jam for two hours."

Regan nearly did snort her response to that. He must think her IQ below 80 to fall for that. Within five minutes they pulled into a small cul-de-sac similar to hers, the house blocks were large, the houses all set back from the street, and hidden behind tall hedges or security fences for extra privacy. The end result, the street was deserted.

Leaning down as if adjusting her shoe, she quickly sent Jordan the name of the street. Sitting up she looked around carefully. It was the sort of street where no one would witness her kidnapping unless they happened to drive past at the exact moment they transferred her from the cab. It was a quiet suburbia, everyone was already at work or school, and there would be little chance of any civilian being caught up in what was coming next, especially if it was done quickly.

Regan steeled herself, settled her breathing and heart rate. She had trained for this. It was her job to stay here until the Sentinels could capture these immoral assholes. She wouldn't let them move her to another vehicle. She had her slim SIG at her back, once at the exchange site she might have the opportunity to take the driver out, truly, though her preference was to knock him out rather than shooting him. No doubt, before moving her they would search her and find her mic, once they found that they'd likely find the earwig and tracking device too. The Sentinels would lose her if they got her into another car.

Too soon he pulled the cab over to the curb. "Why are we stopping here?" she asked wondering how long he'd keep the pretense up.

His hand came into view with a nasty looking stub nose pistol aimed at her chest.

"Not long huh," she muttered.

"Your father's just checking out our back trail to ensure none of your friends are following you. Once he has the area secured, he'll take you to your new home."

Regan looked the driver over thoroughly. He was unshaven and generally unkempt; his dark brown hair was cut short and desperately needed a wash. His clothes were wrinkled and stained. Where was her father finding these guys? Washed up are us?

"Now I've been given strict orders not to shoot you, because, hey you can't run real fast with a bullet in you, now. Can you?" he snickered, obviously enjoying the visual. "But John was a good friend of mine and I've taken his death personally. So it might be worth the trouble I get into if I should have to shoot you."

Regan rolled her eyes, "How many times do I have to tell you morons that if you go into someone's home and try to kidnap them, you have to expect them to fight back. Also get your facts right, I didn't kill either of the idiots that died."

"Regan for Christ's sake! You're supposed to be stalling until we get there, not antagonizing the enemy into shooting you!" Regan flinched at Rafe's rough reprimand in her ear.

Oh so not fair, she couldn't retaliate without giving away that she was in contact with the Sentinels. *Just like a man to take cheap shots at you when you can't respond.*

"Bitch your time is coming. Just remember I'll be there when they strip you naked, toss you out of the cage, and into the park to be hunted down, like the animal you are. You're all the same, trying to stay human, but it only takes a couple of close shots or a small nick before you all shift into animals and run," he sneered. "I'll be sittin' there drinkin' beers while you run for your life. Not that it'll do you any good. It's just a matter of time before someone gets you," his reptilian eyes momentarily lit with enjoyment. "I wonder if you're a screamer. The last one we had whimpered like a beaten mutt at the end."

Regan tuned him out, he was deliberately trying to increase her anxiety, and she was not going to give him the satisfaction. She re-evaluated her situation; if she could take the driver out before her father got here, it would make it easier for the Sentinels to capture her father. Although he was ungroomed, his cold eyes were clear and steady. He was all sinew and muscle from what she could see above the bench seat that separated them. He'd occasionally run his eyes over the quiet street, but they always returned to her, carefully watching. The gun never moved from her chest. Not a lot she could do until he took her out of the car, she might be able to maneuver close enough then, she'd have to bide her time.

Minutes ticked slowly by until the man's cell phone buzzed in the oppressive silence. He held it to his ear without moving his eyes from her, the gun stayed centered on her chest.

"Here," he answered the call, listened for a moment, "OK," he disconnected.

"Time to get out princess, daddy's pulling into the street as I speak."

Her heart spiked, this was it. She tingled as her body started pumping adrenaline into her system. Regan steadied herself mentally; she would not let the sight of her father intimidate her. She was not a child anymore; he had no power over her. She would stay calm and be in control of her actions. He was not taking her by surprise this time and she had help on its way. *I'm ready for this.* Taking a deep breath, she opened her door and stepped out of the cab on the opposite side to the driver. He mirrored her actions holding the gun on her.

"Close the door and step up to the footpath," he directed.

Regan watched carefully for an opportunity to draw her own weapon. Her father was walking into their trap; if she could, she would take this one out. *Come on; take your eyes off me, just for a moment, sweep the surroundings.*

Although he looked a mess, he was obviously a trained soldier, his eyes never moved from her as he exited the car and moved around to her side of the vehicle.

"Face the car and put your hands on the roof."

Regan shrugged philosophically it would have been a bonus

taking him out of the equation with her gun but there was no point getting shot trying to prove herself to Rafe and his soldiers. Placing her hands on the roof, she gritted her teeth as he kicked her feet further apart and proceeded to pat her down. Regan's fingers dug into the roof as the obnoxious prick slowly ran his hands over the zipper of her jeans before cupping her between the legs. He leaned forward so she could feel his hard cock pressing up against her bottom.

"That's right bitch, just stand there, and let Alf have his way with you. I bet'cha love it rough don' ya?"

Lip curling in revulsion, Regan fought the need to slam her head back into his face, but for the gun pressed into her side, she'd ram the cartilage from his nose into his brain.

A white van pulled up behind the cab, the side door opening as it pulled to a halt. Alf pulled back quickly completing his search, removing her phone from her pocket and the gun from the waistband of her jeans.

"Now why would you be carrying this?"

Regan tossed him a look that stated clearly that he was a moron.

"Because my father's trying to kill me?"

Alf grabbed her upper arm in a punishing hold at her sarcasm and shoved her towards the van. The side door slid back fully and her father stepped out, obviously intending to help manhandle her into the van, the driver stayed where he was, engine running.

Now in the light of day with her mind clear of panic, Regan was shocked to see how much her father had aged. She felt a burning hatred for him, but none of the terror and fear of their last meeting. She could almost feel Rafe standing beside her, she wasn't alone anymore, and she drew courage from that.

In the glare of the morning sun, she could see her father's depraved life had left its mark on him. His eyes were sunken, with pouches of lose skin below them. His face was drawn in tight lines, his mouth pulled down, and his lips appearing narrow and bloodless. He looked as if life had treated him harshly, she could only hope. He still held the bulky musculature of his younger days, but there was a hint even the strength he prided himself on, was starting to desert him. His shoulders not as straight as they had been, his hair faded in color to a listless dirty brown. Regan had seen elderly shifters at Eden's Retreat; they held a healthy vitality that her father lacked.

Regan balked, she couldn't let them take her away. *Fuck I hope Alf doesn't shoot me.* Jerking back, she broke Alf's hold on her arm then spinning on the ball of her foot, she kicked out connecting the steel caped toe of her boot to the hand holding the gun. The sound of bone crushing under the force of the impact was heard, before the man's scream of pain was cut off abruptly. Regan saw him crumpling lifelessly to the ground, a gaping hole in his forehead in her peripheral vision as she leaped backward, balanced, and ready to move in any direction. She swung her gaze to her father as the repressed sound of a gunshot with a silencer registered.

"What the hell?" she questioned, when she realized her father had shot his own man.

"Undisciplined. People will investigate the noise."

Regan sprung to the side, barely avoiding his savage strike as he spoke, there was no warning. She danced backward giving herself more space. Her father holstered his gun and came at her again with blurring speed. His body slammed into her knocking her backward. Regan took the shock of the hit and flipped backward with the momentum, rather than hitting the ground. She used her straining muscles to twist her body up and over with inhuman flexibility.

She remembered Rafe's demand that she defend herself not attack, but already she realized her father would overwhelm her if she relied solely on defense, and she'd be gone before Rafe could get here. Defense alone wasn't going to give her enough time.

She leaped back again ceding ground to give herself space to launch her own attack, but her father followed her, a constant blur of motion rushing her. She whirled to the side avoiding a fist, arching her back, narrowly avoiding a crippling punch aimed at her kidney. Twisting to escape a kick aimed at her knee she used all her skill to stay out of his reach, using every trick in her arsenal. Panting she drew air in through her mouth.

Shit! He's fast! She ducked, reversed her momentum, twisted, kicked backwards leaping away, but he followed her giving her no time, no space. *Fuck this!* She surged forward ramming her elbow into his side, twisting away but not quickly enough to avoid a painful blow. It grazed her cheek, her momentum carried her away from the full force, but it still split the skin against the bone. Blood splattered as she swung back in raising her arm, blocking his next strike, before driving the heel of her hand into his nose.

He may have gotten first blood but she was in with her own score now, adrenaline surged through her. For the first time he stepped back, a small break in his aggressive attack. They moved back and forth, a blur of constant motion human eyes would struggle to follow. Regan could hear his breathing roughen with exertion. With vicious intensity, she spun around him and drove the heel of her boot into his ribs, elated as she heard the sound of bone breaking.

But does the old bastard step back, of course not! Regan only had time to brace herself as he rammed into her with his shoulder, knocking her off balance. She called on her fatiguing muscles pushing herself into a flip; she grimaced at the burn as they screamed in protest from over exertion. She had to finish this or she'd slow down, if she did her father would have her. Arching her spin in an inhuman twist, she avoided a slashing blow, dancing out of reach she searched for an opening.

"Thomas stand down!"

As Rafe had sprung from the van, he'd taken in the wonder that was his mate in fighting mode. While her father was all brute strength, Regan was the personification of a panther. Her elegant body flexed and twisted as she flowed from attack to retreat. As he'd moved into position he'd seen her long leg swept up into her father's ribs with crushing force, before she twisted agilely and leapt away. She was fierce, his little warrior, in constant motion. She never offered her father a stationary target.

Thomas stepped back and glanced around to see Rafe and five other Sentinels holding guns on him. His gaze settled briefly on Jordan who held a dart gun loaded with tranquilizer, they meant to take him alive. He looked back at the driver of the van but he had his hands in clear view on the top of the steering wheel, as another sentinel held a gun against his temple.

"Throw your gun out and away from you," Rafe demanded. "Regan move to our van." Personally, he'd love nothing more than to put a bullet in the bastards head, but not in front of Regan.

Regan slowly backed away from her father, keeping a careful eye on him as he reached for his gun. She saw the rage in his eyes and knew. Using every ounce of power left in her flagging muscles, she launched herself towards the yellow cab, intending to use it as cover. The force of the bullet spun her to the side, before the burning pain ripped through her. The sound of another round hitting flesh, barely registered at the back of Regan's mind. Clasping her hand to her wound, she dragged herself behind the cab. Panting she lay on her side shuddering at the ripping agony. Shards of pain radiated from her thigh. Warm, sticky blood ran over the fingers she held to the wound, soaking her jeans. Clenching her teeth she panted through the pain, trying to ride with it rather than fight against it. On some level, she was aware of more shots being fired, of Rafe's roar of rage. She tried to call out, but couldn't seem to catch her breath.

Rafe leaped over the body of Regan's father, they had tried to take him alive, shooting him in the shoulder after he'd shot Regan, but it was as if the man was on PCP or something, he hadn't reacted to being shot, but had gone after Regan. The man had her in his sights when Rafe had shot him in the knee taking him down, but Thomas had kept his gun aimed at Regan. Rafe could only see her boots sticking out from behind the cab but from his position, her father had a direct line of sight. In the instant before Thomas took his second shot at his daughter, Rafe's bullet had taken him in the back of the head killing him instantly.

Fear for his mate drove Rafe as he rounded the car; Regan lay on the dirty asphalt in her own blood. It congealed around her hip, a dark morbid pool. Her cheek was split open, bright red blood trailed down her cheek and neck, soaking into the top of her T-shirt. Her skin was sheened with sweat, but so pale; her healthy tan now a sickly yellow. Holding her pain filled gaze, he knelt at her side.

"Hold on honey, I've got you." Bile rose as he took in his beautiful strong Regan lying in the street. "We'll get you to help in no time." He gently moved her hand from the gunshot, ripping his shirt off he folded it into a pad and pressed it against the raw wound, flinching at her moan, but he had to slow the bleeding. "Baby where else does it hurt?"

She shook her head slightly in response, her eyes taking on a glassy sheen as her body withdrew into shock.

He growled at the realization, she couldn't feel her cheek was sliced open to the bone, because of the searing agony of the gunshot wound. If he could, he'd kill that bastard all over again but slower this time, he'd gotten off too easy.

He turned to see Jordan and Chris heading his way, "Jordan," he barked, "move our van over here. Chris clean up this mess, you'll only have minutes before the police get here. Make sure there is nothing left to tie this to us."

Both men nodded before turning away to follow orders.

Within moments, Jordan slid the van to a stop next to them.

"OK baby we are going to move you now. It's gonna hurt like a son of a bitch. I'm sorry love, but we have to move you before the police arrive."

Regan opened her eyes to meet his worried gaze. She wanted to reassure him she would be fine, but Rafe and Jordan were already lifting her, searing pain crashed into her, ripping consciousness from her grasp.

Rafe and Jordan shifted Regan carefully into the back of the van. Rafe climbed in with her as Jordan clambered behind the wheel and headed for Eden's Retreat, Kylie would be better equipped to help Regan than a human who didn't understand her animal metabolism. Tearing open the first aid kit, he left his folded up shirt on the wound so if any clotting had commenced he wouldn't restart the bleeding, and bandaged it tightly to her thigh, helping her body slow the bleeding. Now that he had time to think about the brief look he'd taken before clamping his T-shirt to the wound, be realized the bullet had torn through the edge of her thigh, rupturing flesh and muscle. It had gouged a channel through her muscled thigh but hadn't hit bone or major blood vessels. He placed some butterfly bandages on her cheek trying to pull the edges back together; he grimaced seeing her flesh already swollen.

He tried to reassure himself she would be fine, but his wolf paced anxiously worrying over her unconscious state. He ran his hand over her looking for any internal swelling or broken bones. He couldn't detect anything, but his medical training was very basic. Using his cell phone, he called Kylie and he filled her in on Regan's condition and their ETA. She listened intently and promised to be ready for them before hanging up. Kylie might have issues with Regan but Rafe knew she wouldn't let that interfere with her care. Helping the sick and injured was her calling; it was as integral as breathing to her.

Rafe monitored Regan's pulse as Jordan wove through traffic, trying to keep himself occupied and the feeling of uselessness at bay. It was steady, which reassured him that he hadn't missed any internal bleeding.

"Don't worry baby we will soon have you fixed up," he continued whispering other nonsense to her as he brushed her damp hair back off her face, needing the contact. Dismayed at Regan's continued inertness he watched her intently, looking for any sign of awareness. Had she hit her head when she fell?

"Come on baby, come back to me."

He kept a hand around her wrist taking her pulse every few minutes, with the other he moved from her hair to run the pad of his thumb over her uninjured cheek.

"You'll be fine sweetheart, Jordan will have us there soon and we'll get you all fixed up."

His wolf prowled restlessly trying to break his hold on it. It wanted out so it could defend Regan and assure itself she would live. It took all Rafe's experience to keep from shifting in the back of the van, but it wouldn't do Regan any good to have a rabid wolf in the van preventing anyone from touching his mate when they arrived.

"We're here Rafe," Jordan called from the front as the van pulled to a smooth stop in front of the clinic.

The side door immediately slid opened and Kylie stepped in. Rafe held stubbornly to Regan's hand; casting him an exasperated glance, she maneuvered around him to assess Regan's injuries. Kylie ran a visual over Regan as she took her blood pressure and pulse. She leaned out of the van to retrieve a mobile drip from the nurse. Within seconds, she had the cannula inserted into the back of Regan's hand and taped into place. She injected morphine into the fluid now trickling into Regan's veins.

"We will give her a couple of minutes for the drugs to take effect then we'll move her." She stepped from the van to ensure the gurney was ready to go. "I can't detect any hemorrhaging but I'll run tests to be certain. I'm confident she will just need stitching up." With a reassuring smile, she gestured for Rafe and the nurse to help carefully move Regan from the van to the gurney so she could be rolled into the clinic. Regan moaned as they moved her. “Don’t worry in a couple of minutes she won’t feel a thing,” she assured Rafe as they finished the transfer.

Rafe stayed out of the way but refused to leave the room as Kylie and her competent staff dealt with Regan’s wounds and assessed her for further injuries. His gut tightened as he watched Kylie repeatedly push needle and thread through Regan’s muscle and flesh as she stitched the gunshot wound, after thoroughly cleaning the site.

As he paced the room Rafe came to the realization he loved his mate. He’d accepted that the mating bond would bind him to her, but what he felt was more than that. It wasn’t just sex, he wanted more he wanted . . . . no, *needed* her in his life every day, he wanted to grow old with her at his side.

When her father shot her, his heart had stopped and hadn’t started again until he’d seen Regan dragging herself behind the taxi. If Regan wasn’t in the world, he didn’t want to be here either. She was strong and courageous; he couldn’t help but admire her. Over the last weeks, that admiration had deepened into a deep and abiding love.

~~~

Sensation returned to Regan in waves. She would hear voices, and then they receded to leave her in peace only to
~~~

wash back in, louder than before. She could now feel someone holding her hand, and felt the comfort of a soft mattress and cool sheets; she tightened her fingers around the hand holding her. A voice whispered of safety, assuring her all was well, she relaxed, she knew she could trust that voice. Time floated as she drifted back and forth, eventually the waves receded leaving her aware. Thoughts returned and she remembered the tearing pain ripping her thigh open, the fight with her father. Where was he? She sat up with a gasp.

"Whoa there. Settle down Regan, your safe now." Rafe gently eased her against his chest as he sat on the edge of the bed. "You're safe, just take a minute," he gently rubbed her back as she rested her forehead against his shoulder.

Regan glanced around, she was back in the same room she'd found herself in the first time she'd woken at Eden's Retreat. She swallowed, trying to moisten her dry mouth. Rafe handed her a cup of water and supported her back as she swallowed a couple of sips, before helping her adjust her pillows so she could sit up.

Rafe smiled into her unfocused eyes as he settled back on the edge of her bed.

"You're pumped full of drugs at the moment so you probably can't feel it, but you have a dozen stitches in your cheek, severe bruising, and a gunshot wound in your thigh, which has been stitched. It tore through some muscle, but there's no bone or tendon damage. You'll have a shit hot scar to brag about though."

She tried to smile at his attempted humor. "My father?"

Clearing his throat, Rafe reached for her hand, he had no idea how Regan would react to her father's death. Yes, she must hate the man for the brutality he inflicted on her and the horror of her mother's death, but he was the last of her family and Rafe had killed him. How did he tell her that even with multiple bullet wounds her father had still gone after her, trying to kill her? He'd left Rafe no choice but to execute him. If Rafe hadn't taken that kill shot, Thomas would have murdered his own daughter. He was obviously insane, who could kill his own child, especially one as special as Regan, with her fierce determination to survive. She refused to be a victim, but also helped other brutalized women defend themselves. Again and again, Jordan had found examples of Regan volunteering her time at women's shelters to teach self-defense.

She might not be able to connect with people emotionally, but she cared. Even when Regan was offered payment, she refused, preferring the money be used to help the women reestablish themselves. Considering Regan only ever took menial jobs and was always paid minimum wage, the temptation for extra money must have been strong, but she never took from charities.

Not only did she teach the women how to defend themselves, but also from the women Jordan had spoken to, Regan helped them gain confidence in their ability to survive, to endure their pasts. Regan might not have connected to the women, but the women had connected to Regan. If she only knew the positive influence she had been, and how much her words and the example her own life was, for the women she taught. They didn't know exactly what had happened in Regan's past, but they all knew she had been victimized, survived, and now stood on her own without relying on anyone. Regan didn't know it, but she had many friends who would jump at the chance to help her if she ever asked. They respected the distance Regan kept, but many of them would love to be invited into Regan's life, their doors would always be open to her.

Rafe rubbed his thumb over her knuckles; he raised his eyes from their joined hands to measure her reaction. "He's dead Regan, I had to kill him. He wouldn't stop going after you, even when we put him down. There was no time, it was either you or him, and I will always choose you – no matter the circumstances."

Regan felt little at the revelation of her father's death. He was a brutal man who had killed off all love she felt for him way before her mother's death. She waited, searching for the grief she should feel, but there was none, maybe some nostalgia for the relationship she should have had with her father, for what could have been. Instead, relief was all she felt; a weight was lifted from her soul at the knowledge that he would never have the power to hurt her again.

“I’d say I’m sorry, but I refuse to lie to you. He was twisted, something was broken in him. What man tries to kill his only daughter when he is surrounded by five Sentinels with guns trained on him?” Rafe questioned roughly.

A lopsided smile pulled at her lips, “A man who would prefer to die in a fight than be captured. His ego wouldn’t allow him to commit suicide so he had to force you to kill him. What better way to force your hand than to go after the unarmed woman?” She leaned into the pillow as tiredness dragged at her. “He probably calculated that if he shot at you or one of the others you’d take him down without killing him, whereas because I was already injured and unarmed, the likelihood of you killing him outright was a high probability.”

She drifted for a time taking comfort from Rafe’s presence. His rough hand held hers and fed her sense of peace. Why she craved contact with this man she didn’t understand. Usually she pulled into herself and found calm when she was centered. Normally she was self-contained, but right now having Rafe with her comforted her and felt too good to reject. Nevertheless, she would have to stand by herself soon, she couldn’t afford to become accustomed to Rafe’s presence in her life, he wasn’t hers for the long term. His mate was out there and she would claim him sooner or later.

She would just take this small time to gather comfort and strength from this remarkable man, and then she would stand-alone again. Joy unfurled in her chest, a tiny flame that grew within her warming her to her soul, no not alone; with her father gone, she could now start the process of moving Ben in with her. She could care for him and assure he grew into the full potential she saw in him. She drifted away, pleased with the possibilities opening for her.

When she next came to, Rafe was still sitting beside her, holding her hand in both of his, looking at her hand as if it could give him the answers he needed. Concern furrowed his brow, but on closer examination, he didn't look as worn down as yesterday.

"Did you get the information you needed from my father's other man?"

With a grimace, he shook his head, "He knew nothing. He was just a local thug they hired to drive the van. He knew they were going to snatch a woman, but that was about it. He was only to drive the van to a secondary point, where you would be transferred to another vehicle. He wasn't even told where that would be."

Rafe felt Regan's disappointment; he held up a hand, "Although it's not the outcome we wanted it has given us time. With your father gone, they have no one to point out shifters. We also have your father's and the taxi driver's phones. Jordan will break the encryption, it is just a matter of time, and then we have three phones with contacts and numbers to track. From there we will be able to trace those involved with *Titan*. So it wasn't a complete bust. We will find them soon. Even without your father, they obviously have the resources to eventually track our communities down." She saw the determination in his eyes, "This time we will act preemptively, I will not wait to see if they find us, but will take the fight to them, and they are not going to survive the reckoning coming their way."

Shaking his head he let the anger go for the time being; he raised Regan's knuckles to his lips and nibbled gently, "But you're involvement is over. I don't think I could survive placing you in danger like that again. I thought my heart would stop when we pulled up and saw you fighting your father. Then when he shot you – God Regan," he closed his eyes, remembering the anguish when he'd reached her to see her lying in her own blood. He hated that she'd been hurt. It had been his call to use her for bait; it was his responsibility to ensure her safety. He'd miscalculated and had been too far away to prevent her father from hurting her again.

Regan could feel Rafe's self-recrimination, like sandpaper against her skin.

"Hey you were there in time to save the day and you killed

the bad guy. Cut yourself some slack," she squeezed his hand.

He shook his head refusing to look at her, "I failed you. If you weren't such a gifted fighter, he would have taken you."

Regan found his remorse uncomfortable; she didn't want him hurting like this. "Rafe look at me," she waited for his chocolate brown eyes to meet hers and sucked in her breath at the deep sorrow there. "Rafe," she whispered, bewildered by his sense of shame. She could see his self-condemnation was tearing at the very fabric of his indomitable character. This had to stop, but what to say? "I had complete faith that you would be there. I knew you were coming and that gave me the confidence to stay and fight."

His eyes dropped from hers again. "Please Rafe, your pain is hurting me, enough of this. You trusted me to hold my own long enough for you to get there, don't take that away from me. I stood toe to toe with my father and he did not beat me. You gave me that opportunity; don't take that victory from me with this self-recrimination. You have done for me what no other ever has. Don't diminish what I did."

Rafe slid from his chair to sit next to her on the bed, "Never Regan," he hushed. "I'd never take that away from you. However, that wasn't your finest moment sweetheart. Your ability to still care for others, after all you've been through is incredible. Helping other women that is your finest moment and your life is awash with moments like that." He leaned forward and brushed his lips across hers, reverently.

Regan swallowed the lump in her throat. No one had ever looked at her with such admiration, as if she were a miracle. His respect fascinated her; he made her feel cherished. Oh boy, how was she supposed to keep her emotions in check around this man? Wistfully she wondered what it would be like to be mated to this man, a warrior, and protector.

He brushed his lips across hers, she felt the affection he held for her, the need to give and take comfort. The sexual burn they felt for each other was there, but for once didn't dominate all other feelings.

"Rafe what are we doing here?" At his raised eyebrow, she gave him a mock punch on the chest. "I don't mean the kissing I mean you and me."

He rubbed his mouth back and forth over hers and smiled against her lips, "Taking a moment to enjoy each other, to savor your courage and rejoice in your survival. It is but a moment in time; don't ruin it worrying about the future. All will work itself out."

Tenderness for this man wound through her and tiredness dragged at her. She tilted her head to the side allowing him to nuzzle against her undamaged cheek as she drifted away again. As she slipped into sleep she thought, they must be some good drugs they're giving me, if I can't stay awake for more than five minutes at a time.

Rafe watched as Regan fell into the deep sleep her body required to heal. The sight of her swollen cheek held together by black stitches tore at his heart, but he took on Regan's admonishment, he would not undermine her courage and self-confidence by allowing her to sense his guilt. Her father had hurt her when she was a child, his to protect and instead he had brutalized her. Now she was Rafe's to protect and he had failed her too. He would hide his shame from his mate, but he would not forget his failure.

Now that she'd awoken and he was reassured she was whole and safe, he needed to let his wolf out. All morning the animal had tried to force the change on him, lunging at the barrier, repeatedly. If Rafe didn't allow the shift soon his wolf would break free on its own. He needed to spend that aggression running or they'd end up starting a fight with another shifter whose control of their animal wasn't as strong as it should be. His wolf was looking for a fight and Rafe needed to let it out before he instigated a challenge with some poor bastard who looked at him the wrong way.

He quickly made his way to the forest, stripping his clothes, he embraced the change and lunged into the woods on all fours, his paws tearing up earth as he raced along the narrow trails that crisscrossed the woods. Reveling in the freedom of his wolf, he laid back his ears and extended his reach, pushing for more speed from his sleekly muscled body. He kept to the grueling pace for hours, feeling the savage turbulence of his wolf slowly settling as he ran. His mate was safe and she would recover.

Eventually he collapsed on his side, sucking in air hard as he recovered. Shifting to his human form, he rolled onto his back, letting the peace of the woods seep into him and contemplated his relationship with Regan. How should he progress their relationship now that her father was taken care of? He would have to reveal they were mates soon. Her first shift could happen any time. If she shifted before he told her, she would be furious that he'd withheld the knowledge. She would believe he had been playing with her, and Regan's response to being hurt was to withdraw back behind that impenetrable wall of hers. That was unacceptable.

His original plan of taking things slow and wining her trust had been sound, but he hadn't been prepared for the punishing desire that consumed him whenever he was close to her. He'd proved again and again, his inability to resist the lure of his mate. They had now consummated the mating numerous times, ensuring her first shift could occur at any time.

His one saving grace was because she had been unaware she was a shifter; she was more disconnected from her cat than a normal shifter would be. Her cat had further to develop, and would take longer than normal to gain enough strength to instigate that first shift. Nevertheless, the question was how long before her first shift? He couldn't risk waiting too long, or she would feel betrayed that he'd kept the knowledge of their mating from her. It was crucial she trusted him, before he revealed his responsibility for leaving her and her mother in Thomas's brutal hands all those years. He prayed that she would be strong enough to forgive him. He wouldn't ask her to finalize the mating through the ceremony until he had exposed himself. His gut churned at the thought of revealing his culpability for her childhood filled with violence. What would he do if she shunned him? Was he strong enough to respect her wish and stay away if she demanded it of him? He shook his head; he could no more walk away from her now than he could stop breathing.

He knew she trusted him on some level or she wouldn't surrender her body so beautifully during their lovemaking. He was sure he also had her cat on his side. She had risen close enough to the surface; his wolf had briefly connected with her a couple of times. He'd discerned her intrigue and interest but if he hurt Regan, he knew her cat would instinctively rise to protect her. He could find himself battling Regan and her cat, if he wasn't careful.

Mulling it all over, he realized he had to reveal they were mates, there was no other recourse. If she shifted before he told her, Regan's justified anger would be a wedge between them. As soon as she was up out of bed, he would explain why he'd hidden from her the knowledge they were mates. Surely, she wouldn't shift in the next couple of days.

He'd allow her as much space and time as she needed to come to terms with the mating. He would continue to woo her and convince her of his love. She was everything to him and he would convince her of it. He was determined to care for her. If Regan was happy, he was happy, it was that simple.

She was meant for him, and she was everything he could desire in a mate, her innate strength, her courage, her willingness to help others. His woman was strong and honorable; she was his equal in every way.

~~~

Regan moved back into her unit at Eden's Retreat. While recovering, she contacted a real estate agent to sell her house. She then rang the alpha's office enquiring about the process involved in formally joining the community and purchasing one of the cottages at Eden's Retreat. The staff member put her on hold for couple of minutes before informing her, the alpha would be over to see her within the hour.

"Hold on I'm......" but they'd already hung up on her. "I'm not prepared for an interview! I just want to know the
~~~

procedure," she continued in exasperation.

CHAPTER 17

So here she was, pacing nervously as she waited for Byron Anderson to make his appearance. Her wounded leg was healing rapidly, each step still caused deep pain within her thigh, but it was manageable. The throb in her cheek was dissipating quickly thanks to her shifter metabolism; hopefully tomorrow, they would remove the stitches, as they were now causing as much pain as the wound itself. She glanced at her reflection in the mirror; she was dressed in a full-length paisley skirt, the only piece of clothing she owned that she could fit over the bandage on her thigh, she wore a moss green tank with it, and her glossy black hair was brushed so it fell down her back. She looked presentable, if you could overlook the fading bruises covering her arms and face and the ugly black stitches pulling at her cheek. She shrugged; nothing she could do about that, she just hoped the alpha wouldn't think she was anything like her father.

Chewing at the quick on her thumb, she stopped to gaze out the window. She needed to convince him she would be an asset to the community here. If he didn't allow her to stay, she would have little chance of obtaining custody of Ben. Why would he accept her though? She had few skills and little money to bring to the community; on top of that, she was a misfit. She didn't behave like other shifters, didn't share their sense of community or need to share every facet of her life with others. She needed her space, she didn't want the other shifters feeling they had the right to hug her and continually touch her. She was like the anti-shifter. Her shoulders slumped, what was normal for them was abhorrent to her, so why would she expect him to accept her?

Her skit flared out as she whirled around at the knock on her door. Glancing at the mirror she tried to pull some hair forward to cover the mess that was her cheek, she grimaced at her reflection. Nothing short of a brown paper bag was going to help. She moved across the floor, opened the door, and looked up and up some more. Holy hell, she'd though Chris was huge, but this guy was close to seven feet and not just tall, he was broad too. She tipped her head to the side as she tried to work out what his shifted form was.

His lips curled up at her considering look, "Grizzly bear."

"Pardon?"

"I'm a grizzly bear when I shift," he clarified. An open grin broke over his craggy features as heat climbed into Regan's cheeks.

"Way to go Regan! Make yourself look like an idiot why don't you?" she muttered to herself as she stepped back and waved him in.

A deep rumble of laughter stopped her self-castigation, "Don't worry Regan, that was not my first impression of you."

Before she could question him on that, he held his broad hand out.

"We've never formally met, I'm Byron Anderson and you're Regan Reynolds," although his hand engulfed hers, he was careful of his strength as they shook hands.

"Shall we sit on the couch near the windows or is it easier on your ribs to sit up at the kitchen table?" The man was obviously used to being in charge, as he took over the position of host.

"Lounge is fine," Regan eased herself down onto the cushions.

"Would you like tea or coffee?" he asked, as he headed to the small kitchenette.

Regan grimaced as she struggled to rise and make him a coffee. Her ribs might only be bruised, but that didn't stop them from hurting like a son of a bitch whenever she sat down.

She watched him rummage through the cabinets looking for coffee as she tried to get to her feet with more grace than a pregnant woman carrying triplets, and saw him raise a hand indicating she should stay seated.

"Sit down woman, you're injured, and I'm the one in desperate need of coffee. I'm capable of making instant coffee, though I'm the first to admit those fandangled machines everyone has now days are beyond me, but this I can handle. Do you want one?" at her headshake, he finished making his own.

It gave Regan a chance to study him unobserved. Now that he'd told her he was a grizzly, she could see it in him. Although tall, his body was proportioned perfectly, he had broad shoulders and a massive chest to complement the height. He had shaggy brown hair that vain men would pay hairdressers a fortune to achieve, but she would bet her last dollar he just got out of the shower and toweled it dry. Even without his height, the man's charisma would draw attention, power radiated from him. She bet he had to bat women away.

His dark brown eyes evaluated her as he came to sit in the lounge chair opposite her, facing the window at her back.

"So you want to join our community?" he prompted.

"Yes – I was just trying to find out the procedure this morning when I rang your office."

Regan watched as he waved his paw... hand, waved his *hand* at her negligently.

"There is no formal process. I only have to accept you. For me to do that, I need to believe you will benefit the community." He paused looking into her eyes, his penetrating gaze felt as though he could see through her protective shield and delve into who she was; it was incredibly hard for Regan to hold his gaze. She didn't want anyone to see behind the face she presented to the world. It felt as if this man could see her every weakness, she was being stripped bare, as he examined her. Nevertheless, Regan sensed she was being tested, and if found wanting, her chances of obtaining custody of Ben would be nil. A fine sheen of sweat covered her body by the time Byron released her gaze and settled back comfortably against the plush leather of the chair. Regan felt as if she'd run a marathon, raw and wrung out. She'd never met anyone with overt psychic powers before, but she'd bet her house Byron Anderson had the ability to see into people's minds, she'd almost felt him sifting though her memories.

"Tell me why you want to become a part of our community."

Regan shifted uncomfortably not at all prepared for this interview. "Well obviously, now that I know about shifters, I want to be a part of this world," she started.

"That might be a minor part of it but you are too self-contained for that to be a major motivation," he cut her off.

His flat statement confirmed her suspicion, he had some sort of ability to read people, and he had seen more than she wanted, when she had held herself open to him. This wasn't a man to fob off; he'd want the truth, and all of it. Regan stared back at him, her ire rising, she hated feeling vulnerable and her automatic reaction to that feeling of being exposed was aggression, if this man wanted the truth, so be it he could have it, in spades.

Sitting up straight Regan nodded at him, "OK Byron here it is. You have a child under your protection that is being systematically abused, not only by his parents but also by the children, and every adult here is guilty of turning a blind eye to the abuse. I will not. I will do everything in my power to help that boy. If that means setting up home here, so I can protect and provide for him – then so be it, that is what I'll do. You people think you have utopia here, but you're no better than humans – turning your backs to that small boy.

Byron's eyes narrowed on her, "You refer to Ben? I've had concern for both him and his mother. I'd hoped by leaving him in her care, she'd come to terms with her past and learn to love him. Moya was gravely wounded, both physically and emotionally; I'm as worried for her as I am for Ben. I had noticed Ben looking better cared for lately, and had hoped Moya had seen the boy was innocent. But now I see it has been your influence." He tapped his fingers on the armrest gazing at her as he thought for a moment, "Maybe it is time to take him out of that situation, I'll have to think on this."

He'd taken some of the wind out of Regan's sails.

He censured her, "But you are wrong in your belief that we think we're better than humans. We are different and have different needs and different problems. No one here would claim to be perfect. I don't believe you think of yourself as such, so perhaps you could be less judgmental of our faults."

Regan flushed at his reprimand, and dipped her head acceding, "You're right I am the last who should judge, but I hate seeing Ben constantly demeaned and denigrated by that woman, and the children here either pretend he doesn't exist or torment him. His life here is hell. Surely there is someone here to advocate for him?"

He smiled at her, "Well there is now, yes?"

She nodded, "Just so you know what you're letting yourself in for, if you allow me to stay, I will be seeking custody of Ben and I'll be doing it soon," she jutted her jaw challengingly.

"You believe you can put down roots here and stay for the long term? To enter Ben's life and then walk away from him because we make you uncomfortable, would be a travesty," his steady gaze pierced the veil of her remnant anger.

"I fully understand that," she responded earnestly, all the last of her resentment draining from her, "but I assure you no matter what happens I will remain a part of Ben's life. I want to look after him and I'm committed to him." She held his gaze as he again delved into her mind; she could literally feel him shifting through her past experiences, obviously trying to determine her motivation and resolve to stay.

"And what does Rafe think about your intention to foster Ben?"

Regan blinked at the question. Shrugging her shoulders, "I haven't discussed it with Rafe. Why would I?"

Byron smiled at her indulgently as if she was a younger cousin, a clueless younger cousin. Laughter lit his brown eyes as he held up his hands, "No reason."

This time Regan tried to see into his mind, but she could read nothing from him but his amusement.

"I'll organize for one of the cabins to be made available for you to rent. I'm happy for you to approach Moya regarding fostering Ben – I believe she will be open to the idea. But, I do insist that you ensure Ben has every opportunity to stay in contact with his mother. A condition of my agreeing to back your push for custody is that you try to foster a positive relationship between Ben and his mother." At her reluctant nod he continued, "That is an open wound that needs healing."

He stood indicating the end of the meeting, "Call by the office this afternoon, I'll make sure my assistant has paperwork and keys ready for you." He held out his hand, "Welcome to Eden's Retreat and the world of shifters, Regan." As one hand engulfed hers, he raised his other to cup her lower wrist and squeezed gently, "You have come a long way in a short time, but you have further to travel, be courageous. Have faith that the path you have started upon will bring you happiness. Don't let old fears hold you back. You are strong enough now to face and deal with what is to come."

Dread washed through her at his warning. What was coming?

Releasing her, he stepped back, "Call me if there's any issue, here's my contact details."

Regan took the card her proffered her and ushered him out, a sense of foreboding settled over her as she closed the door.

That afternoon Regan went to Byron's office and received the keys and papers from his assistant. She wanted to be moved in quickly so she could move forward with having Ben live with her, and away from his abusive mother.

CHAPTER 18

The next day revealed itself to be a beautiful summer's afternoon, as Regan walked across the quad, sunlight filtered through the majestic old trees bordering the vibrant grass; the air was crystal clear and the sky the deepest of indigo blue. It was one of those days where she felt so alive, it seemed to bubble up inside her as she almost floated across the ground, she felt so light and free. She was on her way to meet Ben after school, so they could talk as they walked to training.

In the last couple of days, her body had healed at an amazing speed. The nurse had removed the stitches from her cheek this morning; it had only been three days since the fight with her father. Her ribs were nearly healed, the gunshot wound was painful, but even it was closing and the swelling nearly gone. She'd remarked upon the speed of her recovery to several different people but everyone just shrugged and muttered something about being a shifter. But it didn't make sense; she'd always been a shifter, why start healing quicker now?

A couple of students running off towards the sports fields behind the buildings housing the school snagged her attention. When she saw another small group, rushing after the first two, her radar twanged at their suppressed excitement. She stopped and swung her gaze over the entire area, several other adults had also stopped to watch the students. Something made her gut clench as she watched two more girls head the same direction giggling as one tugged the other to slow her down, obviously not wishing to attract attention. *Too late for that girls*, she thought as she started to follow them.

Regan wasn't the only adult to set off after the girls, she noticed Rafe angling across the quad so he could join her, and a couple of other shifters drifted after the retreating girls. Rafe and Regan met up at the path that led to the sports fields.

"Do you know what's going on?" she asked.

He flashed a quick reassuring smile, "I'd take a guess that a couple of the boys are going to fight. It happens; they have to deal with normal adolescent hormones as well as the extra aggression of their animal. The lead up to our first change is hard on us; our animal wants out and we haven't mastered control of them yet. It can be a tense time and sometimes a good fight is the only way to get the aggression back under control. We just need to ensure there are adults there to supervise and make sure it is an equal match and to stop it if it gets out of hand. We have organized fights for the boys to vent their aggression where we start to teach them skills, as well as techniques for controlling their beast, but boys will be boys and sometimes they can't wait."

At her concerned look, he took her hand and rubbed it against his thigh as they walked. "Don't worry adults are always on the lookout and most are stopped before anyone is seriously hurt."

As they rounded the corner, Regan could see around twenty youngsters surrounding two boys, one of the boys was a head taller than the other and substantially heavier in build. If this was to be a fight, it was going to be an unfair one. It looked like the larger boy was tormenting the smaller, humiliating him in front of his peers. From his cocky manner, the older boy knew he'd easily win.

Regan's contempt for the older boy skyrocketed when she realized it was Ben being tormented. "Oh this is so stopping today," she muttered.

Pulling Rafe to a stop by their joined hands, she turned to him, "Now that they have adult supervision, the boys fight here and now, right?"

Rafe raised his brows in surprise; he'd assumed Regan would want to protect Ben from Peter.

"Sure," he shrugged, "but are you sure you want to put Ben in that position?"

"Oh yeah," she turned and smiled viciously at Peter. Raising her fingers to her mouth, she gave a shrill whistle to gain everyone's attention. More adults had caught up to them and turned to Regan.

"Hey Peter," Regan called as she walked into the circle of silent students, "instead of talking Ben to death, how about a supervised fight here and now? You have the required adult supervision."

Peter looked her over, disbelief shone on his face. He turned to Rafe, "We can fight?" he questioned. Elation filled him at the thought of handing out a thrashing in front of his peers as well as the leader of the Sentinels. It was like a dream come true, he could show his skills to the Sentinel, increase his authority over the other students and get to pound out some of his frustration from class on the insipid kid whose own mother didn't want him. It was obvious no one wanted the kid here at Eden's Retreat, no one ever stood up for him, his own mother walked away whenever she caught Peter tormenting him. The runt wasn't an asset to Eden's Retreat. Peter's own wolf scented an alpha in Ben, but he behaved as an omega and Peter would always treat him as one.

Something about Ben cried out to Peter's wolf to dominate him, or make his life so miserable that he'd leave Eden's Retreat. Ben's lack of assurance was intolerable; they would be a stronger pack without him. To Peter's way of thinking, if he could force Ben's departure, he will have enhanced the pack. And here this woman was giving him permission to thrash the kid in front of his peers. Way to go lady!

Rafe glanced at Ben, "If Ben's willing." He then turned his gaze to Peter "The normal rules apply, no hitting below the belt, no shifting as Ben hasn't attained his first shift yet," he reminded sternly. "You willing Ben?" Rafe prayed the kid would accept, if he refused the other kids would think him a coward and would torment him for it. Shifter kids admired strength and could make life harsh for someone they believed weak. They wouldn't expect him to win, but they would expect him to try.

Again, he wondered at Regan placing Ben in this position, watching her now, he noted his mate didn't appear at all concerned for Ben.

Ben glanced at Regan; she smiled and gave him the thumbs up. Rafe watched as a smile like the rising sun spread across Ben's freckled face. He stood taller, "Yeah sure – why not?"

Regan gave Ben a wink and walked from the ring the gathering crowd had made. Rafe stayed in the center, to act as referee. Once assured both boys were ready, Rafe gave them the signal to start.

Peter immediately rushed Ben, obviously intending to use his greater strength to force him to the ground. Unlike normal boxing, shifters fought in a no holds barred style, they could kick, bite, and hold down an opponent, there were few rules.

Rafe watched as Ben awaited the attack balanced on the balls of his feet, at the last instant he slid to the side, sweeping out a leg he tripped Peter, sending him sprawling face first into the grass. Peter was instantly back on his feet, not giving his adversary any credit he moved in, intending to grab Ben and throw him to the ground for the insult where he no doubt intended to lay into him with his boots. Again, Ben danced out of his reach slipping past Peter; Ben slammed his elbow back into Peter's kidney causing the boy to grunt with pain.

Peter swung out blindly with a clenched fist, catching Ben full in the face. Rafe winced at the sound of cartilage breaking. Ben retreated out of Peter's range instinctively wiping at the blood streaming from his nose. Peter taking advantage of Ben's retreat surged forward and rammed into Ben forcing him to the ground. Rafe prepared to step in, once Peter was in total control of Ben, to ensure he didn't hurt the smaller boy more than was necessary to show all here his dominance. Peter rammed his fists into Ben's stomach and ribs repeatedly.

Even scrutinizing the boys as closely as he was, Rafe didn't witness what move Ben used, but watched as Peter was tossed over Ben's head to land with bone jarring force on his back.

Both boys came to their feet at the same time. "You should have stayed down you little runt," Peter snarled. He rushed Ben, kicking out with his longer legs, aiming his booted heal at Ben's already battered stomach. Ben swept up an arm blocking the kick at the last instant and slammed his elbow into the side of Peter's head as Peter's momentum carried him past Ben. Peter might not be a skilled fighter, but he was a shifter and he was fast and stronger than Ben. At the last instant, even dazed from Ben's shot to the head, he managed to wrap an arm around Ben and dragged him to the ground with him. As he tried to roll over on top of Ben to use his extra weight and strength against his smaller opponent, Ben wedged his foot between them and thrust Peter away, at the same time twisting his flexible spine and flipping to his feet.

A strange hush had fallen over the crowd. The adults were aware they were watching a contest of skill against brute strength. Whereas, before they'd believed they would witness a thumping; now they were seeing a contest.

As Peter tried to gain his feet, Ben danced back in and kicked his feet out from under him, then rammed his boot into Peter's mid section. Peter moaned as the wind was driven from his lungs. Peter tried several more times to gain his feet but Ben was relentless, giving no ground. If Peter tried to stand, Ben would kick his feet out from under him and land another punishing blow. Peter writhed on the ground as he tried to draw air into his abused body.

Wiping at his bleeding nose Ben approached his downed enemy, anger making his copper eyes glow. The temptation to scream his loathing was nearly undeniable. He derived intense pleasure from each kick he delivered. His nemesis was lying right there in front of him, vengeance could be his and no one would blame him for taking it. The hatred twisted inside him.

He looked to Regan, she gave no indication as to what he should do, but the pride that lit her eyes stilled him. This woman had changed his life. She believed in him, she gave her time to him; she trained him, and had made this defeat of his tormentor possible. She had orchestrated this win to be witnessed here and now. Peter would have to endure the humiliation of his defeat in front of this crowd of adults, as well as his peers at the hands of the runt of the school.

Satisfaction poured through him. Never again would he walk away from their taunts or endure the humiliations dealt to him. He'd proved to himself that he could fight back and from now on, he would. Never again would he tolerate their torment without retaliating. Shifters respected strength; he vowed that never again would he cower before them.

He placing his boot on Peter's throat pressing down on his trachea, "Do you yield?" He kept a careful eye on Peter ready to spring back if he attacked. But Peter's need for fighting was quashed, for the time being. At Peter's muttered yes, Ben stepped back and away, signaling the end of the fight.

The crowd clapped and whistled their approval. As Ben took in the spectators, he noticed a couple of the girls from school glancing at him speculatively as they chattered with each other. He accepted congratulations from some of the men who shook his hand, and treated him with respect for the first time in his life. It was uncomfortable, these people seldom acknowledged his existence; he didn't know how to react to their sudden interest. His gaze sought out Regan, reading his trepidation she grinned and shrugged her shoulders helplessly. She didn't know how to deal with these people any better than Ben did.

While Ben was being patched up at the health clinic, Regan filled him in on her plans to move into one of the cottages and live at Eden's Retreat permanently. She'd sounded him out about his interest in moving in with her. She still smiled at his joyful shout of "Hell yeah!" as he'd launched himself at her hugging her tightly.

While she had waited for Ben to have x-rays done on his ribs, Kylie had approached her. Regan had prepared herself for a venomous onslaught but Kylie had stiltedly apologized for her behavior. She'd assured Regan that she and Rafe had only ever been friends. As she'd walked away, she'd given Regan a twisted smile and asked her to let Rafe know that Kylie had organized a transfer to another shifter community, effective immediately. Before Regan could form a response, the woman had walked back into the *staff only* section, effectively cutting off any further contact.

Now as Regan headed to Moya's house to talk to the woman about fostering Ben, she couldn't deny her relief. She'd come to believe Rafe was being truthful regarding his relationship with Kylie. Being a typical male, he'd completely missed that Kylie wanted more than friendship, and although she was relieved that her trust in him had been validated, she still didn't want to become too involved with Rafe. They weren't mates and he had the potential to crush her when he did find the woman destined for him alone. She was afraid if she spent too much time with him, he would become essential to her. She found herself empathizing with Kylie on that score and she had only known the man for weeks not a lifetime like Kylie.

She admired Rafe and trusted him, two things she had thought herself incapable of. If she let him into her heart any further, she'd be devastated when he walked away. It was far better to keep him at a certain distance, than become so entwined that it would rip her apart when he left. She contemplated ending their relationship now, but that idea made her cringe. She wanted to be with him more than she wanted to protect herself from future hurt. She'd been on her own most of her life, why was there this need to entwine herself with this man? She *had* to hold some of herself back if she was to survive their eventual separation.

As she mounted the steps to Moya's house, she wondered again if Moya would be glad to foster Ben out or if she'd spitefully want to keep him? She knocked on the door and waited.

CHAPTER 19

"What do you want?" Moya demanded as she opened the door standing with her arms crossed, blocking entry into the house. "Didn't I tell you not to come back here?" she added belligerently.

"And it's nice to see you too Moya," Regan's voice was syrupy sweet. "Could I come in to discuss Ben with you?" *I can do civil, I can do civil* she chanted to herself. But boy, this woman was a sour piece of work.

"I have nothing to say to you." As Moya went to shut the door in Regan's face Regan thrust her arm out preventing the door from closing.

"Listen lady, I need to talk to you about Ben and you *will* listen to me."

Moya put her shoulder behind the door and tried to thrust it shut, but Regan locked her arm and held her ground refusing to budge.

Grinding her teeth in frustration, Moya stopped her useless pushing and stood up. "You have one minute, then I'm calling the Sentinels to remove you from my property." Again, she stood in the doorway arms crossed over her chest, looking at Regan as if she was a lump of dog shit left on her front step.

Taking a calming breath Regan launched into her prepared spiel. "I'd like to foster Ben. I've organized a cottage here for us, so you can have as much contact with him as you'd like. Think how wonderful it would be for you and your new mate to have the house to yourselves without Ben underfoot. People would understand the two of you wanting a chance to be a couple without Ben and I promise to take good care of him." Regan waited, wondering which way Moya would jump, it didn't take long to find out. Regan nearly tripped over her own feet back peddling as Moya stepped into her space, her face flushed a bright red and her eyes changing to an eerie yellow color as her wolf came close to the surface.

"I don't want that abomination living with me, but I certainly won't let you get your filthy hands on him and twist him into the evil creature your father was. He stays with me and I'll crush the maliciousness out of him. He will not hurt women as your father did," she hissed.

Regan took another step back unnerved by the evangelical

light shining from Moya's crazed eyes. Holding up her hands in a sign of peace she said, "Slow down Moya, what does my father have to do with any of this? I'd never encourage Ben to behave like my father. I'll raise him as my mother raised me, with love."

"What would you know of love," she sneered, "you both have that seed of evil in you. I can smell it. You've obviously fooled Byron with your innocent act, but I know deceit when I see it. I will not allow you to encourage the proliferation of Ben's wickedness. Ben will not follow in his father's footsteps. And I'm the only one who can stop him from doing that, I see the evil that hides behind that quiet exterior he shows the world, but he doesn't fool me!"

Regan watched in a type of horrified fascination as spittle trailed down from the corner of Moya's mouth to her chin. Moya didn't seem to realize it was there, as she glared at Regan as if she was Satan himself.

"Listen to yourself Moya, you need help. Ben is not evil, he is just a kid. You can't blame the child for what the father did to you. He holds no bitterness in him, he doesn't hate you for the way you've mistreated him over the years. But soon he won't care about you at all. You need to seek help and change or you'll lose him completely."

"He needs a firm hand to crush the foulness growing in him. I will not let you influence him. I will not let him hurt others as I was hurt."

Regan took another step back as the disturbed woman stepped into her space again something in her gibberish ranting struck a chord in Regan. *Oh surely not?*

"Moya was it my father who raped you?" she asked softly.

"Don't pretend you didn't already know you vile creature! I will not let you encourage that abomination of mine to become a twisted monster. You are both the same, like drawn to like. No wonder you want control of him. I won't let you, do you hear!"

Regan stopped listening to Moya's ranting, the woman must be having a psychotic break because surely she couldn't be like this all the time, she couldn't hide this from the community. She'd notify Byron that Moya needed her husband at home as soon as she left.

But holy shit! Ben was her half brother, no wonder she felt drawn to him. Joy spilled through her. He was family, she wasn't alone, and she had a brother. She raised a trembling hand to her lips. Nothing would prevent her from obtaining custody of Ben now. If Moya refused to release Ben, Regan would appeal to Byron. She would expose Moya's mistreatment of Ben if she had to. Once Byron was aware of how Moya was abusing Ben, she felt confident he would remove Ben from Moya's poisonous influence. The woman wasn't fit to parent Ben.

Regan shifted her attention back to Moya, who was still spewing on with her warped reality. Standing straight Regan cut across her ranting.

“Hey I’m truly sorry for what my father did to you, but you are blinded by bitterness, if you think Ben is anything like our father. He is an innocent boy who deserves your protection, not your revulsion. Understand this, if you don’t release Ben into my custody, I will ensure he tells anyone who will listen of your mistreatment of him. Imagine how horrified all your friends will be at your behavior, how you’ll be ostracized. Think hard Moya, I’ll be back tomorrow and if I don’t get the answer I want, I’ll be going straight to Byron with Ben to explain exactly what has been going on here, behind closed doors.”

Before Moya could articulate a response, Regan turned and walked away. She hugged herself as she headed back to her rooms where she had left Ben stretched out on the lounge watching T.V. She couldn’t wait to tell him that he was her brother. Hopefully, now he’d trust her more and open to her quicker, because he now had an explanation for her interest in him.

She’d loved Ben before discovering he was her brother, but couldn’t deny she now felt an even tighter bond to him and she knew Ben would feel the same. Even if Moya tried to prevent her fostering Ben, now she knew of the family tie, she would have a greater chance of persuading Byron to transfer Ben's care to her. She didn't want to expose Ben to the mortification of disclosing his mother's treatment, but if that was what they had to do to transfer his custody to her, she would help him endure.

But for tonight they could celebrate finding each other, tomorrow they'd deal with Moya. Regan was running various ways to word the good news to Ben through her mind, when Rafe fell into step beside her.

Rafe had gone back to work while Ben was being treated; knowing Regan wouldn't leave Ben's side. Jordan was closer to breaking the encryption on the phones; as soon as he did, they'd hopefully be able to track the information back to the members of *Titan*. The time pressure had been removed; with Thomas' death, *Titan* no longer had a way of finding shifters. Rafe was confident he and his Sentinels would find the killers and bring justice to them.

He'd arrived at Regan's apartment ready to reveal they were mates, only to find her gone. It was as if fate was moving against him and his sense of urgency was growing. This needed to be done now, before it was too late. His wolf was restless, sensing her first shift was looming. Rafe needed this deception out in the open, before Regan could use it as an excuse to run from him. His wolf's agitation was affecting him, his adrenaline was surging, his heart rate was up, he'd continually paced as he waited for Regan to return. If she shifted without knowing what was happening, the experience would be terrifying for her. The first shift was arduous enough without fear and panic thrown in the mix; he didn't want that for Regan.

Once this hurdle was behind them, it only left his decision to leave her with her father all those years ago, to come between them. But that could come later, one step at a time. He prayed she would be happy they were mates and nothing impeded them moving into a deeper relationship. There would never be another for either of them.

She enjoyed her time with him he knew that. Her dry humor kept him on his toes when she relaxed enough to let it out. Their conversations flowed easily now and silence between them was peaceful. Neither felt the need to search for something to say to fill the quiet.

He'd cursed in frustration when he'd gone to her apartment to find Ben there instead of Regan. Ben had asked him in to wait, but Rafe didn't want to have this discussion with a pre-teen listening in, so he'd elected to wait out front.

His heart picked up further when he saw Regan approaching, the late afternoon sun silhouetted her lithe form. Her black hair shone in the soft light, her skin was brushed a healthy light bronze from her time spent outside. Her simple shirt and jeans hugged her lissome figure. She seemed to almost dance across the lawn towards him. He rubbed his palms up and down his denim-clad thighs as he waited for her.

He wanted this woman and he wanted these obstacles between them removed. They were mates, they were meant to be together. He wanted them to proclaim their bond in the formal ceremony that would mystically bind them. He yearned for the deeper connection that the ceremony would bring to them.

He was tired of this axe hanging over his head. He had a plan and he'd stick to it, but his wolf tempted him to rush things, to bind her to him without her consent. It could be done, but had been taboo for over a hundred years now as women were treated as equals. The man didn't want to force Regan into a mating, but his wolf pushed and pushed, unwilling to wait for Regan to come to them. This was why shifters had to learn how to control their animal instincts, but Rafe's wolf had been riding him for weeks now and the impulse was becoming harder and harder to resist. It was making him short tempered, anger flaring when normally he'd be calm. He was constantly fighting his wolf and it was fraying his control.

"Hey sweetheart," he smiled at her as he fell into step with her, "you look happy enough to have just won the lotto."

Regan smiled radiantly at him, all the blood left his head, and headed for regions south. She'd never smiled so openly before, God he needed this woman tied to him. The urgency was stronger with every hour that passed, and with her so close, it was harder to control.

In a gruff voice, “Care to join me over at my place? I have something I need to talk with you about.”

He was slightly rattled when still smiling she shook her head, “Can I have a rain check on that, I really need to see Ben.”

That was not the response he had anticipated, and a small surge of irritation flared at her rebuff.

Rafe put out his hand to still her as she went to move past him, “No Regan this can’t wait, I should have had this discussion with you days ago, but with everything that’s been going on, this is my first real chance to talk with you and not be interrupted.”

She frowned at him, “Look Rafe whatever it is can wait till tomorrow. I’ve got a lot on my mind right now and as I said I need to talk to Ben.”

His own nerves wound tighter at her refusal to listen to him. He knew he was on edge and his wolf was influencing his response, but knowing that and stopping the anger boiling up were two different things. “I need to talk to you about our relationship. It’s important or I wouldn’t insist.”

“Rafe we don’t have a relationship, we have sex and if you want to talk, we can do so tomorrow.” Regan articulated slowly, "Now let me past, I want to talk to Ben."

His jaw clenched at her dismissive words, his wolf lunged to break free of his hold, a low growl rumbled in his chest. He stepped in front of her as she tried to move past him. "What's so important that you have to discuss with Ben right now?" he questioned softly.

Regan frowned at his restraining hand, what was wrong with him? The tension coming off him was affecting her and her jubilant mood was quickly shifting in the direction of shitty. What was the big deal about talking now? Surely, anything he had to say could wait until tomorrow. She wanted Ben to be the first to hear that they were related but maybe if she explained to Rafe that she intended to foster Ben he would see his discussion could wait until tomorrow, as this was more important.

"OK, just for the sake of moving along here – I'm starting the process of fostering Ben. I've just been to see his mother and now I'd like to continue the discussion with Ben. If you don't mind," she tacked on sarcastically. She looked pointedly at the hand still holding her then back at him.

"You don't think you should have discussed this with me before making such a life changing decision?" he asked incredulously. He was blown away that she would do something so important without talking to him. It wasn't that he had a problem with Ben living with them. He liked the kid and wanted his own kids so one more wasn't the issue. It was that she would make such a momentous decision without even thinking about talking to him. Maybe they weren't as close as he'd believed; maybe he'd been fooling himself that she'd be happy to know they were mates.

Blinking up at him she asked, "Why would I? It's not like we're mates."

"Yes we are," he growled at her too frustrated to censor his words. He knew he wasn't handling this properly. He'd been a fool, thinking he could give her the time she needed to build her trust and come to him; he'd underestimated the primal need to claim what was his. He'd been struggling with his wolf before it had become necessary to use Regan as bait to grab her father, but since he'd done that his wolf had been going crazy. It didn't understand the necessity of placing her in danger, it saw Rafe's decision as a betrayal of their mate, and it now fought him for control with every ounce of its strength. Rafe was being torn apart.

Regan's refusal to confide in him, to include him, pushed him past his limit. He hadn't realized he was so close to the edge, but this woman had the power to jerk at his emotions as no one ever had before. He'd grossly overestimated his ability to control his wolf.

"Yes we are, what?"

"We are mates Regan. That is what I wanted to talk with you

about tonight, I've been trying for days, but as I said things kept getting in the way."

"But we can't be there was no spark, that first day you touched me in my room."

"That wasn't the first time I touched you. You're forgetting the first time we saw each other was at your house when your father was attacking you. You were unconscious when we first touched but trust me sparks flew."

Regan couldn't process what he was saying. She and Rafe were mates? She now had a brother and a mate? Why the hell hadn't he told her when she first woke up? What gave him the right to play God? Fury began to smolder. How dare he withhold this from her? She couldn't cope with him right now; emotions were starting to swirl through her. It was too much. She panted as she tried to drag air into her restricted throat; panic started its insidious attack. She shook her hands trying to stop the tingling sensation in her fingers as she struggled to breathe. Her heart was pounding, trying to burst from her chest, this had to stop, or she'd have a full-blown attack, already fear crept along her spine. *Take control Regan, you've been here before you know how to cope.* And she fell back on old habits. Closing her eyes she forced herself to stamp it down, she could squash the pain and panic. Push the poisonous shards into a black box. She would feel nothing. Cold emptiness was better than this.

Rafe paced back and forth in front of Regan trying to control his own wild temper. He was so engrossed in controlling his own sawing emotions, he didn't witness Regan's struggle.

When he finally locked gazes with her, it was as if all emotion had been sucked from her brilliant blue eyes. They were as dull and lifeless as her voice when she spoke.

"I have nothing to say to you. You had no right to withhold that information from me. Now let me pass."

Rafe had no excuse for what he did next; he couldn't smell the pain and turmoil coming from his mate. It was as if she was an empty vessel and it wasn't good enough. He wanted his mate. She would not hide from him. If that meant she screamed at him fine, good! At least that would show she cared, but he would not tolerate being shut out by this indifferent creature before him.

"Hey, if you're reacting this well to the news we are mates, try this one on. I was given the job of checking on you and your mother when you were just a kid. It was up to me whether you and your mother were brought to Eden's Retreat or left out there with your father. And guess what, I made the decision to leave you with your father." He watched intently as realization washed over her. Nodding "That one broke through you're wall didn't it? Oh yeah now I can see some emotion in there." He waved his hand in a, bring it on gesture. "So come on Regan – let's have it. I'm tired of worrying you'll shut down and walk away from us. I bet you can't tamp down that rising rage boiling inside you this time, huh? No shutting down and walking away from me today baby."

Stepping into her space he didn't stop until he bent down and his nose was touching hers "How's that tactic working for you? Can you keep all that rage squeezed into that closed off box you call a heart?" he asked softly.

Regan shook so hard she thought she might break apart, and shatter into frozen shards of ice. She feared that if she broke, no one would ever be able to put the pieces back together. She would be lost.

Red swirled into black as she was sucked into the past, none of her barriers strong enough to protect her fracturing mind this day. She was lost to the past. Her mother desperately pleading for life drowned out Rafe's tormenting voice.

She couldn't breathe, darkness was crushing her, and she was trapped in the past with her father brutally pummeling her mother. Her mother now down on the floor begging Thomas to stop. Her father's jeering voice melded with Rafe's until they twisted into one.

She lashed out trying desperately to silence the tormenting voice reverberating through her shattered mind.

Rafe stepped back, “What’s up Regan having a bit of trouble with your control?” he continued prodding incessantly at her.

Regan looked up at him from under her lashes, her eyes dark with agony “You want a reaction?” her voice a tormented whisper caused a shiver to run the length of his spine. “I’ll give you a fuckin’ reaction!” she shrieked, kicking him in the gut. As he stepped back from the force of her heel connecting with his abs, she launched herself at him. Hitting, kicking, backhanding, him across the face with both hands, pummeling him with blow after blow. Her attack was uncoordinated, emotion ruling her. It was wild, it was furious, packed with emotion, but lacking the precise timing required to cause serious harm. She was feral, screaming her rage as it roiled within her.

Rafe stood stoically under her attack. Refusing to defend himself from her barrage, blood trickled from his cut lip where she’d first backhanded him.

“My mother died because of you! God, she could be alive but for you!” Regan threw her head back, screaming her torment to the universe. Agony ripped and sliced at her. Tearing at her hair, she yanked chunks from her scalp unaware of the pain. “Why? Why would you leave her with that monster?” turning away before he could answer, she again tipped her head back screaming until her vocal cords tore, and still she screamed, the sound horrendous.

Many of the shifters at the compound had been drawn to the sound of Regan's anguish. Their animals were close to the surface, wanting to protect the distressed female. They gathered in silence, a witness to her suffering. Those closest to her: Jordan, Jen, Steph, Chris, and Ben were there to bear witness to her torment, though it would haunt their dreams for a long time to come. Jordan held Ben back from Regan, wanting to give Rafe a chance to see to his mate.

Rafe's anger had vanished with the first slap to his face, dread settled in. *"What have I done?"* He swallowed his tears, as her raw screams drifted across the hauntingly silent compound. Every shifter had stopped what they were doing at the bleeding agony in her screams. None were immune to her torment. He was dying inside, as he watched her. She would never forgive him. He had lost her. Her heaving sobs tore at his soul, his wolf howled with her.

He'd wanted to provoke a reaction from her, to break through her walls, but not this. God never this. Maybe, maybe this would be a catharsis for her. Maybe she needed this chance to grieve for her mother, but she would never forgive him for his part in her death. His worst nightmare was coming to life in front of him. His mate hated him and would always hate him.

Regan panted with exertion, her voice a raw wound. Wrapping her arms across her stomach, she stumbled to her knees. Her face contorted in agony as she sobbed hoarsely. Pain lashed her blindingly, turning to burning heat, then fading to a smolder, only to lash her again with renewed agony. It would never stop. She burned in misery.

She felt arms gathering her close, and turned to sob into the broad chest, all the fight gone from her. “Breathe Regan.” The gruff voice murmured in her ear. “That is all you have to do right now. Take a breath.” The arms offered her solace. Time meant nothing. She could have stayed there minutes or hours, and still the pain tore at her. Silent tears seeped from beneath her lids. She was unaware that everyone except her closest friends drifted away, heads bowed, hearts heavy for the woman weeping hoarsely into her mate’s chest.

“Come on let’s get you into a warm bath and then bed.” As Rafe stood drawing her to her feet, she became aware it had been Rafe offering her comfort.

Shaking her head, she pushed away from him. Fresh tears trailed down her cheeks to drip from her chin as she looked at him. “I can’t be near you.” Her torn voice dug claws of pain into Rafe’s bruised heart.

“Regan you have to give me a chance to explain what happened that day,” he begged.

Shaking her head, "I can't be near you." She turned from him.

Jordan enclosed her in his arms, looking over the top of her head at Rafe "I'll look after her tonight. She isn't in a state of mind to hear you right now. Trust her to me."

At Rafe's reluctant nod, Jordan swung Regan up into his arms and carried her inside, Ben trailing closely behind. As the door closed behind them, Rafe was left outside in the dark. Tipping his head back, he stared up at the glistening stars, fragmented by the tears distorting his vision. A low moan escaped, filled with remorse, heartache, and self-loathing. As the sound faded into the bleak night, he shifted and ran. Grief and regret his only companions.

CHAPTER 20

Jordan carried Regan into her unit and straight into the bathroom. He adjusted the shower for her, ensuring the water was steaming hot.

"Get in the shower Regan. Ben and I'll be waiting for you when you're ready." Capturing her chin, he made her eyes meet his, "You're not alone anymore." He hugged her tight as another sob tore from her throat.

"Hey. Hey, it will be OK. It will get better, I promise." He held her tight, rubbing her back with his rough hands. Murmuring comforting words, he waited until her sobs died down again. Releasing her, he ran hot water over a washrag, and then holding her face up with one hand, he gently wiped her face with the warm cloth.

"Rafe's betrayal isn't as black and white as he portrayed it to be. I heard everything he said to you tonight. There are mitigating reasons for his actions back then. You know Rafe. He would not knowingly leave a woman and child with someone like your father."

Shaking her head, "I thought I knew him, but after tonight, I don't know him at all."

Squeezing her shoulder, "Yes you do," he urged. "You know he would have protected that little girl and her mother if he'd known." Jordan read the confusion and pain in her bruised eyes.

"Have your shower. When you get out I'll explain exactly what happened back then." He turned her towards the shower with a gentle push and left the room.

"Is she OK?" At the sound of Jordan's entrance, Ben turned from where he'd been staring out the window.

Running his hands over his face Jordan sighed, "She's torn up, but Regan's strong, she'll come through OK," he headed to the kitchen and started going through cupboards pulling out necessities for making Regan a hot chocolate.

"What did Rafe say to her? I've never heard anyone scream like that," Ben asked as he moved to the island bench dividing the small kitchen from the living area. "I didn't know what to do."

"I actually think Regan needed to let all that pain out. She's been carrying that around with her since she was a kid about your age. As to what he said, he told her they were mates and that he was responsible for her mother's death. Which isn't true, but I'll let Regan and Rafe tell you the full story." Jordan took in Ben's reaction, as his shoulders slumped.

Byron had informed Jordan of Regan's intent to approach Moya regarding fostering Ben; he'd wanted Jordan's opinion on Moya's reaction. A part of Jordan's position for the Sentinels was to monitor the members of Eden's Retreat, keeping an ear out for any issues within the community that should be brought to the alpha's attention. Jordan's easygoing personality and genuine interest in people made it easy for him to ferret out issues that might affect the dynamics of the shifters living at Eden's Retreat, and give his alpha the heads up when an issue required his attention.

Ben sank down on one of the stools and lay his head on the bench, "Man what a mess." He'd anticipated moving in with Regan, going so far as to imagine what living with her would be like. He should have known better than to hope, the thought of staying with his mother now was intolerable. How was he going to subjugate himself to her hatred when he'd dared to believe in Regan? He knew he could rely on no one but himself, why had he let her in? He knew Regan having a mate changed everything she'd said to him. Her priority would now be Rafe and he wouldn't want someone else's kid hanging around. Hell, his own mother hated him, how could he expect a stranger to tolerate him underfoot. Rafe wouldn't want him around, anymore that his mom's mate Don had. Had he actually thought someone would *want* him?

He knew better than to hope. Shattered hope hurt more than any physical pain. He'd tell Regan that he'd changed his mind and wanted to stay with his mom. At least that way he didn't have to tip toe around, waiting for Regan to tell him he had to move out.

Ben jerked when Regan slid her arms around him from behind, he'd been so wrapped up in his thoughts he hadn't even heard the shower go off.

"Hey what's wrong? Even I could smell your pain when I entered the room." Her voice was raw.

Before Ben could formulate a reply, Jordan spoke up. "I've just finished telling Ben that you and Rafe are mates, and at this moment Ben is probably trying to formulate some way of stepping out of your life to make room for Rafe, and avoid your rejection of him."

Ben cast Jordan a surly look from under his brows, but Jordan just leaned his hip against the counter as he crossed one long leg over the other and smiled back at him, totally unrepentant.

Regan sat down on the stool next to Ben facing him. “Well he can formulate all he wants, but my little brother will be living with me and once I get guardianship I will never let him go.”

Ben’s heart jolted to a stuttering halt as her words registered. When his heart restarted it raced so hard, he could hear it thundering. Slowly he turned his head, his eyes met hers. Her joy was there for him to read. Even swamped in her anguish over Rafe, her smile for him lit her ravaged face. She was genuinely delighted.

“I’m your brother?” he questioned.

At her happy nod.

“How?”

Shrugging with some resignation, “Same father,” she grimaced.

“Oh,” he took a moment to process the ramification of that revelation.

“He’s dead, yes?”

Regan nodded, “Rafe killed him the other day.”

“Good,” he paused again, studied his fingers splayed on the kitchen bench.

"Sister huh?" he looked her up and down, a smile beginning to tug at his lips.

Regan smiled at him and stood with her arms open wide, "Come, and give your big sister a hug, little brother."

Ben launched himself from his stool into her arms. She laughed as he nearly toppled her over backwards.

Holding him tight she whispered in his ear, "I will never let you go. You are my only family, mine to love."

Pulling back he looked up at her, "But what about Rafe, he may not want me. I don't want to come between you and your mate and some day you will have your own children. You won't need me then."

Regan rubbed her hand across her aching chest at Ben's certainty that she wouldn't want him, once she realized she might one day have her own children. She didn't brush off his concerns, Ben had issues regarding his self-worth, and it would be hard for him to believe she wanted him in her life, especially if Rafe and future children were in the picture, so she formed her response carefully.

"There is no guarantee that Rafe and I will end up together. But if we do, it will be reliant on his unconditional acceptance of you. I will *not* have you hurt again. I don't want to be tied to a man who would try to run off someone I love.

If in the future I have kids, you will treat them as if they are your brothers and sisters and they will treat you the same. I will love you all with the same intensity. I understand your doubts Ben and realize I'll need to prove this to you with actions. But you have to decide if you trust me enough to move in and take a chance, because only time can provide you with the proof you need." She hugged him against her.

He hugged her back clinging for a moment before stepping back. "Yeah, I'll stay with you," with a sardonic smile he shrugged, "I'm not leaving much behind huh?"

Taking a bracing breath, he jerked his thumb over his shoulder towards the bedroom Regan had given him earlier, "I think I'll go listen to some music for a while. Or I can stay out here?" he offered.

Smiling her appreciation, "Nah I'm going to be OK. You go and chill out."

Jordan placed a cup of hot chocolate in front of Regan as she sat back down at the bench. "You're good with him," he observed.

"I had a great teacher." Tracing a finger along one of the veins in the marble kitchen bench she continued, "I always knew my mother loved me, no matter how bad things got.

Sometimes I was so angry with her when she wouldn't leave him, but I always knew she loved me."

Nodding Jordan offered, "She probably knew he was a shifter and would eventually track you down through his paternal bond with you. She could have run from him, but she couldn't take you. You're right not to question her love for you."

She wiped ineffectively at the tears tracking down her face. "How could he leave us there?" she swallowed trying to ease the tight pain in her throat. Everything hurt, she bled inside, raw, serrated wounds she didn't think would ever heal.

Although her mother died eight years ago, it felt as if it had happened today. The pain was as unrelenting and overwhelming as it had been that day. But this time she'd been able to express her grief, her horror, her anger, the dark pain that always clawed at her. Truthfully, right now she was so tired she could fall asleep; to escape this wretched aching sadness, hopefully sleep would allow her a reprieve, at least for a while.

"Ten years ago we had a shifter serial killer on our hands. He was brutally raping women, both shifter and human, before killing them. We had been tracking him for months, by the time Rafe had gone to see your mother; he was killing someone every three days. It was all coming to a head at around that time. None of us were sleeping, every woman lost was unacceptable, and every life lost, destroyed a part of us.

Rafe was on the way to examine the latest crime scene, when he was asked to drop by and see if either you or your mother were shifters. If either of you were, he was instructed to offer you sanctuary at the compound we had at the time. He did a slow drive by, neither of you had the halo of a shifter. You are one of those unique few whose aura doesn't show until you mature or meet your mate, Rafe didn't even know there was such a thing, until he saw your aura developing."

"So because we weren't shifters we deserved to be left with that animal?" she demanded.

"No you didn't deserve that, but we didn't know he was beating you and your mother either. We aren't omnipotent Regan."

"If he'd stopped he might have found out," resentment tainted her rough voice.

Jordan nodded, "Maybe. Maybe not. I bet your mother was pretty good at hiding what was going on. Why would she open up to a stranger?"

"If he had taken the time..."

Jordan cut her off. "He was chasing a murderer – who was

killing a new woman every other day. He drove past, you were laughing as your mother pushed you on a swing in the front yard. Neither of you were shifters, what would you have had him do?"

"He should have come back later; he had to have known my father was violent."

"Your father was cunning. He moved out of shifter run communities when he was young to avoid detection of his perverse nature. He didn't come up on our radar until recently. Moya always refused to say who raped her. If she had we would have been onto him earlier, maybe even saved your mother, but she was too traumatized and has always refused to speak about it."

"So no one ever goes back to check on humans in shifter relationships?" she questioned incredulously.

Jordan shook his head, "Maybe that is something you could do. You would have to discuss it with Byron and Rafe, but maybe you could start a new arm of the Sentinels that investigates shifters that leave the communities, their behavior towards humans they interact with, and the offspring they produce. If you do discover abuse, you could notify the Sentinels to capture the shifter and ensure the human receives the support they need."

Regan's heart pulsed at the idea. It was ideal for her. She

knew how battered women behaved; she had a connection with them because of her past. Maybe she could use the horror she experienced as a child to help others. Abused women sensed a kinship with her. In the past, she had been able to motivate women to improve their situations. This type of work would be an extension to that. She would definitely explore the option with Byron.

Jordan brought her back to the present covering one of her hands with his, “Give the man a chance. He’s a good person and he loves you. If it had been me, or any other Sentinel given that job that day, we all would have made the same decision Rafe did. Don’t blame the man for a fault in our system. If he knew you were suffering, he would have protected you.”

“Even if I can get past him leaving us there and I’m not sure I can, he hid from me that we’re mates. How can I trust him when he kept something to vital from me? He’s lied to me from the moment we met.”

“I know you have a lot to think about Regan, but when you do, be honest with yourself. If Rafe had told you, that you were mates when you first came here, would you have stayed? You would have run from him as fast as you could. He just wanted a chance.”

Exhaustion swamped Regan, she couldn’t think through this

anymore. Her thoughts were all tangled; her body ached.

Jordan could see she was done in; at least she would sleep now.

"You head to bed, I'll check on Ben on my way out and tell him to give you a few minutes to get settled before he goes in to say goodnight to you."

"Regan nodded gratefully as she shambled off towards her bed. She was asleep before Ben entered her room. He sat quietly on the edge of her bed, gazing at her sleeping form, astounded that this woman, his sister, wanted him in her life. He didn't understand it, but he couldn't bring himself to walk away from her. Eventually he left her room returning to his. Lying on top of the comforter, he contemplated where his future might take him now, for the first time he could remember, he looked forward to tomorrow.

~~~

Regan woke up as the sun dusted the horizon with the softest of light. She headed for the shower, her muscles stiff, and her body sore. Her emotions were raw wounds, cycling from fury at Rafe, grief for her mother, hatred for her father, betrayal, loss for the father she'd longed to have. Fury, grief, hate, betrayal, loss, and back to fury. She was a mess and she couldn't stay here; she'd go crazy. No way was she ready to face Rafe, she was too angry and hurt to deal with him,
~~~

and she knew he would want to talk with her. He wasn't a man to sit and wait.

After dressing in comfortably worn in jeans and a black tank top to go with her mood, she checked in on Ben. He was sound asleep, her heart warmed a little at the sight of him lying there peacefully. She left a note for him saying she needed a walk, but would be back that morning to go over their options for legally fostering him.

She called for a taxi to collect her down the block from the entrance to Eden's Retreat, reducing the chances of Rafe finding her. As she waited for the cab, she decided she would start boxing up her belongings at her house and cleaning it. She couldn't stay at her house with Ben in her care, she just wasn't sure she could stay at Eden's Retreat with Rafe there. Maybe once she had custody of Ben, she could move to another shifter commune until she could cope with having Rafe so near. It was something to consider.

At her house, she set to work packing and cleaning cupboards, preparing the house for sale. As she worked, her thoughts constantly turned to Rafe. Even as furious and hurt as she was, she couldn't deny the dismay she felt whenever she considered moving away from Eden's Retreat. Did that mean she would be able to forgive him in time?

Her cat was closer to the surface than ever before. Regan

could easily feel her anxiety and restlessness, almost nervousness. She was affecting Regan's already strung out emotions. Regan could feel her skin itch as if her cat was trying to break through, forcing her to face the fact that soon she would shift into a black panther. The thought was as exhilarating as it was frightening. She hoped she was with Rafe when it happened so he could talk her through it. She stopped scrubbing at the grout in the shower and sat back on her heals as that thought registered. Even this hurt and betrayed, she still wanted his help.

She had just poked her head back into the shower stall when she realized she was no longer alone. Before she could look, blinding pain shot from her exposed back and drove a spike into her brain. Light exploded as her muscles spasmed. *"Rafe!"* her mind screamed before her awareness swirled down into a black abyss.

CHAPTER 21

Rafe had spent the night in the forest, grateful his friends and Steph had left him alone to lick his wounds. Since dawn, he'd been fighting the urge to go to Regan, but now concern for her was driving him, he couldn't stay away any longer. He needed to apologize and find out what he could do to fix things, *if* there was a chance to fix things. Someone had left some clothes and his phone at the main entrance to the forest; he stopped long enough to dress and grab his phone, before heading towards Regan's unit.

Rafe stumbled nearly going to his knees as pain hit him in the back driving a wedge of agony into his skull. Senses jumbled, it took him a moment to realize the pain wasn't his but an echo of Regan's. Christ what had happened? It would take something catastrophic to filter through their fragile mating bond like this.

He sprinted to Regan's apartment, but Ben didn't know

where she was. As he shot towards his office, with Ben running to keep up, his phone rang. Looking at the caller ID he saw Jordan's name.

"Regan's in trouble," he answered the call.

"We know," Jordan responded tersely. "Two men carried her from her house; she was driven away in a white van. The sentinel we had stationed at her house on the off chance someone from *Titan* showed up, followed the van, but they lost him in the city traffic."

"What the fuck was she doing outside Eden's Retreat and why the fuck wasn't I told?"

"Same question I asked the guards at the gate. They're both female cat shifters. So, you can guess how it went down after last night. They empathized with Regan's need to get away for a while. You know what the cats are like, all that solitary shit they go on with. Makes you wonder some times why they live here." He blew out a breath, "And being female they had no inclination to tattle on Regan to you. As far as they're concerned if you hadn't fucked up, Regan wouldn't need to be alone."

"For fucks sake! How old are they? For Christ's sake, we're not a bunch of shopping mall guards here. Our job is to protect our people, and letting one who's been targeted for kidnapping out, without an escort because they're pissed at me, is unforgivable. Tell them to stay the fuck out of my way until I get Regan back. I'll deal with them then." Changing gears, he continued, "Get all the Sentinels up and active. I want them all out there looking for that fucking van within five minutes. Tell me we at least have the tags."

"Yeah we got 'em but how long will they keep her in that van before dumping it?"

"I know, shit. Get everyone out there now; we have to find them before they do that. Where's Arick?" The birds of prey kept almost exclusively to themselves. It was exceedingly rare for one to expose their identity to other shifters, but Arick had been coming and going since he was seventeen. He'd been helping Rafe by flying recon missions trying to locate the hunting ground.

"He's up around the great lakes; I've left him there as we have no idea where they're going to take Regan. Just as much chance it's up that way."

Rafe grunted his agreement and hung up swearing under his breath. Fear was battering at him; he couldn't lose her. He needed to know she was alive in this world, even if she wasn't with him. If she died, he knew he would follow her. He didn't want to be in this world if Regan wasn't in it.

If he ever, no, *when* he got her back, he would control his need to complete the bond with her; a lot of pressure was off him now. He didn't have to worry about her finding out about the mating or his betrayal all those years ago, she knew everything now. She knew the worst.

When he got her back, he'd work out a new strategy to win her over. He couldn't give up, but first he had to get her back. His resolve strengthened, Regan was not going to be hunted down by these bastards. He would be bringing her home. Laying his hand reassuringly on Ben's shoulder, he reassured the silent boy, "I'll bring her home." He held Ben's gaze until Ben nodded grimly in acknowledgement.

Rafe pushed into Jordan's office to find him and Chris bent intently over one of the many screens on Jordan's desk.

"What have you got?" he demanded.

"You're not going to believe this." Jordan moved aside allowing Rafe an unobstructed view of the screen.

Rafe's heart pounded in his chest.

~~~

Regan opened gritty eyes to find herself in a cage, the type you'd transport large dogs in. To sit up she had to angle her head to the side, her other option was to lay curled up as she had been when she'd come to. She tested her arms and legs, nothing was hurt; her gunshot wound ached, but she hadn't damaged it further.
~~~

Looking around the austere room, she counted five other animal cages stacked beside hers. There was a sink and fridge to her left, and a door opposite her cage. No windows, so she assumed she was in a building large enough that she was being held in a central room, or the building was designed purposely without windows. Only reason for that was to prevent people seeing in or out deliberately, and it increased security, if there is no window there is one less point of entry to defend.

Closing her eyes, Regan strained her senses trying to pick up any information she could use to aid her escape. Nervousness nipped at her. *Stay calm Regan, fear will lead to mistakes.* Minutes ticked by as she concentrated. She could only hear the quiet hiss of the air-conditioning and fridge cutting in and out. No outside sound penetrated the walls; she couldn't hear any movement on the other side of the door. The scent of bleach overwhelmed her sensitive nose, and apart from the faint scent of old blood, she gained no hint of where she was, or how many people were outside.

She had to assume she'd been captured by *Titan*, but was she already at the hunting ground or did they still need to transport her? If they still had to transport her, she had a chance of escaping as Justin had. If she was already there, her chances of survival were close to nil. No one else had escaped the hunting grounds, so there was no reason to think she, who hadn't even undergone her first shift yet, would be able to.

She tested all the bars on her cage, but they were unmovable. She examined each joint, but none was the least corroded or weakened in any way.

If only one person was present when they released her from the cage, she could ram the cage door into them the instant the lock released and give herself a chance to overwhelm them. She doubted she'd be that lucky. If they were that inept, more shifters would have escaped. There was nothing in the room she could conceivably use as a weapon, no chairs or tables, no drawers or cupboards that might hold something usable.

They'd taken her watch so she had no idea how long she'd been out. Were Rafe and the other Sentinels aware she'd been captured? Were they searching for her yet? The chill of the cage's steel floor seeped into her. She'd been alone for many years, was this the way she was to die with no one who cared for her, only people who would enjoy her terror, and gain enjoyment from her fear?

She couldn't die now, not when she had just met Ben. He needed her; no one else would love him as she did. If she wasn't there, he'd stay with his mother and she would continue destroying him with her twisted hatred.

She'd made friends and she now desperately wanted to be part of their lives. To see Chris, Jen, and Jordan, mated and with children, to watch Steph torment people with her incessant chatter, to share birthdays and Christmas, to celebrate triumphs and mourn losses. Her breathing chopped at all she would miss, as a bitter weight pressed down on her chest.

And Rafe, here and now with death bearing down on her what did she really feel for him? When she peeled away all the hurt and resentment, what was left? "I want that stupid man," she muttered. He wasn't perfect, he made mistakes, but he was a protector. Everyone at Eden's Retreat respected him. She'd seen how hard he worked, how torn he was at his failure to protect his fellow shifters from *Titan*. He wasn't narcissistic with his power as head of the Sentinels; instead, the responsibilities grounded him, ensured he used his skills and drive to make the world a safer place for shifters and humans.

She felt drawn to him; she'd been misleading herself to think she could walk away. He was a man she could respect, a man she could love. "*Be honest with yourself, you already love him. Even if he is an idiot the way he handled things.*" If she got out of this, she would make sure he understood there would be no more secrets, full disclosure at all times.

Right now she had more to live for, than at any other time in her life. Rafe would be coming after her, her job was to stay alive long enough for him to find her.

Resolve steadied her; she would live no matter what she had to endure. Resolute, she curled up in her cage to conserve her energy and calmed herself to reduce the adrenaline firing up her system; she would need to be sharp at the right time. Her body would need that adrenaline later, now it was time to let her mind and body rest. She had no control over the situation right now; she would need to be at her best to seize any opportunity to escape.

Hours later, the door snigged open, and three men entered. One carried a dart gun pointed at her, another an ugly snub nose pistol, the third was empty handed. Regan sat up slowly studying them. They did nothing to hide their faces, so obviously they weren't worried she would have the opportunity to identify them at a later date.

The one without a weapon approached the cage, the arrogance in which he carried himself indicated he was the leader of this group and accustomed to being in control. All three were lean and muscular, but this man looked harder than the others did. His salt and pepper hair was cut military short. His eyes were arctic blue and merciless. Unlike his subordinates who'd tried to take her previously, this man would not be riled by any verbal jabs she sent his way. If she was reading him right, he wasn't even excited at the prospect of killing her. The other two were. Their heart rates were up and anticipation lit their eyes. No light from within lit this man's eyes as they racked dispassionately over her. The hair stood up on her arms and she could feel her cat rising to the surface, as she watched the man with unblinking eyes.

"Why do you do it?"

His eyes briefly hinted at his surprise, "Hmm you are a calm one aren't you? All the others either wanted to know what happens next or spent their last minutes before the hunt threatening to eviscerate me." His voice was soft and cultured, but as flat as a professor lecturing economics 101 for the twelfth year running.

"I do this because I can. It's taboo, therefore I will do it. There is no one to say no to me and I run these little projects to prove that. I can have anything I want in the world, for now, this entertains me. No doubt, like everything else I will eventually grow bored with it," he shrugged philosophically as if they were discussing becoming bored with tennis at the country club. "But for now it will do until another challenge comes along."

"If you want a challenge you should up the ante and make it just you and me out there."

A humorless smile lifted his firm lips, "Maybe it will come to that one day, but I'm afraid for you it's not going to be today. I've already taken money from a couple of fine gentlemen who are waiting outside to begin the hunt, and I find myself not wanting to disappoint them this day."

Tilting his head to the side, he studied her, "I see you've been talking to our friend that escaped. Told you all about our hunt did he?"

Regan refused to answer.

"It doesn't matter; I'll tell you exactly what is going to happen. You will be released into the park and we will hunt you down and kill you. If you try to jump the fence you will be electrocuted, not enough to kill, just to disable you, we will then return you to your cage here until you are recovered enough to hunt again. The longest anyone has survived out there is five hours." He nodded to her once before turning to leave. "If you have a god, make your peace Regan, for you will not see the sun set this day."

"What if I give you information that will help you kidnap other shifters, will you let me live?" Regan called out desperately, she had to stall the hunt and give Rafe time to find her. She knew he would, if she could only give him long enough.

Those cold eyes flicked over her, "I'm a good judge of character, and you my dear are not like your father. He enjoyed the hunt; you I fear do not have the stomach for cold killing." His smile did nothing but send a shiver down her spine. As her cat struggled to rise closer to the surface, Regan understood she was trying to protect her from the sociopath watching her from the wrong side of the cage.

"I have enough leads and resources to find more shifters without your help. If I were you, I'd take the next few minutes to shift into your animal form. You won't get too far on two legs."

Desperation filled Regan; she had to slow this down. "But I can't shift!"

Stopping at the door he looked back, he tilted his head slightly as he examined her like a scientist viewing a petri dish.

Regan's heart hitched as she rushed in "I only recently met my mate. I'll be able to shift soon but it hasn't happened yet. It could happen any day. Please at least give me a chance," she pressed. Unbidden tears filled her eyes; she didn't want to die. Her heart stopped, as she read the cold rejection in his face before he responded.

"You had better work it out or you will be dead within the hour. You have five minutes before your release."

He left without another glance at her, his two accomplices

followed him out the door, which clicked softly, shut.

~~~

Regan sprinted for her life, panic threatening as she raced. She'd been running for ten minutes down what must have been an old logging track years ago, already her legs, and lungs were feeling the strain. She forced herself to slow down into a pace she could sustain for at least thirty minutes, before having to throttle it back more. She guessed she had another five minutes before they would begin hunting her. Scanning the forest around her, she spied a rocky outcrop to the left that would hide her tracks, maybe giving her an opportunity to lose her pursuers.

She scrambled over the rocks to the top of a small ridge and spied a narrow creek at the bottom. She half slid, half ran down the steep embankment, refraining from grabbing onto any plants as she plunged downward, conscious of reducing the trail she left behind. Once at the bottom she ran along the creek, following it upwards for about five hundred yards, passing several opportunities to leave the creek along granite outcroppings, before deciding to follow one rocky passage. As she ran she studied the terrain, looking for a gully she would be able to climb, wanting to get to higher ground and into the thicker foliage provided by the undergrowth and trees up above. She took her time using the rocks to climb upward, endeavoring to leave the least disturbance for the
~~~

hunters tracking her.

Cresting the top of one of the smaller ridgelines, she stopped just inside the denser shadows offered by the trees. Regan bent at the waist as she tried to regain her breath. Her leg muscles were screaming with pain, her bullet wound felt as if the new scar tissue was ripping, a quick check showed it was holding, but the pain added to her torment. She rubbed her forehead across her shoulder wiping the matted hair off her face, she'd pushed herself as hard as she could trying to put distance between her and the men coming after her. She figured she'd been running for thirty minutes now, which meant the hunters had been out in the park for at least fifteen, how close were they to her? What if he'd lied and hadn't given her a fifteen-minute head start? They could be right behind her. She lifted her head to search the way she'd come anxiously, sweat dripped from her chin as she tried to discern any out of place movement.

Seeing nothing, she let her gaze take in the expanse of wilderness around, from her vantage point near the top of a ridgeline, she could see to the horizon and it was rugged gorge country as far as the eye could see. Massive pines gave away to sections of hardwoods with thick undergrowth. She'd need to keep to those areas, the pines didn't offer enough cover. No roads cut through the trees, she had no idea where they had taken her, but it was obviously a sparsely populated part of the country. If Rafe didn't find her, no one else was going to stumble upon her.

As her heart rate steadied, so too, did the push of her cat to rise, she must be close to her first shift. She'd run faster for longer than she'd ever been able to do before, her animal lending her strength. Her senses were more acute, she could perceive the sound of water moving, and the creek was on the other side of a ridge over a mile away. She could smell various animals in the vicinity, not that she knew what they were, the scents were all too new to her. The one thing she couldn't smell was humans. She leaned against a giant elm tree on the side away from her ascent to hide from those following her. She'd give herself a couple more minutes to recover, before pushing on.

"OK so I'm being hunted and just when I need my wits about me, it looks like I'm going to go through my first change. So what do I know about the change? I saw Rafe do it and it's instantaneous, and from the little I read in the library it feels like a burning rush of adrenaline and I just need to let go of myself. Easy!" she huffed. "This is something else Rafe is going to answer for, if I'd known I'd met my mate I would have found out more about shifting, but did he tell me so I could prepare? Nooo. That would make my life too fuckin' easy wouldn't it?"

She stopped her muttering and listened carefully, before

taking a good look around again, sensing nothing she leaned back against the tree.

"OK puss, I don't know if you can understand this, but if you could put off the shift until we get out of this I'd really appreciate it. I'm lovin' the extra speed and endurance and the nifty ability to smell and hear better, so leave that. But please, please, please, no shifting until we are safe." Regan crossed her fingers hoping she could keep it together; she had no idea if her cat would realize that she was being hunted, and the need to hide. How much control over her cat would she have?

Silently she moved off in a westerly direction aiming away from the buildings where they had released her and into the dense undergrowth. Now she'd take her time taking as much care as possible not to disturb the undergrowth or leave footprints. She hoped she had a large enough head start that she could now be more about stealth than speed.

~~~

By her estimation, she'd been on the move for over two hours now and she was growing in confidence; they hadn't believed she'd live out the hour. As far as she could tell, she was still alone up here. Every minute increased the chance of Rafe finding her; she was starting to believe she might survive this.
~~~

The heavy sound of a rifle report reverberated through Regan as she crashed to the ground, heart jumping in her chest as she frantically looked around. The sound echoed through the mountains, all bird life stopped its constant chattering. Regan's ears filled with the hammering of her heart. They were here. Christ how close were they? She wriggled slowly back under a thicker bush peering anxiously all around her. She understood the shot was to scare her, to intensify her fear and force her into a mistake.

"Assholes, as if I'm not already shitting myself," she whispered to herself, trying to rally her courage. They probably hoped she'd run making an easy target to spot. She needed to decide whether to run and put more distance between her and the shooter, or stay on her present course and move with stealth. The question was how close to her were they? The gunshot hadn't been too close, but with the rifles they were using they didn't need to be close. They could be half a mile away and she'd look like she was across the street in the cross hairs of a scope. Stay or run?

Heart pounding, she crawled forward on her elbows to peer out from under the foliage she was hiding under. Sweat trickled down her spine at the thought that even now someone could be looking at her down the lens of a scope. Apprehension crawled up her spine as minutes ticked by and the birds stayed silent, obviously aware of the predators on the move. The silence pressed heavily exacerbating her fear.

Finally, Regan's nerves couldn't sustain the feeling of being stalked, as she laid waiting like a rabbit in a spotlight. She had to move, even if moving brought her death, she couldn't stand the suspense of staying still any longer. Apprehension seeped from her pores, quivering with the need to escape, anything was better than allowing them to torture her with this slow silent hunt.

Quietly she pushed backwards using the shadowy undergrowth as cover to come out on the far side of the thick stand of trees she'd been hiding in. Hopefully, she was still in front of them; their knowledge of the terrain would allow them to move quicker than her, even with her cat helping her with speed and endurance. More than once, she'd had to backtrack when she'd found herself in a dead end gully.

Keeping low to the ground, she moved in a crouched run careful not to step on any sticks that might snap and give away her location. Her legs were straining painfully as she worked her way up a steep gorge she found herself in, fifteen minutes after that first and only gunshot. Sweat trickled into her eyes as she reached with her fingertips for a hold on the shrub above her to help her up the almost vertical assent. She dared not go back and she didn't like the look of the gully if she continued forward, her cat was urging her to go up and get out of this particular gorge. She was afraid if she didn't get out now, it would only get steeper and she would be trapped.

Her cat was spooked and desperate to get out, Regan had no trouble interpreting her cat's desperation, and it was increasing her own agitation. Once she'd started moving she'd felt better, more in control, but now her cat was rushing the fragile barrier that held her back from shifting. Regan found she had to stop and concentrate on her physical form to prevent the shift. Her cat was terrified and was desperate to be out. It understood they were being hunted, but would Regan keep her reason if she changed, or would the animal take over and expose them by running? Would she have any control, or would she just be a wild animal running on instinct?

Pain exploded along the side of her face as the tree beside her ruptured chunks of bark speared out of the hole left from the bullet. Regan dropped sliding uncontrollably on her side until her heel dug into the shallow dirt and slowed her decent. She took a second to absorb the tearing pain along her bruised and lacerated side. Taking a breath, she scrambled to her feet and raced into the ravine, her panther had been so desperate to avoid. With the shooter above and behind her, she couldn't go back and she couldn't go up. She wiped at the free flowing blood running down her cheek as she raced into the ravine, as she'd feared the sides became steeper as she ran.

CHAPTER 22

As she wove between the trees, she could hear voices above and behind calling out sightings of her to each other. Her heart pounded too fast, she feared it would fail her. Panic raced at her heals as she ran for her life. Her vision was changing all colors leaching away, as her vision became blurred. She couldn't catch her breath, her chest wasn't working properly she stumbled and fell, crashing to the hard ground, losing what breath she had. Agony washed over her. She struggled to regain her feet and fell onto her side; she couldn't stand. Her mind hazed over for an instant, before she realized she was up and moving again. Faster now, her vision was still all wrong, everything was disorientated, making her sick. But she was running, every instinct urging her to race faster.

It was as she dodged around a tree trunk she noticed her black paws and realized she ran on all fours. She'd shifted and now fled as a black panther. After her initial clumsiness, she now felt the power and innate balance of her panther. She also realized that she was still Regan and in control of her thoughts, her cat's primal urges were stronger and she felt more inclined to listen to them in this form. So when her cat suddenly wanted to climb one of the ancient oak trees off to her left Regan went with the desire. Using the power of her hind legs, she sprung up the trunk and then powered her way into the thick canopy, using her claws for purchase. She stalked along a branch and settled into the shadows, a lethal predator in her own right.

Silently she waited for her prey to come to her, she was aware of the hunter walking at the top of the gorge searching for her, but her focus was on the man following her into the deep ravine, trying to push her further in until she was trapped against the shear walls, an easy target for them.

Her cat was confident there were only two men nearby. Hopefully, the others were hunting another section of the park and weren't close enough to interfere. Regan slowly rose to her hunches as her target finally came into view, her blue eyes focused and unblinking. She'd never seen him before; obviously, he has one of the paying clients her captor had not wanted to disappoint. Too bad for him, her captor was about to lose one of his clients, permanently.

She was at all times aware of the hunter moving at the top of the ridge, but her focus stayed on the camouflaged man moving towards her tree. He held his rifle up resting against his shoulder but he wasn't looking through the scope he held his gun just below his eye allowing him to use his peripheral vision rather than the tunnel vision of the scope.

Ten yards from her tree, he stopped and scanned the area, he'd lost sight of her, and maybe his own instincts were kicking in to tell him he had now become the hunted. She could smell his unease and it settled her cat further. She was a predator and natural instinct allowed no self-doubt, today she would hunt and she would kill, as was natural for her kind.

Ever so slowly, the man eased forward, his line wouldn't bring him completely under her tree, but Regan was confident she would still be able to take him down. She eased her weight to the other side of the branch so she would be able to come at him from behind, her blue eyes unblinking, as she watched the hunter move past her position.

Using the lethal power of her hind legs, she launched herself from the tree, hitting him in the center of the back, driving him to the ground. Digging her claws into his back to prevent him from rolling over, she ripped out the side of his throat, before clamping her incisors into the back of his neck and tearing through his spinal column. She held him still as his legs twitched, unaware that the brain directing them was already dead.

She felt no remorse for ending this man's life, he had instigated this life and death struggle, and Regan was determined she would come out alive, if that meant every man here had to die today, so be it. She willed the change back to human; she needed his gun and his radio to hear what the others were doing and to work out how many were hunting her. But nothing happened. She focused on her human form and willed the change, again nothing. *Shit! Shit! How the fuck do I change back? I'm gonna fuckin' kill Rafe myself when I see him. And I'll be ripping Chris's head off too. 'Trust me Regan, Rafe is the one to ask,'* she mimicked in her head. *Obviously, the asshole had known she was Rafe's mate that afternoon she'd asked him about her cat's influence, but had he given her the heads up? No. Mister chuckles obviously found it hilarious, watching her and Rafe stumble around. All men are asses* she thought, flicking her tail in disgust.

A quiet voice issued from the dead man's radio, asking if he had the girl in his sights. Regan willed herself to change back, but once again, nothing happened. She couldn't stay here or she'd end up trapped again. Regretfully she padded silently away from the gun and radio. She backtracked out of the gully intending to circle around and come up behind the man still at the top of the ridge.

She was working her way steadily upwards when she first heard the deep throb of a helicopter. Crouching low she waited, it was traveling low and fast. The thick canopy above prevented her from seeing it, as it flew past her position on a southeasterly trajectory. The engine whined in a high pitch dissonance as the pilot pushed the machine to the limits of its capabilities, as he swung it into a hard landing.

Her heart hammered, was Rafe here already? No one else would have cause to come in so fast and low surely. Now did she work her way back towards the building where it must have landed, or stay near the tracking device she'd lost somewhere in her shift? Her lip curled as the rancid scent of two hunters came to her from the direction the helicopter had landed and brought back the reality that she was still being pursued. Even if it had been Rafe in the helicopter, he was still hours of hard hiking from her. If she could, she would make her way back towards him, but she needed to keep her focus on staying alive. She now had two men coming at her from the east and one that she knew of behind her to the west and still in a higher position.

Looking around her, she decided to change direction, head north, and try to come around behind the single shooter on the higher ground. It would be taking her away from Rafe, if in fact, that was him in the chopper. But if she could take out the single shooter, she might find somewhere to hole up and wait, and see if Rafe was racing towards her at this very instant.

Another hour crept by as Regan slowly, painstakingly worked her way north of the solitary hunter, and carefully worked her way back towards him, coming in from behind. At first he'd been easy to locate as he'd tried several more times to raise the dead man on his radio before finally notifying the others on a different channel that he believed his partner was dead and he was now being stalked. Regan's cat's exceptional hearing had allowed her to follow his voice. Four men had acknowledged his message and he had since stopped talking. He'd been steadily moving in an easterly direction, Regan assumed he was trying to join up with the other hunters.

The pads of her paws allowed Regan to stalk in absolute silence, with her black fur she melted into the shadows, and now was only twenty yards behind her target. Sinking to the ground, she again twitched her ears attempting to hear any other hunters, breathing deeply she drew the scents of the forest into her lungs, shifting through the mire of scents, but she didn't smell any other humans beside the man in front of her. She tried to expand her senses as she was learning to do as a human, but in her cat form that ability seemed retarded as if her cat didn't yet trust the ability and wanted to only rely on physical sensations to help her stay alive.

Her cat was keen for another kill, but Regan tried to temper the desire. Maybe it would be best to stay hidden. Just because she couldn't detect any other hunters, didn't mean they weren't here. But her cat was insistent and Regan was struggling to enforce her will.

She twitched her tail in agitation as she fought her cat's instincts. This was why Regan had been so afraid of shifting, her cat wasn't thinking as a human, she was an animal, aware the man in front of her wanted to kill her, and she was now in a position to terminate the threat. With a last look around, Regan gave into her cat's will and rushed from her hiding place.

The man heard her coming but his reaction was too slow to prevent her barreling into him. He pulled the trigger of his rifle but he didn't have time to aim and the bullet passed by harmlessly. By turning to face her though, he'd brought about his own death as she clamped her jaws around his throat, before her momentum drove him over backwards. She held him on his back as he flailed at her uselessly with his arms and legs. Her maw remained tightly clamped to his throat, suffocating him, as her weight held him down.

Instinct had her rolling off her kill an instant before a bullet plowed into the ground where her head had been. She raced for cover as more bullets kicked up debris around her. Pushing for all her speed and agility, she wove through the trees, trying to be unpredictable as she dodged around trunks using them for cover. She yowled, a mixture of furious anger and terror, as a bullet creased her side. She could hear heavy footsteps crashing through the undergrowth towards her as she raced downwards, away from the spray of bullets and the men coming from behind her.

She could hear the men calling out to each other but she couldn't understand what they were saying over the roar of her thundering heart. Her wounded side burned with fierce pain, but it wasn't slowing her down yet. She had no time to see how bad it was, her full concentration was on keeping her feet under her as she twisted in and out of the trees, plunging down the ravine, frantic to put distance between herself and death.

~~~

Rafe searched the canopy just feet below him as the helicopter's rapid passage disturbed the tree branches as they tore towards the only viable landing spot within a hundred miles of Regan's tracking device. She was down there somewhere, "Hang on baby; we'll have you safe soon."

As the chopper banked sharply to set down in the small
~~~

parking lot next to the single story brick structure, Rafe and his fellow Sentinels spilled from the open doors and sprinted to the building. Chris tried the door, when he found it locked he took one-step back and kicked it in; four other Sentinels, handpicked by Rafe, followed him in. Without a word, the others broke off taking the opposite direction to Chris and Rafe.

A short time later Jordan and his three Sentinels rejoined Chris and Rafe on the far side of the building, they were now inside the fenced hunting grounds.

At Rafe's questioning look Jordan reported, "One man," he shrugged negligently, "we had to kill him he wouldn't surrender. The rest of our side is clear." There was no remorse in Jordan's gold eyes. Good, Rafe did not intend to offer any quarter to these people, not that they would have been given any mercy, even without bringing Regan into it.

The bastards couldn't have picked a more remote inaccessible landscape for their wretched game. Rafe glanced at his sat phone, the screen showed Regan's location within the park. The tracking device hadn't moved for over thirty minutes, he hoped she was holed up somewhere, keeping her head down while she waited for him. He couldn't think of the alternative, the pain would cripple him.

Chris clapped him on the shoulder, "She's alive Rafe, let's go get her."

Rafe nodded, resolving to push the dread and the debilitating fear to the back of his mind. If he didn't he'd make a mistake that could well cost Regan her life, if she were out there fighting to stay alive. Squaring his shoulders, he adjusted the rifle over his shoulder and slid his hand held device into one of the pockets on his black cargo pants freeing his hands; they had a long run ahead of them. Regan's signal was over twenty miles away and this mountainous country was crisscrossed with rugged ravines and dead end gorges. They had all studied the topography maps on the way so they'd be able to avoid wasting time backtracking out of insurmountable fissures.

With a nod from Rafe, they all set off at a ground-eating pace. Rafe's men were supremely fit and their animal nature lent them extra endurance. They were experienced fighters, steady when under pressure; Rafe trusted them at his back and in this fight for his mate's life. They ran for an hour, before splitting up into three teams to come in on Regan's signal from different directions. They carried only minimal equipment in their packs, as they didn't want to sacrifice any speed. Each man carried his own preferred weapons, each team had equipment for abseiling if it became necessary, and basic first aid, apart from that it was all about speed and stealth.

Rafe and Chris, having taken the most direct route were the first Sentinels to close in on Regan's tracking signal. According to his hand held device, they should be on top of her. Both men stayed in the shadows as they scanned for any sign of Regan. Not sensing her nearby, they slowly began scouring the bushes and undergrowth. Chris bent and held the anklet up for Rafe to see; at the same time, Rafe found a piece of Regan's shredded clothes. A short search found the rest of her clothes and paw prints heading down into the ravine. Grimly Rafe silently signaled they'd follow Regan's trail.

As they wound their way soundlessly through the trees Rafe typed a message to the other two teams to spread out from his current location looking for any sign of Regan in cat form. All the Sentinels had hand held computers that would vibrate silently when a message was sent, so as not to alert their enemy to their position.

Chris eyed Rafe sympathetically as they silently followed Regan's tracks down the steep embankment. The man had a lot to make up to his mate for. The unpardonable way he tormented her last night, which lead to her leaving Eden's Retreat unprotected and in turn, being captured, and hunted. Now she'd gone through her first shift with no one to help her through. It was traumatic enough for someone who'd grown up in a shifter community, but for Regan who had no one to teach her or talk her through it, to have gone through her first shift under these circumstances made him grimace. Rafe must be wondering if even the easiest going and gentlest of females would forgive him, nevertheless Regan, with her independent spirit.

~~~

Both men simultaneously increased their pace as the first trace of death hit their nostrils. Within minutes, Rafe was bent over examining the body as Chris kept guard. Rafe's jaw clenched in frustrated anger directed at himself, as he noted the dead man's torn out neck and broken back, a typical big cat kill.

Turning burning eyes to Chris, Rafe asked, "How am I ever going to make this up to her? I failed to protect her and now she's had to kill a man. I have never failed someone so miserably in my entire life, as I've failed Regan at every turn." Every time he convinced himself that he'd be able to earn her forgiveness, something worse happened. Maybe their mating was doomed. Maybe he should step out of her life when he got her back to Eden's Retreat and let her find some happiness with another man. His stomach cramped and he swallowed bile at the thought.

Chris had never seen Rafe anything but confident in his abilities and his decisions; his self-belief that he would come
~~~

out on top in any situation. Seeing him questioning himself and doubting his ability to win Regan, didn't sit well with the big man. Yes, it had been fun to watch Rafe running in circles trying to win Regan over, but he gained no joy from watching this.

"Hey you were given a woman whose character was forged in the fires of hell. Regan will come through this whole. Yes you've fucked up with her, so you better get your head in the game so when we rescue her you can convince her to forgive your sorry ass." He turned Rafe away from the dead body. "Now let's go find your woman before anything else happens to her."

Rafe turned to follow Regan's tracks, but Chris could see the man didn't believe he would win his mate. He was pondering what else he could say, to convince Rafe when both jerked their heads up as someone started shooting.

"Shit they've found her." Rafe scrambled up the steep embankment, sacrificing silence for speed. He knew the other two teams would close in on the shots, without him giving direction. Using trees for support, he hauled himself up and out of the ravine. He raced towards Regan, pumping his arms and legs to gain as much speed as he was capable of.

At another volley of shots, he abandoned his pack and weapons, shifting to his wolf, and sprinted towards Regan, far faster in this form. A slip of grey weaving amongst the trees on silent paws, he was a deadly missile aimed at his mate's tormentors. Red hazed his mind at first; his only intent was to kill. But as he closed in on the area, he gained enough control over his animal to slow down and locate the enemy. He would do his mate no good by getting himself shot before taking out all the hunters.

For now the shooting had stopped, hopefully Regan was holed up somewhere out of sight. He picked up the scent of a male off to his left and adjusted his course to bring himself in from behind. Silently he closed in on his target, his teeth bared in a silent snarl, hatred burning in his coldly focused eyes. Slinking along on his belly, he rounded the trunk of the final tree between him and his prey to see the man was lying prone on the ground looking through his scope meticulously moving his view from shadow to shadow.

Relief crashed through Rafe, the man was still hunting Regan, proof she was alive. He stalked closer to his prey, his eyes a hard unforgiving yellow, as he rushed the final few yards to the prone man, crushing the vertebrae at the base of his skull, killing him before he was even aware he'd become the hunted. Rafe backed away from the body and slunk into nearby bushes, his fur perfectly colored to blend into the undergrowth. He broke away from his next target, his wolf insisting he find Regan now. Trusting his wolf's alarm, he allowed the animal to take control.

Regan backed herself into a small rock crevice, she was exhausted, dehydrated, her mind a muddy tangled mess, and she desperately needed a short rest. Her muscles were trembling, and the wound from her father's gunshot, was causing her right leg to drag slightly, the muscle unable to hold up against the hours that she had now spent running and climbing, in her effort to stay alive.

The new wound on her side burned fiercely, distracting her from what was happening around her. Her cat wanted to hide and lick her wounds for a while, before taking on the men again. Regan however, knew she needed to keep moving, if she stayed, she'd be trapped. But, she also needed her wits about her, she couldn't move around out there without total focus on her surroundings. So just for a few minutes, she'd gather herself. She gently sniffed at her wounded side, it bled freely, while she didn't think any major damage had been done, that didn't negate the pain. The initial shock had worn off now, and her body's first protection against the pain no longer had any affect. Burning pain gouged at her restraint, it was agonizing to stay tucked perfectly still in her small hiding spot.

Panting silently, she watched the forest in her field of vision, she constantly swiveled her ears trying to pick up any sound indicating someone approached her. Time dragged by as she slowly recovered her breath, barbed agony and fear became her world, as the seconds ticked by. Had they tracked her here, were they now moving in on her position? Should she have tried to keep moving, had she brought about her own demise by hiding here? How long did she dare stay and recover? With her wound and the tiredness, that even adrenaline could no longer hold back, how long could she run?

Her head jerked as a jeering voice called, “Here puss, puss. Come out and this will all be over. No more pain, no more running. I’ll make it a clean kill shot. You won’t feel a thing.”

CHAPTER 23

Dismayed, Regan turned her head toward the voice; the rock she hid behind obstructed her view of him, as it must be doing for him. Soon he'd work his way around, until he had a clear shot at her. Then it would all be over. Her eyes darkened with regret. She wanted her time with Rafe to build a life with him and Ben. A raking sob was torn from her chest and now when she so desperately wanted to live, it was to be taken away from her. She swallowed her anguish, but still a soft mewling sound scraped over her raw throat.

"Christ baby don't move," Rafe begged silently as he heard Regan's misery, so much pain, and so much sorrow in that small sound. He wasn't quite close enough to take out his mate's tormentor; he needed Regan to stay put for just a couple more minutes. As he made his way towards the man who was even now unknowingly moving towards Rafe, in his attempt to get a clear shot at Regan, totally unaware he was

moving closer to his own death. Rafe stayed hidden in the shadows as he waited.

Regan refused to sit and wait for death to come to her, if she was going to die it would not be cowering behind a rock. If she was going to do this, she needed to move now, the longer she waited the better shot he would have. The nearest trees that could help provide cover were only five yards away. There was a chance he'd miss or at the very least not get a kill shot if she could move fast enough and weave her way amongst the trees. She was lower to the ground and could race under bushes that humans had to push through.

Slowly she gathered her feet under her, grimacing as the torn flesh in her side started bleeding freely again. She tested her weight on her right leg; she hoped it would hold for a while longer. She carefully mapped out a course she would take. Fixing her focus on the first tree she'd use as cover, then the second if she survived the next few seconds. Closing her eyes, she wished with everything in her being she could hold Rafe and Ben one more time. Blinking tears away, she sent up a prayer to the gods and launched out from behind the rock, a black streak of pure motion.

At the same instant, he pulled the trigger, the hunter's instincts warned of danger behind him. He swung his gun reflexively around to face the threat. But the wolf was on him before he could use the gun to defend himself. Raising one arm to hold the creature off his throat, he grabbed the knife strapped to his thigh, stabbing up towards its underbelly. The animal leaped out of the way, but before the man could gain his feet, the wolf latched onto the arm holding the knife, razor sharp teeth tearing and gouging his flesh. He screamed in agony as he tried to free himself, with his left hand he groped for the Beretta holstered at his other thigh.

Rafe was about to release the man's mangled arm, knowing the torn muscle and tendons now made it useless, and go for his opponent's throat, when a brutal force hit the man, ripping his arm from Rafe's mouth. The black panther tumbled to the ground, but before she could gather herself for the kill, Rafe rushed in ripping out the hunter's throat.. The sleek panther rose to her feet, mouth open, teeth fully bared as she hissed furiously at him. Her blue eyes held no humanity; the animal was in full control, pushing Regan to the background in an effort to protect her.

Rafe stood his ground staying over the dead man as he stared down the infuriated cat facing him. He didn't regret making the kill; it was one heartache he could save Regan from experiencing later. She had killed one man in self-defense, and that was enough; she didn't need the blood of another on her hands. He had killed before and would again; it was a stain on his soul he wished with all his heart he could have saved his mate from carrying.

His beautiful panther was enraged and if he didn't make her accept him as the dominant animal, she'd attack him or any of his men if they got too close to her. Like this, she was a primitive creature, acting on pure instinct. This was the worst thing that could happen to a new shifter, the animal taking total control.

Once a shifter was experienced, it was rare that they lost control like this, but Regan was beyond inexperienced. Not only was this her first shift but she'd never been coached in how to control her animal, and then there were the extenuating circumstances of her first shift with her running for her life, and having to kill to survive. It was no wonder the animal had taken over in an attempt to protect Regan.

It was imperative he find Regan within the infuriated animal facing him down. The longer she stayed in this state the harder it would be to come back. It was well known that shifters who lost control early on, lost confidence and trust in their animal. This then led to them refraining from shifting, and denying their animal any freedom, which in turn hurt them because they were denying a part of who they were. Regan needed to rein in her animal now, otherwise lose the trust in her ability to control her panther.

He watched with coolly calculating eyes, as she paced back

and forth in agitation. She stopped, facing him fully she crouched her front legs slightly, her long tensile tail held straight and low, her hackles up, growling softly she was prepared to attack. Leaning towards her aggressively, he allowed his own growl to rumble in his chest. Hissing she swiped at him before recommencing her pacing, never taking her eyes off him. He didn't back away from her aggression; she needed to know he was the dominant one here.

He allowed another low rumbling growl to fill the air. She paused in her pacing, her whiskers curling forward as she lifted her nose to scent the air. She huffed a racking cough, before with a flick of her tail, she started pacing again. Once again, she kept her eyes on him as she stalked back and forth, but he could read the change in her already, now rather than being indiscriminately furious at every threat to her, she was pissed at him, and if he was reading her correctly, it was personal.

Regan's cat was royally ticked off at Rafe and who could blame her? He'd fucked up in so many ways, he deserved her fury, and he would let her have at him if she wished, but first Regan had to regain full control. He changed back to human, rising to his feet he held her crystal blue gaze. It was a risk as she could overpower him in this form, but he needed her to change back and as long as she didn't intend to kill him outright, she'd need to change to ensure he understood her anger. At least he hoped she wanted to savage him verbally, rather than just rip into him with those sharp fags she was baring at him.

She rushed at him stopping at the last instant to bat fallen debris at him with her front paws before turning her back on him to stalk off a few yards and recommence her pacing. Rafe stood his ground refusing to back away.

"Come on baby, if you want to yell at me and let me know all the ways I've fucked up, you're gonna' have to change back."

Her lip curled at his words, revealing long sharp incisors. She again paced off before turning around and coming back to him. She stared at him.

"You just have to concentrate sweetheart. You have to *want* to be human again, visualize what you look like and the change will wash over you."

He could have cried with relief as he watched the change sweep over her, her personality so strong he never should have worried. He was there to pull her to her feet and couldn't help wrap her in his arms and drag her into the shelter of his body. She allowed it for but a moment, before pulling away.

She stood tall and proud, her small breasts with their berry colored nipples, drew his eye, before his gaze probed her rib cage, following the muscled definition of her stomach to the black curls at the apex of her thighs, and then examining those long legs. His gaze traveled back up, pausing at her wounded side that still trickled fresh blood.

"Before you start, you have to let me look at your wound, if I don't assure myself that you'll be OK I won't take in anything you say." Reading her intention to stop him he followed up "Please baby. I know I have so much to make up to you for, and apologies to give, but please let me check your side, and then the floor is yours."

Regan turned her head stonily away from him but allowed him to inspect the depth of the wound. Once satisfied that although she would again need stitches, it didn't appear life threatening, he ran a finger gently down her averted cheek.

"Thank you sweetheart, my men will be here soon with supplies to bandage it and pain killers until we can get you back home to the doctors." Reluctantly he kept his promise and stepped back away from her stiffly held body, as she obviously didn't want him touching her.

Turning her stony gaze back to him, "Don't you ever make a decision about what would be best for me again. You will come to me and discuss anything that will affect me and together we will decide what to do.. You are not God, and you had no right to withhold the mating from me." She clenched her fists, refusing to give into the impulse to take her anger at his arrogance, out on him physically.

Rafe stared at her as he absorbed her words, holy shit, she was going to give him another chance, and he nearly dropped to his knees in relief. His wolf wanted to howl with the joy of it. He would never make the same mistakes. He closed his eyes and tipped his head back as joy and future possibilities staggered him. Pictures of Regan and him at various stages of their lives passed before his eyes and always whether with children, grandchildren, or celebrations with friends or tender stolen moments with just the two of them, always they were together, inseparable the tight bond of their mateship shining between them. The bands that would form on the skin around their wrists when they dedicated their lives to each other in the mystic mating ritual always apparent in each of his visions. "*Please God don't let me ruin this.*"

Lowering his head, he looked her in the eye so she could read his sincerity, "Done. I have no more secrets and I won't keep anything from you again, I promise," he moved his hand unconsciously over his heart as he made the solemn promise.

She held his gaze making sure he understood if they were going to have a relationship, she wanted the ground rules set up front. Even though she was still furious at his lies and deception, her capture and near death experience had peeled everything back to the bare basics. Yes, she was hurt by his treatment, but if she only had one more day on this planet, did she want Rafe in that day? The answer was yes. She didn't know how long they had to live, there were no guarantees, and she didn't want to waste what she did have wallowing in hurt and resentment. Yes, he'd fucked up; yes, she was going to make sure he knew she would not tolerate it. But, she believed if he gave her his promise not to lie or make decisions on her behalf, his integrity would ensure he stuck to it.

If she hadn't been through the turmoil of today, she would have eventually worked her way through her hurt and anger at Rafe, and forgiven him. Accepting she was going to die, had forced her to put aside her resentment, fear, and bruised feelings. Today she had dealt with a month's worth of angst at Rafe. But she wasn't going to let him off the hook too easily.

"Ben is my brother and he's moving in with me. I will not leave him at his mother's mercy. If you want to be in my life, you have to accept Ben into your heart too. I won't have him feeling unwanted in his own home."

His eyes brightened with pleasure. "He's your brother? Oh sweetheart that's great! I know how lonely you have been without a family. I wish you'd told me last night. My pleasure for you might have prevented my brain from short circuiting."

A genuine smile creased Regan's cheeks at his spontaneous response to the news. She couldn't hide the joy the thought of Ben brought her.

"Sweetheart, I'm overjoyed you've found Ben. If you want custody I'll support you both one hundred percent. My wolf has been interested in him since meeting you, believe me I'd love to have Ben live with us. You are the most important part of my life, if you're not happy I'm not happy. Whatever you need to flourish, it's yours."

"I'd only just found out and thought Ben deserved to know first. You have to remember I had no idea we were mates."

The warmth left her face, "That brings me to the next critical issue for me." Making sure he was fully focused on her again, she continued, "Never. Lie. To. Me. Again." She enunciated each word succinctly. "You know I have trust issues; I will not live with someone I cannot trust."

He captured her face in his large rough palms, his fingers threaded into her tangled, sweat slicked hair, "Regan I've learned the harshest of lessons in the last twenty-four hours. I will never do anything that might make you regret giving us a chance. I will never lie to you again, and that includes by omission."

Releasing her face, he trailed his fingers over her hair gently, reluctant to break contact with her, "I'm not asking you to excuse my behavior, as it is inexcusable, but I want to explain what was going through my head, so you will understand why I'll never behave like that again."

Taking her nod as the consent it was, he continued, "I believed I had to gain your trust before you would even consider entering into a relationship with me. You were so wary of us at first, so to give myself a chance with you I lied about us being mated. But I was afraid when I revealed the lie I would lose your trust and maybe you. On top of that, I couldn't see how you could forgive me for not bringing you and your mother into our community. I couldn't work out how to win you. The more time I spent with you the more I liked and respected you. Then I fell in love and the prospect of losing you drove me insane, but I'd already set my course and knew I'd lose you if I revealed all. It all kept circling in my mind, I was all tangled up,; no matter what I did I risked losing you. Until it all blew up last night. Now you know everything, there is nothing more to hide, and I give my word I'll never try to hide anything from you in the future. Whatever it is, we'll face it together, if you will allow us a chance."

Reading the sincerity in his brown eyes she slowly nodded, "I can see how you got yourself in a mess and I accept that I'd have run a mile at the beginning, but don't ever hurt me like that again Rafe."

Tucking her against his chest, he pressed her head against his heart, "Never Regan, when you hurt, it cuts me like a knife."

Snuggling into his warmth as fatigue again dragged at her, she continued, "We have to come up with a way to ensure that what happened to my mother never happens again. Shifters have to be more responsible for those that leave the communities."

"Baby it broke my heart when I realized what had happened to you and your mother. I'll never forgive myself." He gave her a self-depreciating smile, "I think that's been my biggest problem with courting you. If I can't find a way to forgive myself, how can I expect you to? I'm not making excuses for myself, but it warped all my decisions. When you're ready I'll organize a meeting with Byron and we'll come up with something to ensure it never happens again."

"OK knuckle head, you have your chance, don't blow it."

Rafe groaned with elation, his mate was giving him another chance. His hungry mouth claimed hers in a wild celebratory kiss that revealed his relief and elation. His tongue tangled with hers as he angled her head, allowing him deeper access to her enticing mouth.

The sound of someone clearing their throat brought him back from his dazed hunger for his luscious mate.

"Hey boss man, though I'm lovin' the view of your mate's sumptuous bod, I don't think she'll appreciate showing the whole team her top shelf assets." Chris' voice teased from behind Regan.

She hid her smile as Rafe turned them around, so his large body protected her naked form from Chris' gaze.

"Don't stand there drooling, throw me some clothes and I'd advise you to start looking anywhere but at my mate, unless you want me to let my wolf off the leash."

Regan couldn't help the chuckle that escaped at the growl in his voice.

Rafe caught the clothes Chris threw at him and tenderly helped Regan get dressed in a T-shirt and sweats, they were too big for her, but they covered her to his wolf's satisfaction.

"Nice to see you all in one piece," Chris winked at her as she rolled the gray sweat pants up to her knees to stop them unraveling completely and tripping her up.

"Nice to see you too, big guy," she smiled at him gratefully as Chris handed her a bottle of water once she had her clothes settled.

He ran his hand over her hair gently, telling her without words his joy in finding her alive. She accepted his need to touch by leaning into him briefly, his smile at her gesture sent a spiral of warmth through her.

“What’s our status?” Rafe asked as he dressed in clothes that fitted him to perfection, of course. They couldn’t have brought clothes to fit her could they, nooo that would be too much to expect from a group of men.

“Team three is following one target, he’s trying to outrun us. Good luck with that,” he smiled derisively. “We have three of the enemy dead, including Regan’s kill and this one here.” Turning to Regan, “How many are out here that you know of, short stuff?”

“I’ve only seen four but that doesn’t mean there aren’t more out here.” She shrugged. “Your numbers are out by the way, I killed two. So that means we have four dead and one on the run.”

Both men did a double take at her, “You killed another? Where?” Appreciation lit both men’s eyes as they listened to Regan’s concise directions to the body’s location.

“That’s some woman you’ve got there Rafe,” Chris dipped his head in respect to Regan.

Jordan’s camouflaged form materialized out of the trees.

"Of course our little sister took care of herself. I'm sure if we hadn't found her she'd have killed every asshole here. Isn't that right?" he asked as he pulled her into a tight hard hug, which Regan returned, touched that both Chris and Jordan cared enough to come searching for her. No actually, scratch that, neither of them would have missed the chance to extract revenge on these people. Neither would have sat back at home and missed the reprisal being handed out here today.

"Get your paws off my woman and pass me your first aid kit," Rafe ordered Jordan as he slipped his arm around Regan's waist and tugged her to his side, his wolf uncomfortable with another man near Regan.

Jordan shot Rafe an unrepentant smile as he swung his pack to the ground and pulled out his first aid kit. Winking at Regan as he opened the field kit, "What have you done to yourself this time?" He cast a glare at Chris accusingly, "And why the hell haven't you treated it instead of standing around gasbagging like an old lady?"

He offered the opened kit to Rafe who prepared a local anesthetic, indicating to Jordan he should hold Regan's shirt out of the way while he injected it along the ruptured skin. Rafe's jaw clenched as Regan stood stoically while he injected the fluid along the length of the wound, he hated that Regan had suffered enough pain in her past that she could now stand complacently as he hurt her. Jaw clenched, he cleaned the wound and used butterfly bandages to hold the flesh together until they could reach a doctor to stitch it properly. He was dammed if he was going to stitch her up, he had done it for his men in the past, but he couldn't bring himself to saw a needle back and forth through her flesh. Just looking at her ripped skin infuriated him.

Placing a pad over the wound and using a bandage to hold it there, Rafe gathered Regan into his arms, needing the comfort of her touch. His Regan had suffered enough in her short life, what she had endured would have broken most people.

A Sentinel Regan had never met approached them, dipping his head respectfully to Regan, "Glad to see you alive and in one piece," his low voice rumbled from his deep chest. He wasn't as tall as the other sentinel's Regan had met, but that didn't distract from the danger emitting from his lean frame. The unpleasant looking scar, which ran out of his hairline near the center of his forehead, and traveled diagonally across his face just above his eyebrow to disappear into his hairline again near the top of his ear, added to that sense of danger flowing from him. His eyes constantly probed the surrounding trees and the tilt of his head showed part of his attention was attuned to what was happening in the surrounding forest.

Rafe introduced them, "Regan this is Max, best chopper pilot the Sentinels have ever had. He can pull maneuvers and speeds from our choppers without damaging them that the manufacturers tell us are impossible. None of us has ever figured out how he does it. If we try to imitate him, we always end up with stress fractures or something breaks in the engine."

"None of you listen to what the machine is telling you." Max's exasperated tone indicated he was dealing with belligerent children when it came to this topic. "Chris gave me directions to Regan's other kill. I'll get the bodies together so Regan can view them and tell us if we're missing any beside the one we have on the run." Looking directly at Regan, "Are you in good enough shape to do that now?"

At Regan's nod, the group followed Max through the darkening forest, the sun beginning its decent below the horizon. Regan dispassionately viewed the dead men; she honestly felt no remorse at their deaths, they'd brought this on themselves.

"There are two more that I know of not accounted for here."

"We killed one back at the building you were held in," Jordan showed her a photo he taken to enable him to identify the man later.

Regan nodded it was one of the men who'd come into the

room when she'd been held in that horrid cage.

"That's one of them, but the man who organized this isn't here."

Max explained, "Team three are pursuing the last man who was out here hunting you. There aren't any more fresh human scents up here. There were five men hunting you today and all are accounted for. As soon as Dean and Rick have taken care of him, we'll send a photo to Rafe and you can let us know if it's their leader."

Rafe took control then; he ordered Chris and Jordan to dispose of the bodies in such a way they'd never be found. He then wanted them to go through any personal possessions and the *clubhouse* to find out who these people were and any others involved. No one was to escape their justice. Another chopper was dispatched to bring the rest of the team home, once they'd finished cleaning up here. Max was to fly Rafe and Regan back to Eden's Retreat, as soon as they made their way back to the chopper.

Daylight slowly bled away as they descended the mountain range. As full darkness fell, Regan struggled to keep the sedate pace the two men had set for her. They'd given her protein bars to eat and more water, which had helped for a short time, but Regan's body was beyond fatigued. She concentrated on placing one laden foot in front of the other.

Her thigh muscles trembled at the strain placed on them, as they descended the steep ravines.

Rafe supported her weight when possible; eventually swinging her up into his arms, once they reached flatter terrain. On the way down both he and Max and peppered her with questions learning all they could about *Titan*'s people and operation from her. An hour into their trek Rafe had received a photo of the final hunter. His eyes narrowed with anger when Regan informed him he wasn't the man who'd organized her capture. He confirmed with his men that no other hunters were out in the park, all fresh human scent trails had been accounted for. The only people left alive were shifters.

Cursing under his breath, "Jordan, I don't care what you have to do, but find this bastard. I will not allow him to hurt one more shifter."

Hugging Regan closer to his chest, he increased his pace. *"Would this bastard ever die?"* he questioned himself.

She ran her fingers gently over the lines of tension along his forehead.

"I know what he looks like Rafe. If I have to sit in front of a computer every day for a year, I'll find his photo and we will have him. He won't be able to come back here now we know about this place, so he has nowhere to hunt. You now have the name of the company that leases this place; you'll gain more leads from the identity of these men here today. You will have him soon."

He gave her a quick kiss, "You're right, he won't evade us long."

Not long after the building where they'd held Regan came into sight, Max jogged ahead and cleared it before prepping the chopper for lift off in record time, knowing his boss wanted nothing more than to have his woman home and safe. He'd never been in love, but he could understand the need Rafe felt to remove Regan as quickly as possible from this nightmare.

As the blades wound up to speed, Rafe bent his head over Regan, holding her protectively to his chest, and climbed into the dark machine, which immediately lifted off. Regan was asleep before they'd leveled out and headed for home. Rafe looked down at the woman he held against his heart. Tenderness and a love so strong tightened his chest and brought tears to his eyes. He went so close to losing her today. He laid his cheek gently against her soft hair and repositioned her still closer to him. The future before him now held the promise of love, laughter, and children; deep contentment filled him as he gazed out the window and watched the stars slowly slide across the sky as they raced arrow straight for home.

CHAPTER 24

A gentle night breeze pushed Regan's hair back off her shoulders and down her back as she walked into the center of the circle the residents of Eden's Retreat had formed. She wore a white silk corset top that revealed her delicate cleavage and laced down the back with silver ribbons. Silver threaded through the material of her top and glimmered with each step she took beneath the luminous moon. Her full-length skirt made from the same material, fell in a straight cut with a generous slit up the back allowing her to walk in the strap sandals encasing her feet. All this provided by Rafe for their formal joining ceremony that would mate them permanently.

Glancing sideways, she smiled at Ben who kept pace with her as he escorted her to the two men awaiting them. He returned her smile and squeezed her hand as they stopped beside Rafe. Raising her eyes, she sucked in a breath as she took in the beautiful male before her. He'd dressed in an immaculate black suit with a tie matching the silver that embellished her gown. She melted at the soft glow of love shining from the velvet brown of his eyes. A hush fell over the crowd as Byron stepped in front of them.

"Who gives this woman into this man's keeping?"

Ben raised his chin, "I do."

Giving Ben a reassuring wink, Byron continued, "And by what right do you give this woman away?"

Ben announced clearly for all to hear, "I claim familial rights, Regan is my sister and has asked me to stand with her during this ceremony."

A wave of hushed murmurs traveled through the crowd at Ben's announcement. People subtly searched for Moya in the crowd, her absence from her mate's side, causing another ripple of disquiet amongst the guests.

Regan ignored their reaction as Ben placed her hand in Rafe's outstretched palm; she bent to kiss Ben on the cheek before rubbing hers across his in an open sign of her affection for this boy who was her brother. Love for the man at her side washed through her in a warm wave as Rafe stepped around her and dropped down on one knee to pull Ben into a hug. He whispered something to Ben that even

Regan's hearing couldn't detect. Ben's reaction to Rafe's words was a broad smile and a quick hard hug in return. A momentous step forward for the wary boy Regan had met just over a month ago.

Rafe reclaimed her hand as he returned to his place on her other side and faced Byron.

Byron cleared his throat to hush the murmurs amongst those there to witness the ceremony, "Tonight we celebrate the joining of these two pack mates. This brings joy to us all as it makes our pack stronger." Byron turned his attention from the crowd to Rafe and Regan, he continued in a warm tone, "It's our privilege tonight to bear witness to your binding as mates. As you both know, the only formal words required in your vows are "I pledge myself to you." If there is true intent behind the words, you will feel the magical bond initiate; joining you both for the rest of your lives, binding your souls together. The appearance of the iridescent band beneath the skin of your wrists will signify your intent to cherish each other, no matter if you're granted the easiest of lives or if you have to struggle everyday for your very survival, you will put your mate's needs before your own." He stepped back indicating Regan should begin her vows.

Taking a steadying breath Regan turned to Rafe, "I want you to know how hard I find this, standing before all these people." She held her trembling hand up for him to see; Rafe cupped it in his calloused hands and squeezed encouragingly, proud she was putting herself through what was an ordeal for her so the pack could celebrate their mating. He'd offered to have the ceremony with just Byron, Ben and his parents knowing how hard she would find this, but she'd refused. She truly wanted to fit in at Eden's Retreat and push through her comfort zones. He brought his attention back to his beautiful courageous mate as she continued. "But for you I will continually challenge my limitations. My vows aren't flowery or poetic but they are heartfelt."

Looking into his handsome face her smile wobbled as she met the adoration shining in his eyes, "Once I commit to someone I won't walk away, only death will tear me from you. I declare openly before your parents, family, friends, and pack, I love you with everything I am. I pledge my life to yours."

Rafe moved his hands to cup Regan's face in his broad palms, "Regan you are my world, there is an emptiness in me that only your joy with life can fill. When you laugh, I know no greater joy. It is in my heart to cherish you; to provide what you need to flourish in this life. I will stand with you through the challenges we will face, I will support you in any way you need. I will love you in this life and follow you to the next adventure after death. I pledge myself to you."

He smiled gently as he wiped a single tear from the soft skin of her cheek before turning to the crowd and raising their hands above their heads, so the surrounding shifters could witness the splendor of the bands forming under their skin. A shimmering, midnight blue light sparkled around their joined hands and twined around their wrists. Warmth sunk into Regan's wrist as the lights flared brighter and brighter until her eyes watered from the dazzling brilliance. Then the sparks began to fade and within moments disappeared altogether. Around their wrists were now twin deep blue bands almost like a tattoo, but when she looked closer the color was underneath her skin and held a shimmer of color no tattoo artist could ever hope to imitate.

At the same time, she felt something inside herself shift before warmth poured into her. She looked to Rafe as she realized, it was the mystical bond forming between them she could feel. Rafe's self-satisfied smile assured her he could feel it too. Love for this man who was hers, coursed through her.

Wolf whistles and catcalls rang out from the surrounding crowd as Rafe bent her over his arm and claimed a searing open-mouthed kiss from his mate. Her tongue slid across his, as she relaxed against the arm holding her weight. Lust hit him like a sledgehammer to the back of the head stunning him with its ferocity. He cupped the back of her head as he deepened the kiss and absorbed the delicious taste that was Regan.

"Rafe, your mom and dad are watching this, my man," Byron's rough voice penetrated Rafe's lust filled mind.

He softened the kiss, finally rubbing his lips across Regan's one last time before reluctantly pulling away. Raising her back up, he brushed the back of his knuckles across her flushed cheek, before meeting her dazed eyes. "Sorry sweetheart, I didn't mean to start something we can't finish," he grimaced. "Time to face the crowd, are you ready?"

At her reluctant nod, he moved her under his arm, before turning and holding his hand out for Ben to take. He smiled as the boy latched on, as if to a lifeline. He steered his new family towards his mother and father, who stood first in line to congratulate them.

Regan viewed the older couple with trepidation, *what would they think of her and her inability to mix socially with people, with her need to be alone? Never before had she felt so inept. What should she say to them? God, what if she froze up and couldn't think of anything to say at all?*

Rafe's arm tightened around her protectively, he bent his head to whisper in her ear, "You'll do fine. You don't have to be the life of the party; they aren't expecting a social butterfly. They will love you because of your strength. They admire you already; don't try to be anything but who you are. I love you and they will too. Don't worry, my mother will keep the conversation flowing," he smiled at the tall elegant woman waiting for their attention.

Regan assessed the couple as Rafe introduced her and Ben to them. Rafe's father was an older version of Rafe and wow lucky her, if Rafe aged as well as his father. The woman smiled warmly at her and Ben, she was tall like most shifters but willow thin, and she wore an elegant dress that matched the unusual gold of her eyes. Her thick sable colored hair was cut into a chic style, emphasizing the classic bone structure of her face.

Regan hadn't had the opportunity to meet them before the formal mating, as they'd driven straight from the airport and had only arrived shortly before the ceremony began. It had only been two days since the kidnapping and Rafe had been like a man possessed, to see them mated.

Regan couldn't find it within her to disappoint him, and her near death experience had made her appreciate the need to grab life, and make the most of every day. She loved Rafe and wanted to live with him. She watched Rafe's interactions with Ben carefully and could see he spoke truly of he and his wolf's joy, at having Ben live with them. He constantly involved Ben in their discussions and decisions. He was totally at ease around Ben, didn't try to force a bond with him, seeming happy to wait for it to form naturally with time. Rafe had pointed out to them that he and Regan had a stronger chance of gaining custody of Ben if they were a mated couple. They were still to confront Moya regarding her intentions to oppose Regan's petition to gain custody. They were intent on making sure, if they were forced to go before the council of Elders for custody, they could show they were in a position to provide Ben with a better home environment and support.

To that end as well as preparing for their mating ceremony, they had also moved into one of the available cottages and decorated one of the bedrooms for Ben, taking the time to drive him into the city to one of the big department stores to select his own bed and furnishings. The rest of the house was filled with a combination of Regan and Rafe's furniture. They'd had fun negotiating who's furniture was used and where. They'd laughed as they haggled with each other. Ben had watched them when not at school with a quiet intensity, as if studying a new species. No doubt, he'd never witnessed a couple openly enjoying each other's company. Moya was still hurting and unable to take uninhibited enjoyment from life. It was an indication of Regan's fortitude, that she was able to follow Rafe's lead and tease him as much as he teased her.

Rafe's voice brought her back to the present, "Regan and

Ben, these are my parents, Susan and Dan."

"Rafe has told me so much about you Regan; it's a pleasure to finally meet you." Rafe's mother gathered her into a warm embrace; Regan surprised herself by melting into Susan's comforting arms. Regan felt only warmth and protection emanating from Rafe's mother. Her cat sensed this woman viewed Regan as part of her family and would protect her against all others. She exuded unconditional love and joy, in the mate destiny had chosen for her son.

The raw wound in Regan caused by her mother's absence tore a little more, threatening to shred the joy she'd found in this special day. Her mother should have been here to celebrate her mating, and her absence was never felt more, than as she huddled against Rafe's mother. There was a wanting that couldn't be fulfilled, and hollowness that threatened to swallow her.

Susan gave her a moment to shelter in her arms, before pulling Regan's face away from her shoulder.

"Hush now," she brushed away the silent tears from Regan's cheeks with her thumbs. "Your mother knows you've found your place. She can rest easy now because we will take care of you. Put your sorrow away; honor her memory by celebrating this new chapter in your life. As a fellow mother I know she would want your heart filled with joy today."

Regan scraped a smile together and took a deep breath, "Yes, you're right. She would have loved this and celebrated all night. I just miss her so."

"Of course you do, you love her. But it is a night for rejoicing, so come and meet the rest of our family. I hope you're prepared," she smiled over her shoulder as she led Regan towards a group of twenty odd people standing off to the side, and from what Regan could see tormenting each other.

Regan looked around for Rafe, but he was deep in conversation with his father and Ben, the other shifters who'd been waiting to congratulate them seemed content to mingle amongst themselves, sampling the food and drinks placed on tables scattered throughout the meadow as they waited their turn to congratulate Regan and Rafe.

"Oh, um, I might just wait here for Rafe." Her stomach churned at the thought of facing the rest of Rafe's family without him at her side to ease her into conversations. She hated the thought of these people staring at her, waiting for her to respond to something they said while her mind was a total blank. Yeah sure, she'd told herself she'd be able to handle standing up in front of a crowd of strangers, but she really hadn't considered fully the implication of spending a whole night surrounded by strangers wanting to talk to her, and worse, wanting to touch her as shifters did.

"Nonsense dear, best way to deal with a new family is to jump in the deep end." When she felt Regan's muscles tightening with tension as she led her away from Rafe, Susan turned to her, "Trust me Regan, no one here will make you feel unwanted, we are all different, and all have different strengths and weaknesses. You're one of us now. She slipped her arm through Regan's and pulled her along, an unstoppable force, "Don't worry about trying to remember names tonight, most of the family here are Rafe's uncles, aunts and cousins, but you'll get to know us all over the coming weeks."

"Hey here she is, the girl who's captured Rafe's heart," a male in his early thirties with Rafe's broad frame and muscled physic approached them.

"Grant take good care of our girl, no mischief tonight," Susan admonished, as she released Regan into the shifter's care.

Grant led the reluctant Regan to a table laden with crystal glasses, ice buckets, and with what looked like every variant of wine, spirits, and beer ever created. His sharp features didn't detract from his appeal; his eyes were alive with mischief softening the impact of a face that would otherwise appear harsh. Grant's face didn't carry the maturity the stress of Rafe's job had imprinted on his. "You do realize that now Rafe has mated, the pressure is going to move from him to me, don't you? I'm going to be constantly dodging blind dates arranged by all the aunts and great aunts." The amusement in his voice told of his lack of concern regarding the issue.

"My heart bleeds for you," Regan responded dryly as she took the glass of sparkling wine he passed her.

He grabbed a beer for himself, and then clanked his bottle to her glass, "I suggest you down that before the clan descends on you, a bit of Dutch courage won't hurt."

Regan took him at his word and swallowed a large gulp as the family surrounded them.

Grant introduced her to everyone and thankfully, they were totally into the celebrating part of the evening. Regan relaxed further when Steph dragged an obviously reluctant Jen through the McIntyre clan and to her side.

"Congratulations," Jen muttered before taking up her usual stance with legs spread and arms crossed over her chest, as she assessed the crowed around her.

Steph rolled her eyes in exasperation and stepping out of Grant's hug, turned to Jen, "Jesus Jen you could put a little enthusiasm into it!"

"Stop complaining little girl, you wanted me here, be happy with that."

Giving up for the moment, Steph turned her attention to Regan and with a mercurial grin threw herself at Regan nearly knocking her off her feet. "Welcome to the family! Have you met everyone? I thought the ceremony was fantastic! Hey, there's Derrick! Come on Jen I want you to meet him, I have a feeling you might actually like him."

Grabbing Jen by the arm Steph dragged her off. Shrugging philosophically Jen waved a hand at Regan as she followed Steph into the crowd.

Taking another sip of her wine Regan watched the McIntyre family as they chatted amongst themselves, constantly teasing and taunting one other. It seemed a challenge had been issued as to who could tell Regan the wildest story about Rafe as a boy and young teen, causing her to laugh at the trouble Chris, Jordan, and Rafe seemingly lived for in their teens. Grant kept her glass filled as she sipped at the sweet wine, while listening to their tales. She didn't keep track of how much she was drinking as she relaxed into the evening, laughing with the crowd that had built around her as they tried to outdo each other with outrageous tales about family members and some of the people Regan knew at Eden's Retreat.

When the music started, Jordan came to claim a dance. Feeling carefree and lighthearted from the wine and the laughter Regan followed him into the crowd of dancers and fell in with the beat. She threw her head back and watched the stars swirl as she twirled with the music. Laughter fell from her lips, raising her arms she twisted and turned, swirling with the beat of the music hammering through her. Her cat chuffed with delight wanting out to enjoy the moment amongst the fellow revelers.

~~~

Grant tapped Rafe on the shoulder, "I think you might need to grab your mate and try to walk some of the booze out of her system."

Rafe tried to locate Regan on the dance floor that had been set up. Over the evening he'd claimed several dances and ensured she was happy. For the last couple of hours she'd been enjoying herself and it warmed his heart, he wanted her to be comfortable with his family and friends, without him being there to support her. He'd stopped by several times to steal a kiss while she listened to his cousins and friends with their bullshit stories.

When he couldn't find her immediately, Grant directed his attention to where most of the cousins had gathered to dance at the far edge of the dance floor. Rafe noted that although they weren't looking behind them they were subtly ensuring no one else on the dance floor could see what had Jordan doubled over as he watched someone on the ground. Rafe
~~~

couldn't see what had his friend in stitches but had a bad feeling as he headed over.

"Sorry Rafe, I didn't realize she was such a light weight when it comes to alcohol," Grant muttered as he kept pace with Rafe.

Rafe walked around the crowded dance floor until he passed the last family member obstructing his view of Regan and came to a complete stop. His mate was in panther form and by the looks of it trying to do the tango. She held what had once been a red rose between her sharp teeth, but she'd obviously hit the ground face first more than once, by the look of the rose, which was now, a broken tattered mess hanging limply from her mouth. A thorn had embedded itself near her whiskers and as he watched, she lifted her hind leg to try to scratch it free but toppled onto her side when she lost her balance. Shaking her head, she got back to her feet obviously forgetting the thorn for the moment.

Rafe watched in fascinated horror as she straightened herself out and stood still for a few seconds then her tail started to twitch to the beat of the music, gaining in momentum until it swayed from side to side, then her butt started to sway with the music. He couldn't hold in the laugh that escaped, he'd never seen anything so idiotic. Her rump kept swaying to the beat until she thought she had control, and then she tried to move her feet which got all tangled up and . . . . down she went.

“You’ve gotta’ do something, if anyone else catches an eye full of this she’ll never live it down,” Grant prompted him into action.

Rafe went to his woman rolling his eyes at Jordan who was massaging his ribs, obviously the bastard had laughed so much he was cramping up. He ran his hand down Regan’s back as she gathered herself to stand.

“Hey sweetheart, why don’t you come with me and we’ll have a private dance.”

She swung her head to him and pleasure lit her glazed, slightly crossed eyes.

“Come on,” he helped her to her feet. She trotted drunkenly along beside him, a rough purring sound rumbling in her throat.

He shook his head; it was going to take quite a walk to sober her up. He was nearly at the path that led deep into Eden Retreat’s forest when he noticed Don, Ben’s stepfather angling to cut them off. He’d had one brief conversation with Don since coming back, in which he’d told Don the garbage Moya had sprouted to Regan. Don had been devastated, he’d known Moya was cold towards the boy, but hadn’t realized the extent of her hatred towards her child.

Rafe had been straight up with Don, explaining their intention to claim custody and if Moya and Don opposed them, they'd reluctantly reveal the depth of Moya's mistreatment of Ben to the council of elders who would decide who gained custody. He'd been brutally honest in revealing the neglect and mistreatment Moya had handed out to Ben, before and since mating Don. Rafe had read the man's shame at failing to protect Ben under his own roof. No doubt, he'd justified it to himself somehow but now that he'd been called on it, he'd realized there was no excuse. In fairness to Moya and Don, Rafe had also informed him that they'd be announcing Ben's relationship to Regan during the ceremony.

Rafe stopped just inside the tree line and waited for Don, Regan twined around his legs rubbing her scent across his thighs before heading further along the track waving her tail enticingly at her mate confident he would follow, having missed Don's approach.

"I won't keep you from your mate; I just wanted you to know that I've convinced Moya to release custody of Ben to you and Regan. I believe it's in the best interest for both of them. I'm taking Moya away for a time, maybe permanently. She's agreed to go into counseling and I'm going to be with her every step of the way. Thomas has ruined enough of her life; it's time to claim control back." Don looked away for a moment.

Rafe could empathize with the man, his mate was a troubled woman, and it was no easy road he was about to walk with her.

Looking back at Rafe, "I'm hoping at some future point Moya will want contact with Ben." He squared his shoulders obviously ready to do battle for his mate's right to be involved in her son's life.

"I know Ben will look forward to that time. Maybe when Moya is ready, he could write to her." Rafe knew Ben would want his mother in his life in some capacity. He and Regan would support him in whatever way he needed.

Don looked relieved and held out his hand, "Moya and I'll be leaving tonight, once we've settled, I'll contact you."

Rafe returned his handshake and watched as Don slipped away from the crowded meadow, before turning to follow the enticing scent of his own mate.

He smiled with pure pleasure when he found her leaning back temptingly against the trunk of a giant elm in human form. Obviously, his gutsy mate was having no residual issues regarding shifting from cat to human and back. He never should have doubted his woman; she had the inner strength of tensile steel. She faced her every fear and conquered them with her indomitable spirit.

She crooked a finger at him and he willingly went into her waiting arms. Lifting her so she'd wrap her long legs around his waist, he whispered roughly, "I'll never get enough of you."

He nipped at her lips before racking his teeth along her jaw as he released his aching erection, and then claimed her mouth as he thrust roughly into her with no finesse; thankful, her body was ready for him.

Threading her hands through his hair Regan returned his searing kiss, tangling her tongue with his, heat rushed through her as she met his every thrust. Her inner muscles flexed as their delicious rhythm raced out of their control. It was a frantic joining burning them with its intensity. Again and again, they came together; Regan writhing against Rafe, shuddering as her climax began tearing through her.

Rafe could feel his body tightening readying for release; he leaned back as Regan writhed against him, allowing her to grind against his pelvis, he held tight to her hips as he continued his savage thrusts. He felt her tight sheath convulsing around him, clenching his teeth, he tried to ride out her orgasm, but his body continued its frantic thrusts, his knees weakened as he felt jet after jet explode from him into Regan. He sagged to his knees as Regan continued to writhe through her orgasm, lost in her own ecstasy.

He knelt there still joined to Regan as she collapsed against his chest with her legs still locked behind his lower back.

“Boy I needed that,” she chuckled as she buried her head in the crook of his neck.

He held her tenderly, stealing the occasional sweet kiss, as they both regained their breath; he then slowly pulled her off his member as he stood her back on her feet.

“Unfortunately we’d better get back to the party before someone comes looking for us.” He removed his shirt and helped her thread her arms through the sleeves; the garment fell to her knees.

“Do we have to go back?” she moaned.

“Just for the meal, then we can head into the city for the night. Jordan is going to look after Ben, so we can have a night for just the two of us.”

~~~

Regan leaned back against her mate, contentedly looking around at their friends with sleepy eyes. Amazingly, her wedding outfit hadn’t been destroyed when she’d shifted in it, apart from her panties, which were shredded and were now lodged in Rafe’s pants pocket. The skirt had fallen off
~~~

and Jordan had been quick to unlace the bodice before she'd had a chance to rip it off with her claws. He'd been waiting for them just inside the tree line with her clothes, the shredded panties dangling from his forefinger. He'd handed it all over with a wink and a sly grin, before sauntering back to the ongoing party.

Rafe had told her about Moya and Don, she was glad. Ben wouldn't have to endure the ordeal of revealing his mother's rejection and hopefully Moya would get the help she needed and they could have some sort of relationship in the future.

All her dreams were coming true. Yes, there was still the threat of *Titan* to contain fully. The man with the ice-cold eyes had disappeared but, Regan knew what he looked like, she'd eventually find him. The Sentinels were systematically tracking down participants in the hunts and killing them. None would escape shifter justice. But that was for the future, now was about these people celebrating with her and Rafe.

Using the cover of the long white tablecloth to hide his movements, Rafe slid the smooth material of her skirt until it was rucked up at the back but still falling discreetly over the front of both their legs so the people sitting to the side couldn't see anything untoward. He'd had the dress designed to help fulfill this fantasy, with its long slit up the back allowing the material to be spread out over their legs.

She turned her head to him questioningly, when he encouraged her to rise up a little so he could pull the material of her skirt out from under her so the bare skin of her thighs now touched the rougher fabric of his pants. He smiled innocently and she returned to her conversation with Jordan and Chris who were presently sitting opposite them at the long trestle table.

He then leaned back to release the zipper and button of his pants releasing his aching erection. He then carefully folded the fabric of the back of her skirt over his now exposed erection, so no one glancing down would see that they were now bare to each other. He felt her breath hitch when he rubbed his erection back and forward against the crease of her ass, but she valiantly kept up her end of the conversation. He sat that way for a while allowing her to become accustomed to the feel of him touching her in such a way in public.

Then while Jordan and Chris were focused on another conversation with their fellow Sentinels, Rafe lifted her slightly and allowed his erection to slide between the wet silken folds of her labia. Her wetness immediately coated his erection, making it easy with the slightest adjustment of his hips to slide the head of his erection into her hot opening, and lodge himself just inside. Her gasp brought the others attention back to her. They noted her flushed face and the pinched look on Rafe's face as he forced himself to remain still, when all he wanted to do was thrust upward and drive himself home into the depths of her dripping pussy. Jordan gave him a knowing smirk before continuing the conversation with the others, kindly drawing their attention away from Regan.

Once Rafe felt he had control, he adjusted himself seating himself deep within her body and joined in the conversation with the others while his throbbing erection stayed firmly lodged in Regan's womb. More Sentinels joined them at the table sitting on either side of Rafe and Regan. They'd barely finished congratulating the newlyweds, before both men drew in a long deep breath. With Regan pretending to pay attention to the conversation across the table, both men didn't even try to hide their knowing grins from Rafe. He just gave an innocent *I can't help myself* type of shrug.

How she was supposed to talk with these people, when all she wanted to do was ride up and down on the hard cock embedded in her, she had no idea. Her body was quivering, right on the verge of an orgasm. She was trying desperately to hold off knowing she'd never be able to sit still or keep quiet, if she let it overwhelm her.

She couldn't believe Rafe had done this, the naughtiness of having sex while these people sat around, was making her so hot she could feel her juices running between her thighs where Rafe was joined to her. She knew he'd be able to feel it dripping onto his balls and the seat below them. If either of them moved, the wet sucking sound of sex would give them away completely. No doubt, the men at the table were aware something was going on, but as long as she and Rafe refrained from moving, they wouldn't know exactly what was happening under her skirt and the long tablecloth. Even though she knew she would die of embarrassment if they were caught, the risk of exposure was making her so horny it was all she could do to sit still.

Just as she thought she'd be able to rejoin the conversation, Rafe's rough hand slowly eased her left knee outward and over his thigh, then he did the same with her right, changing the position of his erection inside her so it pressed into the sensitive web of nerves at the top of her womb. She closed her eyes as she once again fought off her climax. Breathing deeply she pushed it back.

An indeterminate time later, her diabolical mate lifted the front of her skirt under the table and as the cold air hit her exposed wetness, a shiver traveled the length of her body. Breathing deeply through her nose, she tried to stay on top of the sensations clawing at her. Rafe then used the fingers of both hands to pull back her outer labia, exposing her throbbing clit to the cool night breeze and that was all it took to send her tumbling over the edge. She closed her eyes leaning back into Rafe as stars swum before her eyes and red heat flashed from her center outward. Clenching her jaw, she withheld her moan of ecstasy. Rafe's cock pulsed with her releasing his seed into her body.

"God I love you," Rafe whispered roughly into her ear.

Turning she pressed a kiss to his lips. "Let's get out of here so we can have some uninhibited fun. This was different but I prefer having you to myself."

Quickly straightening out their clothes, Rafe swung his mate up into his arms and carried her off into the night, with the sound of laughter and wedding night advice being called out to them, from their clan.

"Thank you for taking time to read Predator's Heart. If you enjoyed it, I'd be beyond grateful if you would tell your friends or post a short review on my Facebook page or on the platform you purchased the book through. Word of mouth is an author's best friend.

Thank you so much!

Marian"

ABOUT THE AUTHOR

"Marian Yates lives on the spectacular Sunshine Coast, Queensland, Australia.

Her career has varied from vegetable picker (whilst completing her Bachelor Of Arts majoring in English) to high school teacher, business owner, mother and writer.

Marian writes under the watchful eye of Roxy her faithful Maremma Sheepdog."

www.ingramcontent.com/pod-product-compliance
Lightning Source LLC
Chambersburg PA
CBHW071218250626
47163CB00001B/33